A Circle Sleuth Mystery

Titles by Betty Lucke

FICTION

Circle Sleuth Mystery Series
Circle of Power
Family of the Heart
Secrets of the Past

NONFICTION

Festival Planning Guide:
Creating Community Events with Big Hearts and Small Budgets

A Circle Sleuth Mystery

Betty Lucke

Spearmint Books

Secrets of the Past
A Circle Sleuth Mystery, Book 3

Published by Spearmint Books.

This novel is a work of fiction. Any references to real people, living or dead, business establishments, places, organizations, or events are intended only to give the fiction a sense of reality. These references are used as background in which the fictional characters live, move, and have their being. The fictional law enforcement entities portrayed in this book may or may not reflect how their real-life counterparts function. All other names, places, characters, and incidents portrayed in this book are the product of the author's imagination.

To contact the publisher, please email: spearmintbooks@gmail.com.
Editor: Wendy VanHatten
Cover Design: Tara Baumann
Cover Photos: Jo Pemble, Lauren Filarsky

Library of Congress Cataloging-in-Publication Data

Lucke, Betty, Author
Secrets of the Past: a circle sleuth mystery / Betty Lucke
First Edition Spearmint Books, 2018
Library of Congress Control Number: 2016910487
ISBN 978-0-9884631-4-1

1. Bjornson, Anton (Fictitious Character)—Fiction
2. Mystery—Detective—New Mexico—Santa Fe—Fiction
3. New Mexico—Santa Fe—Fiction
4. Archaeology—Native American—Fiction
5. Dogs—Terriers—Airedales—Fiction
FIC LUC 813.6 DD PS – LCC 1. Title

Printed in The United States of America

Acknowledgements

I wish to thank the following for their expertise and encouragement. The journey with Anton and his friends in the Circle of Sleuths—exploring the characters, bouncing ideas back and forth, and digging deeply into the world of writing fiction has been challenging and rewarding. This mystery is dedicated to the Fiction Writers' Coffee Klatsch folks. Thanks to all who welcomed Anton and Skyla into their lives and helped their story come alive.

Draft and Beta Readers: Emily Brown, Jean Norrbom, Lauren Filarsky, Laurie Rawlinson-Evans, PJ Loomer, Page Frechette, Rachel Lewis, Susan Walsh, the Fiction Writers' Coffee Klatsch, and the members of the Town Square Writer's Group.

Consultants: Don Bestwick, Dotty Schenk, Emily Brown, Jean Norrbom, Kelly Hess, Lauren Filarsky, Laurie Rawlinson-Evans, PJ Loomer, Su Schlagel, Steven Carey, Syl Bestwick, and Weston Loomer.

Editing: Wendy VanHatten

Cover Photos:
Airedale photo by Jo Pemble, GlenRoyal Airedales, Stephentown, NY.
Pecos Mission photo by Lauren Filarsky.

Cover Design: Tara Baumann

PROLOGUE

January 2016

The detective walked into St. Raphael's Care Center and finger-combed his graying brown hair into submission after its tussle with the winter wind. Straightening his tie, his fingers brushing against his body cam, he strode down the hall, stepping aside to accommodate some residents in walkers. He pulled a note from the portfolio he carried to check the room number. Finding the right room, he knocked and entered to find a white-haired lady with a cheery smile sitting in a wheelchair.

"Marilyn Stewart?" he asked. "I'm Lieutenant Pete Schultz from the Santa Fe Police Department."

"Yes, you must be the one who called," she said, reaching out in a firm handshake. "I admit to being very curious. The nurse said you thought I might have information about a case that's dragged on far too long. Please sit. How can I help you?"

"I'll be recording this interview, so I won't have to take so many notes, and it will help me accurately document what you tell me. Is that all right with you?"

"Certainly."

"When I joined the police force in Santa Fe twenty-five years ago, my first case was a kidnapping." Pete settled into a chair. "The child, a six-year-old male, vanished. We've never been able to find out what happened to him."

"I'm afraid I can't be of much help. I moved here recently with my grandson and his family from Montana. I've never been in New Mexico before."

Pete nodded and continued. "Last fall, a young man stopped at the police station and wanted more information about the case. We were surprised, as it is so old. Due to a clerical error we never connected, but I learned his name was Ross Stewart. From Montana. I tried to track him down, but by the time his message reached me, he had already left that state. And then, in an extraordinary coincidence, I saw a group of children performing at St. Raphael's. I spotted a red-headed boy that looked so much like that missing child, I was dumbfounded. That's when I was told your name was Stewart. I'm wondering if you might be related."

"My grandson's name is Ross," she said with a puzzled look on her face. "I've no idea why he would be inquiring about a kidnapping, though. Have you talked with him?"

"I don't know how to get in touch with him. I was hoping you might share his contact information with me."

"Certainly. I can write it down for you." She reached for a small notebook and a pen on her bedside table. "He often stops by to see me about this time of day. Tell me more, Lieutenant."

"The little boy's name was Johnny McCreath. He'd been playing in the park next door to his house with his younger brother when he was snatched. That was 1991. I was struck by the resemblance to your—would it be a great-grandson I saw here?"

"Yes, his name is Matti. How devastating for the parents to have their child stolen." She leaned back. "That's the year Ross came to live with us. He was eight-years old that summer."

Pete blinked and leaned forward. *Mein Gott. The timing even fits.* "Would you like to see the lad's picture? I have it here."

"Of course."

Pete handed her the photograph. Her eyes widened as she gazed at it.

"This child does look a great deal like Matti and like Ross when he was younger." She looked up as a young man entered. "Here's Ross now."

"Hi, Grandma." The man bent down to kiss the woman's cheek. "Who's this?" he asked.

"This is Lieutenant Schultz," said Marilyn. "Santa Fe P.D."

Pete stood to shake Ross's hand, explained why he'd come, and said he'd continue recording their visit if that was agreeable. Ross's attitude was easy-going. Pete was amazed by how strongly Ross reminded him of Cliff McCreath, Johnny's younger brother—and Pete's own son-in-law.

Ross pulled a chair from the other side of the room and folded his six-foot slender length into it.

"I did stop by the police station," said Ross. "I'd met a red-headed guy at the Zozobra Festival that Labor Day weekend. He told me the story. I had some time to kill and thought, why not? When I didn't hear back, I figured you were too busy to bother with idle curiosity like mine."

Marilyn handed him the photo. As he took it, his other hand hovered over it for a few seconds before gently brushing the child's face. When he handed the photo back to Marilyn, his hand shook slightly. "At first, I thought that was my son, Matti. It isn't, though."

"Your grandmother told me you were eight when you went to live with them. Where did you live before that?"

"In Denver—lived there from the time I was born until I went to live with my grandparents when my parents died." He smiled at his grandmother. "I was lucky to have them."

"What brought you to New Mexico?" asked Pete.

"Grandpa died, and Montana winters were increasingly hard on Grandma. Then I saw the job opening in the forest service in Pecos. Melody, my wife, and I thought this climate would be easier for her. I was lucky enough to get the job, and so here we are." He patted his grandmother's hand.

Marilyn handed the photo of Johnny back to Pete. "I'll never forget the summer Ross came to live with us. First his father died in that plane crash—"

Her eyes shot to her grandson, who'd sucked in a breath and leaned back in his chair. "Ross, is something wrong? You just went all pale."

"I'm fine, Grandma. Just got light-headed for a second."

"Must be the altitude. It's more than twice here what it was in Kalispell. Anyway, first his father died, and Ross was so badly injured in that plane crash, and then a month later, my sister had a heart attack and died."

Pete's eyes were on Ross's face as the young man sent another startled look to his grandmother and pulled back slightly. *What is this? Did I imagine that look? From affable to apprehensive in seconds? Was there something in what his grandmother said that made him turn pale?*

"First your father died," Pete said. As he watched, the grandson's expression tightened again slightly at his words.

Ross's blue eyes met his. "What?"

"First your father died," Pete said again.

"You're not thinking I might be that missing kid? That's ridiculous. Can't be."

"Tell me what happened," said Pete quietly.

"We were landing on a lake." Ross stopped. He moistened his lips with his tongue. "I didn't mean to—"

"Tell me what happened," said Pete, watching him intently.

Ross shook his head slightly, almost like a tic. He frowned. "I forgot," he whispered.

"Tell me—"

"The plane crashed. My father died." Ross rubbed his forehead. "I'm sorry. My memory isn't good for much of anything that happened before I woke up in the hospital after that plane crash. When I try, even this many years later, it just brings on a headache."

What just happened? Pete wondered as he left the care center. What triggered the change in Ross? He'd have to review his camera footage later. *Ach du lieber.* He slipped into the language of his parents, as he often did. C*urious. Uncanny resemblances. Or do I just see them because I want to so badly? Doppelgangers—at the very least.*

Chapter One

May 4, 2016

The drone swooped high in the brisk May air, recording light, shadow, and secrets. Its eyes-in-the-sky panned the vista of Santa Fe, New Mexico, in the distance and, nearby, a dust devil skipping across the landscape of sparse junipers and piñons. The eyes caught Drone Tech's Research and Development facility and focused on the two men bent over the drone's controls.

Anton Bjornson, owner of Drone Tech, smiled at the screen. *Uff da.* How sweet it is. He hovered the drone over his business, then sent it up the ridge to where they stood and down the other side of the ridge to curve along another road crossing the undeveloped land below on the edge of the city. He filmed a full-circle panorama. Then he flew it back to them.

As the drone descended, its screen filled with the image of the tall man with dark blond hair working the controls and his young employee watching with a big smile of delight. The rotor draft ruffled the employee's wavy brown hair. The legs on the eight-rotor copter extended for a gentle landing.

Charlie Van Dyken whooped in success. "We did it, Anton. Great maneuvering. I love this job."

"Job? Am I paying you to play around with these babies?"

"Yeah, and very handsomely." Charlie grinned. "Take it up again. I'll pretend I'm a hot-shot movie director, and I've hired you and your drone."

Anton laughed and played along. Charlie's enthusiasm was catching.

"The bad guys are hiding over by that pile of rocks off to your left," Charlie directed. "The guys in the white hats will come riding in toward that rusted-out car body."

"Uff da," Anton said. "Why doesn't somebody clean up that junk?"

"Get into the moment. Pretend it's a movie set. Follow them in."

Anton sent the drone smoothly toward the rocks.

"I found myself saying 'uff da' the other day," said Charlie. "One of the girls I date wondered what the heck that meant."

"What can I say? You hang around folks of Norwegian ancestry long enough, and it comes naturally," said Anton.

"There's a car. Just in time to play the good guys." A plume of dust followed the car as it turned onto the road below them. "He must be drunk. He's weaving all over the road."

On the screen they watched the car slowing. To Anton's surprise, the passenger door opened, and a woman tumbled out. "That had to hurt." He brought the drone closer. The woman struggled to her feet and began running into the brush.

"Those aren't the good guys, Anton!" Charlie grabbed for his cell phone.

Anton followed the drama on the screen. The car stopped. A man got out, sprinted after the woman, caught her, threw her to the ground, and struck her twice with his fist. As he raised his fist again, Anton sent the drone rocketing toward him. The man ducked away, rolled to his feet, and looked toward the drone. The screen captured his look of anger and disbelief in high-resolution clarity. The woman scrambled to her feet, only to stumble and fall as the man grabbed her again.

Like a huge bird of prey, the drone flew back before swooping on an arc above. The man let go of the woman, picked up a rock, and threw it at the menacing copter. Anton sent the drone out of harm's way before diving at the assailant again as he ran to his car and jumped in. The drone circled the car, and the lens zeroed in on the license plate before it was obscured by a cloud of dust with gravel flying everywhere as the car accelerated forward. Anton sent the drone high again as Charlie relayed all of the action to the 911 dispatcher. The drone recorded the woman running into the brush before slumping to the ground. The car reached the highway and disappeared.

In the distance, they heard sirens and saw the red and blue flashing lights of two police cars. One followed their initially relayed directions for the now out-of-sight car. The other searched below them until the policemen found the woman. She stood, awaiting rescue. Anton recalled the drone back to where he and Charlie stood.

"Jesus!" said Anton. "When you conjure up a big motion-picture scene, give me a little more warning next time." The drone landed, and he powered it off.

"She was lucky," said Charlie. "All alone out there. Makes me wonder if he intended for her to survive. What a bastard."

Anton picked up the drone and began folding the rotor arms back so he could carry it. "Thank God we were here. I'd never even thought of using a drone as a weapon to drive someone away before."

"Did you see his face when he looked up at the black monster diving toward him? Good job." Charlie pocketed his phone. "There should be a special place in hell for guys who beat on women. My sister's ex would be the first one I'd throw there."

"Skyla's ex? What happened? She told me she'd been married before, but it didn't work out. I didn't push. I could see it upset her."

"He beat her up. Spent days in the hospital. The trial put her through hell again. He's in prison now, but not nearly for as long as he should be."

"Prison. Jesus. I thought it was usually just jail time."

Charlie looked at him, his eyes smoldering with rage. "He hurt her—a lot. God only knows how bad. She still doesn't want to talk about it."

Anton thought of the beautiful woman he'd been dating ever since Charlie introduced them. Like her younger brother, she was a warm, caring person, occasionally showing a wicked, dry sense of humor. But he'd also sensed some barriers she'd erected, letting people come so close, but no further.

A biting gust of wind hit the ridge top behind his research facility, prompting Anton to zip his jacket a little higher over his polo shirt. He started down the path. When he didn't hear footsteps following, he stopped and turned. "What's wrong?"

Charlie stood above him. His usually friendly smile was absent, his look penetrating. "I know you've been seeing her. Should I ask what your intentions are?"

Anton started to laugh, then realized Charlie was serious. He considered the man in silence for a moment. Charlie was only twenty-five, eight years younger than his thirty-three. He was a friend, at least as much as an employee and employer could be friends. "No, you shouldn't. For one thing, it's early. We enjoy each other's company. But I can assure you I would never hurt a woman. That's not how I'm wired."

Charlie nodded and began his way down the path. "Sorry if I overstepped."

"You're her brother. You should be looking out for her. I respect that." Anton turned as a police car entered the parking lot below. "That didn't take them long. They're already here to talk with us."

Chapter Two

A few days later and miles away, across the Sangre de Cristo mountains that separated Santa Fe from the small communities of Pecos and Glorieta, Buck climbed to the top of a rocky ridge in the Santa Fe National Forest. He saw movement on the road far below. Resting his shotgun on a rock, he pulled his binoculars to his eyes, looking in the direction of Pecos.

A faraway pickup came in view, a cloud of dust rising behind as it wound its way up the forest service road. "It's about time. What the hell have they been doing? Two days I've been digging with no help. Fernando must have a death wish."

He picked up the gun and climbed effortlessly down the steep path to where he'd been working. His constant physical labor had left him in good shape. The altitude no longer fazed him. At the dig site, his own pickup truck was hidden under a stand of ponderosa pines. He wrapped his most recently excavated pot in soft cloths and settled it into the crate with the others under a tarp. His two bosses should be satisfied with this week's work. Three pots, one of them completely intact—a black-on-white—shaped like a football. He'd heard the gallery guy had been excited when his older boss had brought in a black-on-white pot last year.

He went back to his dig near the base of the cliff, adjusted his light in the dim interior under the overhang, and began brushing the soil away from a brown pot with black designs, slowly unearthing it from a corner of the ancient rock shelter. He liked this one. It was broken, but all the pieces seemed to be there. A snake design revealed itself on the curved surface. When he heard the truck drive into the site, bouncing and grinding on the terrain, he stood and went to greet the driver. It was the professor—alone in the vehicle. Buck snorted. Professor. Yeah, like his older boss had ever earned that title. It was just wishful thinking on his part.

"Why haven't you delivered anything yet?" the man said, exiting the truck with a scowl. Approaching Buck, he stopped several feet away and waved a hand back and forth in front of his nose.

Buck knew exactly why the professor had stopped so far away, his nose wrinkling in derision. So, he was a little ripe. What did they expect? No showers or soap here. Just hard work digging and brushing. Buck threw down his brush and stripped off his gloves. "Idiot Fernando hasn't shown up this week. Why isn't he with you? I've been busting my butt here."

"We don't pay you to sit around and look at the scenery. You should be working faster."

"You want sherds or whole pots? It's hard work to dig this stuff out so it stays in one piece. You want it done right? You'll wait for it. Where the hell is Fernando?" Buck snatched off his hat, wiped the sweat off his forehead, and left a streak of grime. He brushed some dust off the brim, caressed the snakeskin hatband, and settled the cowboy hat back on his head.

"Fernando won't be back. There's a warrant out for his arrest."

Buck swore. "Well then, he'd better stay the hell away from here and not come looking for a place to hide. We don't need cops getting nosy around here."

"If the hothead sees Fernando first, he'll wish he was in police custody," said the professor.

"I knew Fernando's short temper would land us in hot water. Now what did he do?"

"Assaulted some woman. Damn fool was out in the middle of nowhere on the other side of Santa Fe. Somebody with a drone filmed the whole thing and called the cops. The woman filed charges."

"Idiot. A drone? Shoulda shot it out of the sky. Do we have to worry about him ratting on us?"

"They have to catch him first. Why would he ask for more trouble? He's in enough already. What's he going to say? By the way, I'm also involved in illegal artifact looting on federal land? Charge me with that, too?"

"If he thought he'd get less time because he ratted, he would."

"No way. He's in trouble in Utah. Same thing. Beat some woman to death. He's wanted there."

"How do you know that?" asked Buck.

"I made it my business to find out." The professor eyed him. "I know things. You, of all people, should realize that."

Buck felt his face flushing. He picked up his tools and returned to the pot emerging from the soil. "So, who's going to help me up here? Find somebody better this time. Fernando was a worthless piece of shit."

He only got a sigh in answer.

Lifting the tarp off the crate, the professor folded it carefully and knelt on it to inspect the contents. His mood seemed to improve as each pot was inspected. The black-on-white brought verbal appreciation. "A canteen," he said.

Buck wondered how much they'd get for that one. "I'll bring them down to the shed tonight. I should have this one out by then."

"Good." The professor rose and inspected his sharply-creased slacks for soil. "I'll get them all off to the gallery. I'll leave your cash in the usual place."

"I should get Fernando's pay, too."

The professor studied him. "I'll think about it."

Chapter Three

Later that afternoon, Anton stood and stretched, looking away from the laptop screens in front of him on the dining room table at Skyla's home in Pecos. Charlie leaned back from the table. Skyla still peered at her screen, totally fascinated by the drone view of Pecos National Historical Park, where she worked as a park ranger.

Anton smiled at Skyla. Both brother and sister had wavy brown hair. Skyla wore hers long, caught back and disciplined when she was in uniform, but often hanging free as it did now when she wasn't working. He sat and focused on the screens again. They had taken videos with the octocopter drone of the ancient dwelling sites. Because the use of drones was illegal in national parks, Anton had applied for a special-use permit and received permission to work with Skyla, as the supervising park ranger, on filming there.

They were checking the two videos they'd taken five hours apart—basically the same pattern each time. Each flight gave the larger context of the interstate, Glorieta Mesa, and Pecos River, before zooming in closer to Pecos NHP and exploring the crumbled Pecos Pueblo walls and the massive remnant of the old mission.

"I'm glad we did this, Anton," said Charlie. "I'd rather learn this stuff now, and not when I have some high-powered film director looking over my shoulder."

"You were smart to suggest it," said Anton, "especially since we've signed the contract with the movie company."

"Charlie told me he'd be working on a film about the Civil War here," said Skyla.

"We begin in a week or so. It's about the Battle of Glorieta Pass," said Charlie. "My job is to give technical support to their cameraman."

"It'll be fun to have you staying in Pecos for a change," said Skyla. "Did any of your friends give you a bad time about living in a monastery?"

"They laughed. Teased me. Said when they saw me again, I'd be wearing a robe and sandals."

"Sandals are okay for the city," said Anton, "but damned impractical for country where you're tromping around cactus and snakes."

"Yeah, and I said I might even cut my hair in a tonsure and would be glad to cut their hair, too," Charlie said with a devilish grin. "Then I told them the monastery made a good business of hosting film crews. Part of their facility is designed to aid movie-making. They'd no idea Pecos was important in New Mexico's film industry."

"This film has the potential for prompting a new demand for our drones," said Anton.

"Ever the businessman?" asked Skyla.

Anton looked at her, wondering if he'd heard a slight derisive tone in her voice. "Success in business doesn't hurt my feelings, but this has been a lot of fun, too." He grinned and winked at Charlie. "I love playing with my toys."

"Isn't that the truth?" said Charlie. "Best job in the world."

Skyla laughed. "You're bad. Both of you. Put some techie gadget in the room, and everyone else could disappear. Although, I'm that way when someone starts talking archaeology."

"You must admit you've enjoyed this." Anton looked back at the monitors. "Look at the difference between these shots above the settlement. You can see all the walls and the outline of the buildings. But here—" He stopped the action and pointed to the later afternoon video. "Why do you suppose this straight dark line is here? It's not on the other one."

"That's a shadow mark," said Skyla. "It means there's an unevenness in the topography there. The angle of the sun when we took this one makes it show up, but not on the other. It could very well be an indication of a wall that's buried. Cool. I wonder if Upton knows that area. He's our park archaeologist. I think you met him? He's older. Gray-haired."

"I remember him," said Anton. "Diminutive in stature, but huge on intellect."

"How about this mark here?" Charlie pointed to a lighter strip in the grassy meadow. "That can't be from shadows."

"Ooh, this is exciting. I think it's a crop mark," she replied, leaning forward to inspect the area.

"What? Somebody mowing marks in the grass?" asked Anton. He intoned the opening notes of the *Twilight Zone* theme.

"Aliens. Marks made by their spacecraft landing. They're comink to take you avayyy." Charlie's fake accent trailed off as they laughed.

Skyla cuffed her brother on the arm. "Get serious. I don't think crop mark was the right term for me to use. Crops are something planted on purpose. It would be more correct to call it a vegetation pattern. Plants grow differently depending on what's beneath the surface. This might mean there's a buried wall here. The roots can't access as much water from the wall area, so the plants are stunted, maybe ripen faster or dry up and appear different."

"And here?" Anton pointed to a darker, circular area.

"That's a different kind of mark. I know there's a kiva in that spot. It hasn't been excavated yet. The roots have more water available in dug-out places and ditches, so the grass grows better."

"You love this, don't you?" asked Anton. Her eyes, like Charlie's, were a striking color—yellow around the pupil, changing to a greenish hazel with a darker rim on the edge of the iris. Right now, her eyes glowed with excitement.

"I do. Sometime I'd like to see somebody film this area with a thermal camera. You can see a lot more of what's buried beneath the surface."

"Beneath the surface?" Charlie asked. "I don't know much about thermal imaging. How does it do that?"

"You know landscape items get heated by the sun and retain heat at different rates. If the sun heats up soil that has buried stones, for example, that area will stay warmer longer than the dry soil without rocks. A thermal camera can record those differences. If you happen to be recording over an ancient settlement, sometimes you can see outlines of structures without digging."

Another techie gadget he could play with. Anton had already been thinking of getting a thermal camera. God love it, this was something he and Skyla would enjoy doing together. With her expertise and his technical ability, they could do some productive exploring.

"Can we show this video to Upton and the park rangers?" asked Skyla. "They'd really like it. We might even think about doing a production to share with the public in our museum. We could put together a script. We shouldn't have a problem getting a special-use permit to film with the drone again."

"I like it," said Anton.

"Yes!" exclaimed Charlie, making a fist and pumping his arm down in agreement.

Skyla pushed back her chair and got up. "It's almost four o'clock. Anybody want a glass of wine before we head on over to Frankie's restaurant?"

"What kind you got?" asked Charlie, getting up to help. "Still have that bottle of Gewürztraminer I saw the other day?"

"Yes, is that okay?"

"Works for me," said Anton. He closed down his computer and looked appreciatively as Charlie carried a plate of cheeses and crackers into the living room.

Anton smiled as Skyla came to him with his wine. He took it and clinked glasses with his friends. "To our video production company." They sat around the low table with the hors d'oeuvres.

"Anton, did they ever catch that guy we filmed attacking the girl?" asked Charlie.

"When was this? What happened?" Skyla asked.

Anton told her the story. "I asked my police friend, Sam, if they got him. They haven't yet. Somebody named Fernando Navarro."

"I feel so sorry for that girl," said Skyla. "It would be very scary for her, knowing he was on the loose, always looking over her shoulder. Jumping at every little noise. I'm really thankful Travis is in prison."

"I'm sure it won't be long before they catch him," said Anton. "The video shows him clear as a bell. They have his license plate number. The girl was able to give them more information. He'll be locked up soon." He looked up as the doorbell rang.

"I wonder who that could be," said Skyla. She crossed to the door and looked through the peephole before opening the door wide. "Come on in. This is a nice surprise." She hugged the woman with red curly hair as she came in. A man in a forest service jacket followed her. Skyla took the bag the man was carrying, looked in, and set it on the floor.

"Hey, Melody, Hoot," Charlie said. "Good to see you again."

"I'd like you to meet Anton Bjornson," Skyla said. "Melody and Ross Stewart."

"Please, call me Hoot," Ross said. "Skyla has told us about you. You have the drone company?"

Anton shook his hand. "That's right. And you must be the forest ranger."

"I wish. Thanks for the promotion," he said with a smile, "but there's only one forest ranger—Brooks is the guy in charge of our office. I'm just the lowly forester."

"We're heading to Frankie's after a bit," said Skyla. "Can you join us?"

"We'd like to," said Melody, "but Grandma has dinner waiting for us. She's got the kids. We just came by to return the crock pot you lent us when ours died. Thanks."

"How are the kids?" asked Skyla.

"Matti just got the cast off his arm yesterday," said Melody.

"What happened?" asked Charlie.

"He was trying to jump from the roof of our shed and catch a tree branch," said Hoot.

"He missed?"

"No, he actually caught the branch he was aiming for on an old willow tree," said Hoot. "But the branch broke and he landed on his arm. I'm just glad his sister didn't try it. She's only three. I'm hoping girls don't try such wild stunts. You have kids?" He looked at Anton.

"I have a daughter who is ten, Sorry, Hoot, girls aren't immune to danger."

"I was afraid of that. What's the worst?"

"I quit counting the number of times she's fallen from her pony, but we make her wear a helmet. She always gets back on. The scariest thing ever was when she was kidnapped last year."

"Kidnapped! Good God," said Hoot. "How'd you get her back?"

"She managed to get away, and except for being scared, she was okay. She kept her wits about her and appealed to the right person for help." Anton touched the scar on the side of his head. "They shot me when I went to where they said she'd be. It was the worst feeling of my life when I realized she'd been kidnapped."

"Is she okay now?" asked Melody.

"She's still leery about going places alone. Maybe a little more clingy. But she has recovered quite well. I don't know that a child ever gets over an experience like that, or their father, either, for that matter."

"To get away by herself," mused Hoot, his eyebrows drawn together in a frown. "Of course, she was older."

Older?" asked Melody.

He looked at her blankly. "I … it was good she wasn't just six or seven. A ten-year old has more savvy."

"True," said Melody. She looked at her watch. "We should be going."

"I would enjoy getting together some time with you two," said Hoot. "Maybe a raincheck on having dinner?"

"We'll look forward to it," said Skyla, closing the door as they left.

"Good folks. I like your friends, Sis," said Charlie. "Frankie's should be open by now. I'm ready to eat."

Chapter Four

Balancing two insulated bags, Skyla kicked her front door shut behind her. She dropped her mail on the kitchen counter and put away the groceries. Living in the rural setting of Pecos suited her, but it was inconvenient to have to go into Santa Fe to find a grocery store of any size with variety, quality, and good prices.

She glanced at the clock. Charlie should be here soon. They were going to Sam Martinez's father's ranch just outside Pecos for dinner. Skyla had deliberately manipulated her brother by telling him they were supposed to arrive earlier. Charlie was habitually late, and she liked to be on time. Skyla wondered who all would be there besides Anton and his ten-year-old daughter, and Sam, his police friend. She'd heard a lot about Anton's daughter, Krista, but hadn't met her yet. The thought was daunting. Charlie knew Krista, though, and he seemed to like her. Said she was a nice kid with her head screwed on straight.

Skyla quickly changed, choosing a blue top of soft fleece to go with her jeans. No telling how warm the ranch house would be, or if they would be outside in the May evening. She brushed out her hair and added blue dangly earrings, loving the way they brushed against her cheeks.

Charlie wasn't here yet. Typical.

She picked up the mail and sorted through it. A bill, advertisements, investment statements. An official-looking envelope was next—from the parole board.

It can't have been that long yet. Maybe they were just letting her know his request had been denied once again. Her fingers shook as she slit the envelope open and unfolded the paper. Glancing quickly at the contents, she sagged against the counter. *Damn. It's way too soon. I'm not ready to have Travis out.* Cold fingers of fear crept into her soul, bringing back the feelings from when he'd beat her and the pain and emptiness that followed. The feeling of diminishment. She'd had to work hard to regain her strength and independence.

He was in the past. *I won't allow any man to have that kind of control over me again. Never ever.*

Rereading the letter, she breathed a sigh of relief, noting that her demand had been met. The conditions of his parole stated that he was not to have any contact with her. Thank God. She never wanted to see him again.

There was a knock on her door, and Charlie came in. "Hi, Sis. Ready?" He came into the kitchen, his cheery expression changing as he looked at her. "What's wrong?"

She handed him the letter in silence. There were things about that night she'd never shared with Charlie, because he was too volatile in her defense. Better that he didn't know. It was just too painful, too personal.

He read it swiftly and swore. "With any luck at all, he won't be living near here." He tossed the letter on the counter and reached out to give her a hug. "It'll be okay. Tonight will be just what you need. Get your mind off that bastard."

"You're right. I won't let him spoil this evening." She picked up her jacket and locked her door behind them. *I must put that letter out of my mind. Focus on the positive. Think about tonight.*

She took a deep breath and looked at Charlie as he started the car. "Anton and I have spent quite a bit of time with Sam and his fiancée, Farah. At first I was confused when we were invited to the ranch. I thought Sam lived in Santa Fe. Are his parents divorced?"

Charlie laughed. "Not at all. They have a home in Santa Fe. That's where they live most of the time. But the ranch is his dad's business, and they have a second home there."

"Have you been to their ranch?" asked Skyla.

"A couple of times. Frank Martinez—that's Sam's father—raises gorgeous Andalusian horses. He also teaches dressage. Students come from all over to work with him. I guess he's fairly well respected in that world."

"Will there be any students at dinner tonight?" she asked.

"Probably not. They have their own living quarters. We'll be in the ranch house."

About ten minutes later, Charlie turned onto the drive leading to the Martinez ranch. He drove past several large barns and corrals with horses, many of them a dapple-gray color. Nearby was a U-shaped building with a central courtyard. They continued on to a parking area near an old, sprawling ranch house. A portal, a covered porch supported by posts with decorative corbels and beams, stretched across the front of the adobe home.

A man, who appeared to be in his fifties, rose from a rocker and came to meet them. "Welcome," he said. "I'm Frank Martinez. I got a text message from Farah a few minutes ago. They're leaving the interstate. Be here any minute."

"Hi. Charlie Van Dyken." Charlie shook Frank's hand. "We've met before. This is my sister, Skyla."

"Good to meet you, Skyla," said Frank. He looked down the road as two SUVs drove in. "Here they are."

Skyla's first impression was happy chaos. Anton and a young blonde girl got out of one vehicle, each with an excited Airedale terrier. From the other car came a patrician-looking man with thick silver hair holding the leash of a more sedate border collie. Because of the strong resemblance to Sam, she figured this man had to be his grandfather.

Sam, a dark-haired man about her own age, got out and held the door for his fiancée, Farah, who was holding a flat food container. A laughing girl, who must be her daughter, and another Airedale burst out of the car. As that third Airedale enthusiastically greeted his littermates, they all ended up in a tangle of leashes. Sam helped Farah extricate herself from the tangle as she held the box high out of harm's way.

"Let them run in the backyard until they've used up some of their energy," said Sam over the barking. "We'll be back in a minute." He led the girls and the dogs off around the house.

Skyla greeted Farah Salib with a hug. Sam had met Farah where she worked as a nursing assistant in the care center where his grandfather had gone after his accident the previous fall. The widow from Syria was about Skyla's own age. She and Anton had had dinner with them several times.

Farah introduced Skyla to Domingo Baca, Sam's grandfather. Soon the girls came running back. Krista gave Charlie a high five.

"Skyla, I'd like you to meet my daughter, Krista," said Anton.

Skyla looked down into blue eyes in an open, smiling face. No attitude, just friendly interest. Her nervousness faded.

"And this is her best friend, Leyla. She's Farah's daughter."

Leyla, a little shorter than Krista, greeted her politely. She was the spitting image of Farah with her curly, brown hair and blue eyes.

"Sam, is your mother coming?" asked Skyla.

"No, she's at home with my kid brothers and little sister. My dad is often here. Mother is usually in town."

"Where do you usually hang out?" asked Charlie.

"I've lived with Dom ever since my grandmother died about ten years ago," said Sam, flashing a smile at him. "We're remodeling and adding on right now. After we're married, Farah and I will live there with my grandfather."

"Our place will be a lot more lively. Something to look forward to," said Dom, as they sat down at the table.

"What does a park ranger do?" asked Krista.

"A large part of what we do is help visitors understand the history of the area. One way we do that is by taking them on tours of the pueblo and the mission."

"Can doggies come on the tour?" asked Krista.

Skyla smiled. "Sure. Pets are welcome on leash."

"Next month when school's out, we'll all go," said Anton.

Chapter Five

Anton watched in enjoyment as dinner progressed. Skyla had drawn both Leyla and Krista into stories of funny happenings at the park. He had wondered how she would get along with his daughter. Skyla was at ease with her and his friends, too. And Dom? He was captivated. Of course, that was a natural. Put a retired history professor into the same room as an archaeology buff, and they'd find lots to talk about.

"How about taking a sunset break before dessert?" asked Frank. "Then we can make ourselves comfortable in the family room."

Anton rose with the others, grabbing his jacket as they went out to the portal. One rocker was already taken by a ranch employee he'd met before, a Native American. His long, dark hair was pulled back and tied at his nape. The top buttons on his shirt were open to show a bone-bead and turquoise choker. In the light of the setting sun, an earring glinted. The man nodded but did not speak as they joined him, continuing to rock in silence.

The portal was built to take advantage of the brilliant New Mexico sunsets. The windmill by the corrals cast a silhouette against the deepening color, its blades turned lazily in the gentle breeze. Krista and Leyla had collected the dogs before they settled down to watch the colors blossom and fade. Twitch, Anton's dog, jumped up and squeezed his way between Anton and Skyla.

As the glory faded, the Native American spoke up. “Sam, there’s a new foal in the stable. Would the girls like to see him?”

“Can we, Daddy?” asked Krista.

Leyla looked hopefully at her mother, who looked at Sam.

“Sure,” said Sam as Anton nodded. The girls skipped off with the man toward the stables.

“Yancy’s okay, Farah,” said Frank. “He’ll watch out for them. He’s worked for me since Sam was about eight years old.”

“Yancy’s a character,” said Sam.

“This portal has been the setting of some very interesting discussions,” said Frank. “Some people might look at Yancy dismissively because of his looks or because of a stereotype they hold, but they should never underestimate him.”

“His face is rather ageless,” said Skyla. “Could be thirty, could be sixty.”

Sam laughed. “I think he’s pushing fifty, but I’ve no idea.”

“Sam, I’ve been wanting to ask you,” said Skyla. “Did they ever catch the man who was beating up the poor woman who Anton and Charlie saw on their drone video?”

“No, not yet. There’s still an APB out for him,” he replied.

Anton saw Skyla rubbing her arms. “Let’s go in,” he said. “It’s chilly now the sun’s down.”

“And I’ve been looking forward to having some of Farah’s pie,” said Sam. “I thought I was full, but I’ve discovered a pie-shaped hole still.”

They were soon polishing off their pie and coffee. The girls had come back, chattering about the sweet, dark foal and how Yancy said it would turn light-colored when it got big.

“How are your wedding plans coming?” Anton asked Farah and Sam. He was surprised to see the look pass between the two of them. Uh-oh. Had he put his foot into it?

“The date is set,” said Farah. “It is on a Saturday—June 25.”

“It’s the place that’s the problem,” said Sam. “Mother has put deposits down on the Basilica and a reception hall and is upset with us because we aren’t moving fast enough.”

Anton glanced over at Sam’s father. He shrugged and put up his hand.

"Don't look at me," said Frank. "I choose my battles, and this one's not mine."

"I'm used to conflict with my mother," said Sam. "God knows I've had enough of it. I'd love to find a good alternative to the Basilica and a huge society wedding, but Farah and I haven't agreed on anything yet. The invitations should go out soon." He put an arm around Farah and pulled her close. "Farah is amazing. She has a spine of steel—yet she's very warm and polite. Mother has definitely met her match."

Anton didn't envy his friend. Sam was the first-born of a mother who was a mover and shaker in Santa Fe society—old Spanish settler family and proud of it. His dad was her silent consort. Occasionally he put his foot down, but this evidently wasn't one of those times.

"Whose wedding is it?" asked Dom.

Anton smiled at the question. Dom had strongly supported his grandson over his daughter while Sam's relationship with the Syrian-immigrant widow grew.

"That's just it," said Sam. "Mind you, I've nothing against getting married in our church, nor does Farah. In some ways we'd prefer it. But we want our wedding to be intimate enough to spend some time with our guests in a meaningful setting. I don't want to put Farah through a stressful occasion where she is overwhelmed by hundreds of strangers. The bride's side of the church would have twenty people with three hundred on the other."

"What are the possibilities?" Anton asked. He listened as Sam and Farah described them. "What would be your ideal number of guests?" He found himself contemplating making an offer to them.

"We have talked about that." Farah looked into Sam's eyes. "Those we want most at our wedding, family and close friends, number about fifty."

"I have a wild idea," Anton said. "What do you think of having your wedding and reception at our home?"

"Seriously?" said Sam, sitting up straighter.

"Oooh! How fun," said Krista. Leyla's face looked hopeful.

"Would that be possible?" Farah asked. "Would fifty people fit? What would Karen say?"

"Karen's my mom," said Anton, glancing at Skyla, making sure she was included in the conversation. His gaze switched back to Sam and Farah. "Mom and I would love it. It'd be cozy, but there's room. It's a big house. The three of us just rattle around in it."

"I know Karen would jump at the opportunity," said Dom. "She had the idea, too, and asked me what I thought. We didn't know how to bring up the subject with you."

Anton raised his eyebrows in surprise as he looked at Dom. "Mom never said anything to me."

Dom shrugged. "We were talking one day when I was visiting. You weren't there at the time." He looked at Skyla. "Dolores, who's my daughter and Sam's mother, will be disappointed at not having a big society wedding to plan, but she has other children with lives to manage."

They all turned to Sam and Farah, who were looking at each other with excitement. "It's certainly a setting that holds meaning for us," Sam said. "Most of our courtship took place there."

"It would be a dream come true," said Farah.

Sam nodded and dropped a kiss on her lips. She drew him closer for a second kiss, then got up to give Anton a hug. "Thank you. It is a perfect solution."

Chapter Six

After dessert, Sam's dad excused himself to meet with his students. The girls settled at the table with their sketchbooks. The others relaxed in the family room in front of a crackling fire. Dom's border collie lay at his feet. Twitch cuddled next to Anton on the couch. On his other side, Anton draped his arm on the back of the couch lightly around Skyla. He found pleasure in occasionally touching her hair, her arm, and neck. She, too, enjoyed the contact if her smiles told true.

Anton told Dom, Sam, and Farah about the Pecos NHP video they'd done.

"I'd love to see it," said Farah. "I was lucky enough to visit several digs in Syria before all of the trouble started. I was fascinated."

"We'd gladly show it to you," said Skyla. "Sometime, I want to hear about those sites you saw."

"Making the video gave me an idea," said Anton. "Suppose you were an Indian who lived in Nambe or Tesuque Pueblo. You wanted to trade goods at the Pecos Pueblo. Would it make sense to take a shortcut through the mountains rather than going all the way to Santa Fe and around through Glorieta Pass?"

"I think it would," said Skyla. "There could have been a campsite halfway to break up the journey."

"Sounds logical," said Dom. "Are you thinking of finding a probable shortcut? Not such a wild idea. Back in the early nineteen-hundreds, the state planned to build a scenic route over the mountains going up the Santa Fe Canyon and somehow connecting to Dalton Canyon, and on to Las Vegas, New Mexico. They even started, but the idea fizzled out eventually."

"I suppose early traders could have started with that same route and come down the river to Pecos," said Skyla.

"I agree," said Dom. "Trial and error would have showed them the best route to take. No Google Earth or USGS topo maps available for them."

Anton laughed and shook his head. "Don't know how they did it. Would have been much easier with drones checking the terrain ahead."

"Are you thinking there might be an ancient campsite up in the Santa Fe National Forest?" asked Skyla.

"Yes, but if I've thought of it, with no archaeological training whatsoever," said Anton, "somebody who knew what they were doing would have been there long ago."

"I'm sure they have been," said Dom. "Certainly some sites have been found. I believe it's equally certain some haven't. It shouldn't stop you from the pleasure of looking—even if you never find a site. I've often wondered if somewhere there wasn't a cache of figures and religious articles some Pecos Indians had hidden away to save them from being destroyed by the Franciscans."

"Makes sense to me," said Anton. "What would you look for in a shortcut, besides a relatively easy route over the mountains?"

"For a campsite, you don't want too high an elevation," said Dom. "Not much higher than eight thousand feet. You'd need a reliable water source, a creek or spring. Even so, they'd have seen a mountain campsite as temporary—maybe used for their hunting and gathering."

"Where would they have chosen to shelter?" asked Anton.

"If I were that Indian," said Dom, "I'd look for water sources first, then a cliff, preferably one with a cave or an overhang. You're not going to find the same kind of geologic features here as you do in the Four Corners area where the cliff dwellers built, but you could augment natural features some with stone walls and adobe."

"A cool puzzle to solve," said Anton. "It would be fun to explore with the goal of finding a site. I'm thinking we might look along the forest service road that goes up to Glorieta Baldy."

"Remember, four hundred years is a long time," said Dom. "There may be some geologic changes to throw off your search. Even if earthquakes aren't likely in the Sangre de Cristos, there are forest fires, which may be followed by landslides. Springs dry up, stream beds move."

"I've a friend who's a helicopter pilot," said Anton. "We could scope out features by air."

"We'd see water sources, certainly," said Skyla, "and cliffs and shelter possibilities."

"How about this for a plan?" said Anton. "First, we'll go exploring, maybe up to the Glorieta Baldy Lookout. Then another day, we'll take a helicopter ride and look for possible spots. We can check them out later, one by one, using a drone. If Hoot and Melody Stewart want to come, we could include them, too."

"That's quite a project," said Dom.

"If we break it up over the next couple of months, it should be doable," said Anton. "What do you think, Skyla?"

"I love the idea of an archaeological site search," she responded. "Count me in."

The girls came over with their sketchbooks and showed off their drawings. Skyla looked impressed by their talent.

"We should be getting back, Sis," said Charlie. "I have to be up at the crack of dawn. The film director is doing some preliminary checking and wants me there."

As they went outside, they heard the plaintive sounds of a Native American flute. At the other end of the portal, Yancy sat playing in the darkness. Several dressage students listened. When he put down his flute, he began to tell stories of his people. His sentences were short, simple. His voice was expressive, enthralling the students with his tales. Then he began another melody.

They paused and listened.

"He's quite good," Skyla said. "We should find a flute player for our video soundtrack. It would pull you right into the setting."

"Do you suppose Yancy would do it?" asked Anton.

Sam shrugged. "Maybe, but I can't predict what he'd do or not. You could ask."

After Skyla said her goodbyes, Anton took her hand and tugged her into the shadows by Charlie's car. Charlie had lingered back on the portal with the others. Anton appreciated his tacit approval, giving them some time alone. The flute melodies followed them, accompanied by the insect sounds of the night.

"I'll call my pilot friend and give him heads up," said Anton.

"I'll talk with Hoot. I can hardly wait. Your idea is wonderful."

"I'm glad you finally had a chance to meet Krista," he said.

"She's delightful and talented. You're doing a good job." She threw her purse in the car and turned into his arms.

He glanced over her head to the others still chatting near the house, then bent, taking her mouth in a leisurely kiss. The world outside seemed to drift away, leaving just the two of them. The warmth of her body nestled against his, her arms drawing him close made him wish for more.

Too soon, Charlie appeared on the other side of the car. "Say goodnight, Skyla."

"I am, Charlie. You're interrupting."

Anton laughed, kissed her once more, and drew a long finger down her cheek. "Will I see you next weekend?"

"Ycs, call me."

After the car was out of sight, Anton went back to the others. The students had left. Dom had joined the group on the portal, and again they talked about the possibility of an ancient site in the mountains.

Yancy seemed uneasy as they shared some of their ideas.

In the dim light, Anton saw a frown on the ageless face. "Yancy, it doesn't look like you're thrilled by our plans."

"I'm not one to tell you what to do." Yancy's voice was somber. "Some things are best left undisturbed. It might attract the wrong kind of interest or bring dangers that you would not expect."

"From whom, Yancy?" said Sam. "You don't believe in witches or evil spirits any more than I do."

Yancy shrugged. "It's not a good idea. I'll say no more."

Anton glanced at Sam, who was rolling his eyes. Strange guy, Yancy. All the same, a shiver went down his back. It was chilly out here.

Chapter Seven

A patrolman waved Sam's car past the crime scene tape at the top of the rise on Old Santa Fe Trail. He parked off to the side of the road behind the crime scene investigation vehicle. Below him the road descended with guardrails on both sides over a dry wash. Traffic was being directed through the area on one lane. Someone had found a good spot for their dirty work, he thought. Though this was a populated area of Santa Fe, the arroyo and the surrounding scrubby vegetation screened it from nearby homes.

The call had come in when he'd first gotten to work. A woman and her dog had found a body. The responding patrol officers notified dispatch when they found the gunshot victim. Pete had assigned Sam to the case—his first homicide as the lead investigator. As Sam picked up his notebook and exited his vehicle, a raised voice drew his attention to a woman dressed in exercise clothes and with her hair tied back. She held the leash of a brindle boxer.

"What do you mean you won't be able to open up both lanes for several hours? That's just not acceptable." The woman shook her finger at the officer.

Sam walked over to the patrolman, who looked relieved at his arrival.

"This is the woman who called in," said the patrolman. "She and her dog found the deceased down off the road." He waved to where the forensics team was just beginning to survey the scene. "Ma'am, this is Detective Martinez."

The patrolman nodded to Sam and left to shepherd a curious neighbor back behind the crime scene tape. The boxer raised his head, looked at Sam, then relaxed again.

"I want you to move that body right now," she said to Sam. "That officer said they might be here for hours. This is a major road. It's a pain to have one lane closed that long."

"We need to find out what happened, ma'am. I'm sure that if you thought it through, you would want us to do a very thorough job. A crime was committed here. You want the person responsible to be caught and prosecuted successfully." He poised his pen over his notebook. "I'll need your name and address."

The woman obliged, pointing up the hill to where he could see the roof of a home among the trees.

"You say your dog brought your attention to the deceased."

"We were out for our morning run. My dog stopped and was all upset. Then I noticed the smell. I thought someone might have hit an animal on the road. Looked over the edge and saw a body there, so I called 911."

"Did you go down there?"

"No, I saw enough from up here. Some things I don't need to look at. Why isn't there an ambulance or something here to haul it away by now? If this were *CSI*, they'd have had it all figured out and done with."

"I'm afraid real detective work would make for a very tedious television show if they filmed the way it actually happens. I think the scriptwriters take a lot of shortcuts. Have to make it exciting, you know."

"Well, I suppose that's true," she admitted.

Sam suggested they move a little way upwind along the road. They sat on the guard rail, and he took notes as she told her story. From there, fresh cool air ruffled their hair. The dog lay on his side.

"Does your property have any surveillance cameras pointing toward the road?"

She shook her head. "Not that see this part of the road. I don't think any of our neighbors do either."

Sam looked at the boxer, now standing, watching an investigator on her way down to the scene. "Boxers are a great breed. Often very alert. Do you remember any unusual behavior in your dog over the past several nights or days?"

"I'm afraid he's been inside with me most of the time."

"Do you walk this area every day?"

"Only a couple of times a week. We hadn't noticed anything unusual before. But now that I think of it, I have seen a lot more of those big black birds flying around."

"Do you know your neighbors? Do you know of any who are especially alert? Who keep an eye on what goes on in the neighborhood?"

"You might try the lady who lives across from me. She's retired. Snoopy, likes to gossip."

"That should do it for now," Sam closed his notebook. "I'll be in touch if I have more questions."

The woman and her dog headed back up the rise to her home. Sam followed the same path the others had taken down to the bottom of the wash. With the leader of his forensics unit, he discussed what they'd found and what their conjectures were. From appearances, a gunshot to the back had ended the man's life. He'd been moved after death and dumped here. Tattoos were partially hidden by the tattered remains of his T-shirt. Jeans and work boots completed his attire. No wallet or ID. He'd been there for a couple of days.

They went back to the road and stood on the asphalt, looking at the dirt at the side of the road. Dog prints were liberally sprinkled in the dusty surface with shoe treads among them. Sam was sure most came from the lady who discovered the body.

As his eyes swept the length of guardrail ahead of him, they stopped. This guardrail had been sideswiped at some time in its history—maybe six months ago if the rust told true. The bolt holding the rail to the posts had been damaged. "Look," said Sam. "Something's caught on the bolt. Looks metallic and round. Could be from when someone hoisted the body over."

"I see it," said the investigator. "We'll document that and secure whatever it is."

Chapter Eight

Skyla stirred the hearty, split-pea and ham soup simmering on her stove and replaced the lid quietly. Then she went back to her living room, where Anton, Charlie, and Yancy were listening to a playback of his Native American flute music. Anton and Charlie were bent over the recording equipment they'd borrowed to get a more professional sound. Yancy's eyes were closed as he listened. She didn't know what vision filled his mind, but the music was evocative.

Yancy had brought two flutes in different keys. When he'd first begun to play, he'd used a higher-pitched flute, but it, too, had a mellow quality. She liked it, but the second was wonderful—a melancholy beauty. She wondered about Yancy. As he'd worked with them, he'd relaxed.

Twitch lay sleeping on the floor. He evidently found the flowing melodies relaxing. They'd wondered how he'd react. They didn't want howling along to be part of the sound track.

The piece came to an end. "That was lovely, Yancy," she said. "You're very talented."

"Thank you, Miss Skyla. I've never heard a recording of my playing. I've learned much today."

"The soup's ready any time. Anton picked up some Asiago cheese and pepper bread to go with it when he came through Santa Fe this morning."

"What's left to record after we eat?" asked Charlie. "Anton and I have something fun to show you after the sun goes down."

"I'd like to try more with the bigger flute," said Anton. "A lot of the Native American flutes I've heard are pitched much higher. I find yours more soothing."

Yancy laughed. "I've tried some of the smaller ones, too, but I play a lot around the horses. They prefer the lower pitched. It attracts them and calms them when they get agitated."

"As I was listening and looking at my notes," Skyla said, "I thought we might add some nature sounds, too. Maybe wind in the branches, the sound of the river, and some songbirds or hawks."

"What about the music for the segment of the mission scenes?" asked Charlie. "Would you use the flute for that, too?"

"Possibly," said Skyla. "I've thought of acapella Gregorian chant. I bet the brothers at the monastery would be pleased to be asked. That might be a good blend. Both the flute and the chant have that flowing, haunting sound."

"I'm curious," said Yancy. "You talk about going up in the mountains to search for an ancient site. Why? You want to hoover?"

"Hoover?" asked Charlie.

"I know that one," said Anton. "It's a term archaeologists use for irresponsible treatment of ancient sites. It means to suck up everything of value without regard for where items came from, or what could be learned, and with total irreverence for the peoples who left them."

"That's definitely not our goal," said Skyla. "That's despicable. No, I want to find out more about the cultures, what they believed, and what legacy they left us."

"Would you dig if you found a site?" asked Yancy.

"No. I wouldn't have access to the resources to do a proper job. To study everything in context. When a dig is done properly, it is done with respect. I like how the park has treated the artifacts that were excavated from Pecos Pueblo. They are preserved with care and placed in a setting that encourages learning and appreciation. Have you ever been to the visitor center, Yancy?"

"Yes. I go to the Jemez annual feast day."

"Someday, I would like you to be a part of one of the tours I do. I could learn something from you, too. Please come."

"What tribe is yours, Yancy?" asked Anton.

"My mother's people are from Jemez Pueblo. My father was Jicarilla Apache."

Anton considered him a long moment. "I'm sure we are all thinking it, but no one has had the nerve to ask you. You sound different from the Yancy, the storyteller we listened to the other night."

Yancy threw back his head and laughed. "I wondered how long it would take you to say something. You are all too polite. Sometimes, with students, I put on an act. Learned it from watching movies. I make their day by being what they expect. Then when I have them reeled in, I challenge them and get into discussions about cultures and stereotypes. They write home about me. I famous Indian." He grinned.

"I love it," Charlie said. "You're in their face. You must get a good laugh out of it."

"I do," Yancy said. "And I've found it to be a good opening. I sit on the portal, playing my flute. They come, sit, and listen. These students come from all over, not just the U.S., but we have international students, too. I have learned a lot from them. I hope they have learned, too, and not just about connecting with their horses and improving their riding."

"That's impressive, Yancy. You're a good reason we shouldn't label people," said Anton. "I'm glad I asked."

"Me, too," said Yancy. "Now I have a favor to ask of you. Can you put the music we recorded on my cell phone?"

"Do you want the soundtrack when it's done, or just the raw recording?" asked Skyla.

"How about recording tonight and soundtrack later?"

"Deal. We can do that," said Anton.

"Tell me about how you started to play the flute," said Skyla.

"I heard someone playing flute at a festival when I was young. I saved up and the next year, I bought one."

"Do you play particular songs or do you make it up as you go along?"

"I listen to Carlos Nakai, Charles Littleleaf, and others. The Jemez Pueblo has a wonderful flute player, too. I learn from them. Sometimes I sit by the river, I listen to the feeling inside me, and I play. It is good when it is in harmony with nature."

"Our video will be much better with your music. Very special," said Skyla.

"I am honored you asked me to share my music. I have thought long about this. Music by itself for the player is good, is healing. But music shared with others connects. One who listens, one who plays, the melodies that came before and ones that come after, the one who makes the flute, nature that gives the gift of wood. It is bigger than one. It puts you in harmony with earth, with past, and with each other."

"That's profound, Yancy," said Anton. "I hadn't thought of music like that before, but I see truth in your words."

Skyla rose and began to clear away the supper. They went back to their recording. The sun was just about down when they finished, and they packed up their equipment.

"And now," Charlie said, "for the surprise. Won't take long." He picked up a couple of small packs and handed one to Anton.

"Charlie made new toys for us," said Anton, as he zipped open the little case to reveal a small quadcopter about five inches across. "These are racing drones. They're amazing. We didn't manufacture these, but they've been specially adapted by Charlie. He's been busy with LED lights and sequencing."

"I might have known," said Skyla. She shook her head at Charlie. "This must be pretty good. I can tell by the gleam in your eye."

Outside, Charlie's drone went up first. Red and blue lights flashed as the little copter zoomed around the yard like a hummingbird. Anton's soon joined it. They chased, hovered, and circled each other in a mock battle. The sound of angry hornet swarms filled the night sky.

Twitch looked up, his tail wagging furiously. He threw his head back. Rah-oooorrr, rowr, rowr, rowr. Skyla began to laugh. The light show with the drones was great, but the canine musical accompaniment was over the top, becoming more enthusiastic as the drones battled on. Yancy was laughing. The drones only had an airtime capacity of about seven minutes. By the time Charlie and Anton brought them down to the sound of the last rowr, rowr, they were laughing, too. Twitch's tail still wagged. He looked very pleased with himself.

"He's never howled at a drone before," said Anton, wiping his eyes. "There must have been something in their frequency that set him off."

"He enjoyed it," said Yancy. "He wasn't howling because his ears hurt, just because he wanted to sing along."

"Those drones are cool," said Skyla. "I can see why you wanted to show them off."

"Cop drones," said Yancy. "That's what I'd call them. All red and blue lights. I don't suppose you could add sirens?"

"Or dog howls," said Skyla.

"What a cool idea," said Charlie with a broad grin. "I'll think about that." He looked at his sister. "Think about sirens anyway." Anton held his cop drone out to Charlie.

Charlie waved his hand. "No, you keep that one. We need practice. Have to improve our act with these cop drones. Upstaged by a dog!" He knelt in front of Twitch and howled. Twitch cocked his head and didn't respond, except to wash Charlie's face with one wet swipe of his tongue.

Skyla laughed again. All in all, the day had been fun and productive. She was looking forward to editing their script, working with the soundtrack, and sharing it with her co-workers. And she liked Charlie's new toys. Her hand rubbed Twitch's head affectionately as they bade Yancy farewell and went back inside.

Chapter Nine

Pete stopped by Sam's desk at the police department. "Got time for us to go over the notes on the homicide you just went out on?"

"Sure," said Sam, getting up to follow Pete to his office. "We've identified him as Fernando Navarro."

"Come on in." Pete pulled out a chair from the round table in his office and sat with his coffee. "Interesting that your case turned out to be the guy Anton caught on his drone video. Any ideas on suspects or motive yet?"

"You knew about his being wanted in Utah for killing a woman. I followed up with the jurisdiction there. Checked to see if any of her relatives might have looked for revenge. Her brothers and others involved were all accounted for during the time period Navarro was killed."

"How about the woman he assaulted here?"

"Ignacia Perez. She was glad he was gone, but again, no leads." Sam listed the different people he'd talked to and the possibilities involved there.

"I've tried to find out where he worked, who he hung around with. Perez said he worked someplace as a digger. She thought it must be in the mountains because he complained about there being no cell reception where they were. They'd be gone days at a time.

She never knew when he'd be coming back. Could be the same day, a week, but most often two or three days later."

"Did she ever meet any of the people he worked with? Would she recognize any of them?"

"She said he mostly worked with somebody called Buck. She didn't know his real name. Never saw any of them."

"What kind of digging?" Pete took a sip of coffee.

"I asked her. Construction? Pools? Irrigation or mining? All she knew was that it was hard, dirty work. I asked her what his clothes were like when he returned. The color of the soil, whether or not they'd been muddy or dry."

"Good questions," said Pete. "Did she know if he drove equipment like a backhoe, or was it hand-digging?"

"He complained about his back, using that shovel all day. She said his jeans were always dusty, with ground-in dirt on the knees. Just the sandy, beige dirt so common around here. I wondered if he was working on a hidden pot grow in the mountains somewhere. Asked her if he ever smoked marijuana. She said she'd never seen him do that, nor had she smelled it on him. He just smoked regular cigarettes. I wrote down the brand he favored."

"Did you ask her if he ever brought home items from his digging ventures?"

"She said every so often he'd come home with an arrowhead. Once he had a broken piece of pottery with a scorpion painted on it. Seemed to like scorpions. One of his identifying marks was a big scorpion tattoo on his bicep."

"What happened to his arrowheads?"

"He took them with him when he moved out. He didn't have much stuff. It all fit into his car."

"Ground-in dirt on the knees. Did the crime lab report say anything about that?"

Sam shuffled the papers in his folder, pulled out the report, and ran his finger down the sections. "Clothing, clothing, here we are. Doesn't say anything about soil. Let me check the pictures. Nothing like ground-in dirt. Just dirt from where he was and what he'd been through."

Pete nodded and got up to refill his coffee.

"Another item from the crime lab report. Analysis found traces of canvas fiber on his clothing."

"Did you ever find his car?" asked Pete.

"No, we haven't. Car keys were in his pocket, though. If he changed the plate, it could be anywhere—even parked in a neighborhood. I've got patrol keeping their eyes open for abandoned vehicles of that make and model."

"Nothing that might help pinpoint where he was killed?" asked Pete.

"No specific trace left at the scene. An interesting bit we found was a torn piece of a canvas tarp with a gold-colored grommet. If they'd transported the body wrapped in a tarp, it could have caught on a damaged part of the guardrail. If the body was dumped in the dark, the killer might not have noticed. Somewhere in the world is the torn tarp, but we don't have it."

"You have no way of knowing if it is connected to your case at this point," said Pete.

Sam sighed. "You're right."

"Let's take another look back at the drone video of his car," said Pete. "See if there were any dents or damage that might help locate it."

Sam pulled up the video on his computer, and they watched. "We lucked out with Anton being in that area filming." He stopped and reversed the video. "I thought I saw something,"

"I see it, too, down low on the right rear fender," said Pete. "Kind of obscured by all the dirt, but it looks like a scorpion."

"I've seen those. Vinyl stickers you can get over the internet. Let's add that to the description of the car. It will narrow it down considerably."

"How hard are they to remove?"

"Easy enough that I should word the description with a 'may have' a scorpion," said Sam. "Anybody with a heat gun can get them off."

Chapter Ten

Dinner with Hoot and Melody should be fun, thought Anton as he parked in Skyla's driveway. The invitation tonight was for a regular family dinner with their two children. They'd heard about Twitch. Melody said to bring him, too. The kids would love him.

"In the back, Twitch." Anton settled his six-month old Airedale onto the back seat of his Honda Pilot. Skyla locked her door and came down the walk to meet him, carrying a flat box and wearing a navy jacket against the chill of the May evening. He smiled, greeted her with a kiss, and opened the car door for her. Her brown hair waved about her shoulders, freed of its disciplined-park-ranger look. He got just a whiff of a clean scent. Was that her shampoo? Nice.

"What's in the box?" he asked.

"Cheesecake," she replied. "Melody's request. I picked it up in Santa Fe. It's hard to come by in Pecos."

"Twitch, sit. Skyla doesn't need you in her face." He got in and backed out of her driveway. "How long have you known Hoot and Melody?"

"I met them last October, just after Hoot began working for the forest service," said Skyla. "I'm glad you'll have a chance to talk. Hoot's been wanting to ask you about drones."

"I never like talking about drones."

"Hah! You and Charlie. I wouldn't even bring up the subject, but at least I'll have Melody to talk with. I've gotten to know what you're like when you get going on drones."

"Are you saying I drone on? I'm hurt."

Skyla shook her head. "You and words."

Anton almost laughed aloud when they arrived and met Hoot's red-headed children. Their heads looked like they were on fire. Matti was a blue-eyed, six-year-old boy. Bonnie, three, seemed a little awed by the tall stranger and the bumptious shaggy dog who stood at her eye level. She watched him from behind her dad's leg, squealing when Twitch managed to wash her face with a swipe of his tongue. By the time dinner was ready, she had warmed up to the pup and was patting him.

The meal was simple: chicken-noodle casserole livened up with mild green chiles and sharp cheddar. Green beans and fruit salad accompanied it. Comfort food, Anton thought with enjoyment. The melt-in-your-mouth cheesecake rounded off the meal before they settled in the family room."

After a while, Melody looked at the children. "It's time to get your jammies on and get ready for bed."

They scampered off with Melody. Soon Bonnie returned in her footie pajamas, dragging a toy plush fox by its foot. Matti followed. "We came to say good night," he said.

Skyla and Anton got good night hugs from Matti and sloppy kisses from Bonnie. Twitch jumped off the couch to get his share of attention.

"Do you need the hall light on tonight, Bonnie?" asked Melody.

"No, monsters don't wike doggies. They won't come out because of Twitch."

When Hoot returned from tucking in his children, he brought a treat for Twitch. "That's for keeping Bonnie's monsters away. Don't know why, but she is frightened of the dark."

"It's good for her to be around Twitch," said Melody. "More wine?" She brought the bottle and filled their glasses.

"Speaking of fears, something interesting happened at work," said Hoot. "Anton, you might not have met Brooks, our forest ranger yet, but he's an owly soul."

"Owly?" asked Skyla.

Hoot laughed. "That's Montana talk for disagreeable. Anyway, last week when a car crashed into a transformer and the power went off, Brooks was in the supply closet, and the door was shut. Made it blacker than the inside of a cow. He had a full-blown panic attack even though it'd been less than a minute before I opened the door. When he calmed down, he said when he was little his dad used to shut him in a dark closet for punishment."

"That's rare, his volunteering anything about his background," said Melody.

"I bet he got angry then," said Skyla, "to cover up his fear."

Hoot nodded. "He'd be pissed if he knew I told anybody about it. Shouldn't matter, though. God knows most kids have fears. I never did get over mine. To this day, when I have to fly, my hands get all sweaty and I'm terrified."

"But that's not unreasonable," said Melody. "You do very well flying, considering."

"Considering?" asked Skyla.

"When I was eight," said Hoot, "I was in an amphibious plane that crash-landed on a lake. My father was killed." He rubbed his head.

When Hoot pulled his hand back, Anton noticed a faded scar that went back into his hairline.

Skyla let out a cry of distress. "Oh, I'm sorry. I never should have asked."

"It's okay. I can fly. I'm just always glad when I'm back on solid ground." Hoot smiled. "That's one reason, Anton, I wanted to talk with you about how drones could be used in forest management. It seems like the best of worlds. The drone could be up—possibly monitoring illegal use of the forests, planning for recovery after a fire, or giving us data on the spread of the damn bark beetles infestation. The drone would do the flying, and I could stay on good old terra firma."

“Skyla and I were thinking of going up to Glorieta Baldy next week. Sam is coming, too. Would that work with your plans? At the least we could map out some areas you wanted to explore further.”

“Love to,” Hoot replied. “I have a special project in mind. Lots of folks cut wood in the national forests around here. With knowledge gleaned from drone exploring, I can figure the best areas to send them to.”

“Now that that’s settled, is anybody up for a game of Scrabble?” asked Melody.

Chapter Eleven

"Very pleasant evening," Anton said as he drove Skyla home. "Good people, good conversation, good food."

"You're just gloating because you beat us all at Scrabble," said Skyla. "You and Charlie—both of you are crazy about word play and puns."

"I like words."

"And what was it with that made-up word? The one you made by adding on to my word, lamb? You almost got away with it."

Anton laughed. "Lamborous. Just wait. Eventually it will make its way into Webster. I know the definition."

"What is it?"

"Are you sure you want to know?"

"Yes."

"It's a feeling, an activity. Encompasses warmth, heavy breathing, maybe just a hint of wickedness, touching and being touched, then a contented glow." He grinned. "I like how it sounds."

She smiled back. "Mmm. I had to ask, didn't I? You're bad, Anton."

He laughed again.

"Mind you, this is not an invitation to get lamborous, but would you like to come in for some coffee?"

"Yes," he replied. "I'm afraid I monopolized conversation tonight with stories about Krista. You've never told me, in the months we've been seeing each other, about how you decided to become a park ranger. Interesting choice."

"Do I hear the unspoken end of that comment? For a woman?" Skyla unlocked her door for them.

He helped her off with her jacket. "I don't think so. I'd encourage anyone to seek out a career that excited and challenged them. What was it that drew you to it?"

He followed her into the kitchen where she set about making coffee. "By the way, I don't think I said, but I like your sweater. That blue green looks good on you."

Skyla smiled and touched the Icelandic design of various blues and whites on the cardigan she wore over a teal turtleneck. "Thanks. Teal is my favorite color. My career? I've always liked nature, being outdoors. And in college, I was fascinated by archaeology, finding out how ancient people lived. Pecos NHP is a dream for me. I can be both a naturalist and share my love of archaeology with others."

While she finished making the coffee, he looked around. He liked the open floor plan of her house. Load-bearing beams between the living room area and the dining / kitchen area incorporated built-in shelves open to both sides. He wandered over to see what treasures she had chosen to display. Native American pottery and baskets were arranged with a blue-and-white vase of tulips and small statues, which he thought might be family heirlooms. A small Dutch boy and girl carrying milk jars, almost salt-and-pepper-shaker size, stood next to taller, elegant Lladró Dutch figures. A well-played-with doll in costume complete with wooden shoes sat nearby in another cubicle with bookends holding storybooks.

Next to a woven Native American basket, a bronze statue of a curled sleeping fox lay, its smooth surface inviting touch. It wasn't the only fox on display, either. She must like them. A Nancy Glazier fox print hung in the living area. The blue and teal shadows in the snow contrasted with the red fox. Skyla had picked up on those colors to coordinate the rest of her décor. He could tell teal was her favorite color.

His favorite fox was the almost-life-sized bronze fox at the end of the hall, sitting on the floor under a slender elvish banner. He wondered, when she finally got the opportunity to visit his home, what she'd think of his gift from his mother when they'd added on to their home. She'd commissioned doors for his suite. They were inspired by the doors of Edoras in the *Lord of the Rings,* but his had more of a dragon and Viking flair.

They sat on the couch with their coffee. "How do you feel about archaeological digs?" asked Anton. "I know there are different viewpoints. Is it better for artifacts to be in museums or should they be left where they were found? Should people have the right to collect them for themselves?"

"I understand the reasons the Native Americans want to keep the burial sites sacred, undisturbed. And I believe we grow from our study of the ancient cultures. I wouldn't want the museums emptied. Those items from the past need to be seen by the public. It disturbs me that sites get plundered for profit with no care for learning. It gets very complicated."

"I can see how fragile or unique artifacts would be better protected in museums."

"True," said Skyla. "It is good to have them there for safekeeping."

"Krista wants to get a storyteller figure for Dom, Sam's grandfather. He's become the storyteller in the Circle Sleuths."

"Now that's different," Skyla said. "The storytellers are modern creations. They're made to be sold. What, if I may ask, are the Circle Sleuths?"

"Remember when I told you about Krista's kidnapping?"

She nodded.

"Well, we Circle Sleuths met and became friends because of that. We worked together to find who did it. That's how I got to know Sam. Our support of each other helped when Dom was attacked. We helped solve that mystery. Since then the Circle has enlarged to take in Dom, Farah, and her daughter. You'll get to meet the rest of the Circle Sleuths when you come for Dom's birthday celebration. I think you'll enjoy them all." He took a sip of his coffee. "Are there any ancient storyteller figures?"

"They're very rare, if there are any. In fact, pottery figures are rare at any of the pueblos where missions were built."

"Let me guess. The Spanish missionaries destroyed them, trying to stamp out the native religion."

"True. That's it exactly." Skyla looked down into her cup and swirled the last of her coffee before looking at him. "You know, I wasn't sure what you'd think of Hoot and Melody's house." She drained her cup and set it aside. "It's only a double-wide trailer. Charlie has told me about your place—how big and beautiful it is."

"Hoot and Melody have in abundance what is valuable." Anton looked at Skyla. "There are houses, and there are homes. Houses are where you reside, show off your possessions, and keep up with the Joneses. A home is where you are surrounded by things you cherish, items with stories because they are connected to those you love. It's where you are accepted for who you are, and where you can be yourself. Home is love and support—Hoot and Melody have that."

"I don't think I've ever heard a man describe the difference like that before. That's quite lovely."

Anton laughed. "It comes right out of my mother's mouth, I confess. It's not original, but I do believe it."

"I think I'll like your mom. If you don't mind my asking, I'm curious, is yours a house or home?"

"I like to believe it's a home. Mom is good at making it homey for our visitors. Houses are kept on display. Homes are used, worn out by active people, dogs, kids, and company. They have books in every room, projects underway, and are places where friends are always welcome."

He set aside his own cup and angled his body toward hers, smoothing her hair back. She turned eagerly into his embrace. All was quiet for a while. Then he felt her beginning to pull back. She stilled his exploring hand by bringing it to her lips for a kiss. He pulled her close, just enjoying the feel of her body against his. Then he stood. Twitch scrambled to his feet.

"I'd better be on my way. Thank you, Skyla. See you soon for our Glorieta Baldy trip."

Chapter Twelve

Anton checked off the items on his list as he surveyed the contents of a couple of backpacks spread across the furniture in the Bjornson family room. He looked up as Krista came in with Shadow.

"I was so excited last night I could hardly sleep," said Krista. She let her dog out and watched him go chasing after Twitch before turning back to her dad. "We get to see Farah's wedding dress fitted. And Leyla's and mine. Gramma's going to take us all shopping and out to lunch."

"Wedding stuff, huh?" Anton smiled as he started replacing the gear and supplies back into the packs. "You should have a fun day."

"Yes. Whatcha doing? Are you going camping?" She watched as he rolled a sleeping bag up tightly.

"No. Skyla, Sam, Hoot, and I are going up to Glorieta Baldy Lookout today. I'll be back tonight. This stuff is what we always keep in our truck, especially when we're going off into the wilderness. It's always good to be prepared. Things happen. Weather changes. I check it every so often. Make sure it's okay and see if anything needs replacing."

"What do you check?"

"Change out foodstuffs. Check the batteries. Make sure my SAT phone is working. I look at my list to make sure nothing's missing."

"What's a SAT phone?"

"Satellite phone. It uses satellites to relay signals. It's handy in areas like the wilderness where there aren't cell phone towers."

"Is Charlie going with you?"

"No, he's started working with the film crew. They'll keep him busy for over a month."

"Is Twitch going with you?"

"Not this time. He's going to stay home with Shadow."

Krista knelt in front of a cupboard in the kitchen and rummaged around. She returned with a small stainless-steel bowl and a sturdy plastic bag of dog kibble. "You should keep this in the gear, too. You might not remember to add it when the dogs come with us."

"Good idea. Thank you for thinking of our furry family," he said, smoothing her long blonde hair away from her face. "They wouldn't be too thrilled with trail mix."

Krista giggled. "They might fight you for the peanut butter and crackers, though."

"You're right. That makes it even more important to have the kibble." He carried the packs out and came back. This time he picked up a cooler from the counter. Krista tagged along with him and watched him stow it in the back of his Ford Raptor.

"What's that you're putting in Thord? More survival stuff?"

"Nope. Maria fixed lunch for us."

"Oooh. I wondered what she was doing. You're going to like it."

Karen, Anton's mother, a tall, elegant blonde in her mid-fifties, came out. "Looks like you're all ready. Good weather. Clear skies. No rain to muck up the dirt roads."

"Or to dampen all that girl stuff you have planned. Give me a hug."

As Anton entered the highway toward downtown Santa Fe, anticipation filled his mind. First stop, pick up Sam, then on to Pecos to pick up Skyla and Hoot. This should be fun—the first of several planned trips testing their site theories. Today's plan was getting an overview of the area. Hoot's forestry experience would be informative. He enjoyed the upbeat attitude of the forester.

The days between his weekend visits to Skyla had dragged. Long phone conversations were good, but no substitute for being with her. He thought their relationship had escalated nicely in the past couple of weeks, though he was encountering challenges he'd never expected. Skyla wasn't impressed by his wealth or tall, Norwegian looks. He was used to women vying for his attention but had always just ignored them. After Sonja's death, it had taken him a long time to even think about dating again. He and Sonja had been blessed, growing up together. Their views had been shaped by each other, and there had never been anyone else for either of them.

He was reluctant to push Skyla, not certain what kind of baggage she carried from her abusive marriage. He knew there was some, but she never volunteered information. They ended most of their evenings on her couch, getting to a certain point, but then she would stop short of the final step. Not the "that's-wrong-before-marriage" stop or the "I-don't-like-how-that-feels" stop, and definitely not teasing, but stop like frozen, panic, insecurity. He supposed this could be like the proverbial turtle and hare race. Slow and steady might win it. He was looking for a lifetime. The prize was worth the investment of care and time, even if he was frustrated.

He set aside his thoughts as he pulled into Sam's driveway to find his friend waiting for him.

"My God," said Anton as he carefully negotiated a turn on the way up the rutty forest service road with rocks poking up at inconvenient points. They'd passed a cattle guard about two miles out of a little mountain community. After that, the road had quickly deteriorated and now—about six miles in—had settled to a bone-rattling rock and roll. "Thord is getting a workout today."

"Ford?" asked Skyla.

Anton laughed. "No, Thord. It's what I call my Ford Raptor. It's a name from a Norse saga. Means son of Viking."

"And I suppose his last name is Ford?" Skyla said with a grin as Anton nodded.

"His full name is Thord T. Ford."

"I'm almost afraid to ask," said Sam. "What does the T stand for?"

Skyla laughed. "You can't see it from the back seat, Sam, but Anton has a devilish twinkle in his eyes."

"Ouch. Sorry, Thord," Anton said as they hit a pothole. "Didn't see that one coming. Mom gave him his middle name. The."

"I knew I should have kept my mouth shut," said Sam. "When you and your mom get going on words and puns, you just don't stop."

"Thord The Ford?" Hoot asked. "Catchy. Anyway, Brooks said the first half of this forest service road was the best. The last three or four miles to the lookout can be pretty challenging. I can see why they don't want you to bring the family car up here. It would never make it."

"Can you imagine this in the rain?" asked Skyla.

"No way in hell," said Anton. "Anyway, our next trip isn't driving. My pilot friend says he can take us in his helicopter on May twenty-seventh. It's a Friday. Can all of you get off work?"

"Oh, darn," said Hoot in mock sadness. "That's the day I have to wash my hair. Can't come."

The others laughed.

"I would like to come when you do the drone trips later though," Hoot said. "As long as I'm on solid earth, I'm fine."

"Glorieta Baldy is way too high for a possible ancient Puebloan site," said Skyla. "I just wanted to see it."

"When can we see the Pecos NHP video you did for the public?" asked Sam. "You honored Yancy by asking him to play the flute."

"It's all done," Skyla said. "The park staff has seen it, but it has to go up the chain of command before it gets seen by the public."

"We could show you our copy," said Anton.

"I'd like to see it, too," said Hoot. "I've thought about your shortcut and site idea. I haven't told anyone about it, except Melody, of course. Going up here today was no secret, and the helicopter trip won't be. I don't think it's a good idea to advertise your reasons though."

"It's not illegal to look," said Skyla, "just to dig and loot. But I think you're right. No one needs to know what we're looking for."

"If I'm along on the drone trips," said Hoot, "we can always tell folks you're helping me check out pest problems or something. A tree cop's job is dealing with pests of the two-legged, four-legged, and the six-legged variety."

"I'm just curious what we can find," said Anton. "It's like figuring out a puzzle."

"Watch it," said Sam. "Pretty soon you'll want to be a detective. We specialize in puzzles."

"Not hardly," said Anton. They reached the old picnic area not far from the tower. "Let's walk the rest of the way."

"I told Brooks I was coming up here today," said Hoot as they neared the steel structure. "He said I should check the place out to see if there's been any recent vandalism."

"He's got you working on your day off?" asked Skyla.

Hoot shrugged. "No big deal. I'm here anyway. Why not?" He craned his neck, looking up at the dilapidated tower. "This thing was built in 1940. It was used until the nineties."

"What happened to the stairs?" asked Sam. Only the handrail and the side stair rails remained in place.

"They took the first couple of flights away to discourage folks from climbing up the tower, but they do it anyway."

"I heard there's a group trying to get it fixed up so it can be rented out for folks to get the experience of being on fire lookout," said Anton.

"That's right. The Friends of the Santa Fe National Forest," said Hoot. "My grandfather was a forest ranger at Flathead Lake in Montana. I spent my summers in places like this. I loved it."

"If you're going up, can we go up with you?" asked Skyla. "I'd love to see the view. Too many trees to get the full three-sixty here."

Hoot nodded. "I'm going up. Just be damn careful. I've no idea how sturdy the wood structure is." As they watched, a bird flew straight through the building on top and perched on a windowsill. "It's obvious the windows have all been broken out."

Soon they were in the lookout, a little out of breath from the exertion and the altitude. Anton looked at Hoot, who was obviously enjoying the experience.

"Look at that view," Hoot said. "We're a little over ten thousand feet. Look! You can even see the interstate way off there and some of the settlements near it. Look at the peaks in the Pecos Wilderness."

"I love the colors," said Skyla. "The green of the trees, stretching away into kind of a dark greeny-blue, and then shades of blue in the distance. The sky is gorgeous today with those puffy clouds."

"I never get tired of seeing the shadows of the clouds chasing across landscape like this," said Anton. He touched Skyla's cheek and smiled. "Your favorite colors, aren't they?"

She smiled back, then chuckled as Sam's stomach rumbled.

He threw up his hands. "What can I say? I know Maria fixed lunch for us. What say we eat?"

"Maria?" asked Skyla.

"Maria is our housekeeper. You'll meet her at Dom's birthday party. And Diego. He keeps the ranch going and takes care of all of mom's alpacas. Maria and Diego are family. They've been with us since before Krista was born."

After eating and exploring more, they started back. Conversation picked up after they reached the better part of the road. It was still a challenge, but Anton breathed easier. He patted the dashboard. "Good job, Thord."

"You talk to your rig?" Hoot asked.

"Sure. Everybody and everything needs encouragement. Thord has feelings, too."

"Does he ever talk back to you?" asked Sam.

Anton laughed. "He does. But not in English. Thord uses a language of lights and icons. Sam, Mom and Krista have been scheming with Farah and Leyla to get Dom a storyteller figure for his birthday. Have you heard anything about that?"

"Leyla cornered me about it. I think it's a great idea—he's the storyteller for the Circle Sleuths. Has been ever since our St. Nicholas celebration." He told Skyla and Hoot about the fun they'd had that day, how the celebration had begun a new tradition for their group, and how much it had meant for the progression of his and Farah's courtship. "A storyteller is something he'd treasure for many reasons. I think we should go for it."

"Skyla, would you like to go with us when we pick one out for him?" asked Anton. "You know more about pottery than we do, and it'd be fun to have you."

"I'd love to," she said.

"Look at all the trees down," said Hoot. "Must have been some strong winter winds here."

"Where do these roads go? Why would they even be built out here in the middle of nowhere?" asked Sam.

Hoot traced his finger across the opened map on his lap. "Damned if I know where they go. Maybe fire access roads. There are several on the map. I'm wondering about that chicken-foot road we just passed going off to the north."

"Chicken-foot?" asked Anton.

Hoot smiled. "That's Montana talk for a road that forks into three. I don't see that one branch marked. I'll have to ask Brooks about it. Part could have been built since the map was printed. Since I only moved here in October, the winter season kept me from exploring. I'll find out eventually."

"Some seem to be well used," said Skyla. "I noticed that one we just passed when we came up."

Buck watched through his binoculars as the Ford Raptor went past. It was sometimes obscured by landscape and trees before appearing again and approaching the curve below his vantage point. On one side of the road, the edge dropped away into a mix of scree and brush for a hundred feet or so. He stood up on the rocks, wishing everybody would just stay the hell away from his mountain. His hand reached for the shotgun next to him before he turned and disappeared back into the trees away from the road.

Chapter Thirteen

A fly flew through the open door and circled the heads of the two men working at a table in the small shed, causing one to jerk his arm in annoyance. "Damn it all to hell. Why do we have to have the door open? It's only the last part of May. Not that hot. Pesky flies. How can I concentrate on these sherds with flies batting all around? The glue was almost set before that damn fly made me move."

"You don't like it? Work somewhere else then. This is my place."

The fly began a futile bouncing off dusty windows, its small taps and never-ending buzzing the only sounds disturbing the quiet for several minutes.

Finally, the glued pieces were braced carefully and set aside to continue drying.

"We may have a problem." The older of the two stood and stretched.

"You always have problems. Now what?"

"Somebody at the park did a drone video of the pueblo remains. Got everybody all excited."

"Already heard that. Somebody who works there talked to somebody else. Word gets around. If you wanted to stop them, and you were clever, you could find a way to fix it so that video would never be seen by the public."

"How the hell would I do that?"

"What I said, *if* you were clever. Anyway, why should we care about some park video?"

"It showed stuff from the air. Indications of settlements—walls, foundations. Even where nothing had been dug yet. God help us if they get the idea of filming on the mountain."

"I wouldn't worry about it. There are no walls here you can see from the air. Who the hell is going to be filming with drones on the mountain?"

"Some idiot who gets the idea from that video. We'd better make damn sure they can't see any sign of us. Buck had the camouflage netting pulled back the other day. Didn't put it back before he left. Might as well take out an ad in the paper. Here we are! I told him if he ever did that again, he'd get his pay docked."

"That lady ranger knows too much about digs. She was up on Glorieta Baldy a couple of days ago."

"How the hell do you know that?"

"I just know. We need to find a way to discourage her. Throw a few roadblocks in her way."

"Don't get any of your hothead ideas again. I don't want to hear of any illegal stuff that'll call attention to us."

"Yes, Mother." He continued his meticulous cleaning of the obsidian spearhead in his hand.

"I'm not your damned mother. Don't be such a smart ass. And leave her alone. What are we going to do about Fernando?"

"Nothing."

"I mean finding a replacement for him."

"I think Buck can handle it by himself."

"Buck isn't going to like hearing that," said the professor, looking up.

"What ain't I gonna like hearing?" said Buck as he came in, carrying a crate.

"Holy—" The professor dropped the sherd he'd been holding in place. "Damn it. Stop sneaking around, will you? How can I fix this with damn interruptions and flies?"

"What don't I want to hear?" said Buck, a little louder.

"We're not replacing Fernando. You got all summer," said the other man working at the table.

Buck slammed the crate down. The pile of potsherds next to the professor rattled. "I've a good mind to quit and let you do your own damn digging."

The professor slid off his chair and moved closer to the door, holding his hand over his nose. "If that'd get rid of the horrible stench that follows you, it would be worth it."

Buck lifted the folded canvas off the crate, revealing several obsidian tools held in place by its weight. "Ain't me that stinks this time. I showered. Somebody borrowed this canvas and hauled God knows what in it. That's what smells."

The professor took another deep breath of air by the door, came back to the table, took the folded canvas gingerly and threw it out the door. "Smells like roadkill."

The other man turned the spearhead over and began polishing it again. "It was."

"I think I will quit."

The younger boss looked up from the spearhead. "That would be a mistake, don't you think, Buck?"

Buck flushed, turned on his heel, and left. They heard his truck leave with a spurt of gravel.

Chapter Fourteen

Excitement about the helicopter trip flooded Skyla's mind. What a treat this was! Anton had really gotten into their shortcut idea, poring over maps and satellite images as they planned their day. They met his pilot friend from college at the Jet Center at the Santa Fe Airport that morning. Sam and his grandfather, Dom, joined them. Anton pulled out the maps again, and they finalized the details as they enjoyed the coffee provided for private pilots and their passengers.

When they walked out on the tarmac to the waiting helicopter, Skyla was surprised. "It's a lot bigger than I thought it would be."

"We use this for executive charters," explained the pilot. "You'll find it comfortable and quiet, yet you shouldn't have trouble following the terrain below with the big windows." He opened the passenger door and gave Dom and Skyla a hand in. Anton and Sam climbed in after.

Luxury surrounded them in the cabin. The pilot handed Anton a headset and gave him a brief lesson in how to use it. As the cabin was separate from the cockpit, Anton would need it to converse with him. The co-pilot was already busy with pre-flight routines.

Their route took them over the mountains east of Santa Fe to the lookout tower at Glorieta Baldy. That was helpful in giving Skyla a sense of where she was. From that point, they roughly followed the forest service road they'd taken the week before as it descended from the peak. It was interesting how the road had been constructed—sticking to the ridge line between the La Cueva and Alamitos canyons. She wondered if the ancient Puebloans had traveled ridgelines as well. Skyla had never thought about that before.

By then, Skyla noticed that Dom had relaxed. He no longer looked alarmed when the helicopter tilted down as it did when they sped up. Sam kept pointing out things to him, asking him questions, and making jokes. Every so often Sam would whistle a tune, which she'd come to expect of him. He probably didn't even know he was doing it.

Anton said that as the crow flies, it might be a hundred yards from the road to some of these interesting spots, but the terrain was rough. To cover that distance, they would have to trek a lot farther than the crow would fly. They decided to explore only one site on the La Cueva Canyon side of the road. They named it Cliff Trail for the track that paralleled the main road for some distance. The terrain there was a lot steeper, the forest thicker, and the road farther from the creek bed.

Maybe if they'd been a serious university team with a grant mandating a site search, they could have checked out more remote areas, but, for their purposes, drone trips would be limited to what they could reach in an afternoon from their vehicle parked along the road. The range of the drone and ability to have a line of sight in controlling it also played a critical role in the areas they targeted.

They saw several possible spots along the Alamitos Canyon side of the road. That canyon featured a set of cliffs along a small creek. They marked two spots along that canyon. One they named Fork, for its proximity to a major split in the road, and the other Scree, as it was not far from where the precipitous drop fell away from the road with little vegetation growing among the rocky rubble.

At one point they saw the road that hadn't been marked on Hoot's map. They'd noted it then. Now, after a word by Anton to the pilot, they detoured slightly to follow it. It didn't appear to be more than a track with no obvious destination before it petered out along a creek. Some hunter or ORV enthusiast probably had a reason to drive it.

Skyla loved watching the meadow grasses blow and the branches whip from the rotor draft on the occasions they were close to the ground. It was cool watching the shadow of the helicopter race along beneath them. Occasionally they saw wildlife—usually deer, once a coyote—but mostly endless treetops. As they came down in altitude, the ponderosas were mixed with piñon, juniper, and grassy meadows.

Skyla made lots of notes, numbering them to coordinate with numbers they wrote on the map. Every so often, Anton would relay some information from the pilot for her to jot down. Time sped by as they craned their necks to the windows, following the terrain below, watching as the two-dimensional information on the maps transformed into 3-D reality. As the mountain roads receded into the distance and they headed home, flying over populated areas, the interstate, and the edge of Santa Fe, Skyla settled back into her seat.

Dom was relaxed now, his apprehension seemingly gone. Skyla was sure he'd find satisfaction in checking this item off his bucket list. Anton had been like a kid with a new toy. This was a gadget to end all gadgets—she knew he'd enjoyed the opportunity to actually be in the machine flying over the terrain rather than just controlling it from the ground.

For Skyla this opportunity had brought to life much she'd dreamed about. Her eyes went to Anton, her gaze caressing his skin. Dare she think about a future with him? Was she brave enough? The coming night and what it might bring filled her mind. Anton wasn't expected home that night. Sam and Anton were supposed to stay at the Martinez ranch. She hoped Anton might be able to spend the whole night with her. In fact, she'd heard him say to Sam, "Expect me when you see me. I've no idea when I'll be in." Sam had just smiled.

Time behaved strangely for Skyla as the afternoon wore on. It flew, the conversations and plans slipping through her fingers like water. Yet it crawled, too. How could it do both?

♦ ❖ ♦

After dinner, Skyla and Anton went to her home. As they came in, the phone was ringing. Skyla crossed quickly to it and picked up the receiver. No answer, yet she'd gotten to it on time. She put it down with a frown.

"Who was it?"

"Nobody. Probably a scam call. I hate those." She poured some wine for them, and they sat on the couch to organize their notes and trace the route on the maps, checking again the three sites they wanted to explore with drones. For each, Anton had noted position and landmarks that would help them locate the sites from the air or ground again.

Skyla looked up from the maps and found Anton's gaze on her.

"You were pretty quiet coming home for a gal who'd just gotten her first taste of aerial archaeology. Was it the flying in the helicopter? You feeling okay?"

"I'm feeling fine. I was distracted. Mind you, I loved it. I'm excited about exploring our sites with the drone." She paused and swallowed. "But I was thinking about you. About us. About tonight."

He raised his eyebrows and then grinned his crooked grin. "Uff da. That's something. I rate higher than a possible archaeological site?"

She tilted her head and looked at him with a teasing smile. "Close."

The maps rested on his lap as he took her hand and played with her fingers before asking, "What were we doing in your thoughts?"

"Remember that word you tried to use in the Scrabble game? Lamborous? That's what we were doing. We'd reached the wicked part." She caught her lower lip between her teeth. Was now the time? Her breath came faster. Was it just being aware of him as a man and what was about to come, or was it also fear? That the step she wanted to take might somehow go past a point of no return, jeopardizing what she'd come to cherish with Anton?

With Travis, she'd taken the initiative early in their marriage, only to have him berate her, figuratively slapping her down for being the instigator. She'd learned to lie acquiescently, feeling guilty about her desires and needs, feeling their problems were her fault. Would Anton be like that, too?

Anton set the maps on the coffee table and slid a hand into her hair to rest it gently on the back of her head. "I like the sound of this."

"I want …" Her voice sounded quavery, even to herself.

"What, my love?"

"I'm afraid. That I can never … when you look at me, you'll wish it was Sonja."

Anton set his hand against her face. "Sonja is part of my past. We were teenagers, innocent, and so long ago. Since then, I've craved being touched, being physical. I've missed that part of my life. Almost seven years—far too many."

"I want to touch you. But Travis—" She looked away, trying to find the words. "You might not like it."

"Skyla, there's so much pent up in me. Touch me how you want to. Believe me, I'll love it. To find you and know you want to love me—I just can't believe how lucky I am."

Should she take that step? She moved her hands over his shoulders. His eyes closed as he leaned closer to her. His lips traveled over her face, his hands gently touching, exploring, giving pleasure. They sank back on the couch. Her lips parted. She cherished this—the warmth, relaxation, just exulting in feelings. Their clothing was brushed or tossed aside.

Then they reached the point where she'd always pulled back, short of the final intimacy.

She sat up.

With the abyss in front of her, she stood, held out her hand, and led him to her bed. She'd left a light dimly glowing when she'd closed her curtains earlier. Now she drew him down beside her on the bed. For a while she just enjoyed his touch, her hand resting quietly on his back. She watched him through half-closed lids. His eyes were open, watching her expression, gauging her reaction to his touch, his expression warm.

She pushed up against his shoulder. The pressure of his body over hers lifted as he dropped back to his side, closing his eyes, his hand still gently stroking her breast. No hint of anger, no words from his lips to scold her for stopping, not even a wheedle, though it was obvious he wanted to continue.

She rose over him, pushing him down to lie on his back. He went easily.

"Let me," she whispered. Tentatively she began to touch him and kiss him in the way she wanted but hadn't dared. In many ways he was so traditional. When it came to technology and computers he was an over-achieving geek, right on the cutting edge, and very successful, but when it came to relationships, manners, and customs, he might as well be living in another century. She wasn't certain he would accept her taking the initiative. Would he, too, believe the man should always be the one in control? His touch brought her back to the present. She smiled and stretched in response.

Anton's expression was tender; a smile played on his lips. He made soft sounds of encouragement, of pleasure, stroking her in return as heat grew between them. Thoughts of Travis evaporated from her mind. Her caresses grew more deliberate. How good it was to be free to touch! There was just this moment—just her, just him, just this wondrous closeness. Tension, release, and climbing again. Sighs and murmurs, salty skin, and slippery places. Then her hand stilled. She watched as his eyes opened.

"Skyla?" A whisper of a question.

It was time.

"Love me," she breathed.

"Loving is for both of us," he said, holding her lightly, pressing her hand against him where she had stilled it.

This time there was no pulling back.

Chapter Fifteen

Buck shouldered the door of the shed open wider, hauled in a crate, and set it down on the work table, raising a small cloud of dust. Overhead fluorescents lit the work area. The two who had hired him were engrossed in cleaning ancient pottery.

One was carefully brushing out the interior of a brown pot with geometric designs in black. "What did you find?"

"One big one, probably a storage jar. Broken, but the pieces are big, and they're all there." Buck lifted off the cloths that hid and protected the crate's contents. "Another knife with an obsidian blade. And two smaller pots I found buried in a corner. I know there's at least one more." He lifted out a pot, set it on the bench, and turned to make room for the latest finds on the shelves that lined one side of the shed.

"We've got another problem," said the professor.

"We wouldn't, if you'd let me take care of her."

"Holy— Back off, just *back off*. You're going to ruin it." The professor half rose from his seat, glaring at the younger boss.

"What's the goddammed problem?"

Buck was wary. He didn't want to be there if they got nasty. The professor always found something to complain about. The younger boss, the hothead, creeped him out, sometimes exploding out of the blue. Now, though, the man quietly put down his brush and picked up the pot Buck had set down, turning it carefully in his hands.

"There was a helicopter up here the other day," the professor said, settling back down. "Flew all over the forest service road. Even followed the track we take into the site. I don't think they spotted anything. I heard rumors of that drone guy talking about filming on the mountain. Looking for possible sites. I don't like it."

"Looking for sites? With drones? For himself?" Buck put the contents from his crate on the bench, put the cloths back into the crate, and set it by the door. "Drones. Shoot 'em down. How hard can it be?"

"Don't be stupid. Anyhow, it'd be like shooting down a flock of damn crows. Can't shoot them all." The professor was annoyed.

"I'd like to try," said his partner.

Buck snorted. It was always funny watching those two squabble. Like little kids. Trouble was, they could go from funny to scary in seconds.

"You idiot. Don't you dare do such a stupid thing. The point is to keep them from knowing we are there."

Buck laughed out loud.

The professor wheeled on him. "And you! Don't be so sloppy about your netting and camouflage."

"If you guys aren't going to dig, get me some damned help," Buck said. "Fernando's been gone for a month. What happened? Did they ever catch him?"

"Somebody killed him," said the other. "He turned up dead in Santa Fe."

"Lucky for us," said Buck.

"Luck had nothing to do with it."

Buck turned sharply to look at the hothead. "Did you?"

The man glared at Buck and stood up. "Just keep your nose clean and remember what happened to him."

"Hey! Cut it out," said the professor. "Buck, I think you ought to keep your activity underneath the overhangs for a while. They shouldn't be able to spot anything there. Anyhow, those areas have been the most productive yet."

"I've had enough of this," said Buck. "I'm heading back up."

"Take a shower before you go back. How can you stand yourself?"

"Who is there to care? Gonna gross out my co-worker? The one who isn't there?" He picked up his crate and slammed the door behind him. Enough of this shit. He liked being alone, but these weeks of solitary digging, with those two hardly ever showing up to help, were getting old. More often now they were getting scary. One of these days, one of them would explode.

And why was he putting up with it? Sure they had something on him, but he was good at disappearing. He certainly wasn't getting rich, but he already had plans to improve that situation. He threw the empty crate on the seat beside him and drove off.

The professor started moving pots on the shelves and peering behind them. *Where is the damn canteen? Why are these guys such hotheads? Shoot down the drones. Yeah, like that'd help. Retirement can't come too soon. Get away from this double life. I want to enjoy myself for a change.*

He moved the new pots aside with begrudging admiration. "I like these latest. These small ones should get good prices." Inside, resentment still seethed, and he had a horrible feeling there was more to his partner's story. "What the hell did you do to Fernando?"

"Who says I did anything?"

"Your sly references about luck."

"It doesn't bother me to have Buck think I would kill someone. Makes him easier to control."

"I don't trust you."

"That doesn't bother me either. Be glad he's gone. That's the end of it. Dead men tell no tales."

The professor set the pot back. "Don't do anything to jeopardize us. This site has been good. Won't be long 'til we reach our pot goal."

"I still liked the Arizona sites better. Anyhow, we leave here, we'll find another site."

"What do you mean *we*? Who found this site anyway?"

"You did. But you were lucky. I could just as easily have found it. Dad taught us well."

"I was always the better student."

"You were a sucking little mama's baby, that's what you were." He looked up and continued in a mocking voice, "Praise me. Didn't I do good? Mommy, praise me."

"Shut up. Go climb in a dark hole. Whose fault is it that we had to leave Arizona? Not mine. If you hadn't been such a damn hothead and ruined it for us, we could still be there. All because you flew off the handle. You've always been that way. I'm tired of it." The professor turned to the crates stacked against the wall and rummaged through them.

"I'm tired of your damn complaints. What the hell are you looking for? Quit banging around."

"There was a canteen. A black-on-white. Football shape. What happened to it?"

"Should be here. Had your provenance papers stuck into it."

"I've checked all the shelves and crates. Did you take it?"

"Hell, no. I think you delivered it already and just forgot. Could be Alzheimer's. You're getting old."

"Shut up. I know I didn't deliver it. Do you suppose he stole it? I don't like Buck being in and out of this shed without one of us here."

"In case you hadn't noticed, he does most of the digging. You and I pull nine-to-fives. It makes sense to have him bring down the pots and store them for us."

"How do we know that he's not skimming off pots that we know nothing about?"

"We don't. You want to babysit and dig alongside him? Go right ahead."

"Forget it. I'll ask him. I have to make a delivery to the little wuss in Santa Fe in a few days. He's getting fidgety."

"When you're ready for my kind of diplomacy, give me a call. I'll take care of it."

"That'll be the day."

Chapter Sixteen

The Circle Sleuths gathered at the Bjornsons' for the Memorial Day weekend. Dom was pleased to be the center of attention this time. He sipped his coffee while he thought. Seventy years old. Friday had been his birthday, and his daughter had organized a celebration at his home. The patriarch. He'd had a good life and looked forward to more. A rewarding career, a daughter and her husband who'd given him certainly the six best grandchildren in the world. And now one of them was soon to be married himself, giving him another granddaughter and a ready-made great-granddaughter.

But this Circle Sleuth gathering—a second birthday celebration—was truly special. He looked around at the faces of those gathered in the Bjornson family room. Pete Schultz, with his gentle humor and easy smile—at least in this setting. Dom had seen this police detective in action with his keen mind and dogged determination. Next to Pete sat his wife, Akiko, whom he'd married while he'd been stationed in Japan.

As Dom watched, Pete's eyes strayed again to Lou, his daughter. Lou, as the King James Bible would put it, was great with child. Dom figured Pete was going to be one proud grandfather. Lou's red-headed husband, Cliff McCreath, sat next to her, holding her hand. Cliff and Sam had been friends since grade school.

Sam would be married soon, and Farah would join their household. Dom couldn't be happier with Sam's choice of wife. Leyla was the frosting on the cake.

Dom smiled in affection as his eyes came to Wilma. Such a generous heart. Wearing yet another outfit of red and purple, she was telling one of her rambling stories. She'd come alive this past year, thrilled to be part of a family she'd always wanted.

The Bjornsons—Karen, Anton, and Krista—three generations. Diego and Maria, loyal members of the Bjornson household for many years. And now Skyla, newly welcomed into the Circle.

There was something wonderful about friends. They stretched him, made him live again—didn't let him sit back in the rocking chair of retirement. They valued his experience.

They were friends, peers, even with their age differences. He loved that. Most of these folks he'd come to know and love because of his terrible accident the previous fall. Tolkien had coined the right word, he thought. Out of something bad, something unexpectedly good had happened, bringing a happy ending. This was eucatastrophe!

His eyes lingered on Karen, the consummate hostess, making sure everyone was taken care of. Karen had brought great joy to him—a serendipity—a closeness, a companionship he didn't even know he'd been looking for. He loved her attitude; found her beautiful inside and out. St. Nicholas day hadn't just been good for Sam's love life, but it had launched Dom into one of his own. Lord, it felt good to be a sexual being again.

Dom chuckled, remembering one night when he and Karen had been surprised by Anton coming home in the wee hours of the morning after being with Skyla. Karen and he had been caught in a goodnight kiss that left little doubt more had been happening than talk. Anton had been positively floored. He'd recovered quickly, though, and didn't seem bent out of shape. A good son.

He put down his coffee cup as Anton and Sam came in with a huge box wrapped in colorful paper and set it carefully on the coffee table. "It takes two of you to carry it?" he asked. "What will I do with something that heavy?"

Sam just started whistling, “He Ain’t Heavy, He’s My Brother.” The others laughed. Leyla’s and Krista’s eyes positively danced with glee.

“Do you know anything about this?” Dom asked Leyla.

She bobbed her head enthusiastically.

“But you already gave me a birthday present.”

“That was from me,” she said before throwing her arms wide to include the Circle. “This is from us.”

Something was up. They all looked like cats with bellyfuls of canaries—very pleased with themselves.

Slowly he undid the wrappings, stretching out the moment. Whatever this was, it couldn’t be better than the shining eyes of the two girls kneeling beside him.

“It was our idea,” said Krista.

“We all chipped in,” said Leyla, bouncing with excitement.

Opening the lid, Dom took off the top protection. “Oh, my. Is this what I think it is?” The top of a pottery head with two little figures clinging to it showed. The wee figures had mouths opened round as if they were singing.

He took out more packing, found more singing children attached to the large central figure, which had his mouth open, too. “A storyteller.”

He took away the rest of the packing. Sam and Anton lifted the figure out and set it on the table. Farah whisked away the wrappings.

“So many children,” said Dom.

“Here we are,” said Pete, pointing to two of the little figures. “These good-looking ones are Akiko and me.”

Cliff pointed to two, one of whom had a cradle board on its back. “Here are Lou and I, and you’ll meet this one in a couple of months.”

Sam and Farah, Leyla and Krista, Anton and Skyla all pointed out their figures. Wilma, Maria, and Diego named theirs, too. Karen pointed to the last one, sitting on the figure’s arm. “That’s me,” she said, “Next to your heart.”

Dom knew his eyes were wet. He felt a lump in his throat. “My God. What a perfect gift. Thank you.” He reached out to touch the little figure Karen had named. “Absolutely wonderful.” Then he turned to her. “I didn’t know I was that much older than you.”

"This has nothing to do with age." Karen smiled at him. "It is the role. You are the storyteller in our lives. You remind us of where we are in history. You keep us grounded in the important things of life."

"Hear, hear," said Sam.

Dom looked into Karen's eyes. "I might relish the history and the role of storyteller. But you provide the setting and the cords that bind this community of Circle Sleuths and the friends they've collected along the way."

"He's right, Mom," said Anton. "I think we need to find a figure for you, too. I've seen some with blankets, surrounding the children almost like enveloping wings. That's your role. The keeper of the community." He winked at Dom. "Then Dom could be one of the baby figures in that storyteller."

"Touché, and thanks," said Karen. "That's a lovely thought."

Dom sat back and looked at the storyteller surrounded by the figures clinging on all sides. "Oh, my."

Then they looked up at a commotion overhead. Excited barking and several Airedales thundering along the balcony and down the stairs signaled a chase underway. Twitch took a flying leap over Gandalf on the stairs and turned to face his sire with his front down, butt up, and tail wagging.

Cliff rose from his chair. "Gandalf, now what do you have?"

Twitch tried to grab whatever the long, blue-green thing was that trailed from Gandalf's mouth. Gandalf growled, warning his offspring away. Wedging into the circle of people, he pranced up to Skyla and dropped the item in her lap, stepped back, and sat.

Dom heard her gasp and saw her face get beet-red as she gathered the teal-colored, lacy bra into a wad in her hands. Surprised laughter broke out all around.

"Gandalf," cried Cliff. "You rascal."

"I forgot to tell you," said Anton, with a huge grin and a little bit of color on his own face. "You need to keep your door shut when Gandalf is here. He likes to snoop in people's luggage, especially for underwear. He knows exactly who it belongs to. He got me once, too."

Chapter Seventeen

Charlie entered the commissary and joined the last of the film-crew members going through the cafeteria line. For the evening meal, the brothers at the monastery often served a hearty stew and fresh, homemade bread. Scarpelli, ahead of him in line, headed with his tray to a lone empty seat at one of the round tables. Predictably, a couple of people from that table got up and moved to another one. In the weeks that Charlie had worked with the film crew, he'd been subjected to too many meals with conversations hijacked by Scarpelli and his tales. How many intrepid Italian ancestors who fought in the Civil War could the man have?

Intrepid. He liked the word. Charlie had always been a voracious reader, and his friendship with Anton had stretched his vocabulary further. They enjoyed puns and the nuances of words.

Charlie sat down next to Scarpelli. "I've been meaning to talk with you. One of the stories that has been passed down in our family was about our great-great-great-grandfather. He fought in the Civil War in the Battle of Antietam. His name was Thaddeus Van Dyken. Have you ever run across that name in your research?"

"No, I can't say that I have." Scarpelli looked bored.

"The story goes that a soldier of Italian ancestry saved his life."

"Really?" Scarpelli's expression perked up. "Do you know the name of the Italian?" He whipped out his cell phone and connected to the internet.

"I remember the name being catchy. Let me think."

"While you're thinking, let me look up your ancestor."

"Please. Thaddeus Van Dyken." Charlie smiled. Baiting Scarpelli was too easy.

The others at the table continued eating while Scarpelli searched. Cameraman Larry Morris gave Charlie a questioning look. Charlie winked at him.

"I can't find a Thaddeus Van Dyken," said Scarpelli.

"Are you spelling it right? There may be a variant spelling. Try v-o-n D-i-j-k-e-n."

Scarpelli's fingers flew over his keypad. "Nothing. Have you remembered the Italian's name?"

"Yes. Decimus et Ultimus. Stands out in one's memory. Tenth and last. His mother must have had it with childbearing. Now what was the last name?"

Scarpelli sat up straighter in his chair. "Barziza! Decimus et Ultimus Barziza. I know that name. He was a famous captain from the Texas Brigade. We believe he was related to the Scarpellis. My mother's brother's great uncle was a Barziza. Do you suppose you and I are related?"

"It's unlikely. Barziza only saved my ancestor's life. It is possible, though, that we are related through some other Civil War hero. Are you related to an officer with the name of Van Wynken?"

Scarpelli stopped eating to check it out. "I can't find that name anywhere in the records. Of course, there are thousands of unknowns who perished in the war. But if he was an officer, you'd think there'd be a record."

"Oh, my. What if it wasn't true? My great-great-grandfather was so inspired by Barziza. Are you sure Van Wynken isn't there? Did you check all of the possible spellings? Maybe the prefix was not separate, but it was made into one word." Charlie watched as Scarpelli labored over his phone.

"I checked all the variants. I know how to do genealogical research. The name isn't there."

"Maybe it was spelled de Blynken."

"That's not even close," complained Scarpelli. "How would you mix up Wynken and Blynken?

Morris coughed and wiped a dribble of stew from his chin.

"That's simple," Charlie said. "Case in point. New Mexico has tons of people named Vaca. Many more are named Baca. It's all in the confusion of how the first letter is pronounced. Is it a voiced consonant or unvoiced? Buh, Vuh—see how close they are? You go back to the conquistadors and you learn Baca and Vaca are the same man."

"Oh, I get what you're saying. Also, it depends on who records the name and how literate they were."

"Well, if you can't find that name, here is another for you to look up. He was an officer, too. A captain. Surely you could find a captain."

"Officers are definitely more likely to show up in the records. What's the name?"

"Hieronymus de Nott."

Someone across the table snorted and began to laugh.

Charlie glared at the laugher. "Hey, Hieronymus is a better name than yours. I love the name Hieronymus. Do you know what it means?"

"I do, actually. It means a sacred name. Jerome would be the closest thing in English."

"I'm impressed, Scarpelli. You certainly know your facts."

"I know because it's my given name. This phone is cutting in and out. Let me go look up Hieronymus Nott on the computer."

"Don't forget the double T," said Charlie. "I'm sure that's important."

"I know what I'm doing," said Scarpelli as he left his plate and went off to the other side of the room where the crew's electronic equipment was set up.

Morris shook his head and grinned. "Charlie, you're bad. Bad to the bone. Wynken, Blynken, and Nott? He's going to kill you."

"Not if he never figures it out. Sounds like Dutch ancestors to me. Who else would go sailing off across the seas in a wooden shoe? Anyhow—what does Scarpelli enjoy more than anything?"

"Finding obscure Italian soldiers who fought in the Civil War."

"And what do we enjoy most?"

"Having Scarpelli off doing his research and not boring us with his endless tales of Italian ancestors."

"Right on." Charlie buttered his last chunk of homemade bread and leaned back in satisfaction. "I rest my case."

A string of expletives came from the equipment area.

"Uh-oh," said Morris. "I think he's figured it out."

A red-faced Scarpelli came charging across the room. "You son of a bitch!" he shouted. "Don't you ever do that again. You people just don't understand. Damn you."

Someone at Charlie's table tittered. Scarpelli rounded on the offender. "You knew what he was doing and you didn't say a thing. You're all a bunch of bastards." He kicked an empty chair, sending it crashing over.

Canby got up from another table and came over. "Now what's got your knickers in a knot, Scarpelli? What the hell is going on?"

Scarpelli's arm shot out, his finger pointing at Charlie. "He's playing me for a fool!"

Canby threw up his hands and rolled his eyes. The tittering at the table erupted into laughter. Scarpelli's face went from red to purple, and he launched himself toward Charlie. Canby grabbed his arm and did some yelling of his own. "Enough. All of you. Goddam it! We have three more weeks of working on this film. Stop it."

The director's glare circled the faces at the table. One by one the smiles left. The director's glare reached Charlie.

This is my fault, Charlie thought. He knew better than to bully someone. It might be funny at the time, but consequences may not be. "I'm sorry." Charlie looked at the furious man held by Canby. "I was out of line."

Canby's grip loosened on the wiry, dark-haired man. "Scarpelli?"

Scarpelli brushed off Canby's hand and yelled at Charlie. "I'm going to kill you!" He strode to the door, turned, glared back at the group, grabbed his arm with his hand and bent his arm up. Then he pushed the door open to crash against the wall and stomped out.

Canby shut his eyes, shook his head slowly, and sighed. "Why me?"

Larry looked at Charlie. “You shouldn’t a done that. But damn, you really had him going. Did you see his face?”

Laughter erupted again from the table.

As people resumed their conversations, Charlie leaned back in his chair and looked at Larry. “Did you ever find out where Scarpelli disappears to at night?”

Larry shook his head. “He won’t say. I think he must have a lover someplace.”

“Heaven help us. Who would fall for him?”

“Somebody he met on an Italian genealogy website,” said Larry.

Charlie laughed. “That would not surprise me.”

Chapter Eighteen

On Thursday morning, June 9, in the back workroom of a small gallery in Santa Fe, two people met in secret. The showroom facing the empty parking lot of the strip mall was still darkened. It was too early for any activity at the nearby businesses.

"I think I should be getting more than you're giving me. How would you get all your pots out of the country if they weren't sent through customs with my replicas?" Gaylord Teller, the gallery owner, rubbed his neck, feeling the tension as he eyed the one who he referred to as a professor. He'd finally dared to broach the subject, after months of warring with himself.

The professor's eyes narrowed momentarily before he settled back in his chair. "Really? What did you have in mind?"

Sweat began to form on Teller's face. He pushed his glasses more firmly onto his nose. He mentioned a percentage. It wasn't quite as high as he wanted, but the inscrutable expression trained on him rattled his nerves. "I'm putting my reputation as a gallery owner at risk here." He laughed. "I'd get a reward for turning you in that would amount to more than what you give me. I know your secrets."

The professor stiffened slightly. "And I know yours. I don't think your risk is very high. In all the years since they've passed the Archaeological Resources Protection Act, they've hardly ever prosecuted anybody. They don't have the will, and they damned sure don't have the manpower. When they catch somebody, it's probation or a slap on the wrist. If you don't mind, I need to make a phone call." The professor stepped outside.

Teller waited. What would he do if the professor said no? Probably roll over and let things go on as they had been. He wasn't doing too badly in this deal; it was just that those pots he'd had to pack and ship were extraordinarily fine. Why shouldn't he get more out of it? Native American artifacts of that quality had to bring a pretty penny in Paris, where they were the rage. Hell, there was even a good market for his replicas there.

The professor returned. "I see your point. How about if I take you out to the site? We've never showed it to anyone before. I guess I could let you have a couple pots. You can choose. They'll be yours to do with as you like."

Teller drew in a quick breath. This was even better than the percentage he'd suggested. "Do you have any more of those black-on-white ones? Intact?"

"A few. Some have been lying in that site untouched for hundreds of years since some trader left them there. Black-on-white, a few animal designs, but mostly geometric patterns. Say yes now before I change my mind. Those pots are worth a fortune."

"Yes, I think we can come to a satisfactory deal." A few of those pots would be a great retirement fund. "When could we go?"

"Right now. Weather is good. It'll be beautiful up there today."

"Now? I'd rather wait a couple of days. I have an appointment with a new artist this afternoon."

"In a few days, I may have changed my mind. Already, I think I'm being too generous. Maybe I should just bring you a pot. I don't know if it's a good idea to let anybody see where the dig is."

"No, I could go now. Let me go home and change."

"You're fine as you are," the professor said with a shrug. "We can drive all the way to the site. We need to go early. Don't want to take the chance of being caught in one of those late afternoon thunderstorms."

This just got better and better. What a fool—the professor was smart at finding artifacts, but not cunning like him. He'd never have showed anybody the source of his treasures. He'd pay close attention to the roads they took. Maybe he could even visit the site himself when it was unoccupied. "I should call my assistant," he said. "She'll wonder why I'm not here."

"Leave her a note. Say you'll see her tomorrow. It's a long way out there and back, and you'll want to get a good look at what we have. Leave your car here. I'll take you to the site."

"Guess I could do that."

"Don't tell her where you're going or who you're with. You don't know me, and I don't know you. And for certain, you don't want anybody else knowing where this site is."

Teller made a mental note as they left the interstate just after Glorieta Pass and turned onto Highway 50. The professor certainly wasn't what the gallery owner called talkative now—only giving a few monosyllabic responses to his questions. He gave up, and they rode in silence.

The professor must have called somebody to meet them. Somewhere in the sleepy community of Glorieta, they stopped. A young muscular fellow met them, and they switched to his four-wheel-drive pickup, which was high off the ground. Owning a gallery was not a physically active business. The owner was short and had a spreading spare tire around his middle. He found it awkward to get his leg up to the step and heave himself into the back seat of the thing.

They turned off the paved road onto a county road. He'd remember the number, but now he began to have second thoughts of ever taking his car up here on his own. The unpaved road wound for miles—the occasional fences, trailers, and small houses showed that someone had attempted to tame parts of this landscape of ponderosa pine and juniper. They crossed a cattle guard. Fences and signs told them they were on national forest land. This rutty, steep road was beyond him—his car would never make it, even if he could tamp down his terror. He was aware of the endless view, but couldn't enjoy it, too busy worrying about the edges and the long drops. He wiped his sweaty palms on his slacks, took off his glasses, and polished the thick lenses with his handkerchief.

As they went higher on the mountain, Teller cringed away from the truck window after catching a glimpse far below of the switchback-filled road they'd just been on. Sweat broke out on his brow. My God, how had they ever found this forsaken place? It was miles and miles from anywhere.

The driver complained. "I thought no one else was supposed to know about this place. Now you're bringing company?"

"Who calls the shots here? Not you, Buck." The professor looked at the gallery owner in the back seat. "Anyway, we need him. And he needs us, right?"

The little man nodded nervously. He didn't like these two. He was way out of his element. The driver looked tough and could hurt him badly if he wanted to. He began to wish he hadn't come.

Buck slowed and turned onto a road that made the first look smooth. It snaked along a creek, through a canyon-like area with pines and blooming wildflowers.

The road all but disappeared. Just now and again did he see a few traces of wheel tracks. Finally, they stopped not far from cliffs rising near a stand of trees. Under screens of netting and camouflage, he saw signs of an organized dig. A trench where they had been working was obscured by brush piled on it. Clever, he thought, to keep anyone seeing signs of digging should they chance to fly over. He stepped down from the truck and stumbled on jelly knees. He was light-headed and wished he'd brought his water bottle. The air was thin up here—must be about eight thousand feet—but it smelled good after being inside that truck.

A stranger pulled up in a truck and parked near them. He slipped on a camouflage jacket, opened the cover on the truck bed, and took out a couple of shovels. "Here," he said in a surly voice. "Pick a spot and scrape the topsoil away. Go gently, you don't want to break anything."

"After a while," the professor said, "I'll show you the pots we've found."

The gallery owner chose a spot between the trench and the cliff, and began to scrape away the soil, soon spotting some potsherds. He looked over to where the others were talking quietly near the pickup. They weren't watching him. He slipped the potsherds into his pocket. The terror of the trip faded, and his excitement grew. One of the pottery fragments was black-on-white with geometric patterns.

Ignoring his shortness of breath, Teller bent and gently brushed some soil away from a bigger sherd. Light glinted on something in the dirt. He knelt and uncovered a piece of obsidian. Was it? Yes! A wonderful arrowhead specimen. He picked it up, glancing back over his shoulder. The stranger had come up behind him. The last thing Gaylord Teller saw was the shovel swinging at him and bright white light. Then, no more. His fingers tightened in a death grip around the perfect arrowhead.

Chapter Nineteen

At the Bjornson ranch, Anton watched the screen as Charlie sent the filming octocopter drone aloft. In first-person view, he saw his mother's alpacas contentedly munching their morning hay. The drone moved on, panning the landscaping around his sprawling home and past the duplex where the housekeeper and the ranch foreman lived. He spotted Krista playing with their two seven-month-old Airedales.

"See if you can capture the dogs," he said.

Charlie zoomed in on their wild, exuberant chase around the yard before bringing the drone back to where they stood. "We did it, Anton. The wobble is all gone. Even on those tight maneuvers, she's smooth as silk."

Anton grinned. "All those hours of tinkering last night did the trick. Good job. Think you can fix it if it starts misbehaving again?"

"Yeah," said Charlie. "I took detailed notes to help the film crew if it happens after we turn it over to them. When we get back to Pecos today, I'll test it again. I know just the area I want to take it—across the river from the monastery."

Krista came over to them with the dogs following. She wore the new T-shirt that Skyla had given to her for her eleventh birthday a few days ago. Skyla had found an airbrush artist at a craft fair and commissioned him to do a whimsical Airedale. Krista had been delighted and immediately dubbed it her Shadow shirt.

"Is it working again?" She made the dogs sit while Anton and Charlie put the drone back in its case.

"It is," Anton replied. "Charlie and I are leaving for work and then Pecos right after breakfast, but I'll be home to go with you to dog training class tonight."

Karen came to the door. "Breakfast," she called.

As they seated themselves in the sunny breakfast room, Krista looked at their guest. "I like your eyes, Charlie. The yellow around the center almost glows when you're happy."

"Thank you, Krista. These eyes run in our family."

"They're sort of like that tiger eye that you wear," said Karen.

Charlie fingered the stone hanging from the leather thong around his neck. "My sister thought so, too. She made this for me."

"Nice." Karen looked at her granddaughter. "Krista, you said happy. Would they change if he were sad?"

"Don't know. I've never seen him sad."

They all laughed, and Anton thought about that comment. Krista had it right. Even when the drone was giving him grief, Charlie loved the challenge of figuring it out. His positive enthusiasm was catching.

"What smells so good?" asked Charlie as they loaded the drone and Charlie's overnight bag into Anton's SUV. Karen handed them a large, bakery-style box.

"Lemony coffeecake for your break at work," she said. "There'll be enough for everyone."

"Mmm," he said. "Anton, we can't leave for Pecos before break. I love lemon."

"We'll make a point of it," said Anton. "Before we leave work, I have to take care of a few things."

"Thank you, guys, so much for letting me spend the night," said Charlie.

"It was more convenient all the way around," said Anton. "I'm glad I came by Pecos yesterday. It helped to see how the drone was behaving, and having the chance to talk with you on the way home let us come up with ideas to fix it."

As they started down the drive, Charlie said, "It'd be nice if my patent award has come. I'd love to show it to Skyla."

"How's the filming going?" asked Anton.

"It's a blast—the whole process. The director has it all in his head—every shot. He has an eye that nails the right detail for historical accuracy. I can hardly wait to see the finished movie. The stuff we did this week was awesome. The footage coming off Glorieta Mesa, following the Union soldiers when they burned the Confederate supply train, was a real kick to do. Of course, the fire will be added later—all computer generated. I've learned a lot on this gig and not just about drones. I never knew before that New Mexico had one of the important Civil War battles."

"The camera man—the one you're training to take over from you—I'll talk to him before I leave today, if I can."

"Good. You'll like Morris."

"Your creativity brought us to where we are with our filming drones, Charlie. Without your innovation, we wouldn't be on that cutting edge. Frankly, some of the excitement had gone out of R and D for me. Working with you has brought it back." He glanced at the younger man and grinned. Anton wasn't the only one at Drone Tech who had been fired up by the young geek. Actually, the thing he had to take care of at work was a surprise celebration—another reason for picking up Charlie from Pecos. His award had come, and everyone was waiting for them. The coffeecake was part of that.

When they got to Drone Tech, they came in the back way. Charlie went to his office to check his mail, and Anton carried the coffeecake down the hall. He grinned as he overheard the young receptionist, standing by the bookkeeper's desk.

"Charlie's eyes are like, awesome. You must have noticed. Do you suppose he wears contacts?" She brushed the hair away from her eye and tucked it behind her ear.

The bookkeeper looked up from her computer screen where she was entering figures into her payroll program. "I doubt it, since he doesn't seem to give a rip about his looks. For certain he doesn't know how a razor functions."

"Oh, you're so dark ages. That unshaven look is hot. He knows it, too. I bet the reason he wears that tiger eye is because he knows it draws attention to his eyes." She held out her hand and centered the diamond ring on her finger. "I wonder if he's dating anyone."

"You're engaged."

"Doesn't stop me from enjoying the scenery, does it?" She laughed and turned to her desk. "Oh, hello, Mr. Bjornson. Can I get anything for you?"

"Good morning. Here's the coffeecake. Everything ready?"

"Yes. Most everybody's there already. I made a pot of coffee, besides putting out a bunch of those different individual coffee things." She lifted the cover of the box. "This coffee cake smells delish. Where did you get it?"

"My mother baked it. It will be delicious. Charlie said he likes lemon."

"Does Charlie know yet that his patent has arrived?" asked the bookkeeper.

"No, I just said I had to take care of a few things here before we headed off to Pecos. He'll be surprised. Remember to pull out the camera, please."

"One step ahead of you, Anton," she replied. "He'll treasure a picture of his getting the award."

Anton retrieved the framed patent award from his office and carried it into the conference room and greeted those already there. Coffee in hand, he went to get Charlie. In a way, Charlie was a lot like himself when he was younger. He thought about the hours he'd spent with him, brainstorming solutions to problems. This patent was from one of Charlie's ideas—innovative, simple, and effective. After months of waiting, it had come.

When they got back to the conference room, Charlie was surprised by the party. Anton gave him the award and enjoyed his awe and excitement. The applause from the others was genuine. They joked about who was going to get the next patent. One of the best parts about Drone Tech was working with folks like Charlie and acknowledging their creative talents. Celebrations like this made for good employees who busted their butts to improve their products. The competitive push resulted in more creativity. It was good all the way around.

The coffeecake disappeared, and the others drifted back to work. Anton and Charlie got into the car to head to Pecos. Charlie held his framed award and was even more animated. “Charles Van Dyken.” Charlie read his name from the award. He propped it on his lap and traced his finger over the glass-protected gold-eagle seal and red ribbon. “Gosh, I sure appreciate all your support in getting this patent. I’m glad you made me keep the log book to document the process, too. This is great. Does it get any better?”

Anton laughed. “The first one is special, but so is each that follows.” His mind wandered, only half hearing Charlie talking about the celebration. Anton thought back to when he’d received his own first patent. What an incredible day that had been! The award held pride of place among several on his office wall now. Eight years ago—his wife, Sonja, was still alive then, and his dad, too. They’d asked his parents to babysit Krista, and they’d gone out to dinner to celebrate.

His attention returned to the present. The drive to Pecos was less than an hour, interstate most of the way to the Pecos NHP visitor center. They entered the gift shop. He’d always liked its décor of large, colorful historical figures against the panorama of a mural. Good design, he thought, educational and attractive.

Skyla waved a hand to them, smiled, and continued talking to a woman by the counter. A black-and-white pot with a shape sort of like a football sat on its wrappings near them. “We have more black-and-white pottery on display.” Skyla led the woman into the adjacent museum room.

Soon she came back, having left the woman to study the displays. She gave Charlie a big hug and Anton a kiss.

“I’m not sure I’ve ever seen pottery in that shape before,” said Anton, indicating the pot still on the counter.

“It’s actually a wonderful piece. The lady just bought it from a private collector and wants more information on this type of pottery. It functioned as a water canteen. It would have been carried by a cord made of yucca fiber through these loops. They probably used a corncob in the neck, much like a cork."

"Clever," said Charlie.

"I've gotten the lady's name and contact information," Skyla snapped several shots of the pot with her phone. "I told her that I'd do some research on it and let her know more."

"I've also got something to show you, Sis." Charlie produced the award and the picture and set them on the counter.

"Oh, your patent came. I'm so proud of you!" Skyla reached out to him with a hug.

Charlie hugged her back, then pulled something from his wallet. "And look." He waved the bonus check he'd received with the award in front of her.

"Good work." Skyla smiled at her brother before touching the tiger eye pendant at his throat. "You're still wearing it."

"Of course. You made it for me." Charlie tucked the check back into his wallet. "I'm going to have a whole wall of these patents one day. Where are your USGS maps? I want to get some."

Skyla pointed to the area, and Anton and Charlie began looking through the maps. The lady finished in the museum, bought a pottery book, packed up her pot, and left.

Another ranger, Claude Frobisher, having just finished giving a tour of the ancestral sites, came in from the back. Anton recognized the reserved, studious-looking fellow. "Good to see you again, Claude."

Claude emitted a sound that could have been agreeable—or not. The glance that he sent Skyla held a hint of disapproval. What was all that about?

"I saw the footage of our park that Charlie did with one of your drones," said Claude. "Fascinating. Really a useful tool when it comes to archaeology, though it can't compete with a good, old-fashioned dig. Skyla, do you know where Upton is?"

"He took an early lunch with the forest service archaeologist. I just saw him drive up."

A short, gray-haired man came in and greeted them.

“Good to see you again, Upton.” Anton shook the archaeologist’s hand. They chatted for a while before Upton went to one of the desks in the small area behind the counter.

Anton and Charlie turned again to the maps. “I want both the—” Charlie’s voice stopped as the bell over the front door tinkled, and he looked at someone entering. “Damn it.” He straightened, letting the maps fall back into their tray, and moved toward his sister, positively bristling.

Anton watched him in surprise. He heard Skyla suck in a breath and saw her demeanor change, also. The man coming toward them was about his own age of early thirties, with pale skin, black hair, and a neatly-trimmed beard. His manner was cocky, bordering on insolent.

Uff da, Anton thought. Who was this?

Chapter Twenty

Anton saw Claude leave his desk and come to stand near Skyla. He wondered if there was a prearranged signal in place, for Upton dropped what he was doing and stood by quietly.

The dark-haired man sneered at Claude. "Well, long time, no see. It's the Clod."

Claude said nothing. He straightened and puffed up a little. His expression took on a subtle change, his jaw clenching.

Skyla was visibly annoyed with the newcomer. "Travis, why are you here?"

"Maybe I just wanted to see you."

"You were told to stay away from me."

"I wanted to give you this." He stopped a couple of yards away from Skyla and opened his hand to reveal a small figurine lying on his palm.

Skyla sucked in a breath. "Oma's Dutch girl! How did—"

"How do you think?" he said with a chilling smile.

Charlie moved forward. The man swung to look at him. "Buzz off, Junior."

"Charlie, no," Skyla said. "I can handle it."

Anton moved to stand between Skyla and her brother, keeping his eyes on the face of the intruder.

"Who's the big ugly?" The man turned to Anton. "Are you her bodyguard?"

"If needed," said Anton. He looked down at the man, figuring he had about five inches on him.

"Is she putting out for you now?"

Jesus, thought Anton. This guy didn't have a good sense of self-preservation. He was just one tightly-reined urge away from being pounded into the ground. "I think it best if you apologize and leave."

They stared at each other for several seconds.

"Go to hell," the man said, before turning to Charlie again. "Someday, when your nanny isn't around, you'll get yours."

Anton put his hand on Charlie's arm, holding him back. He felt the tension vibrating.

The guy turned back to Skyla, his grip tightening on the figure before forcefully flinging it to the floor. The china shattered. Pieces skittered away from them. "You're next," he mouthed to Skyla.

Anton caught Charlie's eye. They bolted forward, each grabbing an arm of the man and dragging him away from Skyla. Claude sprinted forward to open the door. They thrust the man outside. He staggered, caught himself, glared at them, spun on his heel, and strode away.

Anton pulled out his phone and snapped photos of the car and its license number. Claude went back in, leaving Charlie and Anton watching. As the car disappeared down the road in a spurt of gravel, Anton turned to Charlie. "That's Skyla's ex?"

"That bastard! Yes, Travis Cutler." Charlie's words were clipped. "Skyla said he was out on parole. He's not supposed to be anywhere near her."

"Jesus," said Anton. "She's lucky to be rid of him."

"That's for sure. I never met anyone so insanely jealous. Made her life hell." They went back in.

Claude had gone to Skyla and put an arm around her in an awkward gesture of comfort. She shrugged it off and raised one palm toward him in a 'stay away' gesture. He took a step backward. She crossed her arms in front of her, hugging herself.

She stood rigid, face downcast. As Anton came toward her, she turned to him, away from Claude. Over her head, Anton noticed a slight narrowing of the older man's eyes. Fatherly? Or something else?

Then Anton put his arms around Skyla, drawing her close, one hand gently smoothing the tense muscles in her back. Upton got a brush and dustpan, swept up the pieces. and slid them quietly into a wastebasket.

After a few moments, Skyla backed away, rubbing her abdomen lightly as she looked around at the concerned faces. "Sorry about that. It's the first time I've spoken to him since we left the courthouse. Thank you. I'm glad you were here." Her voice quavered.

"Spoken to him? Have you seen him? Is he following you again? He's obsessed," said Charlie. "I should have beaten the crap out of him. Call the cops."

"Your brother is right," said Anton. "They should know."

Skyla lifted her chin. "It's not any of your business!"

"I think it is. He just threatened my woman—"

"I am not *your* woman," she cried. She backed further away, holding both hands up to keep them all back before saying in a smaller voice. "I am my own person."

Ouch, thought Anton. Now he'd done it. "Okay, okay. He threatened someone I care about and one of my employees. It's obvious there's some sort of restraining order in place that he violated."

"How did he get Oma's Dutch girl?" Charlie asked.

That's where he'd seen it before, thought Anton. One of a pair of small figures on the shelves in Skyla's home.

A look of fear crossed her face. She bit her lower lip.

"God Almighty! He got into your house, didn't he?" asked Anton. "If you don't call, I will."

"I don't need some knight in shining armor to help me. I don't want him riled up."

"I'll rile him up," Charlie muttered. "He's violated parole. They'll throw him back in the clink. Then he won't be able to bother you."

"*Men!* Just leave me alone." Skyla's stormy eyes raked them with a glare before the door opened, and a family came into the visitor center, looking a little startled as they realized a drama was unfolding. "I have to get back to work. Go. I'll call. Right now." She pasted a smile on her face for the visitors.

Charlie went back to the map display and picked up the Pecos map that he'd dropped. "I need to buy this first. Do you have the Glorieta quadrangle? We couldn't find it."

"We're out," said Upton. "You might stop by the forest service office if you're going that way. They should have it."

"We're heading there right now," said Charlie, handing him the money.

"Skyla, are you going to be okay?" asked Anton softly.

"I'll be fine. Claude is here, and Upton."

"You'll call?" Anton's fingers gently brushed her cheek. She pulled away but nodded.

"After Anton drops me off at the monastery," said Charlie, "I'm going to take the drone out on the other side of the river to see if our tweaking got all the kinks out of it."

The visiting family went into the museum. Claude's eyes followed them before he went into the office area behind the counter and picked up the phone.

"Charlie, will I still see you tonight?" asked Skyla.

"Yeah. Frankie's." Charlie picked up his award from the counter. "Dinner is on me. Five thirty."

Skyla looked at Anton. "Will you be able to join us?"

Anton looked at her, this prickly, vulnerable woman he felt so protective of. She looked wounded. "As much as I'd like to, I have to get back. Krista and I have a dog training class tonight."

"Okay. Goodbye then."

"Skyla, I mean it." Anton touched her arm. "I want to hear what the cops say. And call me right away if anything else happens. Where Charlie is with the film crew, he has no cell service."

She shot him a glare.

"Please."

She hesitated. "You're way on the other side of Santa Fe."

"True, but I have good friends in law enforcement."

"Please, Sis," Charlie said. "I'd feel better. It might be my hide that needs help."

"I'll talk to you tonight," Anton said. Then he and Charlie turned to leave. He noticed Claude hang up the phone in the office area and wondered if he'd made the call to the authorities himself.

Part way to his car, Anton stopped. He was of two minds. He rubbed one hand over his frown. How he hated leaving Skyla, and yet he had a list of must-dos. Now he had a new item to add to his list.

"Charlie, I'm going to order a little motion-activated nanny-cam for Skyla's house and a camera system that focuses on the outside of her house. I can fix both of them so she can see what is going on with her cell phone. It scares the hell out of me that Travis actually got into her house. That should never have happened."

"I like the idea," said Charlie. "I'll help you install them. Sometimes she can be touchy about a guy trying to help. Sometimes it's fine. She's inconsistent. Drives me up the wall."

"I've noticed. After meeting her ex, I understand more. For now, Charlie, can you do something for me? After your dinner, will you check Skyla's windows and doors?"

"I was thinking the same thing. I think I'll crash on her couch tonight, too. Until I hear that creep is behind bars again, I don't want her alone."

"Thanks. I appreciate that. I'll tell Sam. In fact, I'll text him now. I'll send him the photo of the license plate, too."

Charlie waited until Anton texted Sam. While they stood in the lot, a red car made a grand entrance and parked next to Anton's. Rap with bass vibrations shook everyone and everything. A young man got out and went into the visitor center.

Claude stepped outside. Even from this distance, Anton saw his disapproving frown at the racket. The two young fellows who'd remained in the car asked Charlie if there were any gas stations near. After giving them directions, Charlie and Anton left.

"Good thing I was texting," said Anton. "Conversation against all those decibels would have been worthless."

"All that vibration. That Ford is going to shake apart. God. How can they stand it?"

♦ ❖ ♦

In a few minutes they arrived at the Pecos Forest Service office.

"I wonder if we'll see Hoot," said Anton.

"Have you met the forest ranger yet?"

Anton shook his head. "Just heard about him."

"Brooks is his name. He's a tough one. A follow-the-rules-or-else type. Knows how to throw his weight around."

Anton and Charlie walked in. Hoot rose from the desk and came forward with a smile to greet them.

"We came to find out if you have any USGS Glorieta maps," said Charlie. "I want one for the film crew."

Hoot came up with one, and Charlie paid for it. Shortly after, a tall, muscular man in a ranger uniform came in. Hoot introduced him as his boss, Justin Brooks.

Anton had wondered about this guy Hoot called owly. Brooks was dark-haired, probably in his fifties. He seemed like a high-energy individual. As Anton shook his hand, the calluses and strong grip told him the older man was no stranger to hard work. The lines around his eyes must be from sun. With the sour attitude Anton had heard about, the lines certainly weren't from laughter. Brooks sat down at a desk behind the counter and logged onto the computer.

Charlie talked with Hoot about the filming and then asked, "Have you ever gone over the bridge near the monastery and up onto that hill a bit? I thought I'd take the drone there to test it again in one of those meadows. Got some space to maneuver there."

"Melody and I walk with our kids there occasionally. It's pretty, an out-of-the-way place. Most of the folks here aren't into walking, so it's quiet. It's part of the national forest land."

"You're late leaving for your lunch, Stewart," Brooks said. "Don't think that means you can be late getting back. I have errands to run."

"No, sir." Hoot turned to Anton and Charlie. "You guys eaten yet? I was just going to call Pancho's and order a green chili cheeseburger. They're great."

"We haven't," said Anton. "Pancho's? That's by the Shell station? Good idea."

"It's all take out," said Hoot. "We could bring it back here and eat outside."

While Hoot and Charlie were getting the food, Anton filled up. Yancy came out of the gas station, tucking his wallet back into his pocket. He looked at Anton, hesitated, then came over. A slight frown creased his forehead.

"I want to warn you," Yancy said. "Sam doesn't take me seriously. But something's not right on the mountain. This guy I know—I get bad vibes from him. Even he's frightened, and he's a no-good, mean, ornery jerk. Must be really bad to scare him."

"Do you know what it is that scares him?" asked Anton.

"If he was an Indian, I'd say the witches were after him, but he's white. My father's people would say he'd heard an owl hooting. I'm told he was really spooked last night. Must be strong evil if even Buck could feel it." Yancy looked over at Hoot and Charlie, who were coming out of the restaurant. He lowered his voice and leaned toward Anton. "You and Miss Skyla be careful. It's dangerous up there right now." He turned and got in his jeep.

Anton shook his head as Yancy drove off. Definitely a picturesque character. He turned toward his friends. Delicious smells wafted from the bags the men carried. It had been a long time since breakfast and the lemon coffeecake. He was ready for lunch.

After they ate, they drove the short distance to the monastery and found Charlie's car in the parking lot a short distance from a few film-crew trucks. Parked near them was an older model Maserati.

"Somebody must be a vintage car fan," said Anton.

Charlie laughed. "That's Scarpelli's. Italian-made is all he cares about."

They walked toward the adobe-looking buildings. Someone's gardening talents had created welcoming landscaping with places to sit and reflect. "The guy you are about to meet is Brother Joseph," said Charlie. "He functions as the hidden cog turning the works of the monastery's film-crew-support business. He's good at his job—

content to fade into the background and let the spotlight shine on the flamboyant divas that make up the film crews."

Brother Joseph, a slightly built man with receding sandy-gray hair, rose from his seat in the sun overlooking the parking area and came to meet them. After the introductions, Brother Joseph said, "The crew went into Santa Fe. It's not lively enough here for them on a Friday evening. All except for Scarpelli. He's resting. The altitude makes him suffer."

Charlie took the drone and his duffle, said goodbye, and disappeared toward his room.

Interesting group of folks he'd met today, thought Anton as he left and headed back toward the interstate. Some jovial and interesting. Some creepy and unfriendly, and one downright scary. He'd definitely follow up on whether or not Skyla had made that call and hoped he'd be forgiven for putting his foot in his mouth. He should have known the words 'my woman' would bring a negative, knee-jerk reaction. He hated seeing her so upset. He'd call after he and Krista got home from their dog training.

He glanced at the time. Maybe he'd have time to go over some stuff with Twitch. Good thing his dog was so focused on him, otherwise Krista and Shadow would make them look bad in class. There were never enough hours in the day to accomplish all that needed to be done, especially torn as he was between Skyla in Pecos, his family at home, and the demands of his business.

Krista was doing a wonderful job with her dog. He wondered if Sam had been able to find time to work with Scherzo, his Airedale pup. Adjusting to his new detective position, preparing for his wedding, and remodeling the home he shared with his grandfather to accommodate a wife and child—all this had to put Sam in a serious time crunch.

Chapter Twenty-One

Skyla arrived at Frankie's restaurant a few minutes before five thirty. The spacious room with a high ceiling stretched in front of her. She stepped down past the dark wood railings, following the hostess to a table. The pillars separating the main floor from the side areas twinkled with the small lights wound around them. Light from the clerestory windows and the wagon wheel chandeliers rested on high white walls adorned with two bearskin rugs and several trophy heads of antlered critters. While she wasn't an admirer of some long-dead beast looking down upon her as she dined, she did acknowledge the total atmosphere held a certain charm. What's more, one didn't have to strain to hear conversations at the table, the food was great, and the staff, friendly.

She sat facing the entrance, nodding at some folks she knew. Charlie was never early, habitually arriving seven minutes late, though she didn't know how he managed that. Their mother had said he'd even been born seven minutes into the day after his due date.

As she bent her head to look at the menu, her long brown hair fell forward. She'd taken the time to brush it out to get rid of "hat hair" when she changed. While in her park ranger uniform of utilitarian gray and green, her hair was pulled back. She was proud to wear the uniform, but she loved the sensuous feel of soft fabric against her skin and lustrous jewel-tone colors. Right now, she was wearing a silky blouse in a dark teal. It coordinated with her dangly, beaded earrings—one of her own jewelry creations.

The waitress brought water and took the order for the sampler-plate appetizer she knew Charlie liked and a glass of wine. She glanced at her watch. Five thirty-seven. He should be here about now. The waitress brought her wine. He probably got to talking with the film crew about drones. He didn't seem to notice the passage of time while talking technology.

Five forty-five. Still no Charlie. Why couldn't the man ever be on time? She sent him a text message before sipping her wine and nibbling on the nachos. The tables around her filled up.

Six o'clock. She called him again. His cell phone rang and rang, going to voicemail, where she left a message. Then, even though she knew Charlie would be ticked off at her, she called the monastery. Soon she was connected to Brother Joseph.

"I'm sorry to bother you, but I wonder if you could do me a favor. My brother, Charlie Van Dyken, was supposed to meet me at five thirty, and he hasn't come. Could you knock on his door, maybe check to see if he's fallen asleep?" While he checked, her fingers drummed impatiently on the tablecloth.

"I'm sorry, miss, but there's no sign of him. I did notice that his car is still in the parking lot."

Skyla thanked him and hung up. She called Charlie again, then texted in case he wasn't getting good reception. Cell service was spotty at best in this rural area. Tentacles of worry crept into her mind. Had he fallen? Had he encountered a rattlesnake? What if Travis had run into him?

She'd tried to control herself today, but she'd been petrified by her ex's threat and devastated by the destruction of Oma's figurine. If provoked enough, Charlie's fuse burned fast and furious. She didn't want him to land in serious trouble on her account.

Six fifteen. She took a last sip of wine, apologized to the waitress, and left more than enough money for the bill.

◆ ❖ ◆

She wanted to call Anton, but he would be on his way to dog-training class. He was so far away. She called Hoot and Melody on her way out the door and explained that Charlie had not shown up. "It's not like him. And this was important. We were celebrating his first patent award."

"Tell you what, Skyla, meet me at the monastery," said Hoot. "I know just where he was going to walk with his drone."

Before she drove away, she called Claude. He might be able to help if they needed to search. He didn't answer. She made a quick stop by her house to pull on jeans, sweatshirt, and sturdy shoes. She grabbed a jacket, a flashlight, and was out the door in five minutes. Just a little before six forty-five, filled with concern, she pulled into the monastery parking lot. Hoot was there, talking with Brother Joseph.

"Miss Skyla," Brother Joseph said, "normally, I wouldn't presume to enter a guest's room without their permission, but in this case, I think it might be wise. I saw Charlie earlier this afternoon going toward the river bridge with that drone-case backpack he uses." They walked the short distance to Charlie's room, and the brother opened the door. Charlie's duffle bag was on the bed, still packed. His cell phone and car keys were on the dresser. The framed award and picture lay next to them. No drone was in sight. Brother Joseph spoke briefly with a few of the monks, sending them off to look along the riverbanks both up and down stream. The shadows lengthened as Skyla, Hoot, and Brother Joseph crossed the foot bridge over the Pecos River. They paused midspan, calling Charlie's name and listening. Skyla glanced worriedly toward the sun. By eight fifteen or so, it would set. The month of June brought warm days here, but at seven thousand feet, the nights were chilly.

Skyla was still concerned with the possibility her ex had something to do with Charlie's being missing. "Brother Joseph, did you see anyone else with Charlie or following him to the other side? Any other cars? Maybe somebody stopped to talk with him?"

"No, miss," he answered. "I was out here quite a while after I saw Charlie. There was no one, no cars. I'm sure of it." He took off his glasses and began to polish the thick lenses.

"Charlie was talking about flying his drone in one of the meadows across the bridge, not far from here," said Hoot.

"I know them. We'll check there first," said Brother Joseph.

As they walked along, they called and listened, hoping to hear Charlie's voice.

"Hoot," Skyla said, "my ex came by today and threatened Charlie. You don't suppose he somehow followed him and got into a fight with him?"

"Did your ex know where Charlie was going?" Hoot asked. "If he didn't, he'd never find this place."

"I'm sure we weren't talking about it when Travis was there."

They reached the first clearing and scanned the shadows under the nearby pines, looking for any sign of Charlie, the drone, or the backpack case. They hurried on to the second clearing and repeated their efforts. The sun set, and they turned back in the waning twilight, still calling, listening, and shining their flashlights along the path.

Come on, Charlie, thought Skyla. *Where are you? God, I hope he didn't go chasing after his drone and fall. What if he's unconscious?*

When the sound of the river signaled their return to the bridge, Skyla turned to Hoot. "Do you think I should call in the state police? Get a search and rescue going?"

"Yes," said Hoot. The monk nodded in agreement. "It gets the timeline started. Pulling all the resources together and following protocol takes time. They could put your mind at rest about your ex, too. They can send somebody out to talk with him and ask where he's been since you saw him."

"We'll help in any way we can. They're welcome to set up their base camp here." Brother Joseph hurried ahead to see if the others had found anything along the river. They had not, and the film crew was not yet back from Santa Fe.

Holding back tears, Skyla punched in 911 to begin the process. Then she called Anton.

Chapter Twenty-Two

Across the large room where the dog-training class met, Anton watched Twitch at the end of a long lead, waiting for the command to come. Shadow, Krista's dog, and Scherzo, Sam's dog, sat in the line of ten dogs. Shadow extended a paw toward Scherzo and let out a single enticing bark. Scherzo broke from his sit-stay and responded in play posture, front end down, butt in the air with his tail wagging happily. Both Sam and Krista went to their dogs, put them back in position, and returned to the line of owners. Twitch didn't move; his brown eyes focused on Anton.

One by one, the dogs were recalled until only Twitch was left. When Anton called, he came on the run, skidded on the smooth floor, and crashed into Anton's knees. Then he wriggled back into a crooked sit with a loopy grin, his eyes on his master's, his look adoring. "Good boy, Twitch." He knelt to give his dog a hug.

Sam came over to tease Krista about her dog getting his in trouble. She just laughed.

"Can you come over to the house for coffee?" Sam asked. "Farah baked a pie for us. She and Leyla will be there and, of course, my grandfather."

"Oh, good," said Krista.

"We'd love to," replied Anton. "I'd never turn down a chance to enjoy your fiancée's cooking. Apple pie?"

"Yeah," said Sam. "She decided it was something a good American should learn to make. Pretty soon, she'll have me all fat."

Anton laughed as he looked at Sam's runner's build. "Not a chance as long as you and Scherzo go running every day."

Anton's cell phone rang. He looked at the number. "Hi, Skyla. How was your dinner?" He heard what sounded like a sob. "Skyla? Is something wrong?"

"Do you know where Charlie is?"

"No, he was having dinner with you."

"He never showed up. All of his stuff, his cell phone, and his car are at the monastery. That's where I am now."

"When I left, he was planning on taking the drone across the river for another test run. Haven't heard from him since. Did you check with the brothers? With the film crew?"

"Yes. I might be worrying for nothing; it's probably just a stupid misunderstanding, but it isn't like him. I hope he didn't have a run-in with Travis."

"I'm sure he's okay. Your friend, Hoot, knew the area where Charlie said he was going. Did you call him?"

"I did. He and some of the monks have been looking with me. We finally called the state police to start a search and rescue. They were going to question Travis, too." Her voice quavered. "Oh, God, I was hoping you'd say he called you. I don't know where he could be. I'm worried. I hope he's not hurt."

"I'm coming," said Anton. "I have to take Krista home and pick up some stuff, but I'll be there as soon as I can. Do you know where the search and rescue base will be?"

"Here, at the monastery."

"I'll see you in a little while. We'll find him."

When Anton hung up, he answered the question in Sam and Krista's eyes. "Charlie's missing. That was Skyla. He didn't show up for their dinner tonight. He's dependable—always. He went out walking with the drone."

"Do they have a search party out?"

"She says they just started the search and rescue procedures. They're going out again—across that bridge by the monastery.

How does the process work when a person goes missing like that, Sam? Can you bring in law enforcement right away, or do they have to wait twenty-four hours or something? Somebody was talking about that in reference to that gallery owner who disappeared here in Santa Fe the other day."

"We're on that case. That twenty-four-hour thing is a myth, especially for a missing hiker. It makes sense to look right away in case he's injured. Did she call the state police? They have the jurisdiction in Pecos."

"Yes. You know she's very worried, if she called 911. I'm heading over there to help. If we still haven't found him by sunrise, we can use one of my drones to search from the sky."

"I'll come, too," said Sam. "If we need to stay overnight, we can stay at my dad's ranch, but we'll have to drive separately. I'm on call."

Anton was concerned as he, Krista, and their tired Airedale pups headed home. He wished he'd had the answers for the questions Krista had peppered him with. What could possibly have happened to Charlie? He wasn't familiar with the area. Maybe he just got lost and turned around, wandered out of cell phone range. Surely they'd soon get a call from him at a nearby ranch to come and pick him up. He hoped so.

Then he began to worry. Charlie felt responsible for that drone. If it had gotten away from him and had landed in a treacherous place, he would have tried to retrieve it. He was working for Drone Tech. Anton was ultimately responsible. If Charlie was injured, he might have to fill in for him with the film crew. Anton decided to take the spare filming drone and several batteries with him. Charlie might need a few days to recuperate from a sprained ankle or whatever kept him from returning on his own, but he'd be okay. He was a sensible guy.

An unwanted thought popped into his consciousness. Would somebody have harmed Charlie to steal the drone? The drone was a custom-designed model carrying a high-powered camera—worth a lot to someone with greedy intentions. That didn't even bear thinking about. Too many things could have gone wrong.

And now Skyla was poking around. He didn't want her walking into danger. He began to organize in his mind what he needed to do to get to Pecos as quickly as he could. His SAT phone would be one of the first items he'd pack. He'd never even thought to get one for Charlie. Damn, he should have.

Chapter Twenty-Three

When Anton arrived at the monastery, Skyla flew into his arms. "He hasn't shown up yet?" he asked.

Skyla shook her head against him.

Sam was inside where the Search and Rescue (SAR) team had organized themselves in the common room. Anton introduced himself to the Incident Commander (IC), who was in charge. They'd been busy creating their lost-person profile, calling those who'd seen Charlie that day, and checking places he might have gone. Even though his car was still in the lot, they had a policeman check at Charlie's apartment.

"Can you ping his cell phone and get a GPS signal?" asked Sam.

"His phone is in his room," said Skyla. "Wouldn't do any good."

"Do you have a recent photo of him that we could use?" the IC asked.

Skyla seemed overwhelmed, her mind distracted with worry to answer. "Photo?"

"The patent-awards photo," said Anton, "taken earlier today. He's probably even wearing the same clothes."

"Tell me about this drone and the case he was carrying," said the IC, after he'd gotten a thorough description of the clothes, even down to the brand and size of shoes Charlie'd been wearing. Along with the photo, they'd gotten the shoe dimensions and a tread pattern from the internet. All the information would be shared with the searchers.

Anton chafed under the information gathering. He wanted to *do* something.

"What mental state would you say he was in?" asked the IC.

"Happy, excited over receiving his first patent. Like a kid with a new toy, working with the filming drone," said Anton. "If you're wondering about his being depressed and thinking of harming himself, forget it. That's not how he's wired."

"What kind of area would he look for to fly his drone? Would he try for extreme angles or dangerous places?"

Anton told them about the drone and the maneuvers Charlie would be likely to try. "Almost forgot. The drone has a locater." He took out his cell phone and worked at it for a while. "The battery must be dead. I'm not able to get anything."

"Do you have bloodhounds?" asked Hoot.

"Normally we do have a couple available to us," said the IC, "but there was a SAR going on in the outskirts of Las Cruces, where an old lady with dementia wandered away from her home. I heard they found her okay, but the dogs and handlers need to rest. Maybe by tomorrow afternoon, God willing."

"What did Travis Cutler say when you talked to him?" asked Anton.

"As far as I know, the state police haven't been able to find him yet," said the IC.

Anton looked at Skyla. God, he thought, she looks like she's ready to drop.

The IC spoke to the assistant who was in charge of their radio communications. "Check in with the point guys."

"Point guys?" asked Sam.

"We've looked at the search area and identified spots where he might be apt to show up if he'd gotten disoriented," he said. "People tend to take the easiest route. The terrain kind of dictates where one might go. We've got them at the bridge, at the first meadow, the far end of the second meadow, and up and down stream a ways. Even on the other side of the river, where the road ends near the national forest boundary."

"Is there anything else we can do tonight?" asked Anton, his eyes on a drooping Skyla. "I'm thinking I would like to use one of my drones to search come daylight. Search the meadows where he said he was going."

Skyla looked up at him hopefully.

"I'd like to join him," said Sam.

"Me, too," said Hoot. "And Melody."

"That would be helpful," said the IC. "But with any luck, he'll be found by then."

Anton hoped that would be the case as he said good night to the others and followed Skyla to her home. He sighed. It could be a long night.

♦ ❖ ♦

As the light grew brighter in the eastern sky, Anton and Skyla returned to the monastery parking lot. Sam was already inside. The intent looks on the faces around them showed that the search and rescue was still underway. The monks provided coffee, donuts, and a sandwich buffet for the weary searchers. They found the IC and sipped coffee, waiting until they could talk with him for last-minute guidance and instructions.

Hoot and Melody joined them. Hoot set down his backpack and accepted the coffee Melody handed him.

"Your pack is the same size as Anton's drone one," said Sam when they were ready to leave. "What all do you have in there?"

Hoot adjusted the straps over his shoulders. "Climbing gear. It might come in handy." He watched Anton as he pulled out his maps. "I can handle the map coordination, if you like. Leave your hands free for the drones."

"Thanks," said Anton.

Once they were over the bridge, Anton assembled the drone and sent it aloft. With its first-person view, they could see in real time on the screen what the drone saw. He and Hoot coordinated their patterns, and they moved steadily on the path toward the first meadow. Periodically other team members passed them. No one had seen any sign of Charlie. Sam scanned the ground for tracks and disturbances, though he grumbled. Even knowing what kind of track Charlie would have left, it was hard to tell the searchers' footprints from the searchee's.

No spectacular land formations graced this route—just trees and brush, with rocks and soil in hues of beige forming an austere beauty. Occasionally, broad-tailed hummingbirds divebombed those who dared trespass in their territory. Several deer, one a dappled fawn, skirted them widely on their way down to the river. Anton found himself almost annoyed with them. Didn't they understand the seriousness of the moment? How could the critters go on like it was just another day?

At the first meadow, Anton flew the drone in a grid pattern. Halfway through, he changed to his spare battery. "We have about thirty minutes power on this one."

When the meadow surveillance was completed, they returned to the monastery to pick up fresh batteries and leave the spent ones to recharge.

They ate, refilled their water bottles, and were about ready to leave when Claude Frobisher, the park ranger, walked in. He came over to where they were talking with the IC. He exchanged greetings with the commander and then turned to Skyla.

"I'm sorry I missed your calls last night about Charlie, but I was out of town. Just got back." He turned to welcome another who had entered. "Hello, Brooks," he said as Hoot's boss joined them.

"Still no sign of him?" Brooks asked.

The commander shook his head.

"I wanted to tell you that I heard something yesterday. It might not be important at all, but it would be wrong not to tell," said Brooks. "I ran into a group of young men at the liquor store. They were talking about drones at the check-out counter. One of them said he'd met the guy who flew the filming drone. They wanted to invite him to go up past Tererro with them and said it would be cool to fly the drone along the Pecos there. Another said he'd give anything to have a drone like that."

Anton, already worried about Charlie coming to harm because of the drone, listened intently as Brooks went on.

"I was not impressed with these guys. But maybe they never actually talked with him. I guess it wasn't important after all."

"Holy crap. It might be," said Claude. "I was going past here yesterday afternoon, a little after four o'clock. I saw a car by the gates. Saw the same car full of guys earlier in the day, too, at the park. Had their music up loud enough to make our windows rattle. That's what drew my attention to it. As I passed them on the road here, a young guy shut the trunk and got into the backseat. They took off toward Tererro."

"You've met Charlie," said Brooks. "Was it him?"

"Wasn't paying too much attention. I was just annoyed at the loud music. I was certain the brothers wouldn't like it."

"Do you remember what he was wearing, or what he looked like?" asked the commander.

"Jeans, dark-colored T-shirt. Carried a dark jacket."

Anton glanced at the patent-award photo, which the SAR folks had reproduced and were passing out to the public. Charlie wore a navy T-shirt with Drone Pilot emblazoned on it. He'd had a navy jacket with him, but that wasn't in the photo.

"That surprises me," said Brooks. "I hoped those guys wouldn't find him, but they did seem to know he was staying at the monastery. Anybody could have told them that's where film crews stay."

"Charlie never would have gone off like that," said Skyla. "He was supposed to meet me at five thirty. We were celebrating. He would never have stood me up. Of that, I'm certain."

"Well, he did, didn't he?" said Brooks.

Anton noticed Skyla's face, recoiling like she'd just been slapped. What an insensitive jerk, he thought, adding salt to a fresh wound.

"Can any of you describe this car?" asked the commander. "Or give a more detailed description of the young people?"

Brooks gave brief descriptions and said they bought beer and snack-type foods, but he had no idea of what kind of a car they drove.

"I saw a red Ford Focus," said Claude. "But you'll hear it before you see it."

"We saw that red car yesterday at the park," Anton said, "but Charlie commented on how obnoxious that noise was. He wouldn't go off with them."

"How would you know?" asked Brooks with a scowl.

"He's one of my best employees. Dependable, thoughtful. Task-oriented."

"I'm sure he is when the boss is around."

The IC wrote down all the information they gave him. "I'll pull some of my folks and send them up the highway to check the fishing areas and campgrounds. We'll extend the search further up the river, too. Maybe somebody saw something." He looked at Claude. "Or heard something."

Chapter Twenty-Four

"I want to go back and do the second meadow," said Skyla. "Charlie *didn't* go off with them."

They set off. Folks coming toward them said they'd been radioed that the search was going into a different area and to report back. When Anton's group reached the second meadow, they flew the same methodical pattern.

"Great perspective," Anton said to Hoot, who was coordinating the action with his map. "Look, from this meadow, you'd never know that only one ridge away there's a dirt road. But from up there, you can see it."

"It's surprising to find so many little ranches tucked away down dirt roads here," said Sam. "It's easy to see why drones are so handy when it comes to finding pot fields."

"Hey, what's that?" Anton broke the pattern and hovered the drone near the tops of a couple of ponderosa pines at the far edge of the clearing. "Guys, look! Stuck in the branches. I think that's the drone!"

"Charlie's? Oh, God, please be Charlie's. Does that mean he's nearby?" Skyla asked.

"Looks like it. Doesn't seem to have much damage either. Don't know how the hell we'll ever get it down."

Melody looked at Hoot and smiled.

"Let's see what we can find near there," said Anton. He brought the small drone down next to the tree. The stuck drone could not be seen from the meadow at all. They all peered up into the branches and saw nothing from below.

Hoot set down his pack and unzipped it. He took out a pair of gadgets with straps and buckles. Sam whistled. "When you said climbing gear, I thought you meant, like, for rappelling. You meant for trees."

"Yup. I can get that drone. This tree will be plumb easy. It's how I got the name Hoot. I worked my way through college as a lumberman. They called us Hoot Owls because we got out there working at the crack of dawn. Had to finish before the humidity dropped, and the dryness made it too dangerous to work in the forest with machinery."

Anton liked gadgets, and he was fascinated by Hoot's tree spikes. Each one had a brace that came down the inside of the lower leg, buckled over the calf, passed under the boot, and strapped around his ankle. A wicked-looking spike jutted down from the brace. Then Hoot fastened a harness around his lower torso that had lanyards with rope clamps and carabiners. He looped one lanyard around the tree and hooked the end into the carabiner on his harness. Soon he disappeared up the trunk.

Anton, Skyla, and Sam stepped back to watch from a distance. Melody stayed near the base of the tree.

"He was here," Skyla said. "We need to concentrate our search here."

"Think, Anton," said Sam. "If you were coming here to test your drone, where would you go? What would you do?"

"I'd be coming off the trail where we did, and I'd set down the case and assemble it. If I set the case down in this dirt, you'd see some marks."

"The soil here gets kind of a crust on it after a light rain," said Sam, "then it gets cracky, but underneath, it's soft and powdery. There's been a crowd of searchers through here already, though."

"I'd stay in the open," Anton continued. "Even though the drone has an object-avoidance system, it's still vulnerable to a good wind gust. Let's walk it in a grid pattern." About arm's length from each other, they began going back and forth. Periodically they looked to see Hoot's progress up the tree.

"Wait a minute," said Sam, holding a hand out to stop them as they began their third pass across the clearing. He looked intently at the ground.

"This soil looks a little different. What the heck?" said Anton.

Sam pointed. "Looks like brush marks, like somebody brushed out some tracks."

Anton deliberately took a step, then brought his foot back. "You were saying about cracky edges on the prints? This is *all* powder."

"What happened here?" Sam knelt in the dirt and looked around. "Would there be any reason for Charlie to prepare some kind of landing area, Anton?"

"No, it'd just kick up more dust. Better to have the surface undisturbed."

"Could the rotors have made it look like it was brushed?" Skyla was looking around.

"I don't think so. With eight rotors there's quite a backwash, but this? Unlikely."

Skyla stepped past them and picked up a pine branch. Its needles were dusty and worn. "Could they have used this?" She handed the branch to Sam. He inspected it, then drew it across the dirt at their feet.

"*Voila*," he said. "You've got it."

"Noooo!" Skyla's cry startled them all. She dropped to her knees by a sage plant, reached under the scrubby bush into the dry leaves beneath, and picked up a leather thong with a tiger-eye pendant. Then she held it in her hands, rocking back and forth. Her eyes were scrunched tight. "Charlie!" she wailed.

Anton knelt by her and put his arm around her shaking shoulders. Sam caught his eye and pointed. Several of the sage leaves had dark brown spots. Anton kept Skyla in his arms. Sam took photos with his phone of the plant where she'd found the pendant.

"I got it." The call came from the top of the tree. Anton pulled Skyla to her feet and led her back to the pine. Soon Hoot was back in sight, the drone hanging from another rope attached to his waist. When he was down, Anton disassembled the rotors and folded up the arms. He disconnected the camera and turned his jacket into a makeshift carrying case. He found room in the little search drone case to fit the camera, knowing it would be better protected there.

Sam turned to Skyla, who still clutched the pendant to her breast. "May I see it?" She handed it to him. The clasp was damaged and the leather thong severed near it. Dark stains marked the broken ends. "We should finish searching this meadow." He looked around the group. "Something happened here. I think we should treat this like a crime scene. Anton, if I can borrow your SAT phone, I'm going to call the IC."

Sam told the commander what they'd found—the drone, the pendant, and the disturbed soil. He said they'd like to continue searching with their drone. While they talked, Anton put a fresh battery into his search drone.

Sam hung up and handed the phone back to Anton. "The IC is sending someone up from the monastery to secure the scene until they can get a forensics team in here. They said it was okay to finish the drone search. We can't stop looking for Charlie. Watch where you step. Tell me right away if you see what looks like more brushed soil. Keep your eyes peeled for any tracks that don't seem to belong to searchers, especially vehicle or horse tracks, or fresh droppings."

"We still haven't found the drone control either," said Anton. "It's made out of a dark plastic—bigger and more complicated than the one I'm using now."

"Another thing," said Sam. "I'm sorry, Skyla, but they're going to want to take the pendant as evidence. You'll get it back, but it might be a while."

Skyla sucked in a breath, then nodded.

They continued their search all the way into the thick brush surrounding the clearing but found no more signs of Charlie. Sam took photos of the brushed area, pendant, and any tracks he thought should be recorded. They sent the small drone aloft again and searched until they were sure Charlie was nowhere around. Anton had a bad feeling; he didn't expect to find him here.

When the state trooper arrived, Sam showed him what they'd found, and Skyla surrendered the pendant. Sam asked for permission to take one of the stained sage leaves. He carefully cut one off and secured it in an envelope in his pocket. Anton said he was keeping the drone, as it belonged to his company and would be required by the film crew come Monday.

On their return, Sam carried the smaller drone case. He and Anton held back from the dispirited threesome making their way ahead of them.

"I don't like this, Anton. A person did something to Charlie. Wasn't any kind of predator that attacked him. A human took that branch and tried to hide what happened. I believe that was blood on the bush where the pendant was. And it took violent force to damage the clasp and cord that way."

They trudged on, deep in thought, until Sam asked, "With this drone, where does it record the video footage?"

"The control gets the feed and stores it. But I designed these drones. They use a camera that has a backup microSD card. Whoever tried to hide their actions might not know that. They might think that they got all the footage if they took the control and the tablet."

"Good. I was hoping for that."

"Tonight, we'll take a look at the footage, Sam. Something may show up on it. The cops will want to see it."

The three ahead had stopped to wait for them. Hoot spoke up. "We've been thinking. It could be possible that somebody didn't want Charlie filming what they were doing and harmed him to stop it. I don't think it's a good idea to let anybody know that we have the drone. I mean, the authorities know, but not the public or the press."

"I agree," said Anton, feeling relief. "I think it should be our secret, for now, that we found the drone—and the pendant." He caught Skyla's eyes. She nodded.

They reached the bridge and crossed to the monastery. Anton stowed the drones in his car before going into the command center. It wasn't nearly as busy as it had been in the morning. The commander had been replaced by another trooper, who took their report. Since it was the state police in charge of both the SAR and the forensics team, their report was discreet. They didn't want the public and the press speculating about finding the drone.

They sat, rubbed their weary feet, sipped coffee, and welcomed the sandwiches and fruit provided by the monks. Melody encouraged Skyla to eat to keep up her strength.

The commander's phone rang. He answered, and his posture changed. Anton watched. Not a change to happy, just more alert. Now what?

Chapter Twenty-Five

The room hushed in anticipation. Justin Brooks and Claude Frobisher stopped their conversation near the coffee machine. All eyes went to the commander as he put away his phone, his face somber as he addressed the group. "They've found a body up on the riverbank between Cowles and Tererro."

"It's not Charlie," Skyla said defiantly. "He was *here*."

"I'll go check it out," said Anton, looking at Skyla. "Then we'll be sure. Sam?"

"I'll come with you."

"Melody and I are going to stay here with Skyla," said Hoot.

Sam glanced at Anton as they drove up the road. "I think it's important for us to get up there right away. Sometimes law enforcement can be misled or misdirected. I've a feeling that we should watch what's going on."

After a twenty-minute drive following the Pecos River, they came upon a long line of cars from various law enforcement agencies. Anton parked and they walked up to the activity.

Sam went toward the trooper who seemed to be in charge and showed his credentials. "I'm Sergeant Martinez with the Santa Fe PD. And this is Anton Bjornson, the missing person's employer. Have you identified the body yet?"

"ID in his wallet says Charles Van Dyken."

Anton closed his eyes and felt his energy drain away. God, no. He'd been hoping Charlie might still be alive.

The trooper asked Anton, "I'd like to see your ID, too. Would you be able to identify him?"

Anton nodded and passed his driver's license to the trooper, who jotted down his information next to Sam's.

"Both of you, come with me then." He led the way to an easier descent a short way up the road.

As they neared the body on the rocky shoreline, Anton's hopes plummeted. With all of his being he wanted to push back the clock, to have life go in a different direction. He looked up the cliff to the guardrails and the road beyond. This couldn't be happening. He looked down at the man lying there—at the short brown, wavy hair, the scruffy, unshaven face that their young receptionist at Drone Tech thought was so hot. The eyes were closed—they'd never shine with happiness again.

Anton took a deep breath and said in a broken whisper, "It's Charlie." He stumbled away and sat on a rock at the water's edge, his head in his hands. Numb.

♦ ❖ ♦

Sam looked at his friend, then back at the trooper. "Has he been moved?"

"After they got the first photos and all, they turned him over and pulled him back a little from the water. Nothing else has been touched."

"Is it okay if I take some pictures?"

"Don't see why not. Maybe you'll see something that'll make sense of an accident like this. Damn stupid thing to do. Slip and fall off a cliff. What the hell was he doing up there anyway?"

"Accident?"

"Must've been." The trooper frowned. "You're not thinking he was pushed or something, are you?"

Sam wondered how much he should tell this guy. "I don't know. Seems strange to be out here all alone. No backpack, no water bottle, no hat. I'm told he went missing down by the monastery. Then we heard he'd gotten into a car with some other young people to come up here. Where are they? Makes you wonder, doesn't it?"

"The river prob'ly took his hat. Maybe his water bottle." He looked at Sam from under shaggy, gray eyebrows. "I heard a story, also."

"What's that?"

"I heard that he had some fancy drone with him. Worth a lot of money. Do you suppose they killed him and stole it?"

Sam realized the old trooper wasn't as dumb as he made out to be. He was also fishing for information. He met his eyes. "He didn't just fall, did he?"

"Nope. He had lots of help."

"Who found him?" asked Sam.

"Couple of fishermen. They flagged down a car for help." He pointed up on the road. "They're still here. I suppose you can talk to them."

Careful not to disturb anything, Sam took pictures of the cliff as he studied it, then the area between the base of the cliff and the body. No bloodstains on the cliff that he could see. Nothing looked disturbed. He looked for any trash, metal, glass, or other debris, wondering what injuries might be on the body. He took a few photos of Charlie.

Then he went back up to the road and talked to the two fishermen, standing there with a voyeur's interest, heaping up story details to tell their friends. "Has anything changed in the scene since you first saw him?"

"They pulled him back from the water and turned him over," said one, "so they could see who he was, I guess."

"What do you think happened?"

"I think he must have fallen from the road. Maybe crawled to the water. Just got to the edge. Collapsed and died."

"Did you see anything that might have fallen with him? A backpack for instance?"

They looked at each other.

"It just seems odd," said Sam, "that a guy would be on his own out here in the middle of nowhere without carrying some kind of equipment."

"Didn't see a thing."

Sam followed the path with his eyes from the road to where the body lay. A person would have had to take a huge flying leap to have landed where he did. He didn't see any disturbed soil or weeds between the bottom of the cliff and the body. Couldn't have gotten where he was from rolling with the momentum of a fall. Too many rocks in the way, and the weeds between the cliff and the body were not disturbed. Foul play. Somebody killed him and dumped him. He wondered what hoops he'd have to jump through to see the autopsy report.

He went back to Anton and sat next to him. In silence, they stared at the water tumbling by, cold and clear.

After a while, Anton spoke. "Oh, God, Sam. I don't want to believe it. He was so full of life. Smart, talented, promising future. And Skyla. She's going to be heartbroken. Something's wrong here. He was on the other side of the river. We *know* he was there."

"Do you suppose Travis Cutler killed him?"

"I don't know." He picked up a small rock and flung it into the water. "I worried, Sam, about the possibility that someone killed him for the drone, but they never got the drone. It makes no sense. It must have been Cutler." He looked back at the scene on the riverbank. The medical examiner had arrived. Soon they would take Charlie away. "We have to get back—be with Skyla." They clambered up to the road.

As they left, Sam was still full of questions. "Was there anyone else who may have had it in for Charlie? Someone who was jealous of him?"

"Everybody at work loved him. He was a joy to be around."

"Girlfriends?"

"I know he dated. Never heard of anybody he was serious about."

"How about money? Was he wealthy?"

"I think there was some inheritance from his parents, but not that much. He lived simply."

"Skyla?"

"Bite your tongue, Sam. Those two were close. They were all the family they had left."

"I didn't think she was the problem. But you have to ask."

When they walked into the SAR headquarters, Brother Joseph came to Anton and put a hand on his arm. "They said it was Charlie. But she won't believe it. Not without you saying. Was it him?"

Anton nodded. The brother sagged a bit, then made the sign of the cross, folded his hands, closed his eyes, and began, "*Domine miserere …*"

Across the room, Skyla rose from where she sat with Melody. Anton's feet had lead in them, yet he found himself standing in front of her with no idea how he'd crossed the floor. Hope fled her face and was followed by terrible anguish.

"No," she whispered, shaking her head. "No. He wasn't there. It can't be Charlie."

He reached out, gathering her tense body to his. Dropping his head to hers, he whispered back. "I'm sorry. So sorry. It is Charlie." Tears welled in his own eyes.

"No, no. He wasn't there." She began trembling.

Anton held her tightly. Over her head, he saw Melody's face crumple, and she turned into Hoot's arms.

"Why? Who?" Skyla tilted back her head and looked into his face.

Her eyes were wet, glistening, yellow merging into green, so much like the eyes of Charlie. He swallowed against the ache in his throat, pressed his lips hard together before he reached out to touch her face, his thumb brushing her wet cheek. "Skyla, I don't know. It makes no sense. But I promise you, I will do my best to find out who. And why. For you. For Charlie."

Chapter Twenty-Six

At the Martinez ranch in Pecos, Anton and Sam had the main house to themselves that evening. Sam's dad was at their Santa Fe home. Melody was spending the night at Skyla's house; she didn't want her to be alone.

Anton still moved in a world of disbelief. He put the microSD card from the drone camera into his laptop. What had Charlie captured on the video? Mixed feelings of dread, anxiety, and interest roiled inside him. The first part showed the footage at the Bjornson ranch Charlie had filmed Friday morning. It caught Charlie's exuberance and Anton's own satisfaction as the drone came down. God, was that just yesterday? How could Charlie be gone? He couldn't believe it.

Then the new part, unfolding Charlie's footage in the second meadow. The drone soared high, taking in the clearing and the pines. A family of deer came into view. They moved cautiously, the oblong shapes of their backs showing tan against the scrubby green growth of the clearing. The camera zoomed in, catching the buck's upward glance, and followed his graceful, bounding exit into a thicket. There was an artistry Anton hadn't noticed before about Charlie's filming. Working with the film crew must have been a two-way street. While Charlie had shared his technical expertise, he had learned from them about camera angles, lighting, and drama.

The drone moved higher, catching the ridge beyond the meadow and looking over at a dirt road—little more than tracks between trees. It panned the area in a full circle. The video recorded the tiny figure of Charlie looking at his controls. It moved steadily on over the ridge, then paused over an open area screened by brush from the road. A pickup truck and a man working near it came into view.

Anton exchanged a look with Sam. By God, were they going to see what prompted someone to kill Charlie? The man was digging a long narrow rectangular hole as deep as his thighs. He climbed out of the hole, struggled to pull a shape wrapped in a tarp from the back of the pickup, and dragged it to the opening in the earth. "He's dug a grave," Anton said. "Incredible!"

Sam didn't answer, looking intently at the screen. They saw the guy dump a body out of the tarp into the hole and begin to cover it up. Then the angle of the footage changed from looking directly down on the top of the pickup to more of a side-angle view. The zoom lens brought it closer. Trees obscured the rear end of the truck. Slowly the view moved toward the front end, rounding the fender, just catching the bumper. Suddenly the footage cartwheeled to show sky, trees, sky again, then blurry pine branches. The screen went black.

Sam picked up his phone. "I'm going to call the state police and get this to them. They'll need to secure the scene and dig up that body."

"What'll they do with the microSD card?" asked Anton when Sam had finished his call.

"A trooper will be here in about twenty minutes. When they get the card, they'll extract every bit of information they can find. They'll check out that grave, too."

"Let's watch it again," said Anton, "and write down everything it tells us about these bastards."

They listed all they learned about the man. He wore a camouflage shirt, jeans, gloves, and a cowboy hat. From the sky they couldn't see his face, not even enough to tell what race he was or what color his hair might be. How old? No clues, except that he worked steadily and hard. He was muscular and strong.

"Anton," asked Sam, "why doesn't the digger hear the drone and react?"

"It's up pretty high. Remember the drone I used when you were chasing Wilma's attacker in January in that rocky area? It's like that one—fairly quiet. And the digger is making noise."

The pickup truck was gray or silver. Whatever the color, it was dulled from age or dirt. The truck had a king cab and was built high off the ground—four-wheel drive, adapted to off-road use. The bed of the truck was covered with a four-section, flip-back lid, partly open to show the grooved liner on the bottom. They couldn't make out anything else in the back. The driver's side had a small shape on the doorpost that Anton thought might be a spotlight. The front had what could be a winch bumper.

"If Charlie is their second murder, they might hit the panic button," said Anton. "What would they do to avoid being identified or captured?"

"That's another clue," said Sam. "They, not he. There are at least two. The digger was still working when Charlie was attacked. It's logical the two are connected." He paused. "I don't know enough to say that for a certainty. But to answer your question about what they might do—they could change the appearance of the truck. Lie low. Construct alibis. We've no idea if they're local or not."

"Damn. If he'd only had a few more seconds of filming. I wish we could make out that license plate." Anton went to the end of the video and stopped it just before the drone crashed. He jotted down the time on their notes. The date / time stamp on the video footage said 3:42. That could be the time Charlie was killed. Sam startled him out of his thoughts.

"Son of a gun," Sam said. "A license plate!"

Anton looked at him, the cogs in his brain finally catching up to the conclusion Sam had already reached.

"It *has* a front license plate," explained Sam. "We can't read it, but that means the truck isn't from New Mexico. So, either the gravedigger is from out of state, or he hasn't bothered to get the plates changed after he moved here."

"Where could it be from?"

"Nearby—Texas, Utah, or Colorado. Not very many southern states require front plates, nor do Arizona or Oklahoma."

"Could these guys find out that this video exists?" asked Anton.

"Only if somebody says something. I think the law will be pretty mum about it."

They heard a car drive up and went out to give the state trooper the microSD card, which Sam had put into a sealed envelope with written notes identifying it and establishing the chain of custody. The trooper came inside and inspected the drone and camera.

"I don't see any need to take the drone or camera as evidence," he said. "All that is required is the card. I do need to ask if you viewed the video and if you made a copy."

"We did see the footage," said Sam. "We called you as soon as we realized that this was evidence."

"We didn't make a copy," said Anton, "but, if possible, I would like the card back after the investigation is complete, and it is no longer needed. I'd especially like the earlier portion of the video—my daughter is on that part."

"I will make a note of your request," said the trooper.

When the trooper had gone, Yancy came up to them. They told him that Charlie had been found, murdered. He bowed his head, closed his eyes, and muttered something in a tongue that Anton didn't know.

Anton began to wonder about Skyla's ex, thinking back to the man who had been so obnoxious at the park visitor center. Nothing he had seen ruled him out. Could it be Cutler on the video? Could he be the one burying someone? And there seemed to be an accomplice. It didn't make sense. Who knew?

"Can you find out for me who they buried, Sam?" asked Anton. "Can you find out Charlie's autopsy results? I *need* to help."

"Maybe. I want that information, too." Sam doodled on the notes he'd taken from the video. "Do you have to meet with the film crew tomorrow?"

"Yes, unfortunately, in the morning. I don't want to, but we have a contract with them."

"It's serendipitous that you have a built-in reason to interact with them. You're in an ideal position to learn more. They might be involved. They may know or have seen something. Talk to them. Find out what their secrets are. Find out what they thought of Charlie."

"Haven't thought about it that way. I can do that. I'll be spending quite a few nights there. Their schedule is unpredictable, and Charlie said he was always being hit with script changes." Anton powered off his laptop and zipped it into its case. He leaned back and stretched. Through the open window, he heard the melancholy sound of Yancy's flute. Tonight, it sounded more mournful than ever. Seemed like just yesterday that they'd all been together, recording the flute and playing with the cop drones.

God, he was tired. He rubbed his fingers over his scalp. "Skyla is all alone now, Sam. Life's so fragile. I've thought about it a lot, especially this past year. When Krista was kidnapped, and I was almost killed. Our family was close to being wiped out. It's frightening."

"When Farah came here, she and her daughter were all that was left of their whole family. It had to be tough."

"And now Farah has you. She's part of another family. You never get over it, but you move on." His fingers found the scar on the side of his head and lightly traced it. "Maybe it sounds stupid, Sam, but I don't think Charlie can rest until his killer is caught."

"Doesn't sound stupid to me."

Anton sat for a while in thought, before speaking. "I made a promise to Skyla that I would try to find out who killed Charlie, and why. But I need to do that for me, too. Charlie is … was such a catalyst, a positive force in our company. He needs justice."

"Are you thinking the Circle Sleuths should jump into solving another mystery?"

"Maybe we already have?" Anton looked at Sam's animated face and smiled. "Pete's training is showing. Just like him, you've grabbed onto the puzzle. You're not going to let go until you've figured it out. I saw you in action today." His smile faded. "I could sure use your help."

Later that night as Anton dropped off to sleep, he thought of Skyla. The beauty of Charlie's last video. Grief at the loss of a friend, worker, and brother to Skyla. His heart reached out to her. He'd follow through on his promise. That was important.

Chapter Twenty-Seven

On Sunday morning Anton drove to the monastery for a meeting with the film crew. He knew the director, Elliot Canby, from their earlier meetings when the contract had been drawn up. Brother Joseph pointed out the building where the film crew had gathered.

Anton heard a crash and a loud voice from inside as he reached for the doorknob. “You’re not the director, Scarpelli. I am.”

Anton remembered the name, Scarpelli. He’d been the only crew member remaining behind at the monastery the afternoon Charlie had been killed.

The door swung open and banged against the wall, narrowly missing Anton. A scowling man stormed by him. The voice from inside continued. “The next guy that gets him going will have to replace that door. Can’t you guys just leave him alone?”

Nice introduction, thought Anton. He entered to find the crew sitting in embarrassed silence. A younger man picked up the knocked-over chair and sat back down on his own. From what Anton could see, Canby’s expression was the most unperturbed in the room.

“Bjornson,” the director said, rising to greet him and gesturing to the young man. “This is Larry Morris, our cameraman. He was the one working most closely with Charlie. Damn shame about him getting killed. Damned annoying.”

"Yes, it is," Anton said with a sharp look.

"It's very difficult to lose a friend," said Morris. "He was a good teacher. I, for one, will miss him."

After Anton was introduced to the rest of the crew, he sat down by Canby. "And who was the fellow who left?"

"Scarpelli," answered Canby, confirming Anton's guess. "Walking encyclopedia—he lives, breathes, and speaks Civil War. Don't get him going, Bjornson. He's volatile. I don't know why the studio foisted him on us. If it were left to him, this movie would be a bomb—a boring recitation of facts."

Anton didn't need this. Only Sam's challenge of furthering the investigation, his company's contract, and wanting to honor the effort which Charlie had already put into this project would keep him involved.

But the young man's comments as they talked showed promise, and Anton warmed to the idea of working with Morris. He might be a good source of information about Scarpelli. He wondered where he'd been while Charlie filmed alone.

♦ ❖ ♦

After Anton finished with the crew, Brother Joseph showed him to the room where he'd be staying while working on the film. "I'm afraid Charlie's things are still here. The police have been through them, first to see if there were any clues as to his whereabouts, then to see if there was anything that might point to who murdered him. I told the crew to leave them for you. I thought you'd know how to separate his personal things from work-related, and I trust you to do it right."

Anton sighed. "Of course. I can deliver them to Skyla before I head home tonight. I'll be back tomorrow morning." Anton sorted the belongings and repacked them, thinking all the while about Charlie.

Around noon that day, Hiram Brower, the trooper they'd met at the river, stopped by to see him. Anton answered his questions about Charlie, what they'd done, and who they'd seen in the hours before he was killed. By the time he was finished, it was early afternoon. He called Skyla and told her he was bringing Charlie's things over. She met him at her door. Her hair was drawn back, her face pale with dark shadows under her eyes.

"Have you eaten yet?" he asked as he set Charlie's things inside.

She shook her head. "I wasn't hungry."

"I haven't either. Can we go grab a bite?"

They headed to a restaurant off the interstate on the outskirts of Santa Fe. It was only a short drive, and they both appreciated its quiet anonymity. Over hot soup in a quiet corner, they talked. He didn't tell her that they'd viewed the tape. If it was raw and upsetting to him, it certainly would be for her.

"The state police contacted me and asked me all about Friday," said Skyla. "I asked about Travis. They said they haven't been able to reach him yet. They said they'd call you, too."

"They already have. By the way, you don't have to think about it now, but I can help with Charlie's apartment when you're ready to tackle that."

"Oh, God. I dread the thought. Melody offered to help. I couldn't face it alone. Maybe next week? Thank you."

Anton reached across the table and took her hands, holding them lightly. "I kept Charlie's cop drone. It was in his stuff. It sort of stands in my mind for the good times we shared, his joy in new gadgets, just how much he loved life." He swallowed. "I should have asked you first. If you want it, of course you can have it. That night we flew them was special."

Skyla squeezed his hands. "No, keep it. I wouldn't know how to fly it anyway. I'm glad you have the happy memory."

This next part was tricky. He had to choose his words carefully, or he would end up pushing the wrong buttons again. He took a deep breath and began, "There's something else, too. Before I dropped Charlie off at the monastery, we talked about Travis getting into your house. Charlie was going to come by after your dinner and check all your windows and doors. He said he was going to crash on your couch. He didn't want you alone."

She pulled one of her hands from his to wipe away a tear. She sniffed, then took his hands again.

"You know us. We talked about it and ordered a motion-activated nanny cam for inside your house, and a surveillance camera system for the outside."

She started to pull her hands away, and he tightened his fingers slightly. She relented, letting her hands rest in his. "Skyla, please, listen. He wanted to do it. We can tie it into your cell phone. It gives you more control over who might be in your space."

"I was so frightened when I knew he'd been in my house. I know both of you are being protective." She rubbed her thumbs back and forth across his knuckles. "But this might be okay. I can't say no. I really would feel better."

"Since we ordered them on Friday, they should have already come. Would it be okay if I installed them on Tuesday?"

"Please. And since Ch-Charlie can't do it, would you check my windows when you bring me home?"

After delivering her safely and checking her house, he set off for his own. He called Sam on the way, using his Bluetooth. All Sam could tell him was that the state police had secured the burial site and were processing it. Hadn't heard anything about Travis Cutler, the red Ford Focus, or anything else, for that matter. He hoped to hear about the autopsies on Monday.

When Anton arrived home, he'd barely gotten out of the car before Krista ran to meet him, followed by two energetic, happy Airedales. Krista launched herself at him and he swept her up in his arms, savoring her hug. He'd shared the news of Charlie's death over the phone with them earlier.

She began to cry. "I didn't want Charlie to die."

"I know, sweetheart. He was taken from us way too soon."

He held her and brushed away the tears. Karen came to meet them. "There's coffee on," she said. "Tell us what you can."

"Thanks, Mom." Anton gave her a long hug, grateful for her warmth and comfort.

Chapter Twenty-Eight

Later that night after Krista had gone to bed, Anton packed for a few days' stay in Pecos. Twitch snoozed on the end of his bed, his sleep interrupted by quiet yips and legs moving as though he were running. His puppy habit, for which he'd been named, had not gone away.

Anton finished packing and stretched out in bed. The house grew quiet, and the moon rose, shedding soft light into his room. Anton's last coherent thoughts as he fell asleep were of his daughter.

A few hours later, he awoke, disturbed by a sound. Twitch scrambled to his feet, his tail wagging.

"Daddy?" Little more than a whisper.

"Krista, what's wrong?" He sat up and reached for his robe.

A trembly little voice spoke from his door. "I had a bad dream."

"Should we go make some cocoa, and you can tell me about it?"

Krista sniffed. "Okay."

Soon they were nestled in soft throws on the couch in the family room, cozy in robes and slippers, holding mugs of hot chocolate. Twitch and Shadow curled up with them. "I dreamt a bad person was chasing Charlie, and all of a sudden, it wasn't

Charlie. It was you they were chasing." Her blue eyes reflected misery. "It scared me awake, and I couldn't get back to sleep."

Anton considered what to say. It hadn't been a full year since she'd been kidnapped. She was still a child, frightened by what no child should ever have to experience—being stolen from those she loved. And for weeks afterward the cloud of danger still hung over them. Someone, they'd no idea who or why, had been actively trying to harm them. When that mystery had been solved, Krista had blossomed again. Then this had happened, flinging her back into insecurity.

"Why were they after Charlie, Daddy?"

"Charlie filmed something they wanted kept secret, but we saw it anyway. Soon the police will catch them." How could he find words of comfort for a little girl when he, too, was feeling the threat? "It was a fluke, a chance in a billion that Charlie happened to see what someone tried to hide in the shadows. It's not likely that we will surprise anyone else with secrets." Damn them for spoiling the solo pleasure of soaring above the world, for taking the innocence, the beauty, and tarnishing it with fear.

"But what if you do?"

"What will make you feel better, honey? We can't just hide and stop doing things we love because we're afraid."

"Charlie might've been okay, if he'd had someone else there to watch. Do you have to film alone?"

He supposed he could promise to be with somebody else until the bad guys were caught to allay her fears. "Most of the time, until I'm done in Pecos, the whole film crew will be with me. Lots of people. I'll be safe, Krista."

"Promise you won't go out alone?"

Damn, he didn't want that constraint. But now would he feel the prickle of fear? Be wondering if a shadowy presence lurked behind him when he was out with his drone? "I've got an idea. How about if I take Twitch with me. Do you think he'd let me know if somebody else was there?" Twitch raised his head and looked at him.

Krista licked the whipped-cream mustache off her lip and surprised him with a giggle. "He might jump on them and wash their face, but he'd sure let you know." She considered the option, one hand caressing Shadow's velvety ear. "I think that'd work. We could talk about extra guard training next week at class."

"Good idea. Shadow, too, so I don't have to worry about you, either. So—tomorrow morning when I go back to Pecos, Twitch will go with me?"

"Yes, guard-dog-in-training." She yawned and rubbed her eyes. "I think I'm ready to go back to bed now."

"Will you be able to sleep with no more bad dreams?"

"Yes. I have my own guard dog next to me. He'll scare them away."

Chapter Twenty-Nine

"I don't want to do this, Twitch," said Anton as he took the turnoff for Pecos. "Of course, if it helps find what happened to Charlie, I'd do it in a heartbeat."

Twitch cocked his head at him as if to say he hadn't a clue what his master was talking about, but that was okay. He'd listen anyway.

Anton arrived at the monastery as the crew was preparing to leave for their location near Glorieta Pass. "Twitch, think you can act like a well-behaved, grownup dog?" he asked. He received one woof in answer.

Brother Joseph came eagerly to meet them. "An Airedale. I had one growing up. I must confess that having my own dog is one thing I miss since I took my vows." He knelt in front of Twitch for an enthusiastic welcome.

"When it's not appropriate for him to be with the crew, I'll keep him with me," volunteered Brother Joseph. "It will be a privilege."

Twitch sat down quietly by Anton's knee. "Thanks," said Anton. "Appreciate the offer."

"The scenes we're shooting today are about the fight for Pigeon's Ranch," said Morris as he handed Anton the day's scripts. "I've marked what Canby wants the drone to film."

"Great. I'd like to see the equipment you're bringing. How many batteries? Have you a way of recharging them onsite?" Anton started to assess what Morris knew about drones and their maintenance. In turn, Morris pointed out what the director was likely to ask of them in that day's shoot.

At the site, Anton found the crew had almost completed their set up. It was as if he'd entered the world of the 1860s. Then Scarpelli's querulous voice jolted him out of the setting with complaints about the way the actors were firing their rifles.

"Scarpelli, back off," said Canby. "By the time the edits are done, it'll be perfect. Don't you have any Italian bone to pick with somebody else?"

"Italian?" Anton asked quietly of Morris. "What's that about?"

"Don't ask," cautioned Morris. "You'll hear more than you want to know about Scarpelli's long-dead relatives. According to him, their actions during the Civil War should have merited several chapters in history books but, because of what he thinks is anti-Italian prejudice, weren't included. He's come up with hordes of obscure Italian soldiers and keeps pushing Canby to pay tribute to them."

"Thanks for the warning."

"Also, I don't know if you've noticed, but our director has the same name as the Union commander. Canby gives an inordinate amount of attention to puffing up his ancestor's importance, even giving him some deeds of other Union officers. That drives Scarpelli up the wall. He says he's hired to keep accuracy, and by God, he'll do it."

"Was Scarpelli suffering from altitude sickness on Friday?"

"Not likely. That's just an excuse he uses. Scarpelli doesn't fit in. He goes off somewhere in the evenings."

"But Brother Joseph said he was in his room."

"I'm sure the good brother believes that, but he often misses what goes on. He falls asleep a lot, sitting there in the sun. It's common knowledge. Sometimes I think you could set off a cannon charge and he wouldn't wake up."

Damn, Anton thought, so much for the certainty about the red car not stopping by the monastery. But that might be a moot point. He was pretty sure Charlie had been killed at the second meadow before the time he allegedly got into the red car. He wondered where

Scarpelli went off to. He also wondered about the wisdom of letting Brother Joseph spend too much time alone with Twitch. Unsupervised, a half-grown pup could get into a world of hurt. So far, Twitch was behaving himself.

Canby called for the aerial shots. Anton and Morris concentrated on following the lines of blue and gray as they prepared for and then joined battle. The director had a good eye for camera angles and following the drama. Anton found himself enjoying the challenge and looking forward to seeing the edited version.

"How did Charlie get along with the crew?" asked Anton as they packed up their gear.

Morris laughed. "Everybody liked him. Except Scarpelli. Charlie liked to pull his chain. Used to taunt him about Dutch soldiers who were overlooked by the historians. He'd make up Dutch names and reel off some wild tale about their heroism. He could have had a future in writing. He told great stories. Next thing you know, Scarpelli would be on the internet looking for somebody who never existed. Then he'd come back and say he couldn't find them. Charlie'd say he guessed they weren't important then, but had he ever heard about Van de So and So, and he'd be off on another tale. I had all I could do to keep a straight face. Then Charlie went too far and got him looking up Van Wynken, Van de Blynken and De Nott or something. Finally, Scarpelli caught on. Charlie apologized, but Scarpelli was furious. Flipped us all off. Said he was going to kill him."

Ouch, thought Anton. First day on the job, and now he'd uncovered a reason for the historian to carry a grudge. But was that motive enough for a murder?

♦ ❖ ♦

When they wrapped up their filming that day, Anton spent some time with Skyla. She was exhausted. After checking her windows and doors, he left early. Tomorrow he'd install the cameras. They had arrived.

His spartan room at the monastery was simply decorated with pale blue walls, a plain desk, and a small bureau with a lamp. A picture of Christ hung over the bed. The art was contemporary and showed a dark-haired, robed man carrying a black lamb over his shoulders. Fitting, thought Anton, even provocative. The bedspread was a blue-and-gray striped pattern. Twitch jumped up on the bed with a toy. Soon he lay sprawled across the bed, snoring indelicately. Airedales certainly chose awkward sleeping positions at times.

Anton wished he could relax like that but felt edgy, couldn't concentrate on anything. He decided to call Sam. "What'd you hear today? Anything about who the guy in the grave was?"

"Yeah, it'll be in the papers tomorrow, so I can tell you. It was the missing gallery owner that we've been looking for, Gaylord Teller. Since it was a case that Pete had, I'll hear more tomorrow." Sam paused. "Anton, you're not going to like this. It's likely I'll be working on this case, so I can't tell you what is happening."

"Uff da, Sam. No. I made a promise to help find Charlie's murderer."

"I'm sorry, but that's the way it is."

"I suppose you still want me to tell you if I find anything."

"Of course. Any information might be helpful in nailing his killer."

Anton sighed. "Sounds unfair to me. Damn it, Sam."

"I'm sorry. But when this all gets to the trial stage, you'll be called as a witness. It wouldn't do to have some hotshot defense attorney try to discredit your testimony because you'd colluded with the cops or something. How'd your day with the film crew go?"

"Okay, if you discount film crew politics." Anton punched up the pillows and sat back on the bed. Twitch woke up and moved over to accommodate him. "Some of what I learned, you'll be interested in." He told him about Scarpelli's not having a reliable alibi and Brother Joseph's shortcomings as a witness. "And I uncovered a possible motive for Scarpelli. Charlie mocked him and the others knew it. Scarpelli has a short fuse. They all heard him threaten to kill Charlie."

"So, he could have followed him from the monastery. Motive and opportunity," said Sam. "I'll be sure to pass that on." He paused. "What's that funny noise I hear? Sounds like a dog toy."

Anton laughed. “It is. Twitch is chewing on a squeaky toy. I have him with me.” He told Sam about Krista’s concerns. “Walking him will give me a good excuse for prowling around.”

“True. Well, give the guard-dog-in-training a pat for me,” said Sam. “I’d be interested in those extra training classes with you guys. I’ll talk to you tomorrow.”

Anton plugged his phone into its charger and took Twitch for his walk. He was annoyed with Sam. In his head, he understood why Sam couldn’t tell him, but what was the good of having friends in high places if they wouldn’t help? He was used to being the one in charge, but this time, he wasn’t. Was he being petulant? Maybe? Well, yes.

By the time he got back to his room, his grumbling had changed to productive thought. Who had known that Charlie was going to go to the meadow to fly his drone? Or was it entirely coincidental—they were already there, saw the drone, saw the threat to their secrets, snuck around behind, and killed him?

Who had heard Charlie announce where he was going? He was sure Charlie said it at the visitor center. The pot lady? No, she’d already left. Travis Cutler? When he came in, they’d been looking at the maps. He wouldn’t have heard it. Claude and Upton were there after Cutler left and would have heard.

Then they’d gone to the forest service office. Hoot knew, and Brooks had been sitting there. At the monastery, he’d driven away right after he dropped Charlie off and met Brother Joseph. It was possible the brother knew, and maybe Scarpelli. How was he going to find out anything? None of those were likely.

Who knew their way around that area? Any one of them. His mind went back to Scarpelli. But even if he was volatile, being mocked wasn’t a solid reason to haul off and murder Charlie. It must have been coincidental—someone they didn’t know about. He turned out the light and adjusted the pillows.

How nice if he could be a fly on the wall. He smiled. Gadgets—they intrigued him. Little spy cameras. GPS trackers. If any of these folks raised his suspicions, maybe they would find a fly on the wall.

Chapter Thirty

Lieutenant Pete Schultz called Sam and asked him to come to his office. While Pete waited, his eyes went to Lou and Cliff's wedding picture on the shelf near his desk. He wondered if they'd ever know what happened to Cliff's brother. Several times he'd watched his body cam video of that interview with Ross Stewart and his grandmother. Something had been bothering that young man.

Time just seemed to fly these days—never enough to go back to the Johnny McCreath kidnapping case and dig into the Denver connections he'd unearthed. When could he give it the time he yearned to? And now another homicide investigation beginning. When would it end? He was sure if he dug just a little more…

Sam's knock on his door brought him out of his reverie.

"Good morning, Sam. Multi-agency task force at 0930." Pete sat back in his chair and took a sip of coffee. "You've been on one of these task forces before."

"Is the task force about Gaylord Teller, the gallery owner?"

"Yes, and Charles Van Dyken. The murders are tied together. Tell me again what you learned at the SAR." Pete had already heard the story, but now he was listening in a different context. His ears perked up when Sam added Anton's comments from the night before.

"Sam, it's important for you to keep the facts of the case under your hat. Anton was Van Dyken's boss. It's likely that he will be called as a witness when this eventually goes to trial." He caught the frown on the young man's face.

"*Ach du lieber*," Pete said, slipping into the German phrases that were as natural as breathing to him. "I know you know that, but it's worth repeating. Anton is a Circle Sleuth. You and I are his good friends, and any defense attorney worth his salt will find that out. That's all the more reason to keep our lips zipped."

"I already told him I can't share stuff," said Sam. "He wasn't too pleased, but I think he understands. Where's the meeting?"

"Down on Cerrillos. Hiram Brower's office. He's been around longer than me. He's in charge. You'll enjoy working with Hiram."

"He was the one at the river where they found Van Dyken. At first, I thought he wasn't too sharp. Then I realized he was playing dumb to see what he could get out of me. I liked him."

"That's Hiram. Many don't catch on that quickly and to their peril." Pete smiled in approval. "He's as sharp as they come, but those big, sad, brown eyes fool some into giving him information before they realize what they've done."

Sam followed Pete into Hiram Brower's office, a cluttered, windowless room just large enough for a desk, file cabinets, and a rectangular table with six chairs. A young, square-jawed, shaved-head state trooper was already seated at the table. Hiram rose from his desk and greeted them. Sam noticed the friendly respect between him and Pete.

He turned as an African-American woman, who appeared to be in her early forties, entered. At first, he thought she was tall, but then, as she stood next to him, he realized that her erect posture created that impression. The way she carried herself spoke of quiet authority, a little like royalty who tolerated the presence of lesser beings while still being gracious.

She was followed by the forest ranger he'd met at the SAR. The forest ranger radiated nervous energy. He reminded Sam of a panther, more comfortable in unfettered space, a cat you didn't want to turn your back on.

"Let me introduce everyone," said Hiram, setting his laptop on the table. "The federal portion of our task force—Agent J.D. Purley from the FBI, and Forest Ranger Justin Brooks, from the Pecos District Office."

He gestured toward Pete and Sam. "Lieutenant Schultz, Sergeant Martinez from the Santa Fe PD. This is Storm Olson, State Police." The young trooper stood. "He's working with us on this case."

A thought flashed through Sam's mind. Storm? A trooper? Son of a gun, he has to have been razzed about that. "Olson," he nodded to him.

"Please, call me Storm."

"Storm Trooper," said Brooks with a snicker. "What was your mother thinking?"

"She didn't foresee my choice of career, sir," he said without cracking a smile. "And I was named after my father. He's recently passed away."

"My condolences," said Brooks, "and I'm sorry about your father, too."

Purley rolled her eyes heavenward and took a seat next to Sam.

"Why is Santa Fe here?" asked Brooks, taking the chair nearest the open door. "I don't know how you troopers stand it in these little closed-up rooms. Give me mountains, sky, trees, and open space any day."

Hiram's eyes looked over his glasses as he addressed Brooks. "You and the FBI are here because at least one of the murders happened on federal land. Santa Fe is here because Teller, the gallery owner, was their missing-person case. Olson and I are in charge because we are the local law enforcement in Pecos. We are fortunate in being able to bring all of our resources together to solve these crimes. Let's get started. Agent Purley is a forensics expert. She will tell us what was found in the meadow."

"This site had its challenges," said Purley. "For one thing, the SAR folks had mucked it up quite a bit. I understand that. The state police brought one of their folks to the location where they found the tiger-eye pendant and the spatters, which did turn out to be blood. The drone was recovered from the top of a tree. We have its microSD card."

"I'll tell you about the drone video," said Hiram.

Sam looked at those sitting around the table. He'd seen the video, and, obviously, Storm and Purley had as well. Pete was alert and leaning forward. Brooks sat still. Maybe he'd seen it, too. He showed no reaction. Hiram showed the relevant part of the drone video. All eyes were intent on the computer screen, watching the drama unfold.

"Please note that the time log on the video says three forty-two when it ends. I think we can deduce that is when Van Dyken was attacked."

Hiram passed out some enhanced stills from the video. The pickup truck was first. "We are fortunate in the resolution of this video. Not many crime scenes are caught by movie-quality video. Look at the clarity. This pickup is a silver 2014 GMC Sierra. It is lifted, has a winch bumper high enough to protect the grill, and, even though we can't read the number, has a front license plate. It has a spotlight mounted on the driver's side door. There is a slight dent and scrape on the rear fender. I think we'll have some luck finding this truck when we distribute this picture with a BOLO."

"BOLO?" asked Brooks.

"Sorry. I keep forgetting you don't know police jargon," said Hiram. "BOLO means 'be on look out.' It's essentially the same as an APB."

"If they're smart, they're long gone," said Brooks.

"Possibly," said Hiram, "but we will nonetheless look. Now we come to the digger." He proceeded to talk about the next photos, drawing attention to the man's hat and who might have manufactured it, the manner in which the brim was rolled, and pointing out the hatband. "Rattlesnake," he said. "And we know he is a Caucasian or at least a light-skinned male. We never see his face, but here where he stretched out to pick up the shovel after he'd dumped the body, his wrist shows. We have narrowed down the brand of boots he was wearing to three. We'll send this information out to law enforcement agencies."

Next, Purley told about the investigation of the burial site. "When we got the drone video, I went back to the meadow and tried to see if we could tell how they carried Van Dyken out of there. Back by the path and near the ridge, there were deep footprints. A pair of individuals who were either heavy or were carrying something heavy deviated from the path and walked under the pines, sticking largely to areas covered with pine needles. An untrained person would not have noticed their tracks. Once over the ridge from the meadow, the persons of interest hadn't taken as much care to wipe out their presence." She paused to look around the table.

"Anything that would have had fingerprints?" asked Brooks.

"No, it looks to me like both individuals wore gloves. But one thing stands out distinctly to me. The pickup left tracks, coming and going. But there was a second set of tracks coming and going on the same path. The second set overlaid the first. Not perfectly, but deliberately, I thought. And here is an odd thing. That second vehicle did drive through a wet spot from a spring or seepage. It left a good impression there. We took a cast of that. It had to veer off the main trail to do that. Interesting. You'd think someone with secrets to hide would avoid a wet area. Why go out of their way to leave tracks?"

"Sounds more like a false trail attempt to me," said Pete.

"My thoughts exactly," said Purley. "This second set went to a neighboring ranch. Claude Frobisher, a park ranger, is listed as the owner. As we speak, a few of my agents are interviewing him."

"Frobisher!" said Sam. "He works with Skyla Van Dyken."

Purley continued. "The first set of vehicle prints lead to a path following a fence row and eventually to either County Road B-52 or Cam Lomita, a road that leads back to Pecos. My investigators were no longer able to track them at that point.

Hiram spoke up. "My theory is the diggers killed the second person and thought they were in the clear. The witness was dead. They had the drone control and tablet with the footage. I don't think they knew about the microSD card."

"Now to the excavation of the grave," continued Purley.

"What did you find," asked Pete, "besides Gaylord Teller?"

"His hat. Five cigarette butts. They have been catalogued and kept for future DNA analysis."

Pete pulled out a paper from his portfolio. "I have here a list of Teller's effects that should have been with him. The gallery staff emphasized that he was severely nearsighted and was never without his brown metal-rimmed glasses. He smoked and carried a custom-made lighter—silver with a thunderbird design inlaid with a turquoise stone."

"Neither of those items were found. Do you know what brand he smoked?" asked Purley and noted it when Pete told her.

Hiram picked up some papers from his desk. "I've made copies of the autopsy and crime lab reports for you." He passed them out. "A couple of things I want to highlight. Both individuals were killed in the same manner. They were dealt a blow to the base of the skull, breaking their necks, by something with an edge. Not sharp like a knife, but consistent with a metal fence post or the edge of a shovel. Death was instantaneous."

"Some forensic highlights for Teller. He had potsherds in his pocket and an arrowhead clutched in his hand. The soil in his pockets with the sherds and the soil in the treads of his shoes held a high concentration of pottery dust and fragments. There was a crushed flower in the shoe treads from a plant that grows at a higher altitude than where the body was found. Not alpine, but higher than Pecos.

"We can deduce a connection to a site with grass and wildflowers and in soil associated with an ancient living site. The pottery sherds and arrowhead are the strongest indicators. The plant matter and the soil under his fingernails put him in that area."

"How about Van Dyken's autopsy?" asked Sam.

"He had some soil with pottery dust on his clothing as well," said Hiram, "but we think that might have transferred if they used the same tarp to carry his body as they used for Teller. When Van Dyken was killed, he would have fallen forward. They turned him over, and after death, he was on his back for several hours. When he was dumped, he ended up facedown. The pattern of lividity shows he was moved."

"Schultz, can you give us more background on Teller?" asked Hiram.

"He lived alone in an apartment. His gallery was second rate for Santa Fe—definitely not Canyon Row material. He catered more to the tourist souvenir end. He also had a manufacturing and export operation for fake Indian pottery. He didn't attempt to pass them off as real. He sold some in his gallery and also supplied tourist traps across the Southwest and even exported some to Europe. The real thing was rare in his gallery, though his assistant did point out a couple pots that were in the back, not on display. She thought he may have bought them for his personal collection."

Sam looked around the table. Hiram and Brooks were making a few notes. The FBI agent looked interested. Storm looked a little overwhelmed, like he'd be more comfortable stopping speeders on the interstate, or, Sam thought, maybe that was just his own bias about troopers showing.

"How about security cameras outside his gallery?" asked Hiram.

"They were fakes," said Pete. "Not real. No help there."

"I think," said Hiram, "we are looking at an archaeological connection with these two deaths. We don't yet know where, but it seems Teller was killed at some sort of dig. Unfortunately, Van Dyken might have been in the wrong place at the wrong time and paid the price for seeing them dispose of Teller."

"I don't know that I agree with you," said Brooks. "Teller worked with artifacts. It'd be no surprise to have that kind of material on his clothing. It's more likely that he owed somebody money or stumbled on a marijuana growing operation. The national forest is plagued with them."

"Do you have a list of suspects?" asked Pete.

"Yes, we do," said Hiram. "The unidentified digger. And he worked with at least one other."

"How do you know that?" asked Brooks.

"Easy. Someone attacked Van Dyken while the digger was still burying the body," he answered. "My list also includes Travis Cutler, who is Skyla Van Dyken's former husband. He was heard making threats to her brother." He paused to look down at his notes.

"Have you talked with him yet?" asked Sam.

"He hasn't shown up at his residence since then. We're looking for him. Schultz, can your department help?" He handed Pete a paper with Cutler's information.

Pete nodded and made a few notes on the paper.

"And you said Claude Frobisher?" asked Brooks. "I haven't heard anybody say anything yet about those yahoos in the red Ford Focus. Claude mentioned those."

Sam didn't comment on the red car. It was obvious to him that Van Dyken was killed in the meadow, not on the road past Tererro. "I think the film crew merits some investigation. Especially Jerome Scarpelli, their historian. He was at the monastery, could have followed Van Dyken, and had a motive." He told them what Anton had learned.

"I've talked with most of the folks who were in contact with Van Dyken after he left Drone Tech on Friday. I haven't gotten to the forest service office yet," said Hiram.

Purley nodded. "We could start with you, Brooks. Tell us what you saw and heard when Charles Van Dyken stopped by your office that afternoon."

"Well, purdey little lady, what—"

"Stop right there," interrupted Purley. "That's Agent Purley to you."

Hiram slapped a hand on the table, making everything jump. "Dang it all. We're here to work together. Stay on topic. Brooks, tell us again about those young men you saw."

Brooks related his tale.

"Thank you. I'm going to make some assignments here," said Hiram. "We need to get videos from any surveillance cameras in Pecos that might have relevant footage, especially that liquor store."

Brooks scowled. "I have my own work to do, but I'll try to get those for you. We don't have a list of cameras in the area. It will take quite a bit of leg work."

"Thank you," said Hiram. "I won't ask you to look at all the footage. Just get it to me, and we'll do that. It will be interesting to see if we find that red car, Frobisher, or that pickup truck. Somebody had to travel Highway 63 carrying Van Dyken's body."

Hiram turned to Pete. "Schultz, Martinez, dig into Teller's story. Follow the money, talk with his friends, look into his business dealings, his appointment book—the recent past and the future."

"I've already done a lot of that," Pete said, "but I think his business dealings could use more scrutiny."

"I will follow up with my agents on Frobisher," said Purley. "I'll talk to him and see why that truck was in that area."

"I'll finish talking to all those who last saw Van Dyken, and I'll talk to Scarpelli, too," said Hiram. "And everyone, take your copy of the pickup photo. Try to identify it through your sources. Two last things. First, none of this information we have discussed should be shared with anyone outside our law enforcement contacts, and even then, only those who are absolutely necessary. We don't want leaks compromising our ability to solve and prosecute this case. That being said, we come to the second thing. What information should be shared with the press?"

"How about the archaeological connection?" asked Purley. "Surely the press will talk about Teller's death."

"But they shouldn't know how he died," said Hiram. "I think it'd be a good idea to keep mum about the archaeology part for now."

"The truck photo should be released," said Pete. "We could use the public's help in looking for that. If we can find it, get the license number, we'll have the registration, and the ID of the owner."

"Good," said Hiram, "but don't mention how we came to have the photo."

"I say they're long gone," said Brooks.

"When we find Travis Cutler," said Hiram, "I'll haul him in for questioning."

"I'd like to join you on that, if I may," said Pete.

"I'd welcome you." Hiram looked around the group. "All agreed? I'll schedule a short press briefing. Get started on seeking the identity of the pickup. Thanks. Get moving."

Chapter Thirty-One

Skyla glanced at the clock on the wall of the Pecos NHP visitor center. Almost three thirty. The visitor center closed at five thirty during the summer months. What was taking Claude so long? When he'd called her that morning and asked her to fill in for him, he expected to be gone for a couple of hours. The FBI had some questions for him about what he might know about this murder investigation.

What kind of questions would they be asking Claude? Could she find out? Anton had shared his frustration at not being able to get information from Sam. Maybe she could learn enough from Claude to tell Anton the direction the investigation was taking. But it was so late. Surely the FBI wouldn't be questioning him all this time. Not that she minded working. She enjoyed the kids who'd been scheduled for a tour, and it did help keep her mind off Charlie. She couldn't believe he was gone.

The bell over the door tinkled as Claude came in. A frown creased his forehead, and he moved stiffly like he'd been sitting too long. No tourists were there for the moment.

"I'm sorry, Skyla," he said. "It's been an awful day. Come on into the conference room, and I'll tell you." He closed the door after her against the curious look of the cashier.

Skyla took the chair across from him. "What happened?"

"They seemed to think I had something to do with these murders. But, holy crap, I would never do anything like that."

"Of course, you wouldn't," she said. "Where ever did they get that idea?"

"Somebody stole my truck. It had been driven to the place where they found the body buried."

"Buried? Charlie wasn't buried. They found him on the riverbank."

"It's very strange. Someone had been buried on forest land near my place. I don't know who it was. That's where my truck had been. Whoever stole it brought the truck back. The police had a search warrant and looked all over my ranch and took a bunch of stuff."

"What were they looking for?"

"They went over my pickup truck with a fine-tooth comb. Looked at the ground around it. Checked out my shovels and spades in the old barn. Took an old canvas tarp. All that stuff had been there long enough to get spider webs all over it. I never go in that barn. No animals. Then they took some books." He shook his head. "Holy crap, I don't ever want to go through another experience like that. Those FBI folks are nasty. They're like a dog with a bone—chewing and gnawing on you with questions. Seemed like hours and hours, until you aren't certain of anything anymore."

"FBI? I wondered about that. I thought the state police handled matters in Pecos."

"Oh, they're involved, too, but this happened on federal land. That means FBI. The place is a mess with all their looking. Even had all my dirty clothes out of the laundry basket. Checked my shoes. Even took some mud off the treads of one pair. Crazy if you ask me. Why the hell? Seemed interested in my archaeology stuff. But I deal with archaeology every day. I told them that. It's my job."

"I wonder why? Did they say?"

"They don't tell you anything. After they took me to the station, the questions got worse. Wanted to know when I drove my truck last. I told them I thought it was last week when I got a load of firewood. I try to use my car when I can. Gets better mileage." He looked at her in concern. "I haven't the foggiest idea why. It wasn't my truck in that video. Skyla, I would never have hurt your brother."

"I know you don't have anything to do with this. The idea's ridiculous. Don't worry, Claude."

"But I am worried. Do you suppose those guys in the red Ford Focus followed me? I live all alone out there. What if they thought I knew something? Holy crap, I hope they don't come back." Claude rubbed a hand through his gray hair and straightened the pencils on the table in a row. "They finally let me go. I guess I convinced them there was no way I could have been involved."

"I could have told them that," Skyla said. "I'm sorry they put you through all that."

"Thanks. You'd better be getting on home now. I owe you for filling in for me. I'll do the same for you. I trust the tours went okay?"

"No problems. They were well-behaved. I may take you up on your offer. I need to clean out Charlie's apartment before the end of the month."

"I'd be glad to fill in for you. And, Skyla, I'm here for you, if you need me. If you need protection, or if you just want to talk, please call me." He put a hand over hers on the table.

"Thank you." Skyla moved her hand away and stood up. "I appreciate your offer. And thanks for telling me about your day. I wouldn't worry, if I were you. They'll soon find the killer."

Chapter Thirty-Two

After he finished with the film crew, Anton decided he'd forego the meal at the monastery and invite Skyla to eat with him before he installed the cameras for her. She seemed glad for the suggestion. He called in a to-go order to the restaurant off the interstate. If Twitch hadn't been with him, they could have gone there to eat, but having a fur child with him changed things.

As they ate, he told her about the filming. "I enjoy working with Larry Morris. He's bright and talented."

"Charlie liked him, too." She smiled. "The one he didn't care for was Scarpelli."

Anton rolled his eyes. "I haven't met anybody yet who does like Scarpelli. How did your day go?"

She told him about filling in for Claude and about his upsetting experience being questioned.

"Sam says he can't share anything they learn about the investigation with me," Anton said. "Says I may be called as a witness when it eventually goes to trial. But maybe the kinds of questions Claude got might tell us a little about what direction the police are moving. What were they looking for?"

"They took an old tarp and shovels. Looked at his truck, but he said it wasn't his truck in that video. They were interested in his archaeology books. I don't know what they could learn from those."

Anton didn't say anything, but he began to wonder if archaeology had something to do with the murders. He thought about Claude while he finished his salad.

"Does Claude have a thing for you?" he asked.

She looked startled and laughed. "He's older than my father was. In fact, he sometimes acts fatherly. He likes being around me. Always considerate. He asked me out a couple of times, but that was just co-workers hanging around, doing things together."

Then she paused. "Ye gods and little fishes. I hope that's all it was. Anything more would creep me out."

Anton began to wonder more about Claude, about how sometimes Claude's eyes seemed to follow Skyla. He recognized the signs of male interest. That could also be the reason for the hints of dislike he'd felt from Claude. He shrugged and put down his fork.

When they finished, he installed the nanny cam and the outdoor surveillance cameras. He helped download the apps onto her phone, and they tried them out by having her watch his movements outside when he took Twitch out to relieve himself.

They tinkered with the camera angles, making sure to get the area around the parked vehicles. He thought about asking her if he could access the outdoor cameras on his own cell phone but decided not to. He didn't want to raise that prickly attitude about his protectiveness again.

Then he left to go back to the monastery. He wondered if Travis would be the first person the cameras caught. For once, he was glad the filming kept him at Pecos. He would be close by if Skyla needed him.

Chapter Thirty-Three

In his monastery room that evening, Anton worked on the manual he'd decided was needed to go along with his filming drone. From Charlie's extraordinarily helpful notes and his own experience with Morris, he'd gotten a good grasp on challenges other users might confront. He'd use Morris's help with the language. Because Anton was so immersed in jargon used by techies like himself, he needed someone without his expertise to choose the words that would lead to productive understanding, not confusion. He closed down the computer, satisfied with his work.

His phone rang. "Hi, Sam, what's up? Did you learn anything new that you can tell me?" Anton crossed to the bed, propped up the pillows against the high wooden headboard, kicked off his shoes, and leaned back.

"My guess was right. Pete and I are on the case, along with a couple of state troopers, including the guy we met where Charlie was found. There's also an FBI agent and Brooks. Seems that when a crime happens on federal land, the FBI are the go-to source for forensics."

"Can you share anything?"

"Unfortunately, no, except they isolated and enhanced a still of the pickup truck from the video. They released it to the public. I emailed it to you. Did you see it?"

"Not yet. The rooms here supply the monastic experience—no internet access. I can get it tomorrow. I'm just glad I have reception on my phone. That's been touchy."

"You're not used to that." Sam laughed.

"Got that right. How're the wedding plans coming?"

"Wedding plans are great, thanks to you. Farah and I are sure glad we're having it at your place. Now it's the honeymoon plans that are in jeopardy."

"Why? I thought you had tickets to fly to Virginia."

"The murder investigation. The wedding is the twenty-fifth—only a little over a week away. If we can't wrap things up by then, I can't go."

"Uff da. I bet Farah's not too happy."

"Didn't upset her as much as I thought it would. She's fairly philosophical about it."

"We're already expecting your grandfather, Wilma, and Leyla to stay with us while you're gone," said Anton. Wilma was Farah's self-appointed mother who took care of Leyla while Farah worked. "They can still stay. If the worse comes to worst, and you can't go to Virginia, at least you can have your house to yourselves."

"Thanks. Appreciate that."

Twitch jumped off the bed and looked expectantly at Anton.

"How's your mother adjusting to the idea of her firstborn not having a big whoop-ti-do at the cathedral for a wedding?" Anton reached out to pat Twitch.

"Better than I would have thought. She pitched a fit at first, but she's finding out she can't intimidate Farah. We stayed firm, no more than fifty guests. Your place is perfect for our wedding, Anton."

"Good. It'll be a blast. By the way, I told you that Skyla's ex had gotten into her house to steal the little figure he smashed. Well, the surveillance cameras that Charlie and I ordered for her arrived. I installed them today."

"Smart move. I'll be glad when he's caught."

"I'd better go. Twitch is giving me that look. It's time for a W-A-L-K."

"Can't ignore that. Talk to you later."

Anton got off the bed and filled Twitch's food and water bowls again. His thoughts went back to his challenge. How was he supposed to keep his promise and find out for Skyla who the murdering SOB was? He felt inadequate to the task and didn't like it. One would think Sam could slip him some answers anyway. He clipped on Twitch's leash, stuffed a plastic bag in his pocket, put on his jacket, and picked up a flashlight.

As he walked along the path by the river, Anton remembered he was in a good place to investigate. He was the one with access to the film crew and Brother Joseph. He had access to Skyla and, by extension, to some of her co-workers. Hoot, who knew his way around forest service land, might be helpful. Anton paused while Twitch sniffed some bushes. In the distance, a coyote howled, and another answered. The river tumbled its way by, noisy and swift. Twitch went to the edge, sniffed, and cautiously lapped up a few swallows, until his nose was splashed by the river. He shied away and barked.

Anton patted him and turned to go back, remembering the good times he'd had hiking with Cliff and Gandalf, Twitch's daddy. He perked up. Cliff was another resource for him. A member of the Circle Sleuths who'd be glad to help. Cliff wrote mysteries and would know how sleuths sleuthed and detectives detected. Why not call him? He hadn't seen so much of him recently. Cliff and Lou were all wrapped up in getting ready for their first child. This past year had seen most of his friends moving on with their lives and loves. Finally, he'd found someone again. Skyla just might be the one.

It was still early enough when he got back to call Cliff with his questions.

"Solving a mystery is like an onion," said Cliff.

"How so?"

"As you peel away different layers in detecting," Cliff answered, "new questions emerge. Start with the outside—the big picture. Who are the players? Who had the motive, means, and opportunity? Make a chart. Fill in what you know, and the rest when it becomes available."

"Makes sense."

"Also, as an amateur, you don't have all the constraints that the law does. I'm not saying break the law. I'm saying you can skirt the edges of it in ways cops cannot."

"Like I don't need search warrants to go snooping or spy on somebody."

"Yeah," said Cliff. "It's not going to be like in some mysteries where amateurs solve the crime because they're up against either stupid or corrupt cops. That isn't the case here. Pete and Sam are smart, honest, and hard-working. Pete's experience makes him a formidable detective."

"Is that his son-in-law talking?" Anton joked.

Cliff laughed. "No, and you know it. You'll still need to share stuff with them. As much as it sticks in your craw, because they don't give you information, you will find yourself telling them everything. They have the best chance of catching whoever murdered Charlie and building the case against them so they don't get away with it. It's not a contest—you're working toward the same end. It's just that they have to play by stricter rules."

"So, I can wheedle and be devious?"

"Sure. Remember you have skills and resources they don't. You're super at technology. For example, if you wanted to spy on someone, you would get a little spy camera and do it. If they wanted to do it, they would have to write a search warrant, convince a judge that there was cause for it, requisition the equipment, find somebody who knew how to use it, and do it all legal-like. However, if you come up with information because you spied on them, they can use your answers to give their investigation direction."

After Anton hung up, he thought about Cliff's advice. He got ready for bed and turned the light out. Twitch curled up against his hip. He stroked his wiry fur idly.

Several hours later, he was awakened by a soft, menacing growl. He sat up, realizing someone was at his door, trying a key in the lock. The person began talking to their key, swearing at it for not cooperating. Twitch barked.

"Who put a damn dog in my room? Wha's goin' on?"

Anton recognized the slurred voice. "This isn't your room, Scarpelli," he called. He was damned if he'd open the door to that idiot. He didn't trust him. Anton waited until the stumbling fool had gone to his own room, two doors down. Twitch jumped back on the bed and plopped down. "Thanks, Twitch. Good dog."

The white noise of the river soon lulled him back to sleep.

Chapter Thirty-Four

A temporary lull in customers left Pete and Sam sitting alone at Books and Bearclaws, their favorite go-to coffee-break place.

"*Ach du lieber.* There's an ant in my coffee." Pete looked sadly into his brew.

"That's why I put cream in. The ants show up better. Makes them easier to get out." Sam didn't look up from his notes.

"Hard to dog paddle with six legs. I don't think it's the breaststroke. There, he's stopped." Pete fished out the ant and wiped it on his napkin. He took a sip.

"I can't believe you're going to drink it. They'd give you another cup." Sam waved toward the baristas chatting behind the counter.

"Protein." Pete took a longer swallow.

Sam leaned back in his chair and stretched his arms overhead. "This red Ford Focus thing bothers me. It makes no sense."

"Who started the story in the first place?"

"Somebody at the SAR. Brooks, I think," Sam said. He put his elbows on the table and cradled his latte mug in his hands. He thought back. "No, he was talking about young guys at the liquor store. They'd met the guy with the drone. They wanted him to go with them up to Tererro. Didn't say anything about a car. Then

Frobisher spoke up. He was the first to mention the red Ford. Said he'd seen it at the park."

"So, for all we know, there could be two groups of young men?" said Pete.

"Possibly. Coincidental, but possible." Sam looked up as two men entered. He started whistling the tune from the Andy Griffith show.

Pete smiled and beckoned them over. Hiram came and sat. Storm went to order their coffees.

"Thanks for the fanfare, Martinez," Hiram said. "I needed that. Didn't know we were going to be meeting here today."

"We weren't. Happy coincidence. We were just talking about the red Ford Focus," said Sam.

"Bothers you, too, eh?"

"I'm going to play devil's advocate here," said Pete. "What effect did the red car have on the search?"

"It drew the search away from the meadow," said Sam. "And lessened the possibility that the searchers might find the grave of Teller."

"Do you think the red Ford was a diversion? Intentional?" asked Hiram.

"We know there was a red car," said Sam. "Anton saw it. Frobisher saw it. That was all at the park. Brooks talked with young guys at the liquor store. He didn't see them outside and doesn't know what kind of car they had. It could be a different group of guys."

Storm came over with their coffees and handed one to Hiram before he sat.

"Have you seen any of the surveillance videos yet?" asked Pete.

"The one from the park had the red car," answered Hiram. "It showed Bjornson and Van Dyken and a very brief verbal exchange between them and the red car folks. Nothing more than a few seconds. Couldn't see the license plate of the car." He pulled a map of Pecos from his portfolio and pointed out where Brooks had gotten three other videos from.

"There's a Shell station there." Sam pointed to a spot on Main Street. "Did you get any videos from gas stations?"

"No," said Storm. "Brooks said he got them from the most logical places to him, and he didn't have time to get more."

"My logic would tell me that if you were headed up to Tererro," said Sam, "you'd fill up your tank first. Pecos has the last available gas. There's nothing in Tererro, and the road dead ends there."

Hiram looked at Pete and nodded in approval. "Got a live one here, Pete." Then he looked at Storm. "Where did you say you were going this morning?"

Storm looked puzzled at first, then said, "I was going up to Pecos. Thought I'd stop at the Shell station, maybe the others, and get their surveillance videos from that Friday."

Pete nodded, catching Hiram's eye. "Ditto," he said.

Hiram chuckled.

"I've been thinking," said Pete, "about our distribution of the pickup photo. No results yet, right?" He looked at Hiram, who shook his head. "Then how about if we concentrate in the Pecos area as being the most fertile ground. I'm thinking the gas stations in the area are good places to start. Storm is already going there. And then I'd check with the school bus drivers and alert them. They get around. And maybe the delivery guys, like UPS."

"Good thinking," said Hiram. "I believe we agree that these murders have something to do with an illegal dig. It's likely in this area. There was that flower in Teller's shoe tread. That means somewhere in the mountains. There are only so many roads into those. I think we should focus on those. Check businesses, ranches, or places where people congregate or may have noticed that truck around Glorieta, La Cueva, and Pecos. Maybe up toward Dalton Canyon and Tererro, north of Pecos." He pointed to the areas on his map.

"I agree," said Pete. "My gut feeling is that the murderers are locals. They know their way around."

They each took a section of the area to work on.

"Backtracking a bit," said Sam. "Suppose there was a red Ford Focus of guys involved in this. What would their motive be? What would they gain? If they wanted the drone and killed for it, they were unsuccessful. They got the control, but not the drone."

"And why move the body?" asked Pete. "Why take the control? It's no good without the drone."

"I think our original idea was correct," said Sam. "Van Dyken filmed the burial. He witnessed their secret. They had to get the evidence—the drone control—and silence the witness. It was to their advantage to have the SAR focus somewhere else. So, they moved Van Dyken and set up a red herring, also known as a red car."

"You're heading into dangerous territory there, son," said Hiram. "These are upstanding members of the community. Listen to yourself and the implications of what you just said."

Sam met his gaze steadily. "Have you had the same thought?"

Hiram's bushy brows drew together. He looked at Storm. "We can't say it hasn't crossed our minds."

Pete tapped the monastery location on the map. "While we can't rule out the involvement of the red car just yet, the whole story Frobisher spun is called into question by the time stamp on the end of the video—three forty-two. He said he saw them at four. Doesn't wash."

"Interesting, though," said Sam, "by his own admission, Frobisher was at the monastery near the alleged time of the murder. He had opportunity."

"But wouldn't have had time to get the body up past Tererro to dump it," said Pete. "Of course, the digger could have done that. Odd, all that moving of pickups about that time. How many people were involved in this?"

"Framing Frobisher with the truck bothers me, too," said Hiram. "I talked to Frobisher again about the red Ford Focus. He said he was beginning to think that red car just happened to be in the wrong place at the wrong time. Now he says he doesn't think it had anything to do with anything."

"Framing him may have been a dangerous move on someone's part," said Pete. "Could very well have backfired on them."

"Claude Frobisher bothers me, period," said Sam. "Did Agent Purley question him about an alibi?"

"She did," answered Hiram. "That evening he was with a married woman in Santa Fe. Nesta somebody—last name escapes me at the moment. Met her at seven. Frobisher was all concerned about keeping their affair secret."

"Are Frobisher and Brooks friends?" asked Sam. "Do they spend time together?"

"It hasn't been said, but I'm wondering if Brooks might share what he shouldn't with Frobisher," said Pete. "Brooks is not law enforcement. He might not appreciate the implications of keeping mum."

"Did you notice how quiet Brooks got when Frobisher's name came up?" asked Sam. "Did anybody have their body cam on? It would be interesting to view that part."

"I did," said Pete. "We'll take a look."

"You know, guys, I wonder if any Frobisher-related information should be avoided at our meetings when Brooks is there," said Hiram. "Do you agree?"

All three men nodded in agreement.

"Dang it all anyway," said Hiram, scratching his head. His bushy brows drew together. "Do we have to watch everything we say? How can we operate efficiently like that?"

"There are things that we can discuss in common with everyone," said Pete. "I see a couple of ways we can move on. We can certainly talk about Travis Cutler, Scarpelli, and even look for the red Ford Focus as a group. We can play it like we know there was a clumsy effort to frame Frobisher. We feel for him that he was treated that way, but we consider him an innocent bystander."

"I think I can help give that impression," said Hiram. "I'll mention that the tarp that the FBI took when they served the search warrant didn't seem to have any bearing on the case."

Pete nodded. "Down the road, if it seems wise, we can drop in a false statement or red herring and see who finds out about it. And, if needed, we can meet discreetly at the Santa Fe PD."

"What about Purley?" asked Sam.

"Now that she has all the forensics stuff in our hands," said Hiram, "it is very likely that the FBI will move her on to another case. They don't, as a rule, involve themselves in local murders, and only did so this time because it was on federal land."

"How about thanking Brooks for all his help, but we know he's a busy man," suggested Storm. "Cut the ties and move ahead on our own?"

Pete shook his head. "I'd rather not. I think it's a good idea to keep him involved. We might learn more that way."

"If I don't trust somebody," said Hiram, "I'd rather have them where I can see them, out in the open. But I will take you up on your offer, Pete. We'll meet to discuss our problems at the PD. Dang. How did this get so complicated?"

"Oh, my God," said Storm looking down into his cup. "I have ants in my coffee."

"Protein," said Sam and Pete in unison.

Chapter Thirty-Five

Skyla had been invited by Karen and Anton to spend the night at their home after Charlie's funeral. She'd accepted. It would have been hard to go to a dark, empty house after such a heart-wrenching day.

Long after everybody had gone to bed, Skyla lay awake. Her head ached, and she missed Charlie keenly. Finally, she'd come downstairs through the dark and silent house to get a glass of milk. She sank back in one of the cushy couches in the family room, swallowed some aspirin, and sipped her milk. Her chest felt tight, her nose stuffy, and her throat was one big raw ache.

She thought about Charlie's funeral, the reception afterwards, and the well-meaning folks who sought to console her. One lady in particular stood out. "He's in a better place," she'd said, patting Skyla's arm. Skyla just wanted to smack her. *He should still be here*. Lord knows what she'd murmured in reply. Maybe it didn't matter. Inane phrases by people going through the motions.

A noise on the stairs drew her attention. Oh, dear. She should have gone back up as soon as she'd gotten her milk. As lovely as the Bjornsons had been to her, she wanted to be alone. Didn't even want Anton's company. Maybe they wouldn't notice her sitting in the dark.

Krista flipped on the light. She and her dog, Shadow, came into the family room. Shadow stopped and woofed softly, tail wagging uncertainly as she spotted Skyla.

"Oh, I didn't know anybody was still up." Krista slid open the outside door for her dog. "I fell asleep and forgot to let Shadow out."

Skyla dashed the tears from her cheeks. "Sorry."

"It's okay. Don't be sorry. I was crying, too."

Only then Skyla noticed Krista's red, puffy eyes.

"It hurts, doesn't it, Skyla?"

Skyla nodded. "Yes." Damn. Her eyes welled up again.

Krista let Shadow back in and came over to where Skyla was sitting. "Is it okay to stay with you for a bit, or do you want me to go back to bed?"

"Please, stay." She patted the couch next to her.

"Daddy said Charlie was taken from us far too soon." Krista sat on the couch. "I think it's okay to cry. Gramma said you love someone and if they die, then they're gone. It hurts. You just need to cry."

Shadow put her nose into Skyla's hands. Skyla rubbed the wiry head. This was such an out of the ordinary moment. She didn't know what to say.

"I really liked Charlie. He was so happy. And he made everybody around him happy."

Skyla nodded again, squeezing her eyes shut. Tears ran down her face. A little sob escaped her.

"I think about Mommy sometimes. Well, lots of times. You know what? It's scary."

"Scary?" Skyla looked at the child sitting next to her. "Why scary?"

"Not scary like something bad might happen, but scary … because … because—" Krista ducked her head. A fat teardrop trembled on her lashes before splashing on her shirt. The next few words flew out in a rush. "I can't remember what she looked like. I was only four when she died."

Skyla was startled. "Surely, you must have a picture of your mother."

"Yes, and that helps. I even talk to her picture. But I want to remember."

Such a sad thing to lose your mother so young. "What do you remember best about your mother?"

Krista sat back into the cushions. Shadow jumped up and cuddled next to her. "Being hugged. And she used to comb my hair. I remember that feeling. Especially when all the snarls were gone. It felt so good. She'd let me comb her hair, too. She would hold her head real still. She'd always tell me I did such a good job. I liked combing her hair. It was blonde, like mine. Maybe a little darker. It's funny, when I think of that, then I can see her again." She rubbed Shadow's ears. "I have a picture of Charlie in my head, too."

"You do?"

"The last day he was here. He and Daddy had been flying the big drone. They did a video of our doggies racing around the yard. He was so happy. His eyes glowed. I liked his eyes. I want to remember them. Always. And Gramma made a lemony coffeecake for his patent-award party. He shut his eyes and sniffed a big breath over the box and said how much he loved lemon."

Skyla smiled. "He always did. His favorite pie was lemon. When he was about three, my mom had baked a lemon meringue pie. It was cooling on the kitchen table, on one of those wire racks. He pulled out a chair, climbed up on the table, scooped out handfuls of the filling and ate it. He was a sticky mess. He even had lemon goo in his hair, but he sure enjoyed that pie."

Krista chuckled. "That's a funny story. When I remember the stories, I feel better. I'm still sad. Mommy is still gone, but somehow—" Her face crumpled. "It's kind of like she's there. But it still hurts."

Skyla put her arm around her. "Oh, Krista. I know what you mean." It was a good thing nobody was watching. They were both soggy messes, sniffling. Shadow put her paw on Krista's arm and licked the salty tears from her cheeks. They sat in silence for a while.

"Gramma said something important." Krista's look was serious. "I don't know if your gramma ever told you, so I will. It helps to have pictures and hear stories. Do you have a photo album of Charlie?"

"I'm sure I have lots of pictures. You think I should put them together—an album just of him?"

"Yes, well—him with you and with your parents. And all of the places you loved the best where you had fun with him. That's the first part. And then you have to tell somebody all of the stories about the pictures. Telling is important."

"That's a very good idea. I think it would make it better."

"Can you tell me another Charlie story?"

"I'll tell you one more, if you tell me one more about your mother. Then we'll have to go back to our beds. Deal?"

"Deal."

On the balcony over the family room, Anton rose from where he sat on the top stair and on bare feet went back to his room. Tears ran silently down his own face. For Sonja, for Charlie, Krista or Skyla, for sadness or for joy—he didn't know.

The next morning, Anton and Skyla lingered over breakfast, enjoying their second cup of coffee and the sunlight coming in the window.

"Skyla, I want to thank you for last night. I got up to check on Krista and heard the last bit of your talking. You helped her get through this. She's so young. So vulnerable."

"Your daughter has a generous heart. She helped me, too. Talking with her lifted my spirits."

"I think I'll tell Mom what she said. When you plant seeds, it's nice to know the flower blooms."

"Thank Karen for me, too. Your mother is very wise, and yet she looks so young. It's hard to believe she has a son as old as you."

"She does look good, doesn't she? She just turned fifty-six a while back."

"Ye gods." Skyla looked at him in surprise. "Was she only sixteen when she had you?"

"How old do you think I am, anyway? My folks had me the year after they finished college."

Skyla colored a bit. "I was thinking you were about forty. I mean you have your own business, you've made a success of it and all.'"

"Uff da." Anton grinned at her. "I look that ancient? I just turned thirty-four. Forty? I'm hurt."

Skyla laughed. "Now I'm amazed. You've accomplished a lot more than others your age."

He shrugged. "I enjoy what I do. It's easy to pour energy into something you love. Our timing was right, and we've had great employees."

"I was pleased to see the turnout from Drone Tech yesterday," said Skyla, relieved that he hadn't been offended by her gaffe.

"Charlie was well-liked. It was a good service. I didn't know that you and Charlie had attended the Presbyterian Church."

Skyla shrugged. "When we were growing up in Michigan, we went to the Dutch Reformed Church. We couldn't find one in Santa Fe, so we started going to the Presbyterian. Their theology is similar, and I like their idea of mission. I often work on Sundays, so I haven't attended much."

"Me either. I should, for Krista's sake. I want her to have that background. Mom takes her quite often. I'm bad."

Skyla arched her brow. "Is that because you're often with me on weekends?"

"No, can't use you as an excuse. I fell out of the habit before we met. Cliff and Lou got married in that church. How are the cameras working at your house?"

"I didn't even think of checking yesterday."

"May I take a look?"

She handed him her phone.

"Look, critters." He passed the phone to her so she could watch as several deer roamed through her yard. They stopped to nibble on the shrubbery.

“So that’s what’s been eating my flowers. I should have known.”

“Look. A car is pulling up. What does the date log say?”

“It’s last night—about seven. It’s Upton, carrying something—a bag.” They watched as he rang the bell, waited, then went to the window and peered in. Finally, he left, taking the bag with him. “Wonder what he wanted. He was at the funeral.”

“Heard anything more about Travis yet?”

Skyla grimaced and picked up her coffee. “No, unfortunately.” She held her cup close to her and looked down into it. Her knuckles whitened.

He had the feeling he wasn’t going to like this. “What’s wrong?”

“When Travis got in and stole Oma’s Dutch girl, he also took some photographs I had of myself.”

Anton tensed in his chair. “How did you find out?”

“They came in the mail. It was horrid. He’d disfigured them.” A little shudder crossed her body.

“God Almighty, Skyla!”

She looked up into his eyes. “I called Hiram right away, and he came and took them.”

Anton relaxed a little. “Good. Best thing to do.”

She took the last sip of coffee. “Any word on the pickup in that photo yet?”

“Not that I’ve heard,” said Anton. “Let’s talk about something fun for a change. Do you want to try for a drone exploration on July first?”

“Oh, yes, please. I’d enjoy that immensely.”

They made plans, and then Skyla left.

After seeing Skyla off, Anton came in and sat down at the grand piano in his living room. He hadn’t played much lately. Come to think of it, he hadn’t heard Krista practicing recently either. He’d have to ask how her lessons were going. There never seemed to be enough time. He often reflected about what was going on in his life as he played. Muscle memory seemed to take over and pull from the repertoire tucked away in his mind—pieces learned long ago. Sometimes a series of chords would catch his fancy, and a new melody would emerge. Mostly though, his fingers wandering on the keys didn't create anything that stayed with him.

Feeling relaxed, Anton went upstairs to his office to catch up on work emails, still thinking about Skyla and his promise to find out who murdered Charlie. He was glad the cameras were installed. Maybe more gadgets would help? To keep track of the individuals who might be involved? If he got GPS trackers, how many would he need? Who would they be for? Scarpelli, obviously. Couldn't do anything about Travis. Brooks—just because of his attitude, his knowledge of the area, and knowing where Charlie was going to be. He'd also helped deflect the search away from where Charlie had been killed. In case Claude would someday merit tracking, he'd get one for him. He did think the task force was barking up the wrong tree.

He ordered four waterproof, magnetic, motion-activated trackers. They'd have to be retrieved every two weeks and their batteries recharged and replaced. He also ordered a dog-tag sized tracker, to put on Twitch's collar, adding another for Shadow, just because he knew Krista would want one.

Chapter Thirty-Six

Sam and Pete were already seated at the table with Storm in Hiram's office when Brooks came striding in. Even before Sam could greet him, he said, "How much longer is this going to take? I can't afford to spend time on this. It's summer. In case you hadn't noticed, this is our busy season. You'll never find those guys in the red Ford Focus. I think Travis Cutler did it. You find him, you'll find your answers. He had the motive, and he had the opportunity."

Hiram frowned as he took his place at the table. "We've made some progress on those fronts, Brooks."

Brooks sat in the chair nearest the door. "I'm listening."

"We did find the red Ford Focus, thanks to Storm here," said Hiram. He glanced at his smiling co-worker.

"I checked out more surveillance cameras in Pecos," said Storm. "Hit the jackpot at the Shell station. Not long after Frobisher saw them at the park, they gassed up, bought some snacks, and headed back toward the freeway. Got their license plate from the video. They're from Las Cruces. We tracked them there and had a trooper interview them. They'd been in Denver, spent the night of the ninth at Raton, and were on their way to Carlsbad on June tenth. Checked in at their motel there about seven o'clock. Three men. Said they stopped to eat at some diner in

Vaughn on the way. They didn't have any receipts to prove that, though."

"I confirmed their arrival with the motel. The man at the desk remembered their loud music," said Hiram. "It doesn't appear that they had opportunity to be involved in anything here in Pecos."

"We couldn't find anything to prove or disprove that they had been near the monastery," said Storm, "but Frobisher said he saw the car there a little after four o'clock. Couldn't have been that car. They would have been well on their way to Carlsbad. Just for the hell of it, I asked a trooper to inquire at the diner in Vaughn. The little red car with the loud music was well remembered."

Sam leaned back in satisfaction. "Good work, Storm," he said. Pete looked pleased. Brooks wore a slightly puzzled frown. Maybe he was wondering what they should do next? Sam felt a little sorry for the guy. He was kind of an outsider in this group of cops.

"About Travis Cutler," said Hiram, "he's been stalking Skyla Van Dyken. Elusive son-of-a-bitch. He mailed her some photos he'd stolen from her place. Her images were disfigured. He's one sick individual. Frightening for her. She's had surveillance cameras installed, both in and out of her home."

"Any clue as to where they were mailed from?" asked Pete.

"Santa Rosa, New Mexico. Dropped in a mailbox. We've sent out updates for that BOLO. Now for the next item on the agenda," said Hiram, "and it's good news for a change. Just about half an hour ago, we heard back from our inquiries. We have a positive identification for the driver of the pickup in the drone video." He passed out some papers with photos.

Sam felt his face stretch into a grin. "Son of a gun!"

"How the hell—" said Brooks.

"The information came from two sources," said Hiram. "We worked every place we could think of between Glorieta and up to Dalton Canyon. Finally, Sam talked to a clerk at a dollar store. She remembered the pickup. Said the driver was in quite often. She hated to wait on him, because he smelled bad. Couldn't take a deep breath near him without choking, she said."

"She thought he lived a little ways up the Cueva Road," said Sam. "The last time he was in, she stepped out to get a breath of fresh air and saw him get into that truck. She remembers thinking it was as dirty as he was."

"Then I talked to the school-bus drivers with routes around there," said Hiram. "Good folks, those drivers. One saw that truck quite often and knew where the guy was renting. The kids on his bus thought it was a cool truck, being so high off the ground and having a winch bumper and all. We talked to the landlady and got his name. Bradley Taggeroth, also known as Buck. From Utah. She happened to have several pictures taken at her place with grandkids and all. Turns out one of those photos had the truck, complete with license plate. We contacted the Utah Department of Public Safety and got his driver's license, truck registration, and information. He's had a few run-ins with the law there, but nothing major. We do have his fingerprints."

"Have you talked with him yet?" asked Brooks.

"No, we haven't seen him. He often stays away for a week or so at a time, according to his landlady," said Hiram. "We put out an APB for him. Feel free to distribute this picture. The landlady said she'd let us know when he shows up. We'll blast that area with wanted-for-questioning notices."

"Good work, Hiram," said Pete. "Anything else? I have one matter I want to bring up."

"I don't have anything more," said Hiram. He looked around the table. Storm shook his head.

Sam frowned slightly. "I don't have anything conclusive to tie the cases together, but I see some interesting connections to another homicide I'm working on. The victim's name was Fernando Navarro." He told them about the case and how it had come to their attention. "Navarro worked as a digger somewhere in an area that didn't have cell phone coverage. He worked with somebody called Buck."

Hiram raised his brows. "That is interesting. Keep us posted, Martinez. Anything else?" He looked around the table. "Then go ahead, Pete."

"As you know, I've been plowing through all Gaylord Teller's business papers. I'm finding some interesting stuff. There's a connection in Paris I'm wondering about. He did a lot of business there. I think I'll know more next time we meet."

"Let's meet in two days," said Hiram. "Since you're busy, Brooks, I don't know if we need you. I don't have anything that concerns forestry lands. Do you want to pass on this one?"

"I think I should follow through. Can't have people getting bumped off in the national forest without somebody paying for it. Tourists get freaked out. You might not think of tourists, but they're important to us, you know. I'll be here."

Sam and Pete left and walked to their cars. "You said that on purpose about Teller's papers, didn't you?" asked Sam.

"Turned out just like I thought it would, too," replied Pete. "Brooks is curious as to what it is we're finding."

"Maybe he likes to hear the whole story. Can't stand unsolved mysteries. You think he's talking with Frobisher?"

"Very likely."

"So, are you going to lay out all of the paperwork and what it is you suspect?" asked Sam.

"Hmmpf. Not hardly. I'm still working on ideas, digging through all that. If I do say anything, it'll be some inconsequential drivel."

"Maybe we should drop something in and see if Frobisher reacts. Then we'd know Brooks is a leak," said Sam.

"Good idea. Did you notice that Frobisher was caught in a lie?" asked Pete.

"As a matter of fact, yes. There's no way he could have seen the red car with the loud music at the monastery at four. They were long gone."

Pete nodded. "Maybe we'll focus on Scarpelli next time. Where was he on the night Van Dyken was killed? He still hasn't given us an alibi that can verify his whereabouts."

It was after midnight when Anton, with Twitch on lead, opened his door at the monastery. In his hand he carried one of his new GPS trackers. It was quiet. No windows showed light. Still, he'd taken the precaution to come up with a reason to be out in the parking lot prowling around at that time of night. Bless the wanna-be-private-eye guy who'd made a video for the internet about installing trackers. His advice was to always plan ahead. Make it look like you're supposed to be there. Carry a tire gauge in your shirt pocket and a cloth to get suspicious dirt off your hands. People are generally trusting. Just look confident. Sounded reasonable to him. So, now one of Twitch's toy balls bulged out his pocket. He could always roll it under the car a bit and say Twitch dropped it when they went out for their walk. It would be a good reason for fishing around near the Maserati.

Soon he was back inside and checked to make sure the app was working. He wouldn't need to change the battery in this one, just retrieve the tracker before the film crew wrapped up and left by the Fourth of July weekend. It would be more of a challenge to plant one on Brooks's truck. There were surveillance cameras at the forest service parking lot. He should probably figure out another place to install it. He might ask Hoot. What does a forest ranger do all day? What would be a typical day for him? He'd find a way.

Chapter Thirty-Seven

Skyla looked up as the bell tinkled over the door of the park visitor center and Anton entered. She smiled at him and continued talking with the tourist at the counter. Anton waved to her and went to look over the Pecos area books. Through the window, Skyla could see the girls, Sam, Farah, Dom, and the dogs on the front portal.

"It'll be about fifteen minutes until the tour begins," she told Anton and the interested tourist. "If you like, you can wait on the back portal. We'll start from there."

Dom came in. "I've been on this tour several times. I think this time I'll wait here."

"You won't get bored waiting?" Anton asked.

"Son, there's a bookstore and a museum. How could I possibly be bored?"

As Skyla waited for the tour group to assemble, she watched Krista. She smiled as another family arrived to join their group. Two younger teen boys failed at looking bored, glancing up with shy smiles from their phones. Pre-teens had such mercurial changes of behavior. Krista and Leyla were each part child, part young woman with just a touch of coquette, part interested student—all full of life and exuberance. The girls became giggly, but soon, with the ice-breaking friendliness of the dogs, everyone became acquainted.

Skyla settled her park ranger hat more firmly and stepped into her role of tour guide. She loved this part of her job. How lucky she was to be able to share her excitement about archaeology and piecing together the life of the ancient Puebloans with so many people from different walks of life.

They walked up the gentle slope of the trail toward the top of the ridge. A treeless meadow sloped down and away from them to the east. A low stone wall separated it from the site of the northern pueblo ahead. "The geography of this area contributed significantly to its importance," Skyla said as they gathered around her.

"This grassy area is where the Plains Indians came from the east to trade. They would camp for a few weeks in the meadow to trade their goods: buffalo hides and products, and Alibates flint that was used for making arrowheads and knives. Over this knoll to the north lie the Sangre de Cristo Mountains, the southernmost tip of the Rocky Mountain range. To the west you see mesas. Glorieta Mesa tapers down to a pass. Through that gap, Pueblo Indians from the Rio Grande valley would come to trade, bringing corn, beans, pottery, turquoise, and obsidian. Indians would come up from Mexico with shells, parrot feathers, pottery, and other items to trade. People have moved through this location for ages. First the Indians, then Spanish, and then settlers following the Santa Fe Trail from Missouri. This area was also the site of an important Civil War battle. The Confederate Army was stopped from getting any farther north and west at the Battle of Glorieta Pass. Then came the railroad, Route 66, and now Interstate 25."

She brushed away tendrils of brown hair blowing into her face as she answered questions. The weather was fantastic. The grass on the plain undulated in a light, warm breeze. Cottony white clouds drifted across the cerulean sky.

"What are those wooden poles sticking up?" asked Krista as they followed the rise of the trail. "It looks like a huge sundial." Ahead of them was a round area defined by very low stone walls. Gravelly red dirt covered it. In the center was a rectangular hole with a ladder going down.

"Good observation. It does look like a sundial. This is one of the many ceremonial kivas," said Skyla. "This one has been reconstructed. You may go down if you like."

Krista looked at her dad. He nodded. Sam took the leashes of the three Airedales and stayed up top. The rest carefully descended the ladder. Twitch barked in concern, straining on his leash as Anton disappeared.

Down in the kiva, Skyla pointed out the air shaft opening and the fire pit. She talked about what kind of ceremonies may have happened there.

Krista looked up at the opening. "What happens when it rains?"

"We have a trapdoor that covers the opening." Skyla pointed up. "You can see the hinges there. When you climb up you'll see the door."

"I thought a kiva was a fireplace in a house," said Leyla, rubbing her arms. It was noticeably cooler in the underground space.

Skyla smiled at her. "We do have kiva fireplaces in our homes. That is another definition of the word. It's spelled the same way." She answered more questions before they ascended into the sunlight. Twitch barked excitedly as he watched them climb up the ladder, wriggling happily as Anton took his lead again.

After they finished the tour of the Pueblo and the Spanish mission, they returned to the visitor center. The girls went ahead into the museum. Farah slipped her hand into Sam's. He smiled at her, then turned to Skyla. "Farah and I would like you to join us for dinner tonight at my dad's ranch. I know it's short notice, but I hope you can come."

"I would like to come. I need to go home and change after I finish work."

In the museum, the girls wandered off with Farah, looking at the exhibits and taking turns stepping up to look through the diorama windows. Occasionally they came back with a question for Skyla. "How come some of the arrowheads are pinkish stone, and some are dark and shiny?"

"Remember on the tour I said the Indians brought flint to trade? That's what the pink ones are made of. Do you know about the Valles Caldera in the Jemez Mountains?"

Krista nodded. "It used to be a volcano."

"That's right," said Skyla. "The Indians got obsidian from there to make the shiny ones."

Sam came into the museum and stopped by one of the podiums topped with a plexiglass display cube, his attention riveted on the light-colored ceramic pot inside with reddish-brown and black designs. He beckoned Skyla over. "I'd like to find out more about this type of pottery. Can you tell me how common it was? Maybe what people made it and where it was found?"

Skyla answered his questions.

"This one, too." Sam moved over to another display, this one of a pot with black-on-white designs. "How do you tell what time period it came from?"

She told him briefly about the different types of glazes and paints and pointed out the different styles of lips on the edges of the pots.

Anton appeared surprised by Sam's interest as Skyla pointed out things that the average viewer wouldn't even notice. "You should have seen the pot a lady brought in the day Charlie went missing," Anton finally added. "It was black and white, too. I don't know much about pottery, but this was cool."

"You didn't tell me about a lady with a black-and-white pot," said Sam.

"I didn't know you'd be interested," said Anton. "It didn't have anything to do with Charlie. Skyla can tell you more about it. She looked up information on it for the lady."

"She bought it from somebody who said it had been in their family for a long time," said Skyla. "She didn't know them, just met them outside a hotel in Santa Fe." She told him more about the pot. "I have photos of it on my phone."

"Do you have her contact information?" asked Sam.

"Yes, I do. I emailed her some information on pottery. I can get it for you when I'm through here."

"Please," he said. "And the photos of the lady's pot, too."

Krista came over with Leyla. “Can you tell us what animal it is on that orange and black pot? We think it’s a rabbit, but we aren’t sure.”

“You are right. It’s kind of stylized, isn’t it? Rabbits were important to the Indians for food and clothing.” The girls, Farah, and Sam wandered on to the next display.

“Skyla, why don’t you ride along with us to the ranch?” asked Anton as he followed her to the counter. “I’ll pick you up at your house and bring you back afterward.”

“That’s not necessary. I can drive.”

“I’d feel better if I knew you were okay when you got home. Travis is still on the loose.”

“Oh, here we go again with the knight in shining armor.” Skyla stood straighter.

“What is wrong with someone wanting you to be safe?”

“How can you ask after meeting Travis? He started out being over-protective. I’m not going there again.” Skyla went into the office area behind the counter. The gift shop was quiet. Everyone was still in the museum. The clerk was straightening merchandise over near the restroom doors.

“He wasn’t protective,” said Anton. “He was obsessively possessive. There’s a large difference.”

“Hmpf.”

“Anyway, even knights need somebody to watch their backs. It only makes sense.”

“It’s out of your way.”

“Say yes. I enjoy being with you.”

“Even when we argue? We seem to be good at that.”

“Yes, even then.” He looked at her ears, reached out to the earring display on the counter and touched a pair of dangly leaf ones, making them swing against their card. He took them off the rack and looked down at them, still speaking. “Pretty. I need a little arguing with women in my life. I’m still a son to Mom. I defer to her. At least some of the time. I’m Krista’s parent, and Mom has been sensitive to that. And I’m the boss at work. We have differences of opinion, but everyone is aware of who has the final say. I try to listen and not throw my weight around, but …” He put the earrings back. "Uff da, Skyla. One thing missing in my life is a woman who is my equal, whose opinion carries the same weight as mine. A friend, a peer, call it what you like. You're good for me."

She considered what he said. "You don't give up, do you?"

He shook his head. "It's one of my endearing qualities."

She laughed and straightened several pairs of earrings on the rack, arranging their cards at even distances. "You know it works both ways. There may be a time you need somebody to watch your back."

"I'd welcome your help. Pick you up about five thirty?"

She looked at him. He raised his eyebrows questioningly. She nodded. He grinned the crooked grin that she knew well.

"I should get that information for Sam," said Skyla. "I was surprised by his interest in the pottery. Has he always had an interest in archaeology? Or is there something he's not telling us?"

"Never heard him talk about it. I wondered, too," replied Anton. "Some of his grandfather's interest may have rubbed off on him. But the questions he was asking today weren't general. They centered around those two pieces of pottery."

"The polychrome one and the black-on-white."

"I think there's something he's not telling us. I'm beginning to think archaeology and pottery have something to do with the murders."

Skyla said, "I think it must. You were telling me that trying to solve a mystery is like putting together a big puzzle. Several of our puzzle pieces are about possible digs. The gallery owner, Sam's interest in the pottery, and the pickup truck equipped for traveling off-road. Claude's archaeology books. He didn't tell me which ones, but I know he has some good ones on ancient Puebloan pottery. It makes more sense than anything else."

"When I told Sam the pot had nothing to do with Charlie," said Anton, "perhaps I was wrong. I can't imagine that the lady had anything to do with the murders. I wish we knew more about the person who sold her that pot."

"Let me get her information." She sat down at the computer. Out of the corner of her eye, she saw Sam stop at the counter. "Just on a whim, when I sent her the pottery information, I also attached that truck photo from the police. I apologized for being tardy in getting back to her, but said my brother had been killed over the weekend. They were looking for the driver of that truck as a person of interest who might know something."

Skyla logged on to her email. "Oh, there's a reply from her. Ye gods." She read aloud from the email. "The lady—Patty Lydra is her name—says it looks like the truck belonging to the guy who sold her the pot. She only saw it parked outside the hotel restaurant, but she remembers the spotlight and the funny bumper. She thought it had a Utah plate—had a red arch. She goes on to say she would have stopped at one of the museums or galleries to ask about her pot, but she was busy at her conference. She thought of it when she was passing the Pecos NHP entrance that Friday when she was on her way home."

"Skyla," said Sam, "can you forward your email exchanges with her to me? I'll send them on to the task force."

"Sure. No problem." She exchanged a look with Anton. They were right. It was important.

Chapter Thirty-Eight

The keeper of the community, thought Karen, a title to relish. She enjoyed providing the occasions for these wonderful friends to gather. Sam and Farah's wedding-rehearsal evening at the Bjornson home was special.

The priest was giving an overview of what was to happen and where people would stand or sit. The bridesmaids—Leyla, Krista, and Sam's youngest sister—were listening carefully. Cliff, the best man, was also paying attention. The other two groomsmen, Sam's kid brothers were smirking at something on their phones. Sam turned and gave them a look. Their phones went into their pockets, and they fell into line.

Most people would sit where they pleased tomorrow, but the parents of the groom and Wilma had special places at the front. Wilma had found in Farah and Leyla the daughter and granddaughter she'd never thought to have. And Wilma, being Wilma, basked in the light of the role, letting any criticism crash, break, and flow around her like an ocean wave against a rock.

Karen had seen Dolores's nostrils flare and her lips tighten when she realized that Wilma was seated where the bride's mother would normally sit. She knew Dom had seen her expression, too. As Karen watched from her vantage point in back, Sam's mother,

Dolores, got up from her front-row seat by her husband, Frank, and strode toward them with purpose.

"Uff da," Karen murmured to Dom, "here she comes."

"Can't you do something?" Dolores said in a stage whisper when she reached them. "She's the hired babysitter, the live-in nanny. Can't you put her in her place?"

"She's found her place," Karen replied. "Farah is the daughter she's always dreamed of. You will not take this away from Wilma."

Dom echoed Karen. "She is family. She loves Farah, Leyla, and Sam. She was never blessed as you were. Be happy for her."

Karen's eyes followed Dolores as she marched back to the front. Karen respected her for all the charity work she'd done in Santa Fe, but she didn't think they would ever be close. That was okay.

The priest finished the rehearsal, and they sat down to eat. After a while, Anton turned on his built-in sound system, which brought music to the outside, and they tried the dance floor. The girls needed the practice and so did Stevie, Sam's youngest brother. Farah didn't say much about it, but Karen knew dancing was not a part of her experience, and she'd appreciate the practice, too.

Even though the sky was not dark yet, they turned on the lights. It was magical. Their backyard was transformed into a world of delight. Long strings of tiny lights rained down from several of their tall shade trees. The other trees in the yard boasted shorter strands, lighting the way to their portal where there was comfortable seating. Sturdy poles and a tent-like frame held drapes of sheer material interspersed with more lights. Beneath the frame, workers had installed a parquet floor big enough for six round tables-for-eight and a nice-sized dance floor.

Sam and Farah had hired a professional company to do the lighting and the floor. Tomorrow, a caterer would provide an elaborate dinner buffet, and a DJ would take over the music. They wanted to keep it worry free for the Bjornsons.

Tomorrow afternoon, most of the women would be wearing long dresses. Farah's wedding dress was long, too—simple, modest, and very becoming. She would wear a few flowers in her hair. No veil, no train. The skirt swished nicely, Farah had said, just perfect for dancing. Most of the men would be wearing tuxes. Karen loved the elegance.

She watched her son as he danced with Skyla. She wondered if there was a wedding in their future. Would Skyla make a good mother for Krista? They seemed to get along well. Krista was maybe a wee bit jealous of Leyla, who would now have both a mother and a father. Happy for Leyla, but a little wistful, too.

What would it mean to this house if Anton remarried? She'd always hoped he would. She wanted more grandchildren. She could pull back from her role as stand-in-mother for Krista and relinquish that to his wife. Anton needed to be loved again. He took life so seriously. He came across as someone older than he was. Grief and responsibility had left their mark on her son.

Changes would happen. Karen would give up some of the authority she held now in the household. That was good. She hoped she and Dom could travel. She would love for them to go to Norway. The land of her ancestors called to her. She smiled, thinking she must have genetic memory for fjords, mountains, and crashing coastal waves. Dom had never been to Scandinavia. He'd love it—another setting rich with history to explore.

Would Skyla have the strength to forge a place in the Bjornson home? She'd been married before. There was a painful history there that neither she nor Anton had shared with Karen. Whomever Anton chose would need to be strong to hold her own with a stepdaughter, a mother-in-law, and a housekeeper who'd been a part of their lives for nearly twenty years.

Chapter Thirty-Nine

An hour before sunrise on the wedding day, Anton slipped down to the kitchen, let Twitch out, and brewed a couple cups of coffee. His home was still quiet. With Twitch by his side, he tapped softly on Skyla's door and let himself in with the tray. A little cuddling, time to share thoughts with her—great way to start the day.

"What's the schedule today?" she asked later as they leaned against the headboard, sipping the now tepid coffee.

"Mine's not as complicated as Mom's. The hairstylist and the florist are coming about ten. Maria will fix a lunch buffet. She'll put part of that in the breakfast room and send the rest over to Mom's suite, where all the fussing will be going on. The caterers will be here about noon. Maria will deal with them." He took another sip. "Diego will handle the parking. Sam, his brothers, and Dom should get here after lunch. I told them they could use my room to get ready."

"Do you have to deal with a nervous groom?"

He grinned at her. "Cliff is the best man. He gets to do that. Funny, if there's any drama today, I bet Sam's mother will be behind it. Sam is usually unflappable, but she can rattle him."

"Is there anything special I can do?"

He shrugged. "I'm sure there will be something. Oh, one thing. I have no intention of going anywhere near all those ladies getting ready. You can be the liaison between that madness and the rest of the house."

"That I can do." She smiled at him. "They frighten you, huh?"

"For certain." He drained his cup and set it on the tray. "When the guests start to arrive, Mom and I will be the welcoming party."

He slid off the bed and stretched before giving her another kiss. "See you downstairs." He took the tray and left.

♦ ❖ ♦

So far, so good, Anton thought as he retreated to his room hours later. The only snafu so far had been the florist, who got lost and called Farah. Skyla had brought Farah's cell phone to him, and he'd directed the man successfully back on track. The caterers were here and setting up.

Anton pulled on his wingtip shirt and began buttoning it. He'd get ready now and be out of Sam's way. They'd be here soon. He was reaching for his bowtie when he heard a sharp click from the receiver near his bed, followed by happy giggles from his daughter and Leyla.

"What's that thing Shadow's ball hit?" Leyla's voice came over the speaker.

"It's the baby monitor," Krista's voice replied. "After Charlie was killed, I started having nightmares again. This house is so big, I get scared sometimes that my dad couldn't hear me if I called out. I can turn it on when I want."

Anton crossed to the bed. His finger paused over the off switch as Leyla's voice continued.

"I'm going to like having a dad. Sam's cool. He listens to me."

"I think it's funny," said Krista, "that you'll have an uncle who's just a couple years older than you are. He's cute."

"So's Pete's kid, Rick. I got to dance with both of them last night."

"Me, too," said Krista.

His little girl was thinking about boys already? Anton wasn't ready for that. He sat on the edge of the bed. He knew he should turn the monitor off, but drew his hand back.

"Seriously," said Leyla, "how would you feel if your dad got married?"

"He dated Lou for a while," said Krista. "She would have been a good mom, except it was as plain as anything she was in love with Cliff."

"Do you think he might marry Skyla?"

"Maybe," Krista replied. "I saw him kissing her when we were at Sam's dad's ranch. They keep looking at each other and hold hands a lot."

Leyla giggled. "Like Sam and Mom. Would Skyla make a good mother?"

"Dunno. She'd have to be able to talk about girl stuff. Gramma does that with me now. She told me all about turning into a woman. Gross, but neat, too." She paused. "Yeah, I could talk with Skyla. We talked about my mom and about Charlie one night. It helped."

"I feel good about telling people Sam's my dad. He's, like, cool. How would you feel about telling somebody Skyla was your new mom?"

"I've missed my mom. Skyla would be good. She'd let me do art stuff, too. She makes, like, really neat jewelry. I wonder if she could talk my dad into letting me get my ears pierced? Uff da. He's such a stick-in-the-mud sometimes. Like even more old-fashioned than Gramma."

Anton sat up straighter. *What? Stick-in-the-mud?*

"Would you like a brother or sister? I would."

"It'd be fun." Krista was quiet for a moment. "If your mom and Sam have a baby, or if my dad got married and had a baby—would they like the new baby better than us?"

"Like the new baby would be their whole child? We'd be just half a child?"

Krista giggled. "I think you mean stepchild. Wonder where that name came from. Too confusing. But Sam is adopting you. Isn't that like a whole child? Will he be your real dad?"

"He will. I asked him about it."

"You did? Cool. What did he say?"

"My dad who died was my birth dad. But Sam said adoptive dads love their kids just like birth dads. He said I'm lucky. I've two dads. One died, but he'll always be my dad."

Anton heard his mother's voice. "Krista, I think it's time to put Shadow in the kennel with the other dogs. There's no way those dogs are going to be allowed anywhere near the wedding cake at *this* wedding."

"Okay, Gramma."

"Then you and Leyla can bring your things over to my room. They'll be ready to do your hair soon. Don't forget your shoes."

The voices trailed off. Anton sat a few more minutes. Wow. Marry Skyla? Have a baby with her? Images of her holding his child filled his mind.

And how could Krista be worried about his loving her less if he had another child? They'd have to talk. He went down the hall, stopping in Krista's room to press the off switch on the monitor.

People began arriving. Soon Anton found what his job was: greeting, delivering messages, fetching, carrying, and solving moments of crisis.

Now, as he stood out front, listening to Dolores Martinez rave over his home, he heard the purring of an expensive car approaching. A white sedan came into view with Arturo and Marta Barrena, best friends of Dolores and the owners of the care center where Farah worked. Arturo got out and opened the door for his wife.

Diego came up, his eyes widening at the sight of the Maserati.

"I'm sure you'd be more comfortable handling it yourself, Arturo," said Anton. "We saved a special spot for you." He pointed to a space by itself. Arturo complied.

Dolores, still gushing about the Bjornson home, was speaking to Marta. "Sam wanted an intimate wedding spot, and we knew this would be just perfect. Of course, you will recognize Karen from her work at the Foundation."

Karen came out to lead them into the house.

When they were all out of sight, Diego commented on the car. “Have you ever seen one of these before? Not me. Thanks for suggesting he park it. I wouldn’t want to ding it.”

“I have seen one. Not in Santa Fe, but there’s an Italian guy, Scarpelli, on the film crew. He drives a Maserati. His is not new, though. I can see where Barrena’s son gets his love of fancy cars.”

Skyla walked up to them, wearing a long teal gown. Her hair was pulled back softly, and she wore dangly green-blue earrings.

“Car like Scarpelli’s, huh?” she asked. “That’s funny. It reminds me. I don’t remember seeing it when Hoot and I got to the monastery that night to start looking for Charlie. Brother Joseph said he was there, but his car wasn’t.”

Anton frowned. “It was there when I dropped Charlie off. He commented on it. Are you sure?”

“It’s not exactly a car you can overlook,” she said. “It cries out—look at me. Anyway, there’s another crisis. This one shouldn’t be that difficult. Sam’s little brother forgot his bowtie at home. He’s wondering if you have an extra one.”

“The only ones who haven’t arrived yet are Evelyn and the others from the care center,” said Diego. “You go. I’ll handle them.”

“Thanks, I’ll get it now.” As Anton walked into the house, he wondered where Scarpelli had gone that afternoon. He’d put one of his new GPS trackers on Scarpelli’s car a few days ago, but he hadn’t checked the app to see where he’d been going since he got home. First, he’d deal with the bowtie.

Before he went back outside to mingle with the guests, he took out his cell phone. He checked Scarpelli’s tracker. Odd. Last two nights—outside a casino near Santa Fe. Was Scarpelli into gambling? Morris said he was gone a lot in the evenings. Maybe if he shared that information with Pete, he might get another useful piece of knowledge in return.

♦ ❖ ♦

Anton moved silently along the balcony, stopping when he saw his mother and Dom exchange a lengthy kiss below him near the stairs. His mother smiled brilliantly at Dom before continuing on her way toward the portal. Before Anton could move, Dolores Martinez came around the corner downstairs from the powder room. She must have seen as well.

"Father, what *are* you thinking?" she hissed. "She's young enough to be your daughter!"

"Your math is a little fuzzy, Dolores," Dom said. "And your mother died more than ten years ago. I am still alive. I believe I'm entitled to friends of my own making. Think about it." He turned and went down the hall.

Dolores stood there frowning. Anton started down the stairs. She turned at the sound of his steps and looked up, waiting until he reached the bottom. "You saw? You heard?"

"Yes, I did. We're lucky to have such cool parents." He noticed her jaw flexing as if she were grinding her teeth. He couldn't resist a wicked dig. "You know, if things work out for them, you'll be my stepsister."

Her head jerked back, and her mouth dropped. "My God," she whispered. She stared at him, shaking her head slightly. "I … you … I …"

He waited, curious to see what kind of a comment she was going to hit him with.

"I … I used to wish for a baby brother."

A bark of laughter left his lips at the unexpected answer. "Be careful what you wish for," he said, grinning. "I've known for some time that they were very good friends. I admit I was shocked at first. But I'm happy for them. Mom's been lonely. I mean, she has her weaving, the Foundation, Krista, and me, but it's not enough."

"No, I can see that," she said. She briefly touched his cheek with the back of a manicured nail. "I think I could get used to having a brother. What a day."

"Shall we go join the others?" he asked, crooking an arm to escort her. She took it and went with him. *What a day, indeed.*

As soon as he stepped outside, the DJ came rushing over to him with an urgent whisper. "There's no power."

"No power?" Anton repeated with a frown. He looked at the trees. He'd turned on the tiny lights earlier, but now they were all out. Wonderful. Just what they needed. He followed the DJ back to his station.

One of Sam's police co-workers was there admiring the equipment. "What's wrong?"

"No power," said Anton.

"Probably something simple," he said. "Check the plugs."

Soon they found the problem. An unthinking caterer had unplugged the power strip to put his own in the spot. Anton directed the caterer to the correct outlet and plugged in the cord. To his satisfaction, he saw the lights twinkling again in the trees. He gave a thumbs-up to the DJ.

Now, maybe he could catch Pete and tell him about the Maserati. But Pete was in a discussion with the Barrenas. He didn't want to interrupt that.

Then he noticed the priest had moved to the flower-covered archway in the front of the seats. Well, there'd be time after the ceremony. He wouldn't mention it to Sam at all. The groom didn't need to be bothered. He shouldn't tell Pete right now either. The poor man should be allowed to enjoy this wedding. During Cliff and Lou's wedding, he'd been wound up like a spring. There'd been police all over the place. Anton had never heard the full story on that, but fortunately, there'd been no trouble. He'd catch Pete later.

Anton found Skyla, took her hand, and led her to their seats. Alec came down the aisle with his mother, his father following. Cliff escorted Wilma, who positively floated in happiness beside him. Then Sam, Cliff, Alec, and Stevie came in from the side. Anton smiled as his daughter was the first bridesmaid down the aisle. Her lower lip was caught between her teeth as she concentrated on walking just right, breaking into a huge smile as she reached the front and turned. His little girl was turning into a young lady. Then came Gabriella. Finally, Leyla and Farah.

Sam and Farah had planned this ceremony to include Leyla. When they reached the front, Sam bent and gave Leyla a warm hug. Then she took her mother's hand and placed it in Sam's, before standing next to her. They even mentioned her in the wedding vows, with the words 'family of the heart,' a phrase

Anton knew held meaning for them. Sam promised to be a good father to her and any other children they might be blessed with.

Anton looked down to find Skyla's eyes on him. He smiled and held her hand, daring to hope the future might hold an occasion like this for them.

♦ ❖ ♦

One of the special dances Sam had planned with the DJ was a father-daughter dance. Leyla was self-conscious, but Sam made her laugh, and she was fine. They began, then Anton and Krista joined with the other father-daughter couples. Krista beamed up at him. It was bittersweet; she looked so much like her mother. Her hair was tucked up and coiled somehow, with a circlet of flowers. He wouldn't have missed this dance for the world.

Next to them, Pete was funny, overcoddling Lou, who only had one month to go before delivery and was more into waddling than dancing. Delores danced with Dom. She was all graciousness now, smiling at him as if she hadn't just admonished him.

Then Krista went back to her friends. Anton looked over at Pete, who was talking with one of the guests. Would now be a good time to catch him?

The first strains of a slow dance sent that thought flying from his mind. It was one of his mom's favorites—she must have spoken with the DJ. The mellow voice of Roberta Flack filled the air with "The First Time Ever I Saw Your Face." Anton took Skyla's hand and pulled her onto the floor with him. He noticed Sam and Farah, Dom and Karen, Cliff and Lou, and Pete and Akiko. He smiled—the Circle Sleuths. Then the world fell away, lost to the sheer pleasure of the music enveloping him and Skyla as they moved together.

When he pulled himself back into the present, one moment tumbled into another. It never seemed like the right time to talk with Pete. Toasts, eating, the cutting of the cake, and a dance with a lost-for-words Wilma, overcome with emotion. Then he realized that some of the guests were leaving. Already?

Cliff came up to him. "We're going to be leaving soon."

"You can't stay into the evening?"

"Lou won't say anything, but she's pretty uncomfortable. Achy back and all."

After Cliff and Lou said their goodbyes, Anton looked over at Pete. He and Akiko were talking with Karen. Their kids were nearby. This might be his last chance. He took out his phone and punched in Pete's number. "I've been trying to talk with you all afternoon, but there's always interruptions." Across the space, he saw Pete look at him. "I've something to tell you that I think may be important. I'm not going to bother Sam with it. Can you meet me out by the alpaca pens? Now?"

"Of course. I'll just tell Akiko I'll be gone for a bit."

When they arrived by the alpacas, Anton launched right into his concern. "Skyla and I were talking. It was Barrena's Maserati that jogged our memories. When Charlie and I got to the monastery that afternoon, Scarpelli's Maserati was in the lot. I'm sure of it. When Skyla and Hoot arrived to look for Charlie, it was gone. She's positive. Yet Brother Joseph said Scarpelli wasn't feeling well and was in his room."

Pete's face got what Anton called his hound-on-a-scent look. "Scarpelli told us he was resting. No alibi, other than Brother Joseph."

"And there's something else. I put a GPS tracker on Scarpelli's car."

Pete raised his eyebrows but didn't say anything.

"Morris says he's often gone in the evenings. I tracked his car to a casino. Do you suppose he was there that night, too?" Anton pulled up the app on his phone and showed it to Pete.

"Interesting. I'll check it out." Pete handed the phone back. "Anton, think back to the day Charlie went missing. I know Hiram talked to you, but you were in shock and grieving. It's had time to simmer in your mind. Is there anything else you saw, anyone you talked to? What did you do after you left the park?"

"We went right to the forest service office, spoke with Hoot, got the map, met Brooks. Then we had lunch with Hoot outside the forest service. I filled up at the Shell station, we got take-out from—" Anton paused. "I did talk with somebody else. I'd forgotten. Do you know Yancy, the Indian guy who works for Sam's dad?"

"I've met him. Good storyteller. Fascinating."

"He was at the pump next to me. He warned me again about exploring on the mountain. Yancy mentioned Buck, this guy he knew who was no good. Even he was frightened, he said."

Pete looked startled. "Buck? He mentioned that name? *Mein Gott*."

"Yes, I'm certain. Does it mean anything?"

"We have an APB out for Bradley Taggeroth, also known as Buck. He's the owner of the pickup in the video that Charlie took."

Anton was silent for a moment. "Wow," he finally said.

"Thank you. I'll call Hiram. He'll go talk with Yancy. Let me know if you think of anything else. Even if you don't think it's important."

They turned away from the alpacas as Cliff, Lou, and the rest of Pete's family walked up. Anton chatted briefly before he waved them off and turned to go back. When he got a moment, he'd share with Skyla what he'd learned.

Chapter Forty

The next week reminded Skyla that the summer tourist season was in full swing as the number of folks taking tours of the pueblo and mission increased sharply. The days whirled by. Paperwork took a back seat to the tourists and their questions. On this last day of June, she'd dealt with more than her share of challenges. Now after one last errand, she could go home. She and Anton planned a quiet evening. Tomorrow would be the first of their drone explorations.

Skyla turned the electric cart onto the Pecos Pueblo trail and started off toward the kiva on the rise where the remains of the old pueblo stood. The last of the tourists had departed, and the park settled into age-old silence—just the wind rustling the piñons and the tall grasses near the trail. She drove by the sign that said 'You may encounter rattlesnakes. Avoid and report.' During the summer months, they spotted them about two or three times a week. All the rangers had learned to safely remove and relocate them. Today one had been spotted and the task of dealing with it had gone to Claude.

Skyla slowed as she passed the heavily flowered cholla cactus. This time of year, the magenta blooms were glorious. She looked out over the meadow to her right, imagining it four hundred years ago, filled with tipis and camp fires of Plains Indians traders, their dogs, and livestock. The pueblo on the hill beyond the low stone wall would have been an impressive sight to them. She loved being a part of this sweep of history.

This errand shouldn't take long. The kiva was just a little more than a quarter mile from the visitor center. There had been a phone call from a man who said he'd been on the last tour. She remembered his family. The little kid in the striped shirt had been all over, taxing his parents to keep him out of trouble. The father said the kid had been playing with his wife's cell phone and might have dropped it when he was down in the kiva. Was it possible to go and see if she could find it?

She parked, took her small flashlight, pulled the trapdoor back, and descended into the cool darkness. Her light swept the circular space, the firepit, and the area around the ladder. Nothing. Probably the kid had dropped it somewhere on the trail. Just as she turned off the light and reached for the ladder to climb back up, she heard a noise overhead like someone walking on the roof.

Bang! The trapdoor crashed down, plunging her into darkness. Skyla yelled, "Hey, somebody's down here!" She climbed up and pushed against the trapdoor. It wouldn't move. Somebody or something heavy was on it. She pounded on it and called, "Come on, open the door."

Whoever was there shifted their weight, causing the wood to creak. She took a deep breath to call again when a voice said in a loud whisper, "Bitch." Fingers of fear crept into her blood.

This was no mistake. Who was there? Travis? What the hell was going on? Something smacked down between the ladder poles, followed by noises she couldn't identify. The weight shifted again, then left. Footsteps crunched across the gravelly soil covering the kiva roof. Skyla strained against the door again, but something held it firmly, keeping it from swinging back like it should. She hit the door with the heel of her hand and called again.

She sank back onto the ladder. What to do? Light filtered in through the trapdoor cutouts that accommodated the ladder poles. She climbed down to sit on the firepit wall at the base of the ladder.

Think. She wasn't the last one out of the center. Her car was still in the lot. Her hand reached for her cell phone only to find her pocket empty. Then she pictured where it was—lying on the desk next to her purse in the little office area. She'd had it out to make a call when the office phone rang, and Upton told her that someone wanted to talk with her. Why hadn't she put it back into her pocket?

Silence from outside. They meant to lock her in. It shouldn't have been hard to push the trapdoor back if it were just shut the way it normally was. This was purposefully secured. How, she didn't know.

From her seat on the firepit wall she turned on her flashlight, looking for something that might be used as a wedge or tool to work on opening the trapdoor. The ladder itself was sturdy, bolted in place, built to withstand potential lawsuit-happy tourists. Even as her fingers grasped it, she knew it could not be moved.

The light swept the circular space. Nothing. Perfectly free of any type of debris. Could a rock be worked loose from the firepit? Maybe to pound on the door near the hinges—if she could reach them? Her light shone at the hinges. It would be awkward at best, bracing herself and reaching.

Then she heard someone crossing the roof above, followed by a grating noise. It seemed to come from the top of the vent opening outside. Was this the same person or somebody else? "Help," she called, "I'm trapped here. Can you open the door?"

No voice was heard in reply, but a strange sound came from the opening, like something had been dropped down. The grating noise came again. Now what? It sounded to her like the cap being replaced on the outside opening.

Then she heard the quiet hum of her golf cart, heard its tires turn on the gravel, and the sound recede into the distance. Damn. Now there would be no sign that anything was amiss here.

A soft sound drew her attention back to the rectangular space where the vent entered the kiva near the base of the ladder. She shone her flashlight into the space. Something moved in the shadows. Then she recoiled, jumped back, and stepped up on the ladder.

"Oh, my God!" Skyla whispered as her beam caught a western diamondback rattlesnake, agitated at being dumped ten feet down the chimney-like opening. It slithered its way aggressively across the floor beneath the ladder and into the shadows where it coiled, raising and lowering its triangular head, its tongue moving in and out. She heard the dry, soft sound of the rattles.

Ye gods. Rattlesnakes could climb if they got a 'bellygrip' on a rough surface. She looked at the peeled, weathered, wooden shafts of the ladder next to her. Not smooth enough to push aside her fear. But for the moment, the snake, seeking to deal with this threat to its dignity, didn't seem to know what to do.

It was close to six o'clock. Certainly someone would know that she hadn't gone home yet and would come looking for her. Upton had answered the office phone and knew what it was about—or did he? The archaeologist already had car keys in hand when the call came in, and he'd handed the phone to her and left before knowing why the caller had asked to speak to the lady ranger who had led the last tour.

She thought Claude was still there. But she hadn't told him about the phone call or her destination. She'd taken the cart, thinking to save time. This should have been such an easy errand.

Was there anything like a weapon? She looked at the firepit again. Possibly she could kick loose one of the small rocks on it. But how much damage would that small rock do to a snake, except to make it really mad. She wasn't about to make herself comfortable sitting on the floor now and wait for rescue. Not with that slithery beast who might be seeking warmth or even a way to escape. Maybe the best place to be was on the ladder. Could she brush the snake away with her Stetson if it started to climb? She didn't think it could strike far when it was perched precariously on a ladder. And when her flashlight batteries gave out, what then? She clicked the flashlight off. The light outdoors filtered around the poles. Not much, but as her eyes grew accustomed to the dimness, the snake could be seen on the opposite side of the kiva, minding its own business—for the present.

She looked at the luminous dial on her watch. Six fifteen. Anton was to be at her house just about now. He wouldn't worry right away, but then he'd sound the alarm. Even then he might hesitate, knowing about her independence and how she chafed under his protective attitude. Damn. Skyla wanted him now. She climbed up and pounded on the door again, trying not to panic. Dust motes danced in the gloom. Her hand throbbed. She took off one of her shoes and slammed the heel against the unyielding door. Good. Louder and less painful than with her hand.

Skyla felt in her pocket for a tissue. Her keys! She set to methodically working the wood with her house key around an opening for a pole, sliver by sliver. Still not big enough to get her hand through. Damn. Upton and Claude both carried Swiss Army knives on their belts. She'd thought about getting one, but just hadn't made the effort yet. That would have been a far sight better than her key. Well, now she was motivated.

Light filtered into the kiva and onto the coiled snake by the wall. Periodically she shouted, hoping someone would be coming to look for her. *What would I give for a bottle of water! My mouth is so dry. Keep on sawing*. It seemed that for every sliver that fell to the ground below, one embedded itself in her flesh. Her nails would never be the same; one was torn down to the quick. She discovered that little cuts made almost a half-inch apart, weakened the wood and it would succumb faster.

Time crawled as she worked. The sun set. Twilight filtered into the openings, then gradually disappeared. So black. She checked her watch. Almost nine o'clock. She blinked away tears. Would they find her before morning? Every so often, she turned on her light and checked to see where the snake was. It had moved to the floor by the ladder. Its triangular head twined up, lowered, and twined up again against the pole. Bracing part of its length against the floor, it reached the first rung and slithered along it, its scaly body finding purchase, before reaching for the second. Skyla whimpered and sawed harder with her key.

Chapter Forty-One

Earlier that same evening

Where was Skyla? It was six thirty. She hadn't been at her house when Anton had arrived. He fretted, sitting there with Twitch in his truck outside her home. It wasn't like her to be late. He called her cell phone, left messages and texts. No answers. He called the park number, only to receive the recording about its being closed and the hours. Her car wasn't at her house.

Anton decided to call Hoot and explain the situation. Skyla would yell at him for being overprotective if she found out, but how could he do nothing?

"I'm going to leave a note for her and go over to the park," Anton said when he reached Hoot.

"I'll meet you there. Maybe it's something simple—like she got locked out of her car with her keys and phone inside."

Even though Hoot sounded on the bright side, Anton could tell he was alarmed, too. There were too many similarities to the start of the search for Charlie. He dashed off a note, wedged it where it would be seen but not blow away, and headed to the park. The visitor center parking lot was empty, except for Skyla's car.

Hoot drove up and they tried the doors of the building. Locked. No lights inside. Standing on the front portal near the office window, Anton called her cell phone again. He heard the distinctive ring of her phone from inside. He pressed the disconnect. The phone inside went silent. What had happened?

Who to call? He had to get inside to see if she'd had an accident, or if somebody had been up to no good. The authorities still had the APB out for Travis Cutler. They hadn't been able to locate him since Charlie's murder.

Hoot went around and checked all the doors and even went over to the other set of buildings by the old mission. No one was around. Anton called Sam and explained the situation.

"I'll call Hiram at the state police," Sam said. "He'll know who to call. I'll let Pete know, too. I'm on my way."

Hiram was the first to show up, closely followed by the chief park ranger, who opened the door. They checked all of the rooms, bathrooms, and closets, to no avail. Skyla's cell phone sat on her desk next to her purse, a mute testimony to something being wrong. Anton tried to push aside images of Travis Cutler's vindictive face. He hoped to God he hadn't taken Skyla.

More employees came, alerted by the chief ranger that they were needed for a search. Several state trooper units responded to Hiram's calls. Sam showed up, to Anton's relief.

Upton rushed in, clearly upset. Between gasps, he told about the phone call he'd taken for Skyla. "Holy Toledo. I never should have left until I knew what it was about. The man on the phone said he wanted to talk to the lady ranger who'd led the last tour. Claude was still here. His car was in the lot, too. I thought it'd be okay to leave. I wish I hadn't."

"We haven't been able to get in touch with Claude yet," said the chief ranger. "Let's start on the search." They formed teams to search the garages and work buildings, the convent and mission site, and the grounds around the center. Anton, Sam, and Upton formed the team that was to search half of the ancestral sites trail loop.

And now, as they were just about to start, the sun was setting. Worry gnawed at Anton's stomach.

He put on his jacket against the evening chill and got Twitch from his truck, clipping on his leash. He didn't know if the dog had picked up on his concern or not, but he was uncharacteristically subdued. Upton met them at the rear of the center with an electric cart. They made their way up the path, shining lights into the grasses and along the ancient walls, looking for anything out of the ordinary. They passed the place where the massive remnant of the old mission was silhouetted against the last of the twilight. Repeatedly they called Skyla's name.

Suddenly, Twitch stood on Anton's lap and barked.

"Twitch! Where is Skyla?" said Anton.

Upton stopped the cart. Anton got out and called Skyla's name. Twitch barked again and pulled Anton forward. They heard a muffled cry.

"Help! In the kiva. Help."

"We're coming!" Anton called. He and Sam ran to the kiva with the others following.

"Anton. Oh, thank God. I can't open the door."

Sam grabbed Anton's arm to stop him as they reached the kiva and saw how the trapdoor had been secured. Someone had placed a wide plank over the trapdoor between the ladder poles. It was held in place by an automotive belt wrapped around the poles and fastened tightly by a stick twisted in it and braced against the plank. "Don't touch it, Anton. Fingerprints." He pulled out gloves and tugged them on.

"Hang on, Skyla," said Anton. "We're getting it open."

"There's a rattlesnake down here. Be careful. Oh, Anton." She began to sob.

"Have you been bitten?"

"No, but oh, God. *Get me out*!"

Upton radioed back to the center to tell them Skyla had been found. Sam called out to him, "Have them send Brower from the state police. Tell him it's a crime scene. And send somebody to deal with a rattlesnake."

Upton took Twitch's leash while Sam finished dismantling the makeshift lock. "Holy Toledo," he said, "I would have gone bonkers being shut in there in the dark. Poor thing."

Anton pulled his hands up into his jacket sleeves and, with covered hands, helped lift the belt off the poles. Then he threw back the door and pulled Skyla out into a rib-crushing hug. Tears of relief ran down her cheeks. Twitch stood on his hind legs, trying to reach Skyla's face with his tongue.

Sam pointed down into the kiva. "Anton, look."

Without letting go of Skyla, he looked down. The strong beam from Sam's flashlight showed the rattler on the second rung of the ladder, stretching its way up along the wood to the third. Sam handed the flashlight to Upton, then took out his cell phone. He snapped several pictures of the snake from above.

Anton stepped back, closing his eyes briefly against the brightness of the flashes. Skyla shivered, and Anton became aware of how chilled she felt against him. He wrapped his jacket, warm from his body, around her before taking her in his arms again. He saw the red and blue lights of a police vehicle slowly starting up the narrow trail.

Chapter Forty-Two

Sam watched as Hiram drove up the trail. Lights from the police car and high-powered spotlights flooded the scene. Sam helped the officers section off the area surrounding the kiva with crime tape. Trained eyes discovered where someone had crushed the grass while walking from the nearby ancient wall to the kiva. Just beyond the wall was a flattened patch of grass. Aha, Sam thought, that could have been where the assailant lay in wait for Skyla to arrive. Good chance they left some traces of their presence. The crime tape included a wide area beyond the wall surrounding that spot.

Hoot and the team that had been searching along the other half of the ancestral sites trail came around the loop. Hiram stopped them from entering the taped-off area and told them some of what had happened. Sam noticed he didn't give any details.

Hoot hung back to talk with Skyla and Anton. Hiram greeted him and listened while Hoot told what he knew. "I don't think you need to stay," said Hiram. "I know where to reach you if I have more questions."

"Is it okay if my wife brings some hot soup for Skyla?" Hoot asked.

"I would love that," said Skyla. "Hot soup would be wonderful."

Hiram looked at Hoot. "Yes, send her over."

Hoot jogged away, phone to his ear, his flashlight making a rhythmic bouncing pattern as it disappeared toward the center. Two park employees came to take care of the rattler. The forensics team arrived. Hiram spoke with them before walking away to take a call on his phone.

When Hiram hung up, he said, "Storm and Pete have both arrived. I believe it's time for our task force to start talking with folks. Miss Van Dyken, you'll ride down with me."

She tightened her grip on Anton. Hiram sighed.

"Bjornson, too. And the pooch. And Sam. Might as well start a taxi service."

That's interesting—the *task force* will be interviewing? Sam wondered as he got in the patrol car. *Hiram must think this is related to the murders. Good call. I wonder if Anton and Skyla will realize the significance of that?*

Sam greeted Pete and found that he'd already commandeered the small conference room for their interviews. With the help of the park superintendent, he'd also told the curious employees, still waiting, not to talk with each other about the incident. They'd talk with them all in turn.

Pete pointed at Sam's body cam. "Has that been on?"

Sam nodded. "From when I first got here."

"Good. Keep it on for the interviews."

"Upton," Sam asked, "which phone did the call for Skyla come in on?" Upton pointed out the phone and Sam checked the call history. There was no traceable number for that five-thirty call.

He joined the others in the conference room. Skyla gingerly held a bottle of water in her abused hands. Twitch lay on the floor by Anton.

Hiram said, "There's a medic on his way to look at your hands. Meanwhile, we'd like to hear what happened, starting with your last tour."

"Can Anton stay?" she asked.

Hiram glanced at Pete, who nodded. Sam could tell Anton wouldn't have gone anyway without a fight. After another sip of water, Skyla began her story.

When she finished, Pete asked, "You say the person who locked you in spoke to you? Did you recognize the voice?"

"It was a whisper—hard to tell with just that one word. I think it was a man, but I'm not sure. It could even have been Travis."

"How about the voice on the phone?"

"I know that was a man, and it wasn't my ex. The caller knew about the little kid in the striped shirt on the tour. The caller described him to a T. He asked specifically to speak with me—well, at least, the lady ranger who led the last tour. I thought about that family while I was down there. I don't see how I could have offended them or what kind of grudge they could hold to hurt me like that. Nothing was out of the ordinary. They were pleasant and chatted with me in the gift shop afterwards. They were from western Michigan, where Charlie and I grew up. We talked about places we knew in common."

"Did he tell you how to get in touch with him if you found the phone?" asked Pete.

"Yes. He said they were staying at the KOA campground in Santa Fe. Said he'd call back tomorrow and to keep the phone at the visitor center desk if I found it. They were going to be out tonight. Winston Groothius was his name. I saw it in the guest register. Funny—just had a thought. I knew his name from our conversation here, but he didn't use it during the phone call. Just referred to himself as the father of the kid in the red-striped shirt."

"Could there have been more than one person involved in locking you in?" asked Sam.

Skyla paused to think. "I suppose it could have been possible, but not likely. I only heard the one set of steps on the kiva roof."

"Did you run into anybody on the tour?" asked Pete. "Individuals on their own? People from other tours? Any workers from the mission area? Think back. Who saw your tour group?"

Skyla mentioned Upton, Claude, and one of the maintenance people. She named a few workers in the convent area who'd been putting away their tools for the night. Pete made notes.

"Anything else you want to tell us?" asked Hiram.

"Just that I'm so thankful you found me when you did. I didn't know what to do. The snake had already reached the second rung of the ladder. I was so afraid. I don't know if he was seeking my warmth, or if he knew that up the ladder was the way out. I thought of using my hat to brush him away, but my flashlight was getting dim. Soon I wouldn't have been able to see him." She broke down in tears.

Anton held her closely. "Shhh, it's okay. You're safe, thank God."

"I wished, like Upton and Claude, I had carried a Swiss Army knife—sure would have been better than a key."

"Tomorrow I'll take you to pick one out," said Anton. "If it brings peace of mind and a feeling of being in control, it's worth it."

Skyla considered him. "I think I'd like that."

"Sorry, Bjornson," Pete said. "But where were you between five and six?"

Anton looked startled but laughed and answered anyway. "I was with the film crew until after five, then I showered, shaved, and went to Skyla's. I phoned her several times. Here's my phone. Check the history. I called Hoot and Sam, too. Skyla and I planned to spend the night and leave early tomorrow morning for a trip up the mountain to fly my drone."

"Sam told me about your trip to Glorieta Baldy and your helicopter trip over the mountain," said Pete. "He said you were interested in finding an archaeological site. Have any luck?"

Anton told them about his idea of a shortcut over the mountains. "With my interest in drones and Skyla's in archaeology, we thoroughly enjoyed our trips. We still want to do the drone trip, but probably not tomorrow."

"Who knew about your explorations?" asked Pete.

"Sam, Farah, Dom, Skyla's friend Melody and her husband, for sure. It's no secret. Skyla probably mentioned it to some of the people who work here. It wouldn't surprise me if Upton knew."

Skyla nodded. "Upton and I have talked a lot about our exploring the mountains with drones. He says he would be more interested in drones if he weren't so close to retirement."

"My pilot friend with the helicopter knew," Anton continued. "We didn't ask anyone to keep it quiet. Do you think we should have?"

"I'm just looking at possibilities, casting about for any possible motive," said Pete.

There was a knock on the door. The superintendent looked in. "There's a lady here with a thermos of soup for Skyla. Shall I bring it in? The medic is here, too."

Hiram said, "No, Van Dyken and Bjornson can come out. I've no more questions for them at the moment." He looked at the man in the door. "Has Frobisher showed up yet?" The superintendent shook his head. "Then I think we want to talk with Upton Lawder in ten minutes. If you'd send him in then, please."

While they waited, Sam said, "Whoever did this should be charged with malicious mischief at the minimum. Locked in? With a rattlesnake? That's intended malice. The phone call, the auto belt, the plank, the stick—premeditation. She would have been found tomorrow when they did the next tour, but it might have been too late if she'd been bitten."

Pete nodded, looking down at notes he'd made from Skyla's story. "I think we need to find out about the snake that was caught earlier in the day. Who caught it? What was done with it?"

"And I have some questions for Frobisher when he finally gets his butt over here," said Hiram. "If he was still here at closing time, where the hell was he? But for now, let's agree on questions we need to ask."

"Where were you between five and seven?" said Storm.

"Good place to start," said Hiram. "I'd like to have them tell us in detail about what they did in their job today, where they were, what employees they worked with or took breaks with, any guests they had contact with, and if they saw or heard anything out of the ordinary."

"I'd like to ask them if Skyla was scheduled to work tomorrow," said Pete. "I know the answer is no, but it might be a sneaky way of finding out what they knew about her plans."

"Is Skyla Van Dyken well-liked on staff?" said Storm. "And do you know of anyone with reason to resent or harm her?"

"How about if they've heard anyone fishing for information about her, her friends, habits, or her brother?" said Sam. "We might need to talk with some who weren't on today's schedule."

"Good," said Hiram. "I think I'll go tell Van Dyken she can go home. We can talk to her tomorrow if we need to."

Upton Lawder came in with Hiram when he returned. Sam hadn't paid too much attention to him when they were looking for Skyla. He'd been concerned. Now Sam watched as Lawder entered the brightly lit room and took a seat at the conference table. His receding gray hair was darker than the beard and mustache he wore. His skin had the sun-damaged look of many who make their living outside. He seemed friendly, interested.

Hiram led off with his questions about where he'd been when the tour assembled.

"I was in the office here," Lawder said. "I talked with some folks in the museum, answered their questions."

"Do you remember a family with a little boy in a striped shirt?" asked Hiram.

"Yes, he stood out. He's one of those you have to keep your eye on all the time. He'll find trouble you didn't even know was possible. Nice child, but I'm glad he didn't have to go home with me. He would have tired me out completely."

"This is a small staff here," said Pete. "I would imagine that you all know each other pretty well, know each other's interests and what their plans for their days off are?"

"That's true," he said. "If you're asking about Skyla's plans, I knew she was going off exploring with Anton, using one of his drones tomorrow. We've had quite a few conversations about how drones could help in archaeology."

"Is Skyla Van Dyken well-liked by staff?" asked Storm.

"I would say so," Lawder replied. "Since she had such a horrible time with her ex, there's even a very protective feeling toward her. Especially with Claude. They've always been friends. Every couple of months or so, we all go over to someone's house or a restaurant just to socialize."

"What time did you leave last night?" asked Sam.

"I was on my way out the door when that call came in. I had to go to Santa Fe. Did some grocery shopping. Picked up a prescription. Got my dry cleaning."

"Can anybody verify that?" asked Hiram.

Lawder looked startled. "No, I didn't run into anybody I know. Holy Toledo. I didn't recognize the person who waited on me at the dry cleaners. I'd gotten my uniforms laundered. She might remember uniforms."

"Did you pay by credit card?"

"Why, yes. Oh, I have the receipts at home. Those would have the times on them. But surely you aren't thinking I had anything to do with shutting her in a kiva. Skyla's a co-worker and friend."

"We're asking everyone," said Hiram. "I don't think we need to see those receipts, but I wouldn't throw them away just yet, either."

"No, I won't. But this is upsetting, strange."

When Lawder's interview was done, the task force conferred again before the next employee came in. "He had the opportunity," said Pete, "and quite possibly the means. He would have had to hustle to beat Van Dyken to the kiva, though. Everything would have had to be in place. He's a small man, in his late fifties, I'd say? I don't think he could have done a very good job of holding down the trapdoor while securing it. Unless he had help?"

"There's a thought," said Hiram.

"I've been thinking," said Storm. "Do you suppose we should have the forensics team process the electric carts?"

Pete shook his head. "From what we've learned, the carts have a mish-mash of employee prints and DNA all over them. They were used again in tonight's search. It's not likely that anything we find on them will be helpful."

"Wouldn't it be good to lift prints of the last ones to use the carts?" asked Storm.

Hiram snorted. "Think, man. The last one to use the cart would be the person who drove it in the search. No, that'd be a waste of time."

Sam looked at Storm. His face had reddened clear up onto his shaved scalp. "I'm glad you asked, Storm. I thought of that, too, but Pete told me once that we only have so much time and so many resources at our disposal. We have to pick and choose where we spend them. There *would* be evidence on the cart, but it may not be our most productive place to look."

Storm nodded. "Thanks."

Sam noticed a little smile playing on Pete's lips. "How about volunteers working this afternoon?" asked Sam. "Nobody's mentioned them one way or another."

"Good point," said Pete, making a note.

"Cutler is on the top of my list," said Hiram. "Damn, I wish we could track him down. And that digger, Taggeroth. It's like there's a great hole that swallowed them up."

"If you can get along without me for the next couple of interviews," Pete said, "I'm going to see if I can track down Groothius. I'll make the calls from my car."

Hiram waved him off. "Let us know what you find out. Send in the next one."

Chapter Forty-Three

Pete turned on the computer in his car. While it was booting up, he checked his notes. The names Winston and Meg Groothius were listed in the park guest register along with complimentary remarks about their experience. He called the KOA campground. No one with that name was staying there. He pulled up a list of hotels and motels in the Santa Fe area. On the sixth call he got lucky. He sent a Santa Fe patrolman to the motel to talk with Groothius and see if he wouldn't mind talking with Pete on the phone. Had they been at Pecos NHP that day? The police had reason to believe they may have seen something that would help find a missing person. Had his kid dropped a cell phone at the park that day? Had he called the park about five thirty that evening? No, he hadn't. Would they mind if the patrolman looked at their cell phone history for the afternoon? They were mystified but cooperative. Had they taken pictures at the park? Yes, on their cell phones. Would they mind forwarding them to the police at Pete's email? No problem.

The patrolman helped them with the process. The Groothius family volunteered their contact information. Pete said he was sorry to bother them and thanked them for their help.

After he hung up, Pete reflected on the conversation. He saw no reason to believe the Groothius family was involved in the incident at all. Someone knew about the tour with that active boy and had used that information to sound credible on the phone. Well, now he was even more interested in focusing on the employees who worked that afternoon.

Pete got out of his car, cornered the superintendent, and asked him if there was any possibility of getting some coffee. Yes, instant would be fine. He wasn't particular.

Maybe our perp was too clever this time, Pete thought. Either he was on the tour, or he saw the tour. Pete was just about to enter the conference room, coffee in hand, when Claude Frobisher showed up. *Ach du lieber*. It was getting better and better. The coffee gave him new energy. With keen anticipation he took his chair, ready to engage in a verbal duel.

"What the hell happened?" asked Frobisher. "I got a bunch of messages saying Skyla was missing. Nobody will tell me what happened. Did they find her? What's going on?"

"Where were you between five and seven this evening?" asked Hiram.

"Five? I took some tools back over to the workshop. Some jerk had left them in a mess out here in the breezeway. I cleaned them up and put them where they belonged."

"Did anyone see you in the workshop?"

"No, I was alone."

"How long were you there?"

"Maybe until a quarter to six. What happened?"

"We heard a tourist reported a snake today. Do you know anything about that?" asked Pete, his pencil poised over his notepad.

"That snake? I caught it. Just a small one. Maybe three rattles. I let it go where we usually do, off in an area where tourists don't go."

"You don't kill them?" Pete asked.

"No. Everything, even a rattlesnake, is protected in the national parks," Frobisher replied.

Sam took out his cell phone and scrolled through the latest photos. He enlarged one with his fingers and handed the phone to Pete. Clearly this snake was what he'd call a pretty good size. Six rattles showed. Was it a different snake? Or was Frobisher lying? They had only his word that the snake he'd caught was a small one.

"What did you do when you left the workshop?" asked Hiram.

"Went home, changed out of my uniform, and went to meet a friend in Santa Fe." Frobisher leaned back in his chair and crossed his arms.

"And the name of that friend?"

"Holy crap. I don't think I want to answer that. I don't want her name dragged into anything." Frobisher cleared his throat. "It's rather sensitive. Her husband doesn't know she was with me."

"The name, Frobisher," said Pete. "Police are discreet. Her husband won't find out from us." He looked down at his fingernails and then at the ranger. "Of course, if we had to learn her name the hard way, there's no telling what he might hear."

Frobisher scowled. "Oh, all right."

Pete slid a notepad over to him. "Write down her name and address. Phone number, too."

He started writing.

"And the husband's name," added Pete, inwardly smiling as the man looked up in alarm. "Just so we know who *not* to talk to."

"You still haven't told me what happened," said Frobisher as he shoved the pad back to Pete. "Is Skyla okay? How'd she get away?"

"Get away? Who said anything about getting away?" asked Pete.

"Ahh. Upton. Upton Lawder said she'd been locked in somewhere," said Frobisher.

"Ow," exclaimed Storm with a startled glance at Hiram. "Oh. Excuse me for a minute, will you? I think I have to go pee."

"Take your time. We'll be done here in about fifteen minutes," said Hiram. He picked up the notepad with the woman's contact information and looked at it. A frown crossed his face.

"You're right, Frobisher. She was detained against her will," said Pete.

"Is that all?"

"That's enough," said Pete.

"This woman," said Hiram, tapping the pad. "Same person you were with when Van Dyken was killed."

Frobisher flushed. "So?"

"Just making an observation," said Hiram before continuing with their list of questions.

When Frobisher left, Storm returned. "I talked with Lawder," said Storm. "He said he didn't talk to anybody while he was waiting for everyone to finish talking with us. The super confirmed that. Says since the incident, Lawder was sitting at a desk working on a lecture he has to give."

"Good work, Storm."

"Yeah, I'm learning to translate your kicks on the ankle."

"Much more subtle than a note," said Hiram. "Tomorrow, I'd like you to get the forensic team's information on the automotive belt. Was it a new belt or used one? What vehicle would it have fit? Where are those belts sold? If necessary, have someone help you canvass the area tomorrow. Course, it could have been purchased off the internet. Dang. Too many possibilities. Not enough manpower. Do your best, son."

Sam took out his phone again, found the snake photo, showed it to Hiram and Storm, and said, "When we talk to park visitors, find out if they saw the snake or have pictures of it. Find out if anybody noticed the number of rattles or how long it was. Did anyone watch while Frobisher captured it?"

"All good questions. Sam, take photos of today's guest register. See if you can track down any individuals on it. We're especially interested in their people photos and their snake ones. Ask them if they saw any snakes. Maybe check on Facebook. Sometimes helpful pictures turn up there."

Sam nodded. "That whispered word 'bitch' strikes me as being important. It says something about the mental attitude of the perpetrator. It would make sense to have her ex say it. If someone else said it, well, I'd like to know more about the feelings and attitudes of the employees here."

Hiram nodded. "You're right. Also, I want to ask if the security camera here is aimed to capture license plates of cars in the parking lot."

Pete told them what he'd learned from Groothius. He'd go through the cell phone photos they'd given him. He'd ask Skyla who the various individuals were—tour members, strangers, or employees. "And, guys, there's something that bothers me about this. We believe this attack on Skyla Van Dyken is tied to the murders. I wonder how Anton and Skyla's drone trips threaten them."

"And between you and me," said Hiram, "I've always had a bad feeling about those strange 'in-your-face' double tracks from Frobisher's truck at the burial site. They puzzle me. That whole interrogation of that man just gave me bad vibes. And now he's mixed up in this."

"What do you think?" said Sam. "Should I develop an interest in drones and archaeology and invite myself along on this drone exploration?"

Pete's interest sparked. "I think you might. I don't think Anton and Skyla are aware of what they're getting into."

"And that bothers me," said Sam. "I realize I have to keep mum about our investigation, but I know Anton. We're concerned about Frobisher, yet we can't share that concern with Skyla and Anton. That sucks. They're going to poke around until somebody says ouch and pokes back. These guys don't play nice. I *am* worried."

Pete frowned. "Let's talk about this next time we meet. We need to consider the ramifications. Some things they should know. It worries me, too. *Mein Gott*. Protect and serve. What a tangled web."

Chapter Forty-Four

Anton spent the evening of July 2 with Skyla. The next day was to be the last for filming. Canby had a full schedule and a list of shots he needed before the crew could pack up and leave this location. Anton knew the wake-up call would be early, so he decided to stay at the monastery to let Skyla sleep in.

The night was quiet as he and Twitch got in the car. The stars shone brightly with no city lights to compete. Skyla had no close neighbors but one. As Anton drove away, movement in a car parked nearby caught his eye. The red glow of a cigarette signaled the presence of a shadowy occupant. He frowned, wondering who would be sitting in their car at this time of night out here. His uneasiness grew as he went around the corner. Impulsively he made a U-turn and came back, catching the license plate in his headlights. Uff da. Travis Cutler.

He parked at Skyla's house again and knocked on her door, accompanied by Twitch. Skyla opened it. "Did you forget—"

"It's Travis. He's sitting in a car next door. Watching."

She sucked in a breath, glancing over at the dark car waiting innocuously. "Come in."

Anton waited as she called the cops. She turned out the lights, and together they watched. Suddenly, the headlights in the waiting car switched on, and the engine roared to life. The car left quickly.

Anton didn't know why—maybe he just got tired of waiting or got spooked out. In a way, he was glad Travis was gone, but he really wanted him caught. He knew they wanted to question him about Charlie's murder.

About ten minutes later, a state police car pulled up. As they talked with the trooper, another one arrived to search the neighborhood and the nearby streets. Soon he reported back and said he'd had no luck finding the car. If the guy showed up again, she should let them know ASAP. Then they both left. Skyla locked the door and leaned against it.

Anton looked down at her. She held her lower lip between her teeth. Her rigid stance spoke to him.

"Did he kill Charlie?" Her voice shook.

"I don't know. Maybe." He hadn't told her about what was on the video. Why put her through that? "Or maybe not. Charlie stumbled on somebody's secret."

Skyla pushed away from the door and sagged against him. A small sob escaped.

"Do you want me to stay? The film crew shouldn't need me until seven."

She nodded. "Please."

She was so damn vulnerable, he thought later as he lay beside her. What with losing Charlie, and having this bastard stalking her. The house grew silent. Twitch pedaled and yipped in his sleep on his blanket bed on the floor. Anton finally drifted into an uneasy sleep.

Some time later, he was awakened by a soft growl. He opened his eyes to see Twitch stand up, his stance alert. A digital clock glowed three a.m. Anton threw back the covers and went to look out the front window at the moonlit scene. A shadowy figure stood next to Skyla's car. It appeared Travis was back. Exhaust from his car plumed into the mountain night air.

Anton's hands circled Twitch's muzzle. "Quiet."

"What is it?" Skyla stood next to him.

"Don't turn on the light. He's back; he's by your car."

"Oh, God," she said, punching in 911 on her phone. She talked quietly with the dispatcher as they watched from the dark window.

Anton flinched as Cutler swung a blade at the front tire on her car before going after his. He put his hand on Skyla's arm as Cutler took out another tire, moonlight glinting on the forcefully driven blade. She stayed on the phone, relating the actions to the dispatcher. She hissed in a breath as Travis turned from the cars and came toward her door. Twitch growled again, and Anton covered his muzzle with one hand. "No," he whispered, grabbing the collar and feeling the bristles rise on the Airedale's neck.

His mind raced. What could he use to defend them against that knife if Cutler got in? He let go of Twitch, took a few steps back, and snatched a blanket with a vague idea of somehow disarming him with it. He heard Skyla tell the dispatcher that Cutler was trying to get in. Then she put down the phone and picked up a chair and stood on the other side of the door.

The doorknob turned. He heard a soft expletive from outside before a thunderous kick cracked the door panel. Twitch began barking, deep-throated adult-type barks Anton had never heard from him before. The moonlight caught a wide-eyed Skyla raising the chair over her head.

Just then, quietly and swiftly, two police cars came in sight, blocking the idling car. The troopers opened their doors, and, with guns drawn, ordered Cutler to drop his weapon and put his hands in the air. They heard running steps, saw one of the troopers give chase, heard scuffling noises from the other side of the house, and then loud obscenities.

Anton clipped on Twitch's leash, turned on the porch light, and they watched as the troopers put their handcuffed, belligerent captive in the back of the car. Another trooper arrived to talk with them. No more sleep that night. By the time the troopers had left and the roadside emergency folks had taken care of tire replacements, it was time for breakfast and the day's work.

Chapter Forty-Five

Sam looked up as Hiram, followed by Storm, walked into Pete's office at the Santa Fe Police Department and looked around appreciatively.

"Nice digs, Pete," said Hiram. "Thanks for inviting us. Wasn't sure we were going to get time to meet today, what with it being Fourth of July weekend."

"Can't remember the last time I had the Fourth off," said Pete. "Probably a decade ago."

"Any wisdom for us on how much information we can give Anton and Skyla?" asked Hiram.

"Just shed enough light on what we think is going on to keep them from walking into danger," said Pete. "I'm thinking that the motive for locking Skyla in the kiva is that they didn't want her and Anton up on the mountain. Somebody is threatened by their drone trips. How do they know about those trips and when they are planned?"

"Might be Lawder, might be Frobisher," said Hiram. "Even if they aren't the culprits, they may be passing on information without knowing the danger."

"Can we tell Anton and Skyla not to talk about their trips?" asked Sam. "Give a broad hint that they shouldn't be filming with drones up there until the culprits are caught? Not take their trips at all until it's safe?"

"Good place to start," said Pete. "Skyla and Frobisher know each other well. She would never believe he'd kill her brother."

"Tell Anton, then," said Sam. "He's a little uneasy about Frobisher. At first, he thought Frobisher felt fatherly toward her, but he told me lately he's picked up negative vibes directed at himself. He's wondering if the old man has a thing for Skyla and is getting jealous."

"I will talk to Anton," said Pete. "I'll tell him point blank not to trust Frobisher. We believe he is involved. And to let us know if he sees or hears something that makes him suspicious. Are we okay with that?"

The others nodded.

"We can take Scarpelli off our suspect list for killing Van Dyken," said Pete. "Bjornson has had a GPS tracker on his Maserati and has noticed him several evenings at a Santa Fe casino. We checked back for the afternoon of Van Dyken's murder. Shortly after Van Dyken got back to the monastery, Scarpelli took off. About the time Van Dyken died, Scarpelli had scored a sizable win at the casino."

"Why didn't he tell us that?" complained Hiram. "He could have saved himself a lot of grief."

"He's had a serious gambling problem for a long time," said Pete. "It's landed him in hot water with the studio. They said if he didn't quit, he could kiss his job on this film good-bye. So, he kept it secret."

"Dang it all," said Hiram. "By the way, I talked to Yancy after you called, Pete. Asked him about Buck Taggeroth. He said he didn't know him well at all. Just knew him because Taggeroth rents a room from some cousin of his. Said he was a creepy guy. Didn't care for him or his attitude."

Hiram looked down at his notes. "How about the photos you've collected from the park? Anything interesting?"

Sam pulled several from his portfolio and spread them out on the table. "We haven't had a chance yet to ask Skyla about all the photos, but I thought these might be important."

"Lawder?" asked Storm, pointing to one of a man handing something to a little boy in a striped shirt. "I'm assuming that's the Groothius kid."

Sam nodded. "Lawder's in this one, too." He picked up another photo with a cholla in the foreground. "In the background, by the forest service truck. He's holding a large box. Wonder what's in it? It looks heavy and big enough to be a snake."

"This is interesting," said Pete, pointing to another. "There's the boy in the striped shirt and Frobisher on the back portal as the tour group gathers. Look at his expression. That's a scowl if I ever saw one. He's looking at a pile of tools on the bench. Fits the story he told us."

"And now the last thing on our agenda," said Hiram. "It's been a hell of a weekend. Pete and I were cooped up for hours, talking with that scumball, Travis Cutler."

"He's being held on new violations," said Pete. "Both Anton and Skyla pressed charges from that night. He's not going anywhere soon. Didn't help him that he absconded while on parole, or that he resisted arrest. Got it all on the security camera, including his taking out the car tires and attempting to kick in the door."

"There's no way he can avoid going back to prison," said Hiram.

"What did he say when you asked him where he went after he left the park on the day Van Dyken was killed?" asked Sam.

"Cutler doesn't have an alibi," said Pete, "but insisted he left right away and went to Santa Rosa. That was where he met some girl at a bar. Stayed with her about a week, free-loading. Then he stole some stuff from her and moved on. Went to Texas—somewhere near Amarillo. We're still checking out his stories."

"Then he shacked up with a second woman," said Hiram. "Charmed her and moved in with her. He says he got tired of her, but she started chafing under his jealousness. She called the cops, but he had already split. We checked with them. That's evidently when he came back to New Mexico and started stalking his ex-wife again."

"I've had another development in the Navarro homicide, too," said Sam. "His car showed up. It was in a garage attached to a summer home in the national forest up toward Tererro. The elderly owners don't get up there as often as they used to. When they finally did a few days ago, they discovered that someone had broken into their garage and left the car. The license plate had been changed, but it was Navarro's car. Forensics found pottery dust in the soil on the floor mat consistent with what might be found at an archaeological site."

"I'd be interested in following that case," said Hiram. "Too many dang coincidences."

Pete's phone rang, and he picked it up. He listened, sighed, and turned back to them. "Sorry, Sam and I have to go. *Ach du lieber*. I could learn to hate holidays. Should have been a pizza delivery guy. Work my shift, go home, and forget about it."

Chapter Forty-Six

"I think the third time is the charm," said Anton as he added Hoot's daypack to his and Skyla's already in Thord. "I'm glad you could make it today, Hoot. There's security in numbers. Sam's coming, too. He's meeting us at the cattle guard at the end of the county road."

"I've always liked being out in the forest on my own," said Hoot as he got in the back seat next to Twitch. "But after what happened to Charlie, when the hairs on the back of my neck start to prickle, I pay attention. Melody is spooked, too, even though she's accepted that my job often finds me in the wilderness alone."

"I must admit, there have been times I was glad Twitch was with me," said Anton. "Has Brooks ever asked you about what we're doing with drones?"

"Only to comment that we're damn fools," replied Hoot. "I don't think he likes new technology."

New technology, thought Anton. He'd finally seized an opportunity to attach a tracker to one of Brooks's trucks. Now he needed to come up with the opportunity to change out the battery. That was tough with his limited access.

As Anton drove onto the county road leading into the mountains, he wondered if they were being foolish coming up here. Pete and Sam had hinted that their interest in exploring might be making someone very nervous. They had also said that they should be wary of Claude. He was still on their radar as a person of interest in the murders. Skyla didn't think they were right about that, but in any case, Claude was working today.

It made him feel better that Sam was coming. He'd been surprised when he asked. Surely Sam wouldn't have suggested it if the danger was all that bad. He knew that Sam always carried his gun, even off duty. Another layer of security.

"Does Brooks ever talk about what the task force is doing?" asked Skyla. She sent a sideways look at Anton.

"No, he complains about it being a damn waste of time," said Hoot. "I asked him why he kept on going. He said there are times in forest service work where it pays to play politics. Then he said something odd. If they're going to play on his mountain, he wants to know what they're up to. I suppose he could have meant those who are up to no good, but it sounded more like he wanted to know what the cops were up to."

"Politics? In government jobs? Say it isn't so," said Anton, looking briefly in the rearview mirror at Hoot.

Hoot let out a bark of laughter. "Heard something interesting the other day. Brooks was in his office on the phone. Door was open as usual. He hates being closed in. Anyway, he was talking to somebody about the task force and what they were up to. I didn't hear anything specific."

"Who was he talking to?" asked Anton.

"No idea. Back to what you were saying about the third time," said Hoot. "I know Skyla's being trapped in the kiva put the kibosh on the first try. I didn't know about a second try."

"Scheduling problems," said Skyla. "We thought we'd go last Saturday, but Claude called in sick and asked me to switch days with him. He seems really tired recently. I'm beginning to wonder if he has a health problem. Normally he's even-tempered, but lately he's been crabby. Something is on his mind."

"I had to work last Saturday," said Hoot. "I mentioned that I was going somewhere with you, and Brooks sent me off to the Pecos Wilderness to check out an area for bark beetle infestation. Who knew it'd be easier to get Friday off than Saturday?"

“Claude asked me to work for him again tomorrow,” said Skyla. “I hemmed and hawed, said Anton and I had plans Saturday, but I finally gave in. Made him work for it.” She grinned. “Now I have brownie points for doing him a favor, plus I got what I really wanted, which was today off.”

“Did they ever find out who put that rattlesnake in the kiva?” asked Hoot.

“Haven’t heard,” said Anton.

“They might never know,” said Hoot. “This is the time of year for them. We get calls all the time. I remember Brooks got a call that day from one of our neighbors, who found one by their house. I was surprised when he went and took care of it, rather than telling one of us to go. He must have been in a good mood. Normally he’s plumb owly.”

“I’d just as soon not see any snakes for a while,” said Skyla. “Can we change the subject?”

Anton looked at her. “Sure. I’ve been watching the forecast. We were lucky today. I’d have thought the monsoons would have started by now. They’re late. We could use the rain, but not while we’re driving up here.”

At the cattle guard, Sam was waiting. He threw his pack in the back and got into Thord. Twitch got stuck in the middle of the back seat. In a few miles Anton parked off the road near the site they’d dubbed ‘Cliff Trail.’ This was the highest in altitude and the only site they’d chosen on the La Cueva Canyon side of the road.

There was a track leading down to the spring-fed stream that they followed. Above them, turkey vultures soared, catching the thermals. The temperature was pleasant. Twitch looked eagerly at the squirrels chattering in the trees. He bounced and barked on the end of his leash.

As they walked along, Sam talked about being a new dad, how their remodeling had worked out, and how well Dom had adjusted to having a family around again after ten years in a two-bachelor household. They reached the part of the creek where a cliff rose above it. Anton took out his drone and watched as Hoot assembled it. He nodded in approval as the red-haired forester sent it aloft. They ran it along the cliff but saw no signs of the features that might have supported an ancient campsite. Hoot brought the drone down.

"Hoot, does anybody at the forest service office know you've been practicing with a drone?" asked Anton.

"I hadn't told anybody, but Pecos is a small place with a good grapevine. Matti thought the drone was cool and bragged about it to his class. One first grader's parent works with me, so now everybody knows."

Sam whistled as they walked on, even taking requests for tunes. Anton had always enjoyed Sam's whistling.

"Look!" said Skyla, pointing at some tracks at the edge of the stream. "Mountain lion."

"How do you know?" asked Anton. "Too big for coyote?"

"These aren't from a canine. See how Twitch's claw marks are part of his print? These big ones were made by a cat. Their claws are retracted when they walk." She took a sip from her water bottle.

Anton looked down at his dog in surprise. Twitch was standing stiffly, sniffing the air. Whatever attracted his attention, it wasn't something he wanted to chase. "Look at Twitch. His tail's down, clamped to his butt."

"He's trembling," said Sam.

"What is it, boy?" asked Anton. "What's out there?"

"Eyew." Skyla wrinkled her nose. "Now I smell it, too. Something dead."

They walked a little farther. Twitch stayed right at Anton's side, hanging back a little.

"I see what's upset him," said Hoot, pointing ahead under the brush. "Looks like a cougar kill. A deer."

"How do you know it was a cougar kill?" asked Anton.

"Where it is for one thing," said Hoot. "They like to drag their prey under cover. Coyotes will eat it where it dropped. They're messy, too. Scatter it all over. Cougars keep it together and cover it. See the leaves and dirt clawed over it? That's a cat habit."

"We should leave," said Skyla. "Now."

Anton looked at her in surprise. "Why? You said once they're active mostly at dawn and dusk. This is midday. The smell won't be that bad if we're upwind. We can avoid it and just explore by the cliffs. That's a better location anyway for defense and shelter."

"That's the key word. Shelter," said Skyla. "This time of year, a female cougar should have kittens. It's likely she has made a den near here. She'll be especially dangerous."

"It's not a good idea to mess around an area where a cougar, male or female, has stashed a kill," said Hoot.

"Sounds like good advice," said Sam. "I'm more used to dealing with wild animals of the two-legged kind. I yield to your expertise."

They turned and began walking back to the truck. Twitch seemed quite pleased to be going the other way. He wasn't pulling at his leash. He was in front, stretching it out as far as it would go.

About fifty yards along, Hoot put his hand on Anton's arm and pointed to a tree. "Look."

Anton looked. "What?"

"No, look higher."

Then Anton spotted long, deep scratches on the bark.

"Scratching post," said Hoot.

"Jesus, I can see why you don't want to stay," said Anton. "I'm six foot two. Those scratches are a couple feet taller than me."

They arrived back at the truck. "Plan B," said Anton. "How about if we use the drones in a different area and give Hoot more practice?"

"I would like to take a crack at it, too," said Sam.

They drove to a clearing above the fork on the road to Glorieta Baldy. Anton changed the battery in the drone. Even Skyla flew it. Anton joked with her, that now he'd never get to fly his own drones. She'd be wanting to explore more sites.

"Yeah," she said. "If you get a drone that will map sites, you'll never get your mitts on it. I don't think I'm ready to fly the cop drones yet, though."

"Cop drones?" asked Sam.

They told him about Charlie's adding lights to racing drones.

"That would be a sight to see," Sam said as they gathered their gear and headed back to the truck. "This has been good, guys. Count me in on your next drone trip."

Chapter Forty-Seven

Skyla took the mail from the postman and sifted through the envelopes, putting them in the right person's cubbyhole. One was addressed to her. She saw Patty Lydra on the return label—the pot lady. Wonder what was on her mind? The envelope was too thick to be just a thank-you note.

The top sheet was in Patty's scrawled handwriting.

> I hope you're doing okay. The police contacted me with a series of photos and asked me to pick out the fellow who sold me the pot. I did, but haven't heard anything back. That's frustrating. I like to know how things turn out. Have they caught the guy yet?
>
> Here's an odd thing. I had given my little granddaughter some change—one of each coin. She dropped them in the black-and-white pot. She knew she wasn't supposed to be touching it, so she asked me to get them out. Thank heavens. The quarter, the nickel, and the penny came out right away. The dime didn't. I could hear it in there when I shook it, but something was keeping it from coming out. I got a flashlight and some tweezers. I found these papers. (I'm enclosing copies.)

> Are they important? Does it have something to do with my pot? Does having this paperwork make my pot more valuable?

Skyla looked at the papers. The first she recognized as a handwritten provenance. It did seem to be for the black-and-white canteen, naming the place it had been found sometime in the 1950s and the estimated date of manufacture. The handwriting wasn't like the slanted Palmer cursive writing she associated with folks of her parents' generation. This was upright with distinctive loops.

The second paper was in the same handwriting, but it didn't appear to have anything to do with the pot. It was a daily calendar page with several notes written on it.

"What's so interesting in the mail?" asked Upton.

"Oh, nothing much. I had looked at a friend's ancient artifact. She sent me a copy of the provenance papers."

"May I see?" asked Upton. He took thc proffcrcd papers. "Interesting. Never heard of that site before. What's the calendar about?" He handed them back.

"I don't know yet," Skyla said. "I—"

"Do you have the schedule?"

Skyla turned, startled by Claude's voice right behind her. His eyes were focused on the papers in her hand. She folded them up and returned them to the envelope.

He continued, "I was wondering when that group of scouts was supposed to get here."

"It's on the bulletin board," Skyla said, "where it usually is." She tucked the envelope into a folder on her desk.

"Oh, they put it back then." He went to the bulletin board and traced the arrival time of the scout group with his finger. Then he went into the museum.

"Put it back?" mouthed Skyla to Upton. "Was it gone?"

Upton shrugged. "Can't tell you. By the way, whatever happened to your idea of looking for an archaeological site with drones?"

"It's kind of taken a back seat for a while."

"Well, if you decide to do it, I'd like to hear about it." Upton picked up his keys. "I'm off to lunch."

Skyla took the papers out again, crossed to the copy machine, and made copies. She put all of them into her purse. She'd share them with Anton tonight. He could give Sam the extra copies. Funny, she'd seen loopy handwriting like that someplace before.

Chapter Forty-Eight

Anton looked out Thord's side window as he drove to Pecos after work. In the distance, he saw sheets of rain falling in the mountains. Lightning snaked jagged paths through the sky. He could swear it was almost pink. Thunder rumbled overhead. So much for their planned second drone trip up there tomorrow. Even if there weren't washouts or trees down on the forest service road, it would be slick. The creeks would be full, and the hiking muddy. That's what happened in late July during the monsoon season. He grinned. They'd just have to find something else to do.

By the time he got to Skyla's house, his windshield wipers swished back and forth on the fastest setting, and the rain drummed on Thord's roof. He was glad he didn't have to drive farther. Twitch stood up on the seat beside him, his tail also on the highest setting—for wagging. They ran for the door to Skyla's welcome.

"Mmm, something smells good," he said.

"Hoot, Melody, and the kids are coming over for dinner," said Skyla. "We're having chicken tortilla soup, biscuits, and salad."

"Great. Perfect for this rainy evening. It'll be good to see them."

"Before they get here, I have something to show you," she said. "Patty Lydra, the pot lady, sent these today." She pulled out the papers and showed him Patty's letter. "I made copies of them for you."

Anton dried his hands and took the papers.

"This first one seems to be the provenance for the pot," said Skyla. "It tells when and where it was found and so on. The other one is a page from a daily calendar for Sunday, May 1, of this year. Most of us have a calendar like this at work. Every year, one of our volunteers gives them to the staff as Christmas gifts."

"Do you have a guess as to what the calendar notes are?"

"I think the first refers to the *American Archaeology* magazine. The spring issue had an article on that page about the national parks and preserving artifacts. The phone number seemed familiar to me, so I called it, and it was the New Mexico Historic Preservation Division. The date is for the New Mexico Archaeology Fair. None of these notes would be unusual for an archaeologist, so they may not have any importance at all. I don't have the foggiest notion of what the last note means."

"N. Starbuck, June 10 @ 7. Looks like a normal note to write on a calendar. I would guess someone had a date with N for coffee at Starbucks. Did anybody else see these?"

"Upton was there when I opened the letter. He was curious about it. Claude came in shortly after. He saw them. But he didn't seem interested. He was fussing about where the tour schedule had gotten to. That was odd. It was right on the bulletin board where we always put it."

"Do we have time to scan and send these to Sam before they get here?" asked Anton.

"I think so," she answered, "if we hurry."

They sent the scans of Patty's letter and the papers off.

Then the Stewarts arrived. Melody and Matti ran from the car through the driving rain. Hoot followed carrying Bonnie snuggled under his jacket. She greeted Twitch enthusiastically. Bonnie carried her favorite stuffed animal, her fox, with her. Twitch sniffed at it where it dragged on the floor. Bonnie pointed a finger at him. "No! Weave him awone."

Later, after they ate, and the kids were looking at Skyla's old picture books, Anton found opportunity to talk to Hoot about the drone articles in the forestry magazines he'd borrowed.

"Any more interest in drones at the forest service office?" asked Anton.

"I've kept my mouth shut about it for the time being. Actually, we were kind of walking on eggshells this afternoon. Brooks was on the rampage, finding fault with everything, and the weather meant we couldn't go outside to get away from him."

"What set him off?" asked Anton. "Or doesn't he need a reason?"

"I think a phone call ticked him off. I heard him cussing. His door was open as usual. He said, 'What happens if they put two and two together' or something like that. Then he got up and closed the door."

"Who did it sound like he was talking to? Business call? Or like talking to a friend?" Anton asked.

"Too casual for business. Once he said, 'Yes, Mother,' in a real sarcastic voice. He was impatient and condescending, but then that's typical of him. Such an owly person."

"Mother?"

"I wondered, too. I didn't think his parents were living."

"When I drove by, I saw Upton's car at your office again," said Anton.

"He's helping our archaeologist with a report. Don't know what it's about. Sometimes they leave and go up toward Tererro in a forest service truck. They can be gone for hours. Wouldn't blame them if they just wanted to get away from Brooks for a while. They're good friends. This fall they plan to travel to Europe together. Some kind of symposium, I think."

The children came over to where they sat in the living room. "We found *Koda and the Sami*," said Matti, handing the book to Skyla. "Can you read it to us, please?"

Bonnie clambered up on the couch by Skyla and looked at Anton. "I wike this story. It's about Koda and my fox." She nestled against Skyla, popped a thumb in her mouth, and began rhythmically rubbing one ear of her fox with thumb and finger.

"It's got a boy named Matti," said her brother as he plunked himself down by his sister. "And Polar Bear, Hoot Owl, Rabbit, and a mean old Troll."

"Heads up, Anton," said Hoot. "They will insist you read part of it, too."

Twitch jumped up on Anton's other side, yawned widely, his tongue curling, before putting his head in Anton's lap where he could watch Bonnie.

The thumb came out of her mouth as she giggled. "He has big teeth, wike Polar Bear." Back went the thumb into her mouth.

"Yes, he does," said Anton. "I remember this book from when I was small, and my little girl used to love it."

The thumb popped out again as Bonnie leaned forward to look at Anton. "You have a girl? Is she three wike me?"

"She's eleven. Her name is Krista."

"I must have had a copy of this book before I came to live with my grandparents," said Hoot. "I rediscovered it when Matti was born."

"It's about me," said Matti with a grin.

Bonnie leaned back against Skyla as she began to read. Anton thought it was obvious this was a routine Skyla knew well with the Stewart children. When they got to the part about the storm troll, Bonnie took the book and held it out to Anton. "You read," she commanded.

He grinned and obliged. He remembered how Krista loved little piping voices for the boys and a deep voice for the troll. Bonnie took her thumb out of her mouth again long enough to smile at him when he spoke the troll's lines.

When they got to the last line, about troubles disappearing like smoke from a blown-out candle, Twitch let out a huge doggy sigh. Skyla laughed. "I think he enjoyed it as much as the kids."

"Of course, he did. Smart dog. Good book." Anton smiled back at her.

Bonnie cuddled her fox closer and rubbed her eyes. Melody exchanged a look with Hoot.

After the Stewarts left to get their sleepy kids to bed, Anton walked Twitch. The rain had settled down into a drippy mist. He came back to find Skyla on the phone with Sam. She put him on speaker phone.

"I was just about to ask Skyla if she could go to her office tomorrow and take a look at the calendars," said Sam. "It would be interesting to find if any are missing the May first date."

"These calendars are all over the place," said Anton. "Anyway, think, man. That would draw attention to those papers. It could make them wonder. She can check the day after, when she'll be working anyway. Then they'd never know. And another thing, the papers were already in the pot when the lady brought it by the day Charlie died."

"You're right," Sam replied. "Maybe twenty percent of businesses have calendars like that. I wasn't thinking. I've been distracted lately. Farah has really been upset with politics on television. Me, too. I don't know what the world is coming to."

"Just remember you're making a difference for the better, Sam," said Anton. "I always admired the way you handled the situation with that little bully in Krista's class. Because you cared about his future, he ended up being a happy kid whose actions saved someone's life. If he'd been treated with name calling and derision, I believe he would have gone down the wrong road. He might have joined the gangs. We need more bridge builders, not wall builders."

"Thanks," said Sam. "I needed to hear that. It's just hard to understand how people think sometimes."

"I'll call you day after tomorrow," said Skyla, "and let you know about the calendars."

"Any more drone trips planned?" Sam asked.

"Well, we were thinking tomorrow, but not in this weather," said Anton. "Why? What have you heard?"

"Nothing more. Let me know. I enjoyed the first."

"Will do," said Skyla. "Bye." She put her phone away and turned to Anton. "More coffee? Wine?"

"No, thanks." Anton slid a hand into her hair and leaned toward her. "I know what I'm ready for."

She smiled. "Mmm. You have good ideas, Anton Bjornson."

"I'm not too upset that we don't have to go trudging over the mountain tomorrow. We can sleep in. Wake up side by side. How good is that?"

"Waking up by you? Delicious. Ohh—" Her head tilted back as his lips found the pulse in her neck and drifted lower. Her back arched.

His fingers flicked open a shirt button in his way, and his lips blazed a leisurely trail to where her heart beat. "Sunny tomorrow." He blew lightly on the moisture his kisses had left behind. "With a chance of lamborous." His busy hands cleared the way for more, caressing her curves. "Can't think of a better way to start the day."

"Ye gods, Anton. Yes, oh, yes. I could get used to this."

Sam studied the copies of the papers Patty Lydra had sent. He decided to drop by Pete's house and show them to him. When he arrived, he found Pete and Akiko just finishing a late dinner. Akiko poured Sam some coffee and put a plate of dessert in front of him. Then she left them alone.

Pete looked up from his perusal of the papers.

"On the surface," said Sam, "it looks like the black-and-white pot is legal. It is pre-1979, found on private land. No red flags."

"On the other hand, I'm skeptical." Pete paused, swirling the coffee in his cup. "We know it was sold to her by Buck, who is involved up to his neck in murder."

"I wonder where the hell he is," said Sam. "His landlady hasn't seen him. His stuff is still there. Rent is due next week. APB has been out on him for more than a month."

Pete grunted. "This is like the provenance copies in Teller's files. Same format and handwriting. It's not proof of anything, but it might have something to do with a motive. This ties it to Teller, but it's not his handwriting. This is too precise. Teller's was a scrawl, hard to decipher."

"I'm sure you've noticed the same precise hand on the calendar notes," said Sam.

"Certainly."

"Why did the provenance papers stand out in your mind among all the reams of papers in Teller's files?"

"Teller didn't sell antiquities in his gallery. There was only one file folder with provenance papers, the one with all the invoices to the Paris gallery. It's not typical of his business."

"Whoever wrote on the calendar travels in the archaeological world. Probably subscribes to that magazine."

"We already believe the murders have something to do with a dig." Pete drained the last of his coffee. "It's the rest of the note that intrigues me. N. Starbuck, June 10 @ 7. June 10 was when Charlie was murdered. What or who is N? Or is it N. Starbuck—somebody's name? Is N the north direction—for a particular Starbucks? Should we assume that it was a meeting that took place at a coffee shop?"

"We have a bunch of Starbucks in Santa Fe," Sam said, "and several grocery stores have them and at least one hotel."

"Someone once told me that being a detective was like putting together puzzles. With a real puzzle, you try to put the edges together first. Then you have a good idea where you're going. But with detective work, the edge pieces keep shifting, changing their straight edges into holes that link to a whole other picture." Pete leaned back in his chair and looked at Sam. "We just got another piece of our puzzle in place, but it was just a portal into a new scene." He shook his head sadly. "I should have been a movie theater projectionist. Work my shift, go home. Wouldn't have to worry about getting sucked into strange worlds."

Sam laughed. "You know what would happen? You'd be complaining about how the scripts were written. You'd be saying you could do better. And there you'd be, second guessing the director and burning the midnight oil, writing the perfect script."

Akiko came in behind Pete and rested her hands lightly on his shoulders. "Do you need anything else?"

He covered her hands with his and leaned back against her.

"Thanks, Akiko," said Sam, "but I think we're done detecting for the night. See you tomorrow, Pete."

Chapter Forty-Nine

Anton picked up two small packages, locked his car, and strode toward the FedEx place near downtown Santa Fe. There was another person in line, so he stepped aside to look at some of the greeting cards. It would be handy if they had a good new-baby card. Cliff and Lou's son had been born on the fifth of August. The Circle Sleuths would be gathering on the thirteenth of August at the Bjornsons' to welcome him.

Anton looked up from where he was kneeling by the cards as the customer finished and held the door for a man struggling with a heavy box.

It was Claude. He hadn't looked in Anton's direction. Okay by him. He didn't particularly want to get drawn into a conversation with him.

What was Claude doing here? There was another FedEx place on the other side of Santa Fe closer to Pecos. Anton stayed behind the rack of greeting cards and pretended to be reading them, hanging back until Claude finished and left. The phone rang and the girl at the counter answered. Anton quickly went up to her with his packages. He reached for the forms he needed and filled them out. While he waited for the phone conversation to end, he noticed Customs paperwork and a Paris address on Claude's carton. His eyes widened. It wasn't Claude's name on the paperwork, but it was what he'd carried in. The name was Roger Smith. Who the hell was that?

When the girl got off the phone, he smiled at her as he handed over his packages. "Hello. I like the purple streak in your hair. Last time I was here I remember green."

She smiled back. "I was in a purple mood when I had it done. Next time, maybe I'll try pink."

"I see my friend was just in. More stuff for his sister in France?"

"Yes, Paris. Boy, would I love to go there. He sends them stuff regular."

"He's very thoughtful. I think Jane is fortunate."

She looked over at the package. "Actually, the boxes go to a gallery."

"Oh, I remember she works at a gallery there. Nice lady. A little younger than Roger. Le Chat Noir – wasn't that it?"

"Let me see. No. Something like Gallery de Amerik. I don't know how to say that."

"May I see? Oh, that's Galerie d'Amérique." Anton said it with confidence. He had no clue how a Frenchman would have said it either, but now he'd seen the name and the address. "Have you ever traveled to Europe?"

"No, but someday I want to see Paris, Rome, and Madrid. I'd like to take one of those river cruises, too."

"Well, I hope you get to go. Nice talking to you."

Before he started his car, he wrote himself a note on his phone, recording the name and address in Paris. Was there a Roger Smith, or had Claude made that up? Perhaps he was doing a favor for a friend, but the clerk had identified Claude as a regular customer. How picky was Customs about their paperwork?

He agreed with Cliff's analogy. Peel away one question on the onion and there were three more. This sleuthing sure made one devious.

Look what he'd come to. The other day, he'd chanced upon Brooks's truck at the park visitor center. It was past time to change the battery on that tracker. When he and Twitch drove in, they took the open parking spot next to Brooks. He knelt on the ground and pulled the tracker loose. Twitch was in Thord with the window part-way down. He started to bark, and then Anton had heard the crunch of footsteps on the gravel. Now what, he wondered. Would he be caught red-handed? His back was hiding the gadget in his hand. He quickly slapped the tracker under his own truck.

"Bjornson, what the hell are you doing?" Brooks had asked.

Anton had looked up, slipping the tire gauge out of his pocket. Brooks came toward him with a scowl, his habitual expression. "Oh, hi, Brooks," he'd said. "The low tire pressure light keeps coming and going on my dash. I was checking my tires." He held up the little gauge. "I don't see the problem though. None of my tires were low. I guess I'll have to take it in." Uff da, his hands were filthy. That had been a close call.

♦ ❖ ♦

Books and Bearclaws was his next stop. He'd look for a card there. Maybe he'd get a copy of *Koda and the Sami* for the baby. That book had stood the test of time. He knew Cliff liked it, he certainly had, and the new generation, too, if Krista, Matti, and Bonnie were any indication.

Anton paid for his purchases and picked up the bag when he heard Sam's voice calling to him.

"Yo, Anton."

Anton looked over to the coffee area where Pete and Sam were sitting, looking dapper in their casual jackets and ties.

"Got time for coffee?" asked Pete. "My treat. We're celebrating."

Anton smiled as he ordered his coffee and Sam began whistling a lyrical melody with a Celtic flair to it. He thought it might be one of the songs that Sam, Cliff, and Lou had done when they'd had their Celtic band. Lately, they hadn't had much time to play. The few customers in the bookstore stopped their conversations and listened. He could tell by their smiles they didn't mind.

When Anton sat down with his coffee, he asked, "What was that? It was beautiful."

Sam grinned. "It's 'Sleepsong' lullaby from the Secret Garden album. It's in honor of the bragging you are about to hear from Pete."

Anton laughed. "I'm ready to listen. Pete has every right to be proud of his new grandson."

With a light in his eyes, Pete launched into telling how the new baby had looked right into his eyes, how long he was, how Lou had done so well. And Cliff—rather than being a basket case like some new fathers, he'd been steady, supporting Lou. Pete had been impressed. And what a strong, good-looking baby. There wasn't another in the world like him.

Then Pete choked up. "It's special. My blood, my offspring, heading into a new world, a new future. Look at what's happened in my lifetime. Look at all the challenges that little mite will have to face. He'll see things we've never even dreamed of. How will he navigate those waters?"

Anton noticed Pete's hand actually shaking with emotion.

Then Sam spoke up. "One thing I'll always remember about Cliff and Lou's wedding. When they did the pinning of the tartan, it struck me that this was about two clans, two families uniting. That's how your grandson will navigate all those uncharted waters, my friend. He'll have all the love, all of the good genes, all the wisdom of those two families beside him. You'll see to it that he gets what he needs to grow strong."

"Well put, Sam. No one could have said it better," Anton said. Pete nodded and seemed to regain his composure.

Anton changed the subject to the investigation. "I don't know if you can answer my questions, but I'll ask anyway. Skyla told you what she found when she checked the desk calendars. That page was missing on Upton Lawder's. What does that mean?"

"It's interesting, maybe even provocative, but doesn't prove anything," said Pete. "What do you think?"

"It surprised me," said Anton. "Anything else you can tell me?"

"Not really," said Sam. "Have you heard anything?"

"I did just have an odd encounter with Claude."

"Frobisher? Encounter? Odd? How?" asked Pete.

Anton told him about what he'd learned in the FedEx office. He saw what he called Pete's hound-dog-on-a-scent look when he mentioned the name of the gallery in Paris. Whatever this meant, it definitely held their interest.

"You're not still thinking that Claude had something to do with the murders?" Anton asked. "Skyla can't see that. She told me that somebody tried to frame him. He was really upset after the FBI questioned him. Said his truck wasn't the one in the video."

Sam's eyes flicked to Pete's and back. "What did he say?"

"That his truck wasn't the one in that video."

"When was this?" asked Pete.

"The Tuesday after Charlie was killed, would have been the fourteenth of June." Anton's mind was racing to catch up to whatever they heard in that comment, which hadn't seemed all that remarkable to him. Then it dawned on him. "Jesus. He shouldn't have known about a video, should he?"

Sam shook his head. "How do you suppose he found out?"

"Besides your law enforcement folks, only you, I, Skyla, Hoot, and Melody knew about the video. And only you and I knew what was on it. Wow." Anton leaned back in his chair, shaking his head.

"Exactly," said Pete. "Well, we'll check with the others. Maybe someone didn't know they weren't supposed to mention it. I'm sure that's what it was."

Anton looked at him and nodded. Pete was more interested than he let on. Anton had just found a use for another GPS vehicle tracker he'd ordered. Next chance he had, it would go on Claude's vehicle. And the one he'd retrieved from Scarpelli's car? It may as well go on Upton's. Wouldn't hurt. Might tell him something.

Chapter Fifty

On Saturday, August 13, about a week after Lou and Cliff's baby was born, the Circle Sleuths gathered in the Bjornson home to celebrate. Skyla, now a regular member of their gatherings, arrived just ahead of the new parents. Lou held the blanket-swathed infant. Cliff carried the diaper bag. Gandalf kept inserting his body between the baby and his own curious offspring. When he couldn't block all of the pups, he barked sharply. The pups sat, eyes still fixed on the baby.

A son, thought Anton as he ushered the young family in. Pete and Akiko, proud grandparents, followed.

"What's his name?" asked Leyla.

"We'd like you to meet Douglas Seiji McCreath," said Lou. "The latest addition to the Circle Sleuths."

"They followed our lead, combining their national heritages to come up with names," said Pete with a broad smile.

"If we'd had a girl, she would have gotten German and British names." Cliff's face wore a teasing grin. "I was thinking maybe Brunhilde Boadicea."

"In your dreams, Cliff." Lou smiled as a little hand extended from the blanket.

"Uff da. You wouldn't do that to a child." Karen laughed as she took the baby from Lou. "He's so precious. Look at all that dark hair."

"Not as black as Lou's," said Krista. She looked at everyone hovering over the baby. "It's more the color of Pete's—brown with red lights—at least where Pete's hair isn't gray."

"Or gone—like the part that has disappeared off his forehead," said Sam.

"It's wavy like Pete's," said Leyla. "Not straight like Lou's. Not curly like Cliff's."

"*Ja*, he'll be handsome like me, too," said the proud grandfather.

"But it is messy like Cliff's," said Krista. "Look how it's sticking out all over." She reached out and touched a tiny hand. Immediately the fingers curled around one of hers. "Oh, look. He's strong. Can I hold him?"

"Sit down first," said Karen, getting the nod of approval from Lou. They showed Krista how to hold him to protect his head as Anton watched. *She should have been a big sister. How careful she is.* His reverie was interrupted by Skyla touching his arm.

"Gandalf is all worried," she said. "Shall we send the dogs to the backyard for a while?"

"Good idea," said Anton. He threw a couple of toys into the yard, sparking a game of chase. Gandalf obediently went out but ignored the toys, took up his post by the door, and sat looking in.

"It looks like Gandalf is adjusting pretty well to having a baby in the house," said Sam.

Cliff smiled. "He's fascinated. Every time Dougie fusses, he worries until one of us comes."

Later Anton took the baby. He cradled the baby's head in his long fingers and rested the little body on his lap facing him. Blue eyes looked at him. He heard a hiccup and smiled as a bubble grew and popped. A son, he thought. How lucky they were. The little guy, freed from his blankets, kicked tiny feet.

"Hi, Dougie." Anton touched the baby-soft cheek with an index finger. "Has your daddy started you on the bagpipes yet? No? Well, maybe it's early. Give him a couple of weeks. You might have to grow a little bigger first. I don't think your fingers are ready for the chanter yet." He talked more nonsense to the baby before looking up to see Skyla's eyes on him. He smiled. "Want to hold him?"

She nodded and took the infant, cuddling him to her breast. Her hand gently smoothed back the dark, unruly hair. Her smile was misty. After a bit, the baby turned his head back and forth, rooted at her breast, fussed and gave a little cry, becoming more insistent.

Lou was watching and took him back. "He's hungry. We'll be back in a little bit." She left with the baby.

Skyla excused herself and went down the hall toward Karen's weaving studio. When she didn't return, Anton followed, concerned why she was gone so long. He looked in the empty studio, at the open bathroom door, and went back to the hall. A door stood ajar, where the hall ended near a window seat. He saw Skyla sitting outside on the portal. She looked bereft. He walked outside, touched her shoulder, and asked, "Want to go for a walk?"

She nodded. "I'm sorry. I didn't know how much it would bother me. Holding a baby. After." She walked on, head down. He felt like she was crawling into herself, pushing him away.

"After?" he asked quietly.

She looked up, her beautiful eyes awash in tears.

"Skyla," he murmured, pulling her close to him. He looked back. They had walked out of the view of the house.

"It hurts so bad." She sniffed, and a tear ran down her cheek. He guided her over to one of the large boulders along the trail and sat, pulling her down on his lap.

"Do you want to tell me?"

She covered her face with her hands before tipping her head back, eyes shut tight. Tears coursed down her cheeks. Her hands slid down to cover her mouth as sob after sob wracked her body. What caused such misery? He wrapped his arms around her in silence, just holding her, supporting her until the sobs stopped. His own eyes grew wet. How could he help?

"When Travis beat me …" Her voice was reedy, soft.

Oh, no. He dreaded what was coming and ached for her.

"I was five months pregnant. I lost my baby." She rocked back and forth in misery within his loose hold. "Just now, feeling that precious little life, feeling him nuzzle at my breast, I felt so empty."

"Skyla, I'm so sorry."

"I should have protected him."

"I know, I know."

"Oh, Anton, I never even got to hold him."

"I know."

"You *don't* know." She scrambled from his lap and stood looking down at him. "He murdered my baby, my son. I couldn't save him." She turned away, hugging her arms, standing rigidly.

"I *know* how you feel," he said.

"You *don't* know how I feel. You've never lost a child. Your child is living, breathing." She spun around, glared at him with wet, green eyes, and jabbed her finger at him with each sentence. "You can hug her, talk with her, celebrate birthdays with her, laugh with her, and thank God for her. You. Do. Not. KNOW." Her rising voice ended in a huge shuddering sob, followed by silence.

KNOW, know, know. Her last word echoed in his mind. Slowly he stood, transfixed by the anguish on her face. "I *know*." Words he'd never intended to speak aloud came up from his depths, and he heard himself say them. "When Sonja was killed in that car accident, it wasn't an accident. Her car was deliberately pushed over the cliff. She—"

He swallowed hard. "I've never told anyone this. Not Mom, not Krista. I never intended to tell anyone. To speak it …"

He closed his eyes and felt the raw ache in his throat. "Oh, God. To speak it—would make it real. No pretending it hadn't happened. I couldn't bear it. I couldn't lose our child as well as Sonja. She was carrying our baby. No one knew. We had just found out the day before. It was such a wonderful secret. Then she was gone. I couldn't tell. Couldn't say the words."

His throat worked, and he shook his head back and forth, saying in a whisper, "They were gone. My wife. My child. My unborn child."

She looked at him in shock, then threw her arms around him, holding him tightly. "I'm sorry."

"Skyla. The pain. Our babies. Who would they have become? Their futures … stolen. It hurts."

She spoke against his chest. "Anton, you can cry for them. They are lost, yes, but still a part of us. They always will be. Shh, it's okay."

He had no idea how long they stood there, each finding comfort and strength in the other. When he finally stepped back, he studied her face, this woman his soul seemed to embrace. "Skyla, I love you."

She looked up. With a thumb she dried his cheek, before her hand went behind his neck. She pulled him down for a soft kiss. "I know. I love you, too."

A warm, pine-scented breeze caressed them and moved on as they stood in each other's arms. One of the pups barked, echoed by another. Distant voices and laughter reached his ears, bringing him back to the present.

He smiled, drew a finger down her cheek, then took her hand. "Uff da. Look at us. We've damage to repair here. Can't have two tear-stained folks at a celebration. Come with me." He took her around through the piñons outside their fence to the other side of the house and up a flight of stairs. "This is my room," he said. "Bathroom's there. You first."

He noticed her eager look around, very interested in seeing his personal space. Even though she'd stayed in his home several times, he'd never brought her into his room. He thought of the first time he saw her home, saw the clues that told him more about her. What would she think of his almost medieval décor—the *Lord of the Rings* inspired touches. He'd appreciated the elven banner at her place. Would she find it ironic that his was mostly Rohan with a touch of Viking thrown in?

He didn't rush when it was his turn. He needed time to regain his emotional equilibrium. When he came out, feeling better from the cold water splashed on his face, he found her by his bed holding the picture of Sonja from his nightstand.

"Krista looks a lot like her mother. She was beautiful." She set the picture down and looked back at the outside door. "Shall we go out and around and come in the other way?"

Anton took her hand. "Why not just come down with me?"

"What will they think?"

"They'll probably think we've been getting lamborous. Do you mind?"

She smiled back, one delicate brow raised. "Mmm. Okay, let them think it. I don't mind at all."

As they passed through Anton's carved doors, Skyla looked at them curiously, her free hand tracing the Celtic knots and the gilded dragons. "There must be a story about these."

"There is," he said, smiling at her. "Mom commissioned them for me when we remodeled. I've always loved *The Lord of the Rings.* There was a time when I was young and enamored of the power I had. It began to go to my head. These doors, like the ones at Edoras, remind me that with power comes responsibility. Theoden's people saw him as their king, but the flip side of that was that his life was devoted to taking care of his people, even though it meant leading them into battle and to his death. These doors are beautiful, but humbling."

He led her past guest rooms, Krista's room, along the balcony, and down the broad staircase. As they walked into the family room, Karen handed them glasses of wine. Farah smiled at them, and Anton caught a wink from Sam. Cliff held the sleeping baby on his lap, his and Lou's attention totally focused on their son.

"Now that everyone's here," said Karen. "I think Lou and Cliff should tackle that pile of gifts."

The mood was definitely jovial now, thought Anton. Dougie would certainly be a well-dressed baby. Pete and Akiko had come up with three onesie outfits, a kimono-looking creation and a blue tartan romper suit. The last one they took out of the box was a German outfit made to look like lederhosen with embroidered straps on the shirt part of the onesie.

Karen and Dom had snooped around and found a furniture item Cliff and Lou still needed. They had added a little outfit with *Uff Da* emblazoned on the front. Everybody laughed at that gift. Anton thought it was a good place to start. "I'll start encouraging him now," he said. "Maybe uff da will be his first words. Mama and dada are so common, so trite. Surely your child could say something special."

To go with the *Koda and the Sami* book, Anton had chosen a baby carrier that either Lou or Cliff could strap on and carry Dougie. He knew Cliff liked to get out and hike. That seemed to him a very practical gift. He watched Cliff as he opened up the book. Anton remembered seeing the Koda toy with the battery-operated lantern and the stuffed fox sitting on one of Cliff's shelves.

"Thanks, Anton," Cliff said. "This is special. This book has always been important to me. It will hold a place in Dougie's heart, too."

Lou reached over and squeezed Cliff's hand. They exchanged a smile and a look that made Anton feel like he'd chosen exactly the right thing.

Skyla set her glass down and rose from her place next to him. Anton looked at her with questioningly. She smiled at him, crossed to Cliff, and said, "If you don't mind, I'd like to hold him again." She took Dougie carefully and sat, her face glowing. She held a tiny foot, smoothing each pink toe.

Anton's heart seemed to swell beneath his ribs. She knew his innermost secret. It was odd, but some of the pain had been nudged aside. In its place something blossomed, new and promising. A flicker of hope. He was more certain than ever that Skyla should be his wife. He'd been looking at rings. Now he'd go ahead, make his purchase, and find the perfect moment to ask her.

Chapter Fifty-One

Anton was stunned at her reaction to his proposal. Only three days had passed since they'd revealed their secrets about losing a child to each other. There was no doubt in his mind that they were meant for each other. Now, sitting next to Skyla on her couch, Anton looked at her in disbelief. "You don't want to marry me?"

"I don't want to marry anyone again. Ever."

"I thought you loved me."

"I do love you."

"You love me. Just not enough to marry me."

"That's putting it all wrong. Living together is what people choose nowadays. It's the norm."

"Skyla, I want to marry you. I want the 'til-death-do-us-part. I want it all, the commitment. I want you to be Krista's mother. And, God willing, I want us to have more children."

"I would like us to have children."

"Well, then, marry me."

"I can't."

"Why? What have you got against marriage?"

"That piece of paper, that ceremony—it changes people. It's the relationship that's important. Anton, don't take this the wrong way. I love you. I do want to live with you. But I just don't want to marry."

"How do you think marriage would change me? Seriously, I want to know."

"I won't be owned by anybody again. I am my own person."

"This is 2016. We don't live in a medieval society. Husbands don't own wives."

"They do. That piece of paper says a woman belongs to her husband. He controls her."

"Maybe that's what Travis thought. Sorry, Skyla, but he was a twisted individual. I believe marriage is a partnership. Anyhow, there's more than me involved here. I have a child. I want to set a good example. I want her to believe in marriage. It's what I want for her someday."

"I think she'd be okay with our living together. Probably half the kids in her class are in homes where the parents aren't married."

"More's the pity for them. I think they are missing out. But it's not my place to say what's right for those families. For me, I want marriage. I want the commitment."

"I will live with you, be a mother to Krista, love you for the rest of my days, bear and love your children, and grow old with you. But I will not marry you."

He leaned back and closed his eyes, setting the fingertips of one hand over his mouth. He shook his head slowly. Strange, why was he aware of his breathing all of a sudden? He felt his lungs draw in short breaths through parted lips, he heard his exhales in bursts of tiny sighs.

"Anton, please understand," Skyla whispered. "We can live together. We don't need that piece of paper."

A weight seemed to settle over him like the leaden apron before an x-ray at the dentist's office. He opened his eyes. Her look was uncertain, her eyes very green, glistening with unshed tears. Reaching out one hand, he cupped her cheek. She leaned into his hand and closed her eyes. One tear escaped. His thumb gently brushed it away.

"I think I should leave now. Maybe we need some space."

"I don't want to lose you," she whispered.

All you have to do is say yes, and I'll be yours for a lifetime. The words remained unuttered. Instead he said something inane about they had a lot to think about.

How had it all gone so wrong?

He drove away quietly.

Chapter Fifty-Two

Dom came in to the Bjornsons' through the door by Karen's studio and heard the piano from the living room. Sounded like a Beethoven piece, slow and somber. Must be Anton playing. Didn't sound anything like what Krista had been working on for her lessons. The piece was full of emotion and not entirely free of klunker notes.

The music followed him into Karen's studio, where he paused and watched her working the big loom. Her brow furrowed as she wove the blended colors into her tapestry. She looked up and smiled. He crossed to her and kissed her upturned cheek.

"Be right with you when I finish this section." Karen's fingers deftly threaded the colors into the warp strands.

"Take your time," he said. "I never get tired of seeing you work your magic. I don't know how you keep it all straight. It's so complicated and it comes out so beautifully for you." He straddled a chair and rested his arms on the back. He noticed the absence of her normal sparkle. The frown that flitted across her face from time to time didn't seem to relate to her weaving. What was with this household today? First the melancholy piano, now her mood.

"Something's troubling you, *mi corazón.* Anything wrong?"

Karen sighed. "It's Anton. Two nights ago, when he left here to have dinner with Skyla, he was lit up like a candle inside.

Happy. Filled with anticipation. I heard his car come back later. Quite early. The sun hadn't even gone down yet. He just went up the back stairs to his room. Did he say anything to you at all when you saw him yesterday?"

"No," answered Dom. "It was odd. He acted like he was on autopilot."

"Krista came to me this morning in tears. She said he'd told her he was going to ask Skyla to marry him."

"I thought so. She must have said no."

"How can that be? What woman in her right mind would turn him down?"

He smiled at her. "That's a proud mother talking. What did Krista say?"

"Poor child. Anton hasn't told her anything. She got a worm in her mind that it's her fault that Skyla might have said no because she didn't want to be her mother."

"I hope you convinced her that wasn't the case."

"I tried." Karen frowned. "I wish he could find a wife to love and who loves him."

"Maybe all it needs is a little more time. Skyla was in an abusive marriage. She had the strength to leave him. But obviously she was badly hurt by the experience."

"He takes things so seriously. Anton never wants to burden anybody with his troubles. He needs somebody to talk to."

"Karen, are you asking me to talk to him?"

"If you're comfortable with it. Yes, I think you could help."

Anton closed the lid on the piano as the last notes faded away. He headed to the portal and sank back into the cushions of a chair. Twitch brought him a tug toy, but Anton ignored him.

What happened to his dream? He wanted a wife, more children. He wanted Skyla to be their mother. How did it all go so wrong?

Anton took the ring out of his pocket. He traced the comet-shaped insets of spiderweb turquoise pushing against the center diamond, their tails tapering around and out of sight on the platinum band. The ring he'd chosen because it looked so much like one she'd love. She hadn't even known it was waiting in his pocket for the right moment.

If it were just him, he'd probably give in, and they could live together. But there was Krista. And his mom. Or were they just excuses? He wanted Skyla to say before God and the whole world that she had chosen him. That she loved him—with all his faults. That she loved him enough to make that leap of faith.

And that was not what she wanted to say. Maybe there was someone else for him. Maybe this was not working out with Skyla for a reason. He leaned forward, elbows on knees, closed his eyes, and hung his head, fist tightening around the ring. He didn't even want to think about it. He couldn't imagine feeling for anyone else what he felt for her.

He wasn't about to give up. She was the one for him. How could he convince her? If she was his other half, was he being petty in asking for marriage? But he believed in marriage. He felt so alone.

It was a miracle she'd accepted him as much as she had. It couldn't have been easy for her to love again. He hurt for her. What to do? How could he prove to her she could trust him?

He'd screwed up. Not only with Skyla, but he'd been such a jerk to Krista and Mom. Hadn't told them what was going on. He'd have to talk to them soon. Even now, it had been so long he was embarrassed.

Grow up, Anton. Do a little rebuilding here. Maybe you can make it work. Nobody ever said relationships were easy.

Dom came out on the portal and closed the door quietly. He looked at Karen's son sitting there, bent over, thirty-four, going on ninety by his looks. "Anton, would it help to talk? I don't want to intrude, but sometimes it helps to have somebody listen."

"I'm sorry, Dom." He raised his head. "I haven't been very good company lately. But I could use somebody to bounce ideas off."

"Do you want to tell me what happened?"

Anton sighed and leaned back in his chair. “I asked Skyla to marry me. She says she doesn’t want to get married again. She says she wants to live with me, but not marry me.”

“And that wasn’t what you wanted to hear.”

“No, I want the commitment. I want the ceremony. I want it all. I overheard Krista say I’m old-fashioned. Maybe she’s right. How could I give in and settle for living with her?” He rubbed his forehead with fingers and thumb.

“I’ve been thinking of how to tell Krista,” Anton continued, “and of all the questions she’ll ask if Skyla comes to live with us. Where would she sleep? Will she be my mother? Do you have to be married before you have babies? What do I call her? Do I have to do what she says? Jesus. She’ll be a teenager soon. As sure as God made little green apples, she’s going to challenge me. I think it’d be easier if Skyla were my wife.”

“Did she give you reasons for not wanting to marry you?”

“That bastard she was married to really hurt her. She says the piece of paper changes people. But I’m not like that. I would never hurt her.”

“So, you’re feeling hurt that she doesn’t trust you?”

Anton nodded. “I guess my ego got bruised. I didn’t handle this at all well. It never even occurred to me that she would say no.” He handed the ring to Dom. “I had this for her. Didn’t even get a chance to show it to her.”

“Beautiful. It looks like her.” Dom touched the turquoise and handed it back. “What’s the worst thing that could happen?”

“Breaking it off. Not seeing her again.” Anton turned the ring around and around, looking down at it. “And not just because of me. It might be harder than ever for her to love again. It was incredibly brave of her to get involved with someone again after being hurt so bad.”

“Do you believe she’s the right one for you?”

“I do.”

“What’s the best thing that could happen?”

Anton smiled. “Her saying yes and finding joy in it.”

“What would have to happen before that could come true?”

"You're good, Dom." Anton looked over at him. "Have you been practicing with Sam?"

Dom chuckled. "Ten years ago, when my wife died, my daughter insisted that I not live alone. Sam volunteered to be the one to move in. Dolores thought it would be a sacrifice for him, but it has turned out to be a blessing. We talk a lot, Sam and I. It's worked both ways. There have been rough spots in those ten years for both of us."

"What would have to happen? First, we have to talk. Maybe I could talk her into being engaged. We wouldn't have to set a wedding date yet. But she would live with us as my fiancée. Maybe after a while she would be ready for marriage."

"And she would move to this place?" Dom indicated their surroundings with a sweep of his hand.

"Why, yes, of course." Anton's brow furrowed in thought. "I made another assumption, didn't I? She's made herself a lovely home. How did it get this complicated? One of the reasons I'm ready for marriage is that I'm tired of that forty-five-minute trip back from Pecos in the middle of the night. I want to wake up with her in my bed. But that means she'd have the forty-five-minute commute to her job."

"You wouldn't expect her to give up her job?"

"Hell, no." Anton was startled. "Her job means a lot to her. She loves it."

"Have you discussed that with her?"

Anton's look grew sheepish. "No, I was too busy hearing she didn't want to marry me. I guess that would be a good place to begin. I mean, that's almost neutral territory. Living together or married, we'd still have to make those decisions."

"There's one more thing. Karen said that Krista came to her in tears this morning. She figured out that Skyla said no to you. But somehow she got the idea that it must be her fault because Skyla didn't want to be her mother."

"Oh, God, I've got to talk to her. That's not the problem at all. I should have said something much sooner. Thanks, Dom."

Chapter Fifty-Three

Skyla's phone rang. She left the food she'd been pushing around on her plate and slid off the stool at her kitchen counter to answer it. Could it be Anton? She looked at the number.

"Oh, hi, Melody."

"Hoot and I were wondering if you and Anton could come over for dinner on Saturday night."

Skyla slumped in silence back onto the stool. She thought she was all cried out, but evidently not. More tears rolled down her cheeks.

"Hello? Are you still there? Skyla?"

"Oh, Melody," she said. "I told him I couldn't marry him, and he left." The last word trailed off into a sob. "I've been so miserable."

"Skyla, I'm coming over. Right now. Hoot is here. He'll watch the kids."

"No, you don't have to. I'll get through it." Oh damn. She was talking to the dial tone.

Minutes later Melody came in, gave her a big hug, and listened as Skyla told her story through tears.

"Do you love Anton?"

"Yes, very much." Finding a few crumbs on the table, she pushed them into a pile.

"Why don't you want to marry him?"

"A man changes when he gets that piece of paper." She arranged the crumbs into a long line.

"Skyla, you are a strong woman. I think your fears about someone else treating you like that despicable asshole did are all out of proportion. Can I talk some sense to you?"

Skyla sat up straighter. "Melody, I've never heard you use the a-word before."

"In this case, I think it's deserved. Do you really think Anton will change his spots when he has that piece of paper? Travis put on an act. He got what he wanted and then dropped the act."

"But what if he does? I'm stuck. I can't go through all that again." She sent the crumbs flying with a swipe of her hand.

"Anton is not Travis. What was his marriage with his first wife like? Did you ever see or hear anything that tells you that Anton would not be as loving to you after you were married as he is now?"

"No, but men hide things until it's too late."

"Do you think Hoot changed his spots when he married me? Would Charlie have become abusive if he got married?"

"Of course not." Skyla glared at Melody. Sometimes friends could be annoying, especially when they hit you with cogent arguments.

"Travis was a rotten human being. Don't judge other men by him. Do you have any tea?"

Skyla got to her feet and set the water on to heat.

"I've seen you with our kids. I imagine you'd love some of your own. Would you?"

"Yes." She set a small pitcher of milk on the table.

"Can you see Anton as their father?"

"Oh, yes."

"Can you see yourself being Krista's mother?"

Skyla nodded. "She's a great kid. He's doing a wonderful job as her dad."

"Have you ever thought that is one reason he wants to marry you, not just live with you? He has a child he loves. I've seen live-in couples and their kids. They don't have the same security as the married ones do. Marriages aren't perfect, by any means, but there's something in that legal piece of paper that tells the kids something. Hoot and I are committed to making our marriage work. When we made that promise, we had no idea of what life had in store for us. We still can't say what the future holds, but, by God, we will face it together. How can that not help our kids?"

"Okay, I admit I'd love to have Anton be my child's father." Skyla poured the tea.

"Say you did live together and had a child. Then you decided you didn't want to live with him anymore or maybe he found someone who did want to marry him. You'd want to take your child with you. He would fight tooth and nail to keep that child. It would tear you all apart."

"You don't hold back when you talk sense, do you?"

"Not about something this important." Melody poured some milk into her tea. "You've told me about his spread, how beautiful it is."

"And that's another thing. Anton is a powerful man and wealthy. Sometimes wealth creates attitude. It makes them think they're more important than you. They can do what they want because they have money. I don't trust that."

"Have you ever seen him throw his weight around and look down on others?" Melody sipped her tea and leaned back.

"Well, no. Come to think of it, Charlie never mentioned an attitude like that either."

"Tell me again who lives there with him."

"His mother and his daughter. Maria and Diego live there, too, but they each have their own house."

"Pretend a minute. Anton has invited you to live with him. Off you go. Into a house where three females have already carved out their space. That's enough to make the strongest woman shake in fear. First there's his daughter. She would have to share her father's attention with you. She's going to be a teenager in a few years. I can just hear her yelling, 'You aren't my mother. I don't have to do what you say.' If you and Anton disagree over discipline, he has the edge. He is her father. You have no legal status. You are just his lover."

“Melody, that’s pretty crass. I’d be more than that.”

“Would you? Sounds like a good way to drive a wedge between you and Anton. And then there’s his mother. You wouldn’t even be her daughter-in-law. Would she end up resenting you? Thinking you weren’t good enough for her son?”

“You make it sound awful.”

“I’m not done yet. There’s the housekeeper. You told me she’s worked there for a long time. They’ve worked things out well between them. Anton says to her, ‘this is what I want you to do,’ and she will do it. She’s the employee. But what would your status be? If you say, ‘this is what I want you to do,’ what will she think? You’re not her employer. You’re only his lover. In her mind, you are beneath her. You diminish his status in her eyes. She never thought he would do that to them, and she is not as happy there as she once was.”

“Damn. Don’t even say it. Another wedge. How did you figure all this out? Where did it all come from?”

Melody huffed a little laugh. “I lived it. I was the bratty teenager in just such a household. It was hell. When I finally got out of high school, I left there like a shot. Hoot and I met in college. We spent a lot of time talking with his grandparents. They taught me so much about good relationships.” She reached out and put her hand lightly on Skyla’s wrist. “Talk to Anton. It’s not going to be easy. Everybody has conflict, but it’s worth it.”

“Whatever happened to your family?”

“The housekeeper quit. My dad and his live-in split. She took the kids they’d had. My grandmother died without ever seeing her grandchildren, my half-sisters, again.”

Anton got behind the wheel for another forty-five-minute commute from his home. The ring was tucked into his pocket again. He’d called Skyla, asked if they could talk. She seemed eager, said she’d been so miserable without him. Before he left, he’d talked first with Krista, then with his mother. She told him not to worry about Krista and to take the time he needed, even if he had to be there all night. Not too subtle, he thought, but definitely encouraging.

After an eternity he was at Skyla's door. No sooner had she opened it, but they were wrapped in each other's arms. He savored the warmth, the light scent that was hers alone, and the feel of her heart beating against him.

"I made some coffee," Skyla said. She drew out of his arms and shut the door. "I don't know why I'm so nervous."

"I do. For the same reason I'm nervous. This is important, and it's uncharted territory, at least for us. I worry about getting it right after I messed up. I want to hear your thoughts. I want to tell you what I've learned. We'll work this out, Skyla."

They talked while the coffee grew cold in the cups, while the shadows lengthened, and the sun called it a day. He told her he'd gone to Dom for advice. She said she'd had a good talking to by Melody. She talked about her fears. He talked about his hopes, his desires. They talked about where they'd live, about their careers and plans for the future. They talked about the children they both wanted, about what they'd need to raise those children to be strong happy adults.

"I should give in and marry you," she began, "but—"

He leaned forward and put a finger over her lips. "Skyla, don't say that. I don't want you to *give in.* That's capitulating, and it's putting me in control. If and when you decide you want to marry me, I want you to because you love me so much that you can't live without me. That you're willing to spit in the face of fate. That you are saying yes, not because of what you might lose, but what you will gain. I want you to be so filled with such joy at the idea, that giving in never crosses your mind. Then we'll marry."

She smiled, a slow smile that lit up her face.

"I have something to ask you, Skyla. It's sort of the same question, but different." He took a deep breath and took her hands in his. "Will you be engaged to marry me? Can you promise that someday in the future you will take me as your husband? That someday, when you are ready to take that leap of faith, you will be my wife?"

He didn't know how it was possible, but her smile grew even bigger. He couldn't look away from her. She tugged her hands from his and slowly put them on his cheeks. She drew closer, looked at his lips, then met his gaze again.

"Hold onto your hat, Anton Bjornson. You just became an engaged man. Yes, I will take you as my fiancé and someday as my husband."

"Oh, Skyla, it's not my hat I'm wanting to hold on to." He drew her close and reveled in the feel of her body close to his. "With your promise, I can wait. We will work it out. I love you so much."

It was only later that Anton remembered the ring in his pocket. He reached over the edge of the bed and picked his jeans off the floor to retrieve it.

He'd been right. She did love the ring. It looked great on her finger. God willing, it wouldn't be too long before it would be joined by the shaped circlet that snugged up against it with all the tiny diamonds, and he could wear the matching turquoise-inlaid band that said he was hers. The rough spots still existed, but the important thing was that they were together. They had time.

Chapter Fifty-Four

"We're off to the mountains. Drone exploration number two," said Anton with a smile a week later. "Weather's wonderful. No thunderstorms forecast. No disasters last night to disrupt our trip." He got into his pickup. Skyla sat beside him; Sam, Twitch, and Scherzo were in the back seat.

"Upton asked me what I was doing today," said Skyla.

"What did you tell him?" asked Sam.

"Just hanging around. Laundry. Errands. Typical Saturday. There's another odd thing about Upton. The other day, he handed me a letter—addressed to me—from Patty Lydra. It had been opened. This time it was a thank-you note. He said it was in his box like that."

"Was he telling the truth, or do you think he opened it?" asked Anton.

"Do you think there might have been something else besides the thank-you note when Patty sent it?" asked Sam.

"I don't know. There have been times in the past when I got something in my box and opened it, only to find somebody had stuck it in the wrong box and it wasn't addressed to me. I just had a funny feeling about it. So, when we made plans for today, I didn't tell anybody. I don't think Upton would be a problem, but I didn't want him to say something, even innocently, that would tell folks where we were exploring with a drone."

"Dom and Farah know," said Sam.

"So does Mom," said Anton. "It makes sense to have someone know where you are and when to expect you back when you head off like this."

They reached their destination, the site they'd dubbed Scree, parked under some pines near the forest service road, and started off cross-country with Twitch and Scherzo on leads. The route they planned had the gentlest slope into the Alamitos Canyon. All three had loaded the maps and apps onto their smartphones, which meant their GPS signals should work even without cell towers. Anton had his map and compass as backup. This site was the lowest in altitude of their targeted sites—and the one farthest from the forest service road.

"By the way, congrats from both of us on your engagement," Sam said as they walked along. "Have you set a wedding date yet?"

"Thank you. Not yet. We aren't in a rush," said Anton, reaching out to take Skyla's hand.

"We'll have a party to formally announce our engagement," said Skyla. "Maybe sometime after Labor Day." She smiled up at Anton.

"We'll look forward to that," said Sam. "Wow. Labor Day. Son of a gun. Just think. This time last year, I didn't even know Farah. Now she's my wife. And I have a daughter. Double wow."

As they hiked along, they looked back. The scree area was big enough so that it was often visible. Their route skirted that steep drop-off next to the road. Periodically they stopped in the shade, sipping water, while Anton checked out the route ahead with his drone. Puffy white clouds passed overhead. Anton felt the breeze, warm and dry enough to get rid of his film of sweat, but not oven-like. They paused for their third stop while Anton sent the drone high for an overview. Sam watched the screen over Anton's shoulder while whistling an upbeat tune.

"What's that?" asked Sam, breaking off his whistle and pointing to the screen. From this angle, looking back on the precipitous drop of rubble, something odd reflected the light.

Anton zoomed in. “Looks like something off a car. Is that a bumper?” He sent the drone to look from a different angle.

“There’s something else,” Skyla said. “Something shiny. It doesn’t look like it belongs there. Looks like a side mirror or something.”

“Follow the line downhill from the bumper to the mirror, if that’s what that thing was,” said Sam. “Then pan lower and look around.”

As Anton did, they saw more debris and what could be bits of glass reflecting the sunlight. Then, in a small rocky ravine, almost hidden by brush, they spotted the remains of a vehicle.

“That doesn’t look good,” said Skyla. “Wouldn’t we’d have heard about it, if there’d been an accident out here?”

Sam and Anton were looking intently at the screen. Anton maneuvered the drone closer, zooming in on the wreck.

“Not if no one knew,” said Sam. “Looks like a pickup. You can see by the vegetation and the mud it’s been there for a while, but it’s not rusted. It’s silver.” His voice trailed off.

“Are you thinking what I’m thinking?” asked Anton. “Buck?”

Skyla sucked in a breath and looked at Sam.

He nodded. “Could be. I think we should work our way down and check it out. But it’ll mean we won’t get to look for our ancient site.”

Anton looked at Skyla.

“We should check,” she said. “You’ll need me to hold the dogs when we get down there.”

Sam borrowed Anton’s SAT phone and called Hiram. Anton brought the drone back slowly, checking for the easiest way down, which appeared to be going ahead on their present route and then backtracking to the base of the scree. When the vehicle was in sight, Skyla stayed back with Twitch and Scherzo.

As he and Sam approached the vehicle, Anton’s nose wrinkled at the odor that lingered. He noticed Sam’s grimace. Their suspicions were correct—the number on the Utah license plate confirmed it was Buck’s pickup. They went back to Skyla in the open where they could get satellite reception and called Hiram again. He was already on his way, but he would summon the forensics team and alert the coroner.

After their calls, Sam went back to see what he could learn without disturbing anything. The passenger compartment was badly crumpled, but still intact. Anton went with him part way before stopping. The exposed underbelly of the pickup tilted skyward. "Uff da, I don't even want to look."

Sam went ahead, took out his cell phone, and snapped some pictures of the vehicle with its identifying plate, the remains, and the location. They returned to Skyla.

"Damned unpleasant," said Sam. "Glad I'm not the one who has to get all this out of here."

From where they sat at the base of the scree, not far from the rocky ravine, they could look up to the forest service road. They waved at the police car when it came in sight above them. Sam called Hiram again to guide him and the forensics team on the best approach down to where they were. When they arrived, Sam told them how they happened to spot the wreck. After Hiram had had a chance to examine the scene, they hiked back up to the road with him.

"I'm getting too damn old to do this," Hiram complained after he'd caught his breath, "but I'm glad you found it. This may break the case wide open." He took another swig of water and recapped his bottle.

Anton poured some water into a container for the dogs. Maybe he and Skyla would hear something interesting if they waited a bit.

They heard a vehicle coming down the road toward them. Soon Brooks pulled up next to the collection of police vehicles and got out.

"What's going on?" he asked. "Hiram, Sam, what are you doing here?"

"We spotted a pickup that had gone off the road a while back. They're checking it out now," said Sam.

"How'd you happen to find it? I didn't know there'd been a wreck there, and my job takes me back and forth on this road all the time."

"We were hiking," said Anton. He didn't feel the need to go into the fact that they were using a drone. He'd put the drone out of sight in his tool box. Skyla wasn't talkative either, staying where she was seated on a rock, holding the dogs' leashes.

"Why so many people and cars? Isn't the coroner enough?" asked Brooks.

Interesting, thought Anton. He just assumed there was a body down there. Didn't even ask if there was.

"Accident reconstruction," said Hiram. "It's their job to determine what happened and why. Make positive identification and so on. You'll be interested to know that's Buck Taggeroth's truck down there. Presumably that's why we haven't been able to find him."

"Well," said Brooks, "that kind of wraps up your case, doesn't it? You got your killer."

"Too soon to call it quits," said Hiram. "He wasn't working alone, remember? But, for all we know, there may be more than one set of remains there. You available for a task-force meeting Tuesday?"

"What time? Earlier the better. I got things to do."

"Nine o'clock. My office."

Anton watched as Brooks drove away. He hadn't told anyone that he'd put a GPS tracker on Brooks's truck. He would be interested to see where Brooks went now that he knew about Buck.

"You guys ready to go?" he asked.

"Hiram, do you mind if we leave you?" asked Sam.

"Naw, I'm going to call Pete and Storm. See you Tuesday?"

"Yes, sir. At 0900," answered Sam.

Even the dogs were subdued on the way back. They flopped on the back seat by Sam.

"This accident means we'll never be able to ask Buck what he knew about Charlie's death," said Skyla. "I was hoping he could tell us."

Anton's glance caught Sam's eyes in the rearview mirror. "It wouldn't surprise me if they found this was no accident. I'm thinking it could be another murder."

"I'm thinking you're right," said Sam. "These are not nice folks to deal with."

♦ ❖ ♦

When Anton had opportunity, he checked his trackers. When he purchased them, he had some sort of vague idea they might help. He was getting data, but he had no clue what to do with it. Patterns were emerging, though, and anything he could learn about their habits might pay off. Upton was a regular at the forest service office, usually stopping there once a day. Hoot said he and the forest service archaeologist were good friends.

Brooks, not surprisingly, was often on the county road that became the forest service road going up to Glorieta Baldy. Since his vehicle was there nights, he must live there. Just by listening to Hoot, he'd learned Brooks's schedule. Either the man was a workaholic or he had something going on in the mountains. That interested Anton.

It got even more interesting when he began tracking Claude. It was easier to get the tracker on Claude's car as it wasn't unusual for Anton's car to be seen at the park. Quite unremarkable, as a matter of fact. One thing he noticed—Claude and Brooks were often in the same place at the same time.

A couple of times Claude had made a round trip directly from the beginning of the forest service road near Pecos to the FedEx place in Santa Fe and then back again. It definitely wasn't the most convenient shipping place for him. He thought the starting point must be Brooks's place. Strange pair to be friends.

Brooks had gone home after he'd left them at the crash site. Soon Claude had joined him there. What that meant or didn't mean was beyond him.

Chapter Fifty-Five

Sam looked around the group gathered in Hiram's office on Tuesday morning. They were still waiting for Brooks when they heard noises in the hall. Brooks walked in and took the chair they'd left for him by the door.

"Where's the purdey lady?" he asked.

"Agent Purley is on another assignment." Hiram frowned at Brooks, then shuffled his notes on the table. "Well, folks, glad you could come. I know you are all busy with the Labor Day weekend coming up. We'll try to make this short."

"As you know, Buck Taggeroth's truck was found on Saturday. One set of remains. At this point they appear to be his; ID was on him. Cowboy hat with the rattlesnake band was there—crushed, but there. They'll confirm the identity later, possibly from fingerprints or dental records."

"Was he dead before his truck went off the road?" asked Pete.

Brooks straightened slightly. "What do you mean? Do you think he went off the road because of a heart attack or something?"

"I'm simply saying that we're investigating two murders here. Could be a third. Can't just make assumptions."

"No," said Hiram, "the cause of death was attributed to the accident. But—" He paused for emphasis. "Forensics also found tool marks on the brake-line hose. They were able to prove the line had been cut. Someone intended for him to go off that drop."

"It was homicide then," said Pete.

"Apparently," said Hiram. "That truck contained some interesting items. In the bed, or what was left of it, they found lots of wooden crates. Pottery sherds. Tools you'd associate with a dig. No surprise there."

"Most interesting to me," said Storm, "was they found a drone control and tablet. I took pictures of them and showed them to Anton. He says they matched Van Dyken's. Forensics was able to confirm that by recovering the video."

"Pete, you'll be interested to know that Teller's custom-made lighter was found in Taggeroth's pocket."

"I guess you have your killer," said Brooks. "There's the proof."

"There's more than one killer," said Hiram. "Taggeroth didn't cut his own brake line and go driving off that cliff. We were lucky in identifying him as the man in the video as early as we did in June. Soon we would have had him in custody. It's my theory that someone was afraid Taggeroth would squeal on them. They couldn't let that happen."

"What else did you find?" asked Sam.

"A canvas tarp," said Hiram. "I believe it's the one we've been looking for since we saw that video of Teller being dumped in the grave. Had gold metal grommets. One was missing. Forensics is checking the DNA from blood, bodily fluids, and hair caught on that canvas."

Sam sat up straighter. "Son of a gun! Was a little piece of canvas torn away as well?"

"Yes," said Hiram. He slid a photo across the table to Sam.

Sam pulled up a file from his computer, found a photo, and compared Hiram's photo to it.

"What's that from?" asked Brooks. "It looks like Martinez has a picture of what's missing on the tarp that Hiram found."

"Exactly," said Sam. "I will be very interested in the DNA analysis for any traces on that tarp." He exchanged a look with Pete.

"What else did you find?" Brooks pulled at his collar like it was too tight.

“Fingerprints from the cab interior. Prints from more than one person. We should have those results back two weeks from today.”

“It takes that long?” asked Brooks.

“Labor Day holiday coming up. Slows down the system,” said Hiram.

“Surely after all the time he’s been down there,” said Brooks, “you can’t get fingerprints. Don’t they deteriorate or something? Anyhow, any number of people could have ridden in that truck with him. Doesn’t mean they were involved in murder.”

“Forensics has some pretty amazing tricks when it comes to getting fingerprints,” said Sam. “That amount of time won’t stop them.”

“Any other questions?” asked Hiram. “I think we’ll see this wrapped up soon.”

“I came all the way for that?” grumbled Brooks. “This has been a waste of time. I got things to do.” He walked out the open door.

Sam heard the sound of the forest ranger’s boot heels receding down the hall. He looked at the others still sitting at the table.

“Interesting.” said Pete to Hiram. “You and I know that you can’t predict precisely when we’ll get fingerprint information back. I’m assuming you said two weeks from today for a reason.”

“Brooks doesn’t know we can’t be precise. I’m thinking the word will leak to our culprit, and things will escalate.”

“We’ve known ever since the eighth of August that Brooks was leaking information to Frobisher,” said Pete. “No other way he could have known about a video with a pickup.”

“I’d say that quite soon now Brooks will tell Frobisher about the two weeks,” said Hiram, looking at his watch. “I expect that will make him very nervous. Nothing like a little stress to lead to mistakes.”

“Can’t come too soon for me,” said Pete, rising from the table.

“Dang right,” said Hiram. “What’s on your agenda today?”

“Digging,” said Sam. “Archives of antiquities looting. We’re both at it.”

“I think we’ll hit Starbucks on the way back,” said Pete. “Puzzle pieces are easier to fit together if you have coffee.”

“Keep in touch.”

Chapter Fifty-Six

The two men worked diligently at the dig site. One was in the trench where Buck had found the last pots and knives. The professor was farther back under the overhang. He was examining the rock wall at the back of the recess. He frowned and picked at a crack in a rock.

"I could weep when I think of all the artifacts that Buck must have stolen from us before he split," he said as he picked away. "That black-on-white canteen was one of the best we've ever found. Gone. Damn him."

"It's because of his carelessness that we have to move on." The other knelt to brush away dirt from pottery. "Damn. Only a broken sherd. All we have time for now is intact items. Did you get your ticket?"

"Of course." The professor knocked a stone against the surface he was inspecting. "It's horrible. While we were thinking Buck had absconded, he was lying dead at the bottom of the scree. It's amazing we never knew."

"He still stole a bunch from us. I don't feel sorry for him. You can thank me any time."

"Toss me that trowel. Thank you for what?"

The digger in the trench tossed the trowel to land in the dirt by the professor. "What do you think?"

The professor picked up the trowel and then grew still. "Holy— You cut his brake line. You killed him. Damn you. That's four. I can hardly wait to be done with you. You fly off the handle, and the cops get closer and closer. I had nothing to do with any of those deaths."

"Just what did you think was going to happen when you brought that little wuss up here in June?" The hothead climbed out of the trench and stood looking down at the other. "You called, asked for my advice. You got what you wanted, even though you are too squeamish to admit it. You knew what would happen."

"Dammit. I did not!" The professor jammed the butt end of the trowel into the chink he'd been enlarging. A rock loosened and fell into a space beyond. He stopped, transfixed by the empty darkness.

The younger man looked at the professor and took a step back. "What the hell are you doing? You're going to dig out the wrong thing, and it will all come down."

"My God, I don't believe it. This wasn't solid rock. It's a wall. There's a space behind it. I wondered why it didn't feel right. Something was off. I think it opens into a cave."

"What's in it?"

The professor lay on his stomach and shone the light through the opening he'd created. He worked more with the trowel.

The other moved back toward the daylight.

"I see some pots," the professor said, peering into the opening. "They could be for grain, maybe for carrying water. Come and see."

"I don't like caves."

"Holy— This could even be better than what Buck found earlier. I wonder how far back it goes. I'll have to take away more of this wall."

"I'm not getting anywhere near that."

"Oh, for God's sake. You afraid it's going to collapse? This earth hasn't moved in 400 years. It's not going to move now."

"I don't like caves. Never have. Bats."

"Since when have bats bothered you? No bats. It's dry as a bone. Just dark. That's your problem. We don't have much time. We should be out of here in ten days. Damn. Wish we'd seen this earlier." The professor dug around a stone. "If I can get these stones out, I might get the opening large enough to crawl in. Clever the way they were mortared in to make it look solid."

He shone the light in, then reached his hand into the opening as far as he could reach. He felt in the darkness. "I knew I saw something." He pulled his fist out, opening his hand. "Look, look. A turquoise bead." He looked back at his partner near the opening. "Holy crap, why are you just standing there? If you're not going to help with this wall, at least make yourself useful. Get some crates. Haul these stones out of our way. Damn. I hate running out of time just when good stuff shows up."

Chapter Fifty-Seven

Anton pulled Thord off to the side of the forest service road near the best route to get them to the site they'd named "Fork." He glanced at the sky. The bright sun that shone upon them a short while ago had become hazy.

"Are you sure you want to do this today?" asked Anton. "Pete and Sam would be unhappy if they knew. It's not without danger. They still haven't caught who murdered Charlie. We can turn back."

"I know, but it's already September," said Skyla. "Soon we won't be able to poke around up here. I hate to wait for spring."

"I called Sam. I was going to ask him if he wanted to go with us, but he said he was swamped at work. Said they were almost to the point of making arrests in two of his cases. So I ended up not even mentioning it to him." Anton picked up Twitch's leash. "It's not going to be as hot today. Better for hiking."

Skyla motioned toward the distant peaks of the Pecos Wilderness as they adjusted their daypacks and began walking. "It's neat the way the clouds pour over the peaks and cuddle them."

"We may be glad we brought our jackets. I told Mom we'd be home or call her by five or so."

Anton mentally checked off a list of what they'd brought on their hike. He had his SAT phone. They had their cell phones with their downloaded maps and built-in GPS signals. Their daypacks contained the essentials, plenty of water, and the lunches Skyla had prepared. He had an extra drone battery, too.

When he'd been getting ready for today, Anton had checked the drone they planned to use—the same one used for the SAR. Tucked in its big case was a little case with a cop drone. It had been in there ever since Charlie's things from the monastery had been delivered to Skyla. He'd opened it up, held it in his hands. Almost forgotten, the drone was a bittersweet memory of that night they had flown them. They'd laughed so hard. God, he missed Charlie. He zipped it back into its case and set it aside. Then on a whim, he'd picked it up again, changed the batteries, and tucked it into his pack. Maybe it was silly to bring it, but it didn't take up much room and weighed less than five ounces.

Both of them had enjoyed the challenges of this ancient-site quest. They didn't really expect to find one, but it had been fun looking and fun talking with Dom about their trips. Skyla's enthusiasm for archaeology was contagious. Anton grinned—Skyla would soon want a drone of her own.

When they reached the creek in Alamitos Canyon, Anton assembled his drone. "Canyon" was a rather over-impressive term for the topography here. The creek was still flowing but easily crossed with a jump. Anton wondered if it was spring-fed or just carrying the remnant of the July and August monsoon runoff.

Twitch ran ahead of them on a loose lead. They flew the drone along the creek over the tree tops, getting the lay of the land. They walked toward the cliffs on the far side of the creek. Skyla looked down to where erosion had made a wee gully. She picked up something shiny. "Look, Anton. An obsidian arrowhead!"

He brought the drone down, and they sat by the gully. Skyla photographed the arrowhead as it lay on Anton's palm. Then they put it back where they'd found it.

They searched more and eventually found some potsherds on the ground below a place where the cliff developed a terrace before descending more steeply to the creek bed. Many years ago, a few pines had taken root on that ledge and now stood tall. Smaller pines clung to the slope. Carefully, using the zoom lens on the drone,

Anton ran it along the cliff. They saw a more gentle approach to the area and climbed up to the shelf of rock and soil.

Ahead of them was an overhang, screened by pine trunks challenging the cliff and the ledge to find enough purchase for their roots. With a flashlight, they illuminated the recess, too small to be called a cave. It looked like some animal had been using it for a den at some point, but there was no fresh scat. The undisturbed weeds reaching for the scant light told the story of an abandoned home for anything bigger than squirrels. Indeed, it would be hard for a grown person to access the area. The trees guarded it well.

Twitch was interested in the squirrels, but Anton kept a tight grip on his leash. With the flashlight beam splitting the gloom of the shallow cave, Skyla let out a cry of delight. Almost obscured by dirt and plant matter, stones formed a low, man-made wall that perhaps once had shielded the cave. Not indicative of any large settlement, but maybe it had been a stop-over place for ancient peoples as they traveled over the mountain.

They took pictures with their cell phones. "Ye gods and little fishes. What a delicious find," said Skyla.

"We don't know who lived here or why. It would be nice if these stones could talk."

She smiled at him. "They do. We have a photo of the arrowhead. I can figure a date from the style, and it will at least tell me if it belonged to an Ancestral Pueblo or a nomadic Athabascan people."

Anton peered past the trunks. "Doesn't seem large enough to live in."

"Could have been a storage area," said Skyla. "We don't know how big this bench was four hundred years ago, either."

"It's eroded since these trees began to grow. Look how the roots are showing on the edge. And they're pulling up some near the cliff."

"This one pine is really leaning," said Skyla. "Almost at a forty-five-degree angle."

Twitch lunged after a ground squirrel that scurried to safety near the leaning tree on the ledge. He snuffled and dug at the hole. Pine needles and dirt flew behind him. Coughing as the cloud of dust suddenly enveloped her, Skyla pulled him back. "That squirrel is safe from you, boy." She bent to look where he had dug away the layer of pine needles, knelt, and picked up a handful of fresh soil, sifting it through her fingers.

Anton grinned at her. She was like a child kneeling in front of gaily wrapped Christmas packages who couldn't stop smiling. What was so interesting?

"Hang on to Twitch for a minute." With her hands free, Skyla poked in the soil near the hole. "Look at these little stone chips concentrated in this area. They aren't from any rocks around here. Some are flint, some obsidian." She looked up at him with excitement. "I wonder if someone used to sit under this little overhang, knapping."

"Napping?"

"Knapping with a K. Making arrowheads and other stone tools," she replied. "Hold out your hand." She sifted through more of the soil, found several rock chips, and laid them on his palm. Then she took a photo.

"Do you want to take some to show Dom? Would it be possible to get them dated?"

She shook her head. "No, we have the photo to show him. These artifacts have much more scientific value when left in place. They belong here. As far as dating goes, I can get a good idea from the arrowhead style."

Anton tossed the glassy chips back in the dirt. "Time buried them pretty deeply. It took the tree roots, a few good gully-washers, ground squirrels, and then Twitch to bring them to light."

As Anton moved in the narrow space, his head bumped a low branch. He stumbled on the uneven surface and put out a hand to brace himself against the tree. It moved under his weight. Skyla caught at him to steady him. "Uff da," he said. "That tree is fixing to come down soon."

They looked around the area, snapped a few more photos and made notes before climbing back down to explore more of the canyon. Dappled shade covered most of the area. Occasionally, jays scolded overhead and ground squirrels gave warning chucks, piercing the peace of the setting. Skyla and Anton sat on rocks near the creek to eat their late lunch. The sky was overcast; white had replaced the blue of morning. The air was decidedly damper. It felt good to be in the sunlight, even filtered as it was.

"Let's follow the other branch of the streambed up for a way." Anton tucked away his lunch wrappings in his daypack. "It's bigger. This peters out not far from here. Then we'd better head back. I didn't see it on the forecast, but it looks like some weather's moving in."

Snap. Was that a twig being stepped on? He looked up toward the top of the cliff. He motioned to Skyla to be quiet. They both listened. Nothing. He must have imagined it. Either that or a pine cone had fallen. He turned again to his drone.

"No more filming?" asked Skyla as she watched him fold up the drone and put it carefully in his backpack.

"Battery's low."

"This has been such a good day," Skyla said. "We actually found what could be a shortcut site."

"What will you do, now that we have?"

"I'd like to talk with Upton and maybe somebody from the Center for New Mexico Archaeology."

"Do you suppose they'd do a dig here?"

Skyla shrugged. "Funding is pretty scarce, so I doubt it." She hefted the straps of her pack over her shoulders and frowned. "But I'm thinking. Maybe it's not a good idea to say anything to anybody right now. Until they've caught the killer."

They crossed the little creek to the other side, where walking was easier, and followed it upstream with Twitch exploring ahead on lead. Anton noticed tracks near the gentle flow of the creek. Deer tracks were abundant.

Skyla reached down and picked up a small potsherd with a polychrome design from where it had lain half-covered in the silt. "This site might be bigger than we thought. Do you suppose there might be more ahead?"

Anton grasped her arm. A tingle of alarm went down his spine. “Look!” Fresh boot tracks, not all made by the same person, had joined the animal tracks.

A rabbit flashed by, flushed from its hiding place behind some weeds. Too late, Anton thought to tighten his grip on the leash. Twitch pulled it out of his hand. He was soon out of sight upstream, gone after the little rabbit running for his life.

“Twitch, come!” Anton shouted.

Chapter Fifty-Eight

Anton and Skyla followed Twitch around a bend in the creek. The canyon wasn't as deep here. On their left, scrubby junipers and pines dug their roots among the boulders leading up a rise. On the right across the creek, the same cliff formation they'd been exploring continued on in a curve. Overhangs featured in this new area as well, but the bench under these overhangs was wider on the far end and narrowed to a small ledge near them. On the left where the terrain near the creek widened out, a white pickup truck was parked almost hidden by the ponderosas.

"Oh. My. God." said Skyla. Dig signs were obvious. A step-ladder descended into a wide trench, camouflage netting draped overhead, and they realized they had found the site where the looters had been plundering. Rocks formed a natural protective overhang. Shadows obscured what could be a cave. A wooden crate and several tools lay on the ground nearby.

A figure straightened in the shadows and emerged from underneath the cliff overhang into the light. At first, Anton didn't recognize the man wearing a sweatshirt, jeans, and a baseball cap turned backwards. Then he turned toward them. Jesus, he thought. Brooks.

“Getting crowded up here,” Brooks said. “Just found this dig. You two know anything about it?” He bent and picked up a shotgun from the ground.

“No, we’re just out for a hike,” said Anton as he stepped between Skyla and Brooks. “We’re looking for my dog. He took off chasing a rabbit.” He cleared his throat. “Do you mind pointing that thing somewhere else?” This guy made his skin prickle. With a hand behind his back, he motioned for Skyla to back away. Her fingers closed around his, and they backed toward the rocks and brush.

“Dogs have to be on leash in the national forest,” said Brooks. “I could cite you.”

“He has a leash on,” said Anton, taking another step back. “He pulled away. We’ll keep looking for him.” Out of the corner of his eye, he noticed they’d reached a good-sized boulder. “Good luck catching whoever was working here.”

Anton tensed as Brooks’s other hand went to the gun. “Duck!” he cried to Skyla. They dove behind the rock, hearing the chk chk sound of a round being chambered. Boom. The slug glanced off the rock, sending sharp splinters flying.

Chk chk. Boom.

Anton and Skyla kept low behind the rocks, scrambling up the slope. Chk chk. Another loud report reverberated through the canyon. Anton felt something hit his backpack, knocking him off balance to his knees. He stumbled, got up, and pressed on.

Behind them another shot, then silence. They continued working their way up, ducking from cover to cover, but didn’t hear any sound of pursuit. Then came sounds that chilled Anton’s soul. A bark from a happy Airedale. Chk chk. Shouting. A shot. A terrified yelp suddenly cut off, and then silence. Anton looked at Skyla in horror. Had Twitch been shot?

As Anton and Skyla reached the top of the slope, he heard more shots. What? thought Anton, these shots didn’t even sound like they came from the same gun. Sounded like more of a loud crack.

Taking cover, they peered over a rock in the shadow of the brush and looked down toward the creek. Brooks had retreated to the overhang. Was he reloading? Anton couldn’t see anyone else, but shots were still being fired. Brooks acted like he was the one being shot at.

"What's going on?" whispered Skyla. Her eyes were huge in her pale face. "Who's shooting at Brooks?"

"I've no idea," he said, "but I think we should take advantage of it to get away."

"Twitch?" asked Skyla.

"God, I don't know." Anton closed his eyes against the pain. "I don't know if that bastard killed him or what. He has a tracker on his collar, but it might not work in this rough terrain with all the pines." He looked down at the site again, blinking to clear his eyes. It was still blurry. Then he realized the cloud cover had dropped. The misty dampness swirled in wayward wisps, coming and going.

Skyla pulled her binoculars from her pack. "No sign of him," she whispered, "from this angle anyway. We can see, but we're in a cloud. Brooks is still hunkered down."

Below them, the gunfire ceased. They watched, but Brooks stayed put near the overhang.

"Come on," said Anton quietly. "Let's get out of here before somebody starts after us."

Skyla backed away from their overlook, keeping low and quiet to avoid being noticed. Beside her Anton adjusted his pack straps on his shoulders.

"This feels weird," he whispered, frowning.

She glanced at his pack. "Something's hanging— Ye gods, Anton. One of the shots hit your pack."

He slung the backpack off his shoulders. "God Almighty," he hissed. "I knew something happened. Didn't know what. Threw me off balance."

"Are you hurt?"

The upper part of the pack sprouted downy feathers from the rolled-up jacket inside. Sharp bits of plastic poked through it. Shredded lunch wrappings trailed down from the ruined mess.

"No, I'm not hurt." Anton picked at a plastic propeller. "This drone will never fly again." He carefully rummaged through the destruction. "Jesus! The SAT phone! Hope it still works."

He pulled the phone out of the pack from where it had rested next to his back. "Looks okay." He turned it on, then smiled. "We're in luck. That's the worst thing he could have hit."

Skyla touched his cheek. "Not the worst thing." She drew him close to her. "Not at all. Ye gods, that hit was way too close to you."

She held him, offering a silent prayer for their safety, then pulled back.

"I wish we knew about Twitch," he whispered. "Watch Brooks for a minute while I get out from underneath these pines and get a signal." He crept quietly down the slope.

Behind her screen of pine branches, she peered down at Brooks as he hung back under the overhang. There was no sign of Twitch. What would it do to Anton if he felt he had to abandon Twitch? After they'd shared the loss of their babies, she realized how Anton had kept the pain of his lost child inside. He might think he'd bottled it up to shield himself, but he'd wanted to protect his mother and daughter from more hurt.

And here, on the mountain, he would try to get her to safety. She knew it would haunt him to leave Twitch, but he would never say, because that's who he was. Every time he walked through the doors of his suite, he was reminded of responsibility. He would take the pain inside himself in order to protect those he loved.

Why had she ever hesitated when he'd asked her to marry him? She looked down at the ring on her hand. He was Anton. Fierce protector. Not cut from the same bolt of cloth as her ex. Different as night from day.

Her decision was crystal clear in her mind. They would make a least one try to see what had happened to Twitch. Knowing his pup's fate, even if sad, would help. Otherwise it would gnaw on him.

Anton came back. "Come on," he whispered, beckoning her down from her vantage point.

"We're not leaving without Twitch," she said softly.

"We have to," he whispered.

"We'll get your truck," she said, "come back, and hide the truck in the brush by the fork. We'll look one last time. If Brooks's pickup is gone, and no one else is there, we'll go down and check. We can't just leave him."

"And if Brooks passes us on our way back?" He shook his head. "I want to go back, but I can't risk you."

"Anton Bjornson, all day long you've been putting yourself between me and danger. I know you're protective. You fear losing those you love. I understand that." She swallowed hard.

"You'd even die for me if you had to," she said, "but you want me to be your mate. To stand by your side. Well, that's where I'm standing. Not behind you. I have the right to risk my life for yours, too."

"Put it in perspective, Skyla. He's only a d-dog." His voice broke.

She stepped toward him and put a hand on his face. "Yes, he's a dog. A puppy that adores you. He's dependent on you. And you love him."

"We can't."

"One thing you have taught me. Take a chance for love. Or avoid risk and watch what you love dissolve before your eyes. We can do this. We don't have to behave rashly. We'll weigh our chances and arm ourselves with what we have."

"He's got a damn gun. Fat chance we'd have with just a knife."

"You're forgetting. Our biggest asset in this battle is that we're together. Mates. A team." Her gaze was steady. "We *will* go back." She pushed away from him. "Or maybe I'll go back. I can't risk you."

In silence she watched him. Finally, he held out his hand. "You're a strong, stubborn woman, Skyla Van Dyken. God help us. We'll go back."

"Wait! I heard something," she whispered close to his ear.

"Somebody else is coming."

Chapter Fifty-Nine

As Anton and Skyla crept back to the top of the ridge and watched, two men emerged from the fog near Brooks. The one in front moved unsteadily with his hands on top of his head. Claude followed and held a rifle pointed toward that man. With a jolt of surprise, Anton recognized Yancy.

They heard Claude yell, "What the hell's going on? First, I hear you shooting at something, then this crazy Indian starts shooting at you. I hit him over the head. Might have hit him too hard. He's acting stupid—or maybe he is stupid."

"God Almighty, Brooks *and* Claude are the looters," whispered Anton. "It must have been Yancy who kept Brooks pinned down. He's hurt." From his vantage point, he saw the side of Yancy's head was red with blood.

"What should we do?"

"It's more than Twitch now. It's imperative that we help Yancy. I'll call Sam and get help started up the mountain. Then we'll come up with a plan." He stepped down away from the pines again to make another call.

In a few minutes he was back. "Not much time. They'll kill Yancy."

Below them, Yancy seemed to have passed out. Claude rolled him over the edge of the trench, out of sight. Then they pulled their ladder from the trench, gathered their tools and seemed to be trying to erase evidence of their presence from the site, stuffing their belongings in crates. The voices of Claude and Brooks reached their hearing intermittently. Much of what they said was in anger, and Anton had no trouble hearing that.

"What weapons do we have?" asked Skyla.

"My hunting knife. Good stout branches. Not much."

"My Swiss Army knife. If only you had your drone. That would distract them."

"Hey!" Anton smiled. "Just remembered. I do have a drone." He dug deeper in his pack, past the destruction of the big drone. He pulled out the small case. "Charlie's cop drone. Came across it when I was getting ready. Don't know why, but I kept it in here."

Skyla closed her eyes, then blinked rapidly. "Use it." She put her hands over Anton's as he held the little drone case. "Those flashing lights in the fog? Even better than the big one."

"For Charlie. You're right. He'd have loved it."

"I've thought of another way to distract them," Skyla whispered. "I'll sneak down the other way to their trucks. While you've got the drone up, I'll get to both trucks, jam branches between the seats and the horns and set them off."

He looked at her, pausing in his quick assembly of the little drone. "One horn will do just as well. Do that and get the hell away. I'm thinking they'll come on the run to see who's there."

"How long will the cop drone work?"

"About six minutes," Anton replied. "Leave the stuff from the packs behind. Take only the first aid kit, some water. On your way down, get the branch to jam into the horn, and a big one for yourself."

She nodded. "Give me maybe ten minutes to get to the truck. I won't do anything until I hear the drone."

"Oh, Skyla. Be safe." He drew her into his arms, and they held each other close. A final kiss, and they began to work their separate ways down to creek level.

⬧ ❖ ⬧

"What the hell?" yelled Claude. "There's a damn dog lying in the trench. What'd you do? Shoot him?"

"He came running at me. Tried to attack me. I clubbed him with the shotgun. He fell in there. Don't know if he's dead or not."

"Where the hell did he come from?"

"That drone guy. Said he ran off from them."

"The drone guy? Them? What do you mean—*them*?" Claude's voice rose again. "Is that who you were shooting at? Anton? And *Skyla? You were shooting at Skyla?"*

"So what if I was?" bellowed Brooks. "They *found* us. They found the site. You idiot. You want them to tell everyone? They need killing!"

"You're the idiot. Can't you get it through your thick head that the more bodies you leave behind, the more police will be looking for us. No. More. Killing."

"Try and stop me!" yelled Brooks. "Damn little Mama's boy. I'm going after them."

"We need to get the hell out of here. Even now it might be too late. Grab what you can. We're leaving."

"The stuff we just found. It's all good. Won't take long. Then I'll shoot the Indian, and we'll go."

"Holy crap. No more killing. Leave the damn Indian alone. Anyhow, we're getting out. Now. Forget the cave."

Brooks picked up the shotgun. "He can't live."

Claude leaned toward him, shaking his fist at the taller man. "I swear. Enough. You kill one more person, and I'll club you and throw you into that cave. I'll seal it up and leave you in the dark." He took a step forward. Brooks backed away. Claude kept advancing, his long-held venom thrusting aside his normal civil voice. "You'll wake up and you won't be able to breathe. No air. *Tons* of earth, *pressing* in on you. Can't breathe. In the dark. Until you die. All alone—*in the dark."*

"Shut up!"

"In the DARK."

Suddenly Brooks reversed his hold on the gun, swung it against Claude, who raised an arm to deflect the blow, but still took a hit on the side of the head. He fell back and lay still.

Brooks stood in shock. "No. I didn't mean it." He knelt by Claude and shook him. "Get up. Get up!"

A new sound reached Anton's ears as he crept silently down and gained the protection of the big rocks where they'd first been shot at. What the heck was that? Very softly came the plaintive sounds of Yancy's flute. *I don't believe it. He can't be playing. It must be the recording on his cell phone.*

"What the hell?" Brooks left Claude and looked down into the trench. "What are you doing? Oh, God. The Indian is still as death. He's not moving. Where's that sound coming from? What is going on? Stop that. I'll kill you now." Chk chk.

Anton sent the little cop drone high. The flashing blue and red lights appeared in the whiteness of the fog. The angry, bee-swarm noise filled the air. Brooks wheeled to see what new threat came at him from the sky. The copter came toward him, tilting and zipping up and down, back and forth.

Then Anton heard a sound to make his heart glad—a mournful howl from the trench as Twitch reacted again to the sound of the drone, hesitantly at first, but growing in strength. "Ruurrowhr, rowr, rowr."

Anton circled the drone around Brooks above his head, thinking it might help if Brooks got dizzy while he was looking up at it. Brooks pointed the weapon at the copter. Boom! Anton zoomed it back and forth. Sideways. Up and down. Chk chk. Boom. Chk chk. The little copter zoomed toward him. Brooks blasted it. It streaked away, the swarming noise halted, the LED lights flashing before plummeting to the ground. A few feeble blue and red flashes marked where it hit before it went dark. Chk chk. No shot. Chk chk. Brooks swore and fumbled in futility at his belt.

Anton tensed, waiting to see what he would do next.

Then he heard the sweet sound of the truck horn blaring. Emergency flashers on the truck started. Brooks spun around, and ran toward his pickup, holding his shotgun like a club. Anton ran toward the trench and slid the ladder over the edge. He found

Yancy sitting up. Anton glanced at Claude motionless on the ground nearby. He helped Yancy climb out, then went down and lifted Twitch out. The dog was all over both of them, barking happily.

The sound of the blaring horn gave way to a truck engine roaring to life, tires spinning as Brooks sped away, bouncing down the track away from the dig site. Anton cautiously approached Claude.

"He's still breathing, but I think he's been knocked out," said Yancy.

"His arm looks odd. It may be broken."

They tied his feet together as a precaution, secured his good arm, and frisked him for any weapon. Skyla came running up and flew into Anton's arms. In the distance, he heard the sirens as the police made their way up the mountain. He let go of Skyla and picked up Twitch's trailing leash.

"Yancy, how did you happen to be up here?" asked Anton.

"Ever since Buck was found, I've been poking around on this mountain. I was here before you arrived this morning—had just found this site. Heard somebody coming, so I hid up on top of the cliff. Heard you prowling around and talking. Know you found something, too."

"I thought I heard a twig snap above us."

"Careless on my part," said Yancy. "I had been keeping an eye on Brooks, but the other one showing up surprised me."

"How's your head where he hit you?" asked Skyla.

"I'll have a headache for a while. Head wounds always bleed a lot. I'm sure it looks worse than it is. He never actually knocked me out. I was pretending to be more hurt than I was, to buy time into getting away."

"You're lucky you weren't killed. You saved our lives. Thank you," said Skyla.

"They needed to be stopped. They're destroying a site important to my people. The spirits are uneasy here. What will the authorities do, Miss Skyla?"

"There's protocol they must follow. My guess is that they'll get the evidence they need to prosecute Brooks and Claude.

Archaeologists will try to figure out a dollar amount for the damage that's been done. They'll confer with several of the Pueblos, including Jemez about what they wish. I think they'll map it, document it, and then backfill it to protect it. The location will be kept secret."

"Good. I'll be right back," said Yancy, picking his rifle up from where Claude had been piling his possessions. He handed it to Anton. "You know how to use this?"

Anton nodded. Yancy fished some rounds out of his cargo pants and handed them to him. Then from another pocket he took a SAT phone.

"Yancy, ye gods," said Skyla. "They didn't even take your phones?"

Yancy laughed. "That Claude fell for my act. Never underestimate inscrutable Indian. I live in the same century as they do. The SAT phone won't work down here, but when I get to the road, I'll call Sam. Tell him where we are. My jeep's hidden nearby. You keep watch?"

Anton nodded. "I don't think we should move Claude. He's still out. Don't know how badly he was hurt. We'll stay with him."

"I'll show the medics the way," said Yancy. "Then they can take that piece of shit away."

Chapter Sixty

Yancy walked away into the wispy fog. Soon they heard the sound of his jeep starting. They kept their eyes on Claude, but he remained motionless. Twitch settled by Anton's side. Anton gently explored the wound on the Airedale's head. He thought the dog was going to be all right, but as soon as they could, he was going to have a vet check him out. Then he took out his phone and tried to follow the GPS tracker on Brooks's truck, but the signal wasn't clear.

Soon they saw the lights of the police cars coming slowly down the track, following Yancy's jeep. Sam and Storm were the first to arrive.

"It's sure good to see you," Sam said. "We knew there were two villains, but we only caught Brooks just now. He's in a state. Not talking. Keeps muttering he didn't mean it. We didn't know where Frobisher was or what had happened to you. Then Yancy called and said you were okay. Said Frobisher was knocked out."

"Brooks clobbered him," said Anton. "Helped even the odds a bit."

The medics arrived and went to Claude. He moaned and showed signs of coming around. One medic checked out Yancy. They made arrangements to get his jeep home and get him to the hospital to take care of his scalp wound.

Sam went with Anton back up to where they'd kept an eye on Brooks to get the things they'd left there. When Sam saw the state of Anton's backpack, he shook his head in disbelief. "The good Lord was looking after you." He shook his head and gripped Anton's shoulder hard.

They took Anton and Skyla to where Thord waited for them by the side of the road, and then followed them down. They passed out of the cloud hugging the mountain to where Pete and Hiram waited to welcome them by the beginning of the forest service road. A New Mexico State Police Mobile Command Post vehicle was parked there, antennas raised for communication. Anton took the time to call his mom and Krista to let them know they were all right and would be home as soon as they could.

First Skyla, then Anton was taken into the command center to be debriefed on their experience. What had they seen? What had Brooks and Frobisher done and said? At that point Anton showed off his backpack again and told them about Yancy. He said he believed that Brooks had wanted to kill Yancy, but Claude intervened and was hit. He also showed them what Brooks had done to Twitch.

By the time the interviews were over, darkness was falling. They learned briefly about the police discoveries and the escalation of the investigation.

"When you called, after Brooks shot at you," said Pete, "Hiram put roadblocks into place on all the roads leading from the mountains—especially this one and the ones that come out by Dalton Canyon. Brooks knows all the roads in the national forest like the back of his hand. But Hiram has been around here a long time, too, and knew who else had that knowledge. We knew Brooks lived right near here and that he'd probably head home."

"That was some quick organizing," said Skyla.

"We had a head start," said Pete. "A great many puzzle pieces fell into place earlier today."

"We'd already gotten search warrants for both men's homes," said Hiram. "Everything they needed to escape—passports, airplane tickets, money, luggage—all were waiting for them, and so were we. Forensics is busy at both now. They'll take on the dig site come daylight."

"I just about had a heart attack," said Pete, "when I found out you were exploring the mountain with your drone today. I couldn't reach you by phone. I finally called Karen. Said it was important. That we'd learned some information that told us you were in danger."

"She and Dom told us where you were," said Sam.

"Several things came to light," said Pete. "We laid a whole bunch of related papers on the table and brainstormed about them. Tried to figure where they fit. That little piece of paper Frobisher had written his alibi on for the kiva incident fell out of my notes and into place—literally. There it was—that same distinctive upright, loopy handwriting that was on the provenance papers and the note that Patty Lydra sent us."

"That's where I'd seen it before," said Skyla. "We get so used to emails and computer-written stuff, that we don't see cursive writing much anymore."

"I'll tell you more later, but a clincher was when we found out Frobisher and Brooks were stepbrothers."

"Stepbrothers!" cried Anton.

"*Ja*, Brooks's father married Frobisher's mother when the boys were teenagers," said Pete.

"Then another clincher," said Sam. "We got the forensics report on Buck's truck. Frobisher's prints were all over the front passenger area. Gaylord Teller's were in the back seat."

"I'm concerned that none of the information about the dig site gets leaked to the public before law enforcement and the archaeologists have it taken care of," said Skyla.

"Nothing about the location and precious little about their activities will ever see daylight. It's the murder of four people that is the crime the public will hear about," said Hiram.

"We'll get together in a few days," said Pete. "I'm sure we can tell you more when the dust settles. For now, just get your dog checked out and get on home. Karen and Krista will be glad to see you hale and hearty. Dom, too. He's there."

Gratefully, Anton turned Thord toward home. Twitch stretched out on the back seat. Twilight gave way to darkness, hiding the secrets on the mountain once more. They didn't know all the answers yet, but Charlie's killers had been caught.

Chapter Sixty-One

Anton and Skyla made arrangements to meet Sam, Pete, Hiram, and Storm at a Starbucks not far off the interstate in Santa Fe late Monday afternoon. That morning's papers included the story detailing the capture of the pair suspected of murder, complete with pictures of Frobisher and Brooks.

When they arrived and everyone had gotten their coffees, Hiram spoke up. "I'm sure you're curious as to what we found on that mountain. We talked to Yancy earlier and checked to see how he was doing."

"How is he?" asked Skyla.

"He's fine. Tough fellow. Good acting ability." A little smile played on Hiram's face. "I could learn a thing or two from that man."

Anton and Skyla listened as the story unfolded. "I'm still worried about the ancient site," said Skyla. "Yancy will be, too. We'd just as soon the knowledge doesn't go further than you. Dom and Karen know, but no one else will. The archaeologists who deal with it will keep their silence. That's the way we want it. Let it rest."

"I think we can promise that," said Pete. The others nodded.

Then Hiram took up the tale. "We spoke briefly with Frobisher. He's in the hospital, under guard. His arm is broken, but deflecting the blow as he did may have saved his life. He still took a hard knock to his head. When he recovers from his concussion, we'll learn more, but he did confirm some of what we had figured. For instance, after he saw the papers Patty Lydra sent, he stole that calendar page from Lawder's calendar. Frobisher appears very bitter, blaming most of his trouble on the hothead, as he refers to Brooks. Says Brooks killed all four men."

"Brooks would've killed Yancy, if Claude had let him," said Anton. "Do you think Claude'll be cooperative?"

"My guess is yes," answered Hiram. "Brooks is in jail, under suicide watch. I think he was disappointed to be taken alive." He shook his head; his shaggy brows drew together. "He won't manage at all well, being in a confined space. They've had to keep him sedated. Went into a full-blown panic attack—white, sweaty, shaking. He might not be able to cope with being cooped up in a small space. It's a sad day when two fellows, who had so much going for them, end up as they have. It's hard for me to understand."

"The relationship and their background might explain some of that," said Pete. "In my research on antiquities looting, we hit on a gold mine. Both the Frobisher name and the Brooks name burped up in some of those old files from the sixties and seventies. It turns out those were the parents."

"I went at it from another angle and got to the same conclusion," said Sam. "We backtracked in Frobisher's life—his career, schooling, family. Just recently we came across an article that led to the surprising fact that the two were step-brothers. Then we started digging into Brooks, as well. They grew up in the Four Corners area. Both parents were rugged-outdoor types. Both had histories of collecting antiquities. Definitely of the finders-keepers school mentality who believed artifacts were theirs for the taking. Strong personalities. Very individualistic and anti-government."

"Why work in government then?" asked Anton.

Pete glanced at him. "Old Man Brooks thought the best way to handle the government was to toady up to those in charge, work your way up to a position of power, then use that power and your inside information to game the system to your own advantage. That was his pattern. It finally caught up with him, and rather than pay the price, he and his wife fled the country when the boys were college age. They created new identities. The old man and his wife died over a decade ago, but a half-sister is the Paris connection. She runs the French gallery."

"The one that Claude was sending the packages to?" asked Anton.

"Ja, that was an important puzzle piece for us to find." Pete smiled at Anton. "It tied Teller's gallery to Frobisher."

"It really makes me angry," said Skyla. "Why on earth would someone take the trouble to excel in their career and use it in that foul way? It's not easy to be selected, to rise in the ranks, and reach that position of trust."

"Some people have twisted minds," said Sam. "There are bad apples that rise to power in law enforcement, too. Maybe every profession, for all I know. I do think Frobisher had a lot of inner conflict over what he was doing. He had to rationalize his actions a lot. Find someone else to blame."

"Was it Claude who locked me in with the snake?"

"No, that was Brooks," said Hiram. "Your friend, Hoot, said that Brooks had been called out that day to deal with a rattler. It wasn't uncommon for there to be forest service trucks around the park. It wasn't notable to have someone walking around in a forest service uniform. You expect to see them, so you accept them without thinking."

"Did you ever find Teller's glasses?" asked Pete.

"Found those, too, when they processed the looted site yesterday. Kind of hidden in the grass, not far from the trench."

"One thing that always puzzled me," said Storm, "was the bit about using Frobisher's truck to make that second set of tracks. Why'd they do that?"

"I'm guessing that idea came from Brooks," said Pete. "Even in his concussed state, Frobisher was complaining about that. Brooks must have been pretty sure they could make it look like somebody was framing Frobisher, but that he could get out of it. After all, he did have an alibi for the time of the murder."

"The note on the calendar, the N Starbucks," said Sam. "That referred to Frobisher's lady friend. Her first name was Nesta and that's where they met."

"It was dangerous, though, for Brooks to try that gambit of framing Frobisher," said Pete. "From that time on, we were suspicious of him, but didn't have the proof to charge him."

"What a waste," said Hiram. "It's a heavy blow to the forest service office in Pecos and to the park, too. Makes it tough on those who do the right thing."

"I'm sorry that Pete and I couldn't have been more cooperative in letting you know what was going on," said Sam. "It bothered me."

"Likewise," said Pete. "We finally hashed that out and began sharing more, especially when we realized that you and the looters were on a collision course because of your quest to find a shortcut site."

"I was in awe over your ability to feed us information, really helpful information, even when we didn't reciprocate," said Sam.

"I didn't like it," said Anton, "but that doesn't mean I didn't understand why. You had to make some tough choices, and we wanted to do everything we could to make sure that Charlie received justice." He reached out to Skyla's hand.

"It's worth saying, Sam," Anton continued, "even though the Circle Sleuths didn't meet specifically to discuss this case like we did for Krista's kidnapping and somewhat for Dom's adventure at the care center, I still felt supported by everyone. That includes you and Pete, too."

"Thanks, guys," Skyla said. "It gives me hope, even after those two destroyed so many lives. I thank God there are people like you who do care about doing the right thing."

Chapter Sixty-Two

Anton and Skyla had awoken early on the day of their engagement party. Very early, and very lamborous. It was still dark outside. Then Anton had put on his jeans, gone down to let Twitch out, and made them some coffee. When he came back, Twitch at his heels, Skyla sat up in bed. He slid in next to her.

God, she's beautiful, he thought. Her eyes were shining and happy. Was it the afterglow of their lovemaking or anticipation for their celebration tonight?

"Tell me about what December is usually like here," she said. "I know that December 6 will be a big celebration for St. Nicholas. Are there any other events in December that I should know about?"

"Just Christmas. December 26 will probably be the Airedale terrier walk again. Last year Twitch and Shadow weren't old enough. And staff parties. No date set yet for Drone Tech's. Will there be a staff party for the park?"

"Probably, but on a weekday. Do you have anything scheduled for the seventeenth? It's a Saturday."

"Nothing. Why? Shall we save it for something special?"

"Yes," she replied, taking his cup and placing it next to hers. "Very special. I'm thinking, that if you like the idea, that could be our wedding day."

Stunned, he looked at her. "Oh, love! It would be perfect. You're sure you're ready?"

"Very sure." Her strikingly beautiful eyes looked confidently into his. "I want to say before the world that you are an honorable man. I trust you. I give myself freely into your keeping, and I accept your freely given self into my keeping."

He slid his fingers into her hair, tracing her face, lost in her eyes bright with confidence, feeling his own smile grow, and knew he must be floating. He pulled her close and gave a laugh of pure happiness.

The sun shone brightly into their room before they came back to earth. "There are three people that we should tell before tonight," she said as they left the room. "Krista, your mom, and Maria."

When they told them, Krista squealed with delight. She jumped up from the table and gave Skyla a big hug. "Now I'll have a father and a *mother* again. I can hardly wait to tell Leyla."

Karen, too, got up to give warm, long hugs—first her son and then Skyla. She had tears in her eyes. "Skyla, I bless the day when Charlie introduced Anton to you. I am thrilled that you will be my daughter-in-law in truth soon. You have made my son very happy. This is such welcome news."

"Anton was a schoolboy when I joined this household," said Maria when it came time for her hug. "Diego and I have been honored to be a part of this family. I'm so glad Anton found you, Skyla. You are just who he and Krista need."

Later that afternoon, Hoot drove his family through the gates of the Bjornson Ranch and started up the drive. Soon a large, sprawling adobe home came into view. Along their left, they passed corrals with a few horses standing quietly, curious about visitors. Past the corrals were pens with alpacas. A few outbuildings, a duplex, and they arrived at the house.

He'd known Anton was wealthy; he'd heard Skyla talk about his spread. She'd told Melody what Anton said of houses and homes, and Melody had shared that with him. Still, he was a little intimidated. But then Anton and Skyla came out to greet them. Anton's mother gave them warm welcomes. Sam and Farah were there, Leyla, Krista, and Dom. These were folks he respected, admired, and whose friendship he enjoyed. He looked forward to meeting the rest of the Circle Sleuths.

Matti and Bonnie danced with excitement at seeing Twitch and the other Airedales again. Krista and Leyla took the two little redheads off to see the critters before following the group back to the house.

Hoot and Melody stood at the back door, laughing at the antics of the Airedales and the oddly marked border collie as they played in the yard with Matti, Bonnie, and the girls. He was aware of more people arriving but stayed watching the children.

He heard Anton's voice behind him. "Akiko, Pete, I don't know if you've ever met Melody and Hoot."

Hoot turned to find his wife shaking the hand of a woman of Japanese ancestry. "Pleased to meet you, Akiko," she said.

"And her husband, Pete."

Hoot raised his eyebrows as he looked at the man standing next to Akiko. He'd met him before. This was Pete? The detective he'd heard so much about? The one whom the Circle Sleuths held in such esteem? Lieutenant Schultz—that was his name. In January, Schultz had come to visit his grandmother. He'd been there, too, and Pete had asked them all kind of questions, told him about the little boy who'd been kidnapped twenty-five years earlier. Hoot had tried to convince the lieutenant that it couldn't be him. That he was older than that missing boy, and that his father had been killed in a plane crash when they were coming to visit his grandparents. A strange uneasiness had accompanied that interview.

Now it was like he was standing outside himself, watching himself as he shook the man's hand. "Lieutenant Schultz."

"Ross Stewart, if I remember," said Pete. "Good to see you again."

"So formal," said Anton. "Have you met before?"

"Briefly," said Pete. "In different circumstances. I've heard you talk about Hoot many times during the last several months. I had no idea what his …" Pete cleared his throat, "real name was."

Anton went on with the introductions. "You've heard us talk about Lou and Cliff, but I don't know if you've ever met. Lou is Pete and Akiko's daughter. This is her husband, Cliff McCreath. And this is the youngest member of the Circle Sleuths. Dougie McCreath."

Hoot looked away from Pete to a woman holding a baby with a head of dark hair that stuck out all over. From them he looked over into a pair of shocked blue eyes. Blue eyes on a man with messy, curly hair, even redder than his own.

"We met once," said Cliff. "In Santa Fe at the Labor Day festival last year."

Why was he feeling this way? Hoot almost felt panicky. Like other times when something triggered something in his head. It seemed a thought was waiting to pounce on him. But the words wouldn't come together. He couldn't let it get to him. He felt his wife's hand slide into his.

"Hoot, honey, are you okay? You've gone all pale."

He shook his head as if to clear it and squeezed her hand. "I'm okay," he lied. "Just a little headache."

The back door opened, and the girls came in with Matti and Bonnie. Krista cocked her head and looked at the two red-headed men. "Hoot, when I met you," she said, "I thought you reminded me of somebody. Now I know who. You look a lot like Cliff."

Melody had taken the hands of the two little redheads. "These are our children, Matti and Bonnie."

Hoot felt like his ears were buzzing. He looked back at Pete. Pete was looking at his son-in-law as he met the children. Cliff's mouth hung open a bit as he looked down at Matti.

"My God," Cliff said. "He's just like I remember Johnny."

Hoot had to do something. Had to stop this madness, this yammering on about this missing boy. It unnerved him.

"I admit it's strange," Hoot said, bristling a little as Cliff stared at Matti. Matti sidled a little closer to his mother. "I know the story of your brother. I know you've never stopped looking for him. But we're not related."

Karen stepped forward. "They say that everyone has a doppelganger, someone who looks like them. I would venture that you two are related generations back. Families emigrate, move around. Maybe when you've had time to get acquainted, you'll find that you are tenth cousins or something. You are probably both descended from the same ancestors in some small Scottish village."

Anton came forward with a tray of wine glasses. "Don't let these folks give you a hard time, Hoot. Now that everyone is here, we have some toasts coming."

Hoot accepted the wine, nodded his thanks to Anton and his mother, grateful for their interrupting what could have grown into a more awkward moment. Krista and Leyla had small glasses of grape juice for his kids and themselves.

Hoot smiled reassuringly at Melody and tried to focus on what Anton was saying, to listen to the announcements. His voice automatically joined with the others in the chorus of best wishes, of cheers, of *skål*. That funny feeling, almost like panic, was receding. He blinked, and the feeling of being outside himself seemed to go away.

The radiant faces of Skyla and Anton captured his attention with one more announcement.

"There's another day we'd like to share with you," said Skyla. "We would like you all to be with us again on December seventeenth when we celebrate our marriage."

Next to him Melody said, "Yes!" A big grin split her face. Whistles, cheers, and applause broke out. Hoot followed Melody forward as she moved to hug Skyla.

Chapter Sixty-Three

"Anton, I need to see the site in the mountains again. To see what it looks like, now that the archaeologists have finished. I feel like we need closure."

Anton reached across the breakfast table and took Skyla's hand. After he'd taken Krista to meet the school bus and returned, they'd lingered over their second cup of coffee. He'd taken the day off to spend it with her. "Do you want to go today? Roads are still open. Next week will be busy with Thanksgiving."

She looked outside. The bare branches of the trees were defined against the November sky, a fair blue. It was crisp, but dry. "Yes, I would." She met his eyes. "Would it be okay if we took Yancy with us?"

He nodded. "I think it would be important for him. He connects a spirituality to places that I don't fully understand. I'll call him."

When they picked Yancy up, he was carrying one of his flute cases. He got into the backseat of Thord. After he greeted them, he was quiet. Anton thought they all were preoccupied, thinking of all the violence they'd experienced there in September, a little leery of what the archaeologists might have done to the place to put its secrets back into hiding.

They followed the track that the looters had used. The archaeologists had gone that way, too. They parked and walked.

Yancy carried his flute case slung over his shoulder. Anton carried his daypack.

The site was almost unrecognizable. Fresh soil covered the area where the trench had been dug out. Rocks and soil covered the area near the overhang. Where erosion might be a problem, mulch and other controls had been utilized. All traces of the looters were gone. A few young pine trees raised their branches to the sky where none had been in September.

"They've done a good job," said Skyla. "It won't be long until this will look like nothing ever happened here."

Yancy walked along the cliff. He bent and picked something up, tucked it into his fanny pack, and came quietly back.

"Let's see if they did anything to the first site we found," said Skyla. They all followed the creek around the corner.

The first difference they saw was not man-made, but the work of nature. Wind and gravity had finally taken down the leaning pine tree, which now lay across the tiny creek. They clambered up onto the bench where it had once stood. Broken roots and loose rock partially filled the hole where the pine's shallow roots had hung on.

Though the archaeologists had worked to hide the traces of this site, too, now part of the depression with the ancient wall was more exposed. Broken roots among the flat stones and crumbling mortar showed how it had been disturbed. A shadow lay behind it. Anton took off his daypack and got his flashlight. He shone it into the darkness. "Skyla, Yancy, look!"

They hunkered down low to see what the light beam discovered. Someone long ago had dug out this little cavity, hidden their treasure away in darkness, and walled it shut. Tucked back at arm's length were a few pots, and a jumble of pottery figures in a heap, like they had been placed there in a long-ago-disintegrated basket.

Skyla reached out reverent hands to the small figure nearest them and picked it up. It was a female with two smaller figures attached. Crudely, but lovingly made. All had open round mouths. "Ye gods," she whispered. "It's almost like a storyteller. It's beautiful."

Anton looked at her as she cradled the figure in her hands. Her eyes were shining in awe. He thought he would always carry that picture in his mind.

She handed the figure to Yancy. He sat in silence, holding it, eyes closed, then passed it on to Anton. He held it for a while, thinking about the four hundred years since hands had held this figure. Then he handed it back to Skyla.

Anton took several photos on his phone—the dugout hiding place, the figures within, and the little figure held by Skyla. Dom and Karen would see these shots, but they would remain hidden from the rest of the world. Then Anton reached in and put the figure next to the other figures.

"We should cover it over," said Skyla. Anton nodded. She looked at Yancy.

"Yes," he said.

Anton got a shovel from his truck. Just before they started to fill in the dugout, Yancy took something from his fanny pack and held it on his palm—the mangled remains of the cop drone. He reached in and laid it next to the figures.

"Yancy," Skyla said. "I'm surprised that you would leave that bit of technology with the ancient relics."

"It, too, is part of the past," he said somberly, but with a twinkle in his eyes. "Someone someday will wonder and will come up with wild ideas about how that got there. Charlie's spirit would find it amusing."

Anton chuckled. "It belongs there. You're right. He would love it." He smiled at Skyla.

Her eyes were wet, but she nodded. "Yes."

They filled the dugout in with soil and rocks and erased their traces. When they were finished, Yancy said, "I feel a song in me that must be played. Do we have the time?"

"All the time you need, Yancy. This place waits for your song."

Yancy went to sit by the creek on the downed pine. Skyla and Anton remained sitting in silence. Anton put his arm around Skyla, thinking of the lost voices. Charlie would always be missed, but the good times would live on in their memories. Skyla had moved on from her failed marriage. Travis no longer had the power to control or put her down.

Their own marriage would be celebrated soon. He had hope that one day they would welcome a child or two of their own. He thought of the promise he'd made to Skyla. Fulfilled now. Charlie's murderers were caught. His spirit at rest. How much I owe him, bringing back my zest for life, introducing me to Skyla, and starting us on life together. So much.

Peace, at peace. Skyla thought she would have a different attitude now toward the artifacts displayed in the museum. "I'm grateful we've had a glimpse into the life here," she said. "I wonder about the individuals who had taken these figures to safety, what happened to them, and how their journey ended."

Anton smiled. "I do know that your imagination will make them come alive for people when you give the tours now."

"They seem close here," she said. "Maybe it's fanciful of me, but they do."

"Who, my love?"

"The ancient ones who journeyed here. And also those whom we lost. Sonja. Your unborn babe. My son. And Charlie. It feels complete, somehow."

"Mm-hmm. The mood has changed," he said. "Do you feel it? The evil has gone. The music is cleansing it."

The wind blew through the trees; hawks soared high above on the thermals. The squirrels chattered. The sound of Yancy's flute floated through the canyon. Music came to him, through him. Familiar melodies. Traditional tunes handed down through generations. Melodies he'd played for the video of the ancient sites, and his own creations that welled up from within, mixing new and old.

The final notes wafted into memory. Yancy walked back to the truck in silence. Anton and Skyla followed, hand in hand, leaving the place in peace.

A wisp of wind stirred the top of the dusty soil, sending it spiraling away. Another wisp circled back, bringing seeds with downy wings to rest. A squirrel busied himself burying pine nuts in the loose soil. Winter would weather this place, the seeds would take root, and spring would bring new life.

The mountain drifted back to slumber. Once again, its secrets were folded into hiding, and hushed were the voices from the past.

About the Author

Betty Lucke holds a Bachelor's degree in elementary education from Macalester College, St. Paul, MN, and the Master of Religious Education and the Master of Divinity degrees from Princeton Theological Seminary, Princeton, NJ. She has fond memories of summers worked in New Mexico. She lives in northern California with her husband and a Welsh terrier.

She is a co-founder of the Town Square Writers, a weekly writing group associated with the public library.

www.ingramcontent.com/pod-product-compliance
Lightning Source LLC
Chambersburg PA
CBHW070545260626
47161CB00002B/512

* 9 7 8 0 9 8 8 4 6 3 1 4 1 *